PSYCHIC SPAWN

A NOVEL BY
Ryder Syvertsen and Adrian Fletcher

POPULAR LIBRARY

An Imprint of Warner Books, Inc.

A Warner Communications Company

POPULAR LIBRARY EDITION

Copyright © 1987 by Ryder Syvertsen & Adrian Fletcher
All rights reserved.

Popular Library® and the fanciful P design are registered
trademarks of Warner Books, Inc.

Cover design by Barbara Buck
Cover illustration by Mark & Stephanie Gerber

Popular Library books are published by
Warner Books, Inc.
666 Fifth Avenue
New York, N.Y. 10103

 A Warner Communications Company

Printed in the United States of America

First Printing: October, 1987

10 9 8 7 6 5 4 3 2 1

THE WILL THAT KILLS

▶   ▶   ▶   ▶   ▶

Brandon's father went from his knees to his back, rolling on the wooden floor of the raquetball court, clutching his chest with his left hand and reaching toward Brandon with his right. His mind screamed, *Brandon, help me! The pills!* but no words came out.

Brandon stared down at him, unmoving, a slight smile playing on his lips. His eyes were strangely radiant. Arthur glimpsed the five children on the other side of the glass. They were staring at him, too, not moving. For God's sakes, why weren't they helping him?

An odd, stray thought surfaced through the haze of pain. *My God, they want me to die!*

ATTENTION: SCHOOLS AND CORPORATIONS

POPULAR LIBRARY books are available at quantity discounts with bulk purchase for educational, business, or sales promotional use. For information, please write to SPECIAL SALES DEPARTMENT, POPULAR LIBRARY, 666 FIFTH AVENUE, NEW YORK, N Y 10103

**ARE THERE POPULAR LIBRARY BOOKS
YOU WANT BUT CANNOT FIND IN YOUR LOCAL STORES?**

You can get any POPULAR LIBRARY title in print. Simply send title and retail price, plus 50¢ per order and 50¢ per copy to cover mailing and handling costs for each book desired. New York State and California residents add applicable sales tax. Enclose check or money order only, no cash please, to POPULAR LIBRARY, P. O. BOX 690, NEW YORK, N Y 10019

CHAPTER One

Bavaria, April 1945.

Lieutenant James Ryan, twenty-four, United States Army Air Force, looked around his underground prison and wondered: Are the Nazis going to kill me? What *is* this place?

He was in a cell measuring about eight by ten feet, hewn out of a granite wall and lit by a single bare bulb strung from the ceiling. It seemed to be part of a fortress carved deep inside a mountain, completely hidden from the outside world. It was huge, packed with odd rooms filled with scientific-looking equipment—he had glimpsed some on the hasty trip to his cell. And it was populated with hundreds of men and women, some in uniforms, some in laboratory smocks.

He was surprised he was still alive. The C-47 he had been piloting on a supplies run for troops in the Rhine Valley had been shot down by German Messerschmitts that had climbed out of the cloud-shrouded valleys of the Bavarian Alps. He had no idea what happened to the rest of his squadron, including the P-51 Mustang fighter escorts.

Ryan sighed and stood up. He didn't know how long he'd been in the cell—many hours, he was certain. He had slept off and on.

He flexed his arm muscles. His whole body ached from the impact of his crash through the thick Bavarian forest. Had any of his buddies made it down? If so, were they captured, too, held somewhere else in this subterranean place?

Christ, he thought, *all those bombing missions in the B-17s, and I have to get shot down on a milk run.*

He went to the iron bars. "Hey!" he shouted. "Is anybody here?" His words echoed along the narrow corridor and came back on him.

He thought of his twenty-three-year-old wife, Rachel, and their four-year-old son, Bobby, who were in Akron, Ohio. Rachel's last letter had said they were praying and waiting for Daddy to come home. That's all Ryan lived for.

I'll get out of here, Rachel—I promise I will.

He heard heavy footsteps approaching. A stern young man flanked by two guards materialized out of the shadows from beyond the light. The young man wore an angry expression, but Ryan had a feeling he looked this way all the time.

"*Sprechen Sie Deutsch?*" he demanded of Ryan.

Ryan tried to look blank. He wasn't about to admit that he understood and spoke some German—thanks to his wife's Frankfurt-born grandmother, who lived with them.

The young man stared intently at him, eyes boring through him. He was tall and sinewy, with short blond hair and a pale, bony face that was so lean it was almost gaunt. His blue eyes were set in hollows that added to the intensity of his gaze. He was dressed in charcoal gray trousers, a khaki shirt, and a loose white jacket, the kind doctors wore.

Ryan wondered if the young man really was a doctor, and had been sent to check him for injuries. He couldn't be much older than Ryan himself.

He pulled back from the cell bars but didn't let go. He had a well-earned reputation for being fearless, but there was something about the young man that made him extremely uneasy.

The German's gaze didn't waver from Ryan's eyes. The man said, *"Darf ich Ihnen eine Zigarette anbieten?"*

Would I like a cigarette, translated Ryan silently. Damn, would I like one!

His captors had stripped him of his leather aviator's jacket, which contained his pack of unfiltered Chesterfields. Ryan was having a nicotine fit. He practically licked his lips at the thought.

Instead, he feigned he did not comprehend.

The Nazi twisted his thin mouth into a half smile. He said, in English, "I see you do understand me, Lt. James Ryan. I see it in your eyes. You cannot fool me."

Ryan admitted nothing. "Where am I?"

"Gehen Sie Hose und Onterhose aus!"

Ryan squawked. This Nazi prick had just ordered him to take off his trousers and shorts. He was no doctor, and Ryan was damned if he'd let himself be buggered by a pervert! He tightened his grip on the bars until his knuckles went white.

The blond German snickered. "I thought you'd object. Very well, Lieutenant, I'll play your charade and speak English. I don't have time to waste on you. Take off all your clothes, immediately." He nodded to the guards, who opened the cell door and allowed him to enter. The guards followed him in. Suddenly the small room was very crowded.

Without realizing it, Ryan took several steps backward. Then he stopped and squared his shoulders. His sore muscles protested.

Ryan was slightly over six feet in height, and he looked eyeball to eyeball with the young German. He had more flesh on his frame than the German—hard, muscled flesh—but he felt oddly vulnerable. There was something about the man, an unpleasant aura that swept out around him. Ryan wanted to stay out of his way. His instinctive reaction angered him.

Damned if I'm going to let some Nazi punk bulldoze me, he told himself. "Who are you?" he said out loud. "What is this joint?"

"My name is Hans Messner. *Doctor* Messner. And it is I who will ask the questions. Take off your clothes."

Ryan started to protest anew, but Messner cut him off. "You Americans are so preoccupied with sex. I have no interest of that kind in you. Do as I say, immediately!"

The guards snapped their short-barreled submachine guns to Ryan's chest level. Either he was going to undress himself, or they were going to undress his corpse. Slowly he undid the buttons of his shirt and unzipped his trousers. Presently he was standing with nothing on but his dog tags.

Messner ran an appraising eye up and down his body. It gave Ryan the willies, and a hot flush of embarrassment spread below the tanned skin of his face. He felt like a piece of meat on display, and he still wasn't convinced he wouldn't be buggered. He'd heard stories about the unnatural sexual preferences of a lot of German soldiers. It was humiliating standing here like this. He had expected to be tortured, not humiliated. If he got out of here—*when* he got out of here, he corrected himself—he sure as hell wouldn't say a thing about this. He wondered if the guards were getting their jollies, but got no hints from their cold eyes and grim mouths.

Messner reached out and with both bony hands began probing and feeling, avoiding the skin that was already blackening from bruises from Ryan's fall. "It is not out of kindness that I avoid your bruises," he informed Ryan. "I simply do not like to touch bad flesh, the same way I would not touch spoiled parts of an apple."

Ryan shuddered. This German's touch made him queasy, and he sounded like he was rowing with one oar in the water.

Messner poked at the American from all sides. "You are in excellent condition, Lieutenant. A well-proportioned build, firm flesh. Mid-twenties, I'd say. Hmmm..."

Ryan dropped his eyes. He noticed the German had a large brown birthmark in the shape of a diamond, just above his left elbow on the outside of the arm. He preoccupied himself with it to take his mind off the discomfort of the man's poking.

Messner came around from behind and peered into Ryan's face. Ryan stared into ice-blue eyes that had no more warmth than a glacier. Messner's white skin was stretched taut from cheekbone to cheekbone. The nose was sharp, the nostrils deep. Despite his apparent youth, tiny scowl lines showed on the forehead and around the thin lips. The face was devoid of marks that indicated laughter or happiness.

Messner pulled down Ryan's lower eyelids and then raised his upper lids. "Good characteristics... gray eyes, sand-colored hair, square jaw.... Open your mouth."

Ryan obeyed.

Messner pulled back his lips to expose his teeth and gums. "You have unusually good teeth in the front, but I see gold in the back—"

Shit, that's what this creep wants—the gold crowns. He's going to pull my teeth out!

"—you have not taken proper care of your teeth," Messner finished. "Overall, you are a nice specimen." The German stepped back. "You may get dressed."

Ryan almost sighed with relief. He couldn't get his clothes back on fast enough. "What is this—a laboratory exam?"

"As a matter of fact, it is, but only to satisfy my curiosity. If you were German, I could make use of you. Americans I have no need for. You will be executed."

Ryan went cold. His skin prickled. Surely they would torture and interrogate him first. If only he could prolong his life until he figured out a way to escape. There *must* be a way out of here, he thought.

For God's sakes, the war was supposed to be nearly over! Germany was on her knees. He couldn't survive this long without making it all the way.

He said stiffly, "I demand to be treated according to the Geneva convention—"

"You have blundered into an A-1 security area. You will

be executed. Save your breath, Ryan." Messner spun on his heel to go. On the other side of the cell, he stopped and turned around. "Perhaps, Lieutenant, I can make use of you—for a while. Don't get your hopes up about staying alive, but your death will be delayed if you cooperate."

"If you think I'll divulge classified military information—"

Messner seemed amused. "You delude yourself if you think you know anything of interest to me. I am curious about your *abilities*, Ryan, not your worthless military information."

Ryan was caught short. "My abilities for *what*?"

But Messner ignored him, speaking rapidly instead to one of the guards. The guard slung his machine gun onto his shoulder and unhooked a pair of handcuffs from his uniform belt. He yanked Ryan's arms painfully behind his back.

Ryan protested. "Wait a minute! What about that cigarette you promised?"

Messner gave him a hard look and addressed the burly guard again. Ryan's hands were pulled around in front of him and cuffed.

At least I might have a fighting chance with my hands in front of me, Ryan thought.

The guard reached into a pocket and drew out a crumpled pack of German cigarettes and a box of matches. He stuffed a cigarette between his thick lips and lit it, then held it out for Ryan.

"That's all you've got—Nazi weed? What happened to my own smokes?" Ryan didn't get an answer. He took the cigarette between his teeth and inhaled deeply. The tobacco was tarry and stale, but he was grateful for it. He inhaled again, and then Messner took the cigarette away from him and stepped on it.

"Hey!"

"Smoking is forbidden in most parts of this facility," Messner said. "We must go. Now."

The guards closed in around Ryan, each taking an arm

and shoving him forward out of the cell. Jesus, they *were* going to torture him. That's what Messner meant—his ability to withstand pain.

The guards walked him at a quick pace into an arched granite corridor hewn out of the living rock of the mountain, and lit every few feet by bare light bulbs strung along the apex of the arch. Messner was already well ahead, going at a fast clip. Ryan looked around, tried to absorb details. They passed other corridors, and he cast quick looks in both directions. All passages were lit with rows of bare bulbs on the ceilings. Men and women passed them, carrying clipboards and racks of test tubes, nodded deferentially to Messner. Some of them wore Nazi uniforms and some wore white lab coats. Ryan saw open rooms with more scientific equipment that reminded him of chemistry lab in high school. He read the signs on closed doors, but they told him little: *no smoking . . . authorized access only . . . caution . . .* Then they passed a red door that read, *Vorsicht! Lebensgefahr!*

"Caution! Danger of death"? What on earth was going on in *there*?

But the guards bustled Ryan by the door before he could speculate.

Just as they passed a door labeled "No Trespassing," it opened and a man in a purple jacket emerged. Then Ryan realized the jacket was white but looked purple in the violet light that came from within the room. Ryan glimpsed a glass partition inside. On the other side of the glass were rows of silvery metal cylinders—very cold, judging from what looked like coatings of frost on them. They didn't look like bombs. But what are they?

The man in the smock stopped Messner. They conversed in low tones, the man gesturing toward the room with the cylinders. Ryan strained to hear but caught only fragments of the rapidly spoken German. The man was concerned about temperatures and light because too much of one and not enough of the other—Ryan wasn't sure which—was detrimental to whatever was in the cylinders.

Maybe they *are* bombs, Ryan thought. Some new secret weapon. Maybe this place had something to do with those V-2 rocket missiles the Germans had just developed. Or maybe the canisters held gas. That was it! The Germans had developed a new poisonous gas.

And maybe they were going to test it on *him*. Ryan's stomach felt like a mass of jelly.

He was prodded on. He had no sense of bearings—they kept turning down one corridor after another—left, right, left. The corridors all looked alike. The place was huge, a maze. Or else they were going in circles.

The only other open door they passed revealed people of indeterminate sex, wearing white smocks and black hair nets, bent over microscopes. The smell of formaldehyde reminded Ryan of his biology lab in high school. He glimpsed large vitric jars sitting on a stainless steel counter, but he could not identify the oddly shaped objects that floated in the formaldehyde.

Messner was stopped again, this time by a woman who brandished a large, brown folder, from which she extracted an X ray. The image was of a man's pelvic area. She was asking permission for something—an operation, Ryan guessed. But Messner held up the X ray to the bare bulb light and shook his head. The woman didn't argue. She replaced the X ray in her folder, made a slight bow, and continued on her way.

Nobody seems to argue with this guy, Ryan thought.

At last Messner stopped in front of a steel door painted brown and inserted a key in the lock. He strode in. The guards followed, dumping Ryan unceremoniously on a straight-backed wooden chair at a rectangular table. The table was strange. It was partitioned so that a person sitting at one end could not see who was sitting, if anyone, at the opposite end.

"Herr Gruber!" Messner called. A pock-faced, balding man with round wire spectacles appeared from a cubicle in a corner. Messner pointed to Ryan. "Give him the Zener test for latency."

"Zener test? What are you talking about?" Ryan didn't have the foggiest idea what was meant by "latency."

Messner peered down at him. "You Americans like to play cards, no? Are you a gambler, Lieutenant? Do you try to guess what hand your opponent holds in a game of poker?"

Ryan wasn't sure how to respond. If this was interrogation, it wasn't anything like what the Army had prepared him for. "I guess I play a little stud," he said warily.

"You guess. Good for you. That is exactly what you will do now—make educated guesses. See, we have an interesting little card game for you." Messner took a pack of cards from the pock-faced man and displayed them to Ryan. They looked like flash cards for elementary school children. Each card had a single symbol on it—a square, a triangle, a circle, a pair of wavy lines, or a cross.

"These are Zener cards. Herr Gruber will sit on the other side of the partition. He will pick a card and think about its symbol. He will concentrate very hard to hold a picture of it in his mind. You will sit on the other side and try to determine what symbol he is thinking about."

"Are you kidding?"

"You do not take this seriously?"

"This is nothing but a parlor game. Besides that, I can't read his mind!"

"Maybe you don't realize that you can. That is what we want to find out."

Ryan shook his head in bewilderment and mumbled, "Loco, man. Pure loco."

"'Loco'? Ah, yes, 'crazy.' Far from it, Lieuteuant Ryan. You are wondering why do I not torture and interrogate you for military information. Military information is worthless to me. *This* information is priceless. Proceed. You will have to speak your beginner's German. Herr Gruber understands no English."

"But—"

Messner and one of the guards exited, leaving him looking up at the ugly Herr Gruber with his pocked face and double chin. The remaining guard took up a station by the door, his submachine gun ready. For the first time, Ryan noticed a nasty scar that ran the length of one cheek.

The room seemed suddenly cold. Gruber scrawled a few lines on the paper attached to his clipboard and then stared at Ryan.

Ryan grimaced. He did not want to use German. It was a barbaric tongue, the language of bloodthirsty Huns. Besides, he wasn't convinced Gruber didn't understand English. Didn't all foreigners, if English was spoken slowly enough? He said to Gruber, "You don't have to give me the fish eye."

Gruber set down his clipboard on the other side of the partition. He picked up the cards and began sorting through them. *"Ich verstehe nicht,"* he growled.

"Okay, I gotcha, you don't understand." Ryan sighed and put his elbows on the table. He was jumpy, and desperate for another cigarette. *"Zigaretten!"* he shouted. *"Geben Sie mir Zigaretten!"*

Dr. Josef Mengele waited impatiently for his colleague by the main exit, a lift that went to the surface of the mountain hideaway. He was anxious to get out of this place. With the Allies closing in, he hated being underground. Damn it, where *was* Hans? He was usually punctual. Mengele paced back and forth, his small frame hunched in the heavy overcoat.

Unlike some of the Nazi officers around him who refused to admit the Reich might be defeated, Mengele was a realist. He had a contingency plan. He would not sacrifice himself in some useless last stand. He had seen the handwriting on the wall the previous November, when Himmler had ordered the deathworks shut down at Auschwitz. Mengele had been loathe to do it, and even more reluctant to give up his engrossing medical research with twins, but he could see that it was time to preserve what he could of his work and get out of the crumbling German empire. He had done more than turn off the gas showers and end the mass executions by firing squads—he had abandoned his post as *Lagerarzt* and slipped out of Auschwitz in the dead of night just before Christmas. He had fled Poland and gone underground back in Germany, prepared to survive at all costs—and so would Messner if the young man followed his instructions—so that work on the Reich's most important project, *Die Wunderkinder* would continue, somewhere, somehow.

Everything of *Die Wunderkinder* was here at the fortress. Mengele worried about its safety but Hans remained unperturbed by the changing tides of the war. Mengele sighed as his boot heels clicked against the granite. Perhaps he did worry too much. Wasn't the fortress well-hidden, and wasn't it specially reinforced to withstand surface bomb explosions?

But the Luftwaffe no longer controlled the skies even over Germany, thanks to the ineptness of Hermann Göring. Der Führer should have gotten rid of Göring sooner!

Mengele fidgeted and pulled at his dark mustache. He did not like waiting. Perhaps Hans needed a reminder about *discipline*. He continued pacing back and forth, the leather of his polished jackboots creaking with every step. The four guards around him—Mengele went everywhere these days with guards—stood at attention, eyes staring straight ahead.

Before Mengele's irritation blossomed into anger, Messner appeared, marching down the cold granite corridor. Like Mengele, he was dressed for the trip up to the outside, wearing a heavy, khaki-colored wool trench coat and black leather gloves.

Mengele narrowed his eyes in disapproval of his lateness.

"My apologies, Josef," Messner said in a voice that indicated he wasn't sorry at all. "I had to take care of that American flier we captured."

"You've executed him?"

Messner shook his head. "Not yet. I'm giving him the Zener test for latent extrasensory ability."

Mengele was not pleased to hear this. "You're wasting the

time and resources of the Reich. The prisoner is of no value to us—have him shot immediately!"

Messner coolly regarded him. He was much taller than Mengele, and was fair to Mengele's dark. And unlike Mengele—as well as Hitler and a host of other ranking officers of the Third Reich—he was the perfect embodiment of the exalted Aryan characteristics. That, plus his brilliance and stubborn nature, enabled him to do as he pleased most of the time.

Messner replied, "It does no harm to give him a few tests. We have never evaluated an American. After we've won the war, we may want to incorporate some American specimen into the Project."

After we've won the war! Did Hans, preoccupied in his subterranean laboratory, have no idea how badly the war was going for the Reich, how panicked were its officers, how paranoid was der Führer—why, the man hadn't set foot outside his Berlin bunker since January! The Americans had crossed the Rhine and were pushing deep into Germany; the Russians had just seized Vienna. And the air assaults from the Americans and British were growing worse every day, with bigger and bigger bombs.

But this was neither the time nor the place to discuss such matters, in front of the guards. What Mengele had to say might be construed as treason. Even in these chaotic days, it was still possible to be shot for the slightest hint of disloyalty. He still had his contingency plan to consider.

"You may give the American a few tests," he agreed grudgingly. "Then shoot him."

"Yes, sir."

With the guards, they squeezed into the lift, a small metal cage on a cable that ran on a track between the outside of the mountain and the center of the laboratory. The track inclined at a steep, forty-five-degree angle.

Mengele pushed the start button and the cage began its slow, jerky ascent. Once outside, a car would take them down a narrow, rutted road that wound through the mountains to a hidden airstrip nearby. An old Fokker, a relic of the previous world war and all the Reich could spare for noncombat flights, waited there to ferry Mengele away.

On Mengele's standing order, Hans always accompanied him to and from the airstrip. Mengele never explained why, but it was one of his precautions against assassination attempts by the guards. The inner circles of the Reich were rife with plots and counterplots. No one could be trusted. The guards, he noticed, seemed fearful of Messner. Even the Totenkopf, the Death's Head Corps, which Mengele had sent from Auschwitz. The Totenkopf were SS rejects, the acknowledged scum of the Reich, and it took an extremely tough man to discipline and command them. Yet these men at the laboratory followed Messner's orders as meekly as lambs.

Mengele glanced at his colleague, once again speculating on the mystical power he possessed to make others obey. Hans was deeply absorbed in thought. He was, Mengele guessed, preoccupied with the American flier.

He, on the other hand, was preoccupied with saving himself and *Die Wunderkinder* from destruction by the Allies. In his opinion, the genetics project was the most important work undertaken by the Reich—far more important than expanding the borders of Germany, or beating other nations into submission, or disposing of the world's degenerates at the death camps. But Hitler's commitment to *Die Wunderkinder* was weakening, despite his obsession with creating the Master Race.

Mengele could not allow his beautiful project to suffer. *Die Wunderkinder* was the key to the future of the Master Race.

The project had its beginnings long before Hitler rose to supreme power and began his war campaigns. It was created by a Munich doctor by the name of Kurt Schmidt, who was fascinated by spiritual mediums, hypnotism and "extrasensory phenomena" such as clairvoyance and telepathy. It was his theory that extrasensory perception was not some strange gift handed randomly to individuals by a capricious God, but was an ability that lay dormant within every person. Some individuals were born with this ability naturally awakened; others could awaken it through rigorous training; and some remained psychically asleep their entire lives.

It was also Dr. Schmidt's theory that if a man and a woman who were both endowed with naturally awakened psychic gifts were to mate, then their offspring would have the same, if not superior, ability. Dr. Schmidt felt the world would be vastly improved if all human beings possessed and used these rare talents.

It was all a matter of genetics. Carefully controlled breeding.

Dr. Schmidt set about to test his theory. He scoured Germany for a group of test subjects and paid them handsomely to conceive children out of wedlock "in the name of science." Since times were bad, he got a fair number of takers. Some of the tests did yield remarkable offspring— quiet babies with large, mesmerizing eyes, in whose reflection Dr. Schmidt was certain was the manifestation of extrasensory power.

The doctor's ambitious scheme called for generations of breeding—the children from the first test group would be mated with other psychic-positive persons he found. Eventually, he hypothesized, he would achieve the "ultimate human," someone whose mind was developed to its full potential.

But Dr. Schmidt was so far ahead of his time that his ideas were scorned and derided, and he could not get funding for his research. Until he came to the attention of Dr. Otmar von Verschuer, a professor at the University of Frankfurt am Main, who was widely published in his views of racial science. Luckily for Mengele and the Reich, and unluckily for Schmidt, von Verschuer promoted the Munich doctor to Adolf Hitler, a man fascinated by both the occult aspect of Schmidt's work and by its potential for the Master Race plan.

Hitler was enormously impressed by Schmidt's scattered

results. When he consolidated his power as the ruler of the Third Reich, he incorporated Schmidt's work into his grand blueprint for eugenics. For a place in which to conduct secret research, Hitler had the Bavarian fortress built out of a series of natural caves. He made unlimited funds available —nothing was begrudged *Die Wunderkinder*, as the project came to be called.

Mengele remembered old Dr. Schmidt. Grateful for Hitler's support, but stubborn and disagreeable, wanting to do things his way instead of Hitler's way. Der führer had taken care of that problem. After the doctor was arrested on false charges of treason—he died soon after in prison—Otmar von Verschuer lobbied successfully for *Die Wunderkinder* to be given to his favorite student, Josef Mengele.

And rightfully so, thought Mengele as the cage ground toward the surface. *It was destined to be mine, considering my degrees in medicine and anthropology, and my commitment to the Master Race!*

Just short of the surface, the cage stalled. Cursing, the guard at the controls worked the gearshift and stabbed at different buttons. Josef felt his temper, always short, begin to fray.

"It's the generator," said Messner. "It's been troublesome."

"Damn it, fix it! You shouldn't be so sloppy."

Messner did not respond. The guard succeeded in restarting the cage, and they resumed their ascent. Within moments, they reached the top and the cage jerked to a stop. A guard spun the wheel of the steel door to the surface of the earth, and pushed it open. Cold night air rushed in at them, a welcome relief from the stuffiness below. Mengele breathed deeply as he stepped out. Overhead, stars sparkled like gems in a clear black sky, and a gibbous moon hung low over an icy peak.

Black metallic paint glinted nearby; it was the Mercedes waiting to take them to the airstrip. Leather boots crunched on the hard-packed snow as Mengele and Messner climbed into the back seat and one of the guards got behind the wheel. The engine sputtered and caught. The trip would be slow on the twisting mountain roads because they would not travel with headlights on. The other guards from the fortress would wait behind for Messner to come back. Hans did not share Mengele's fears of assassination.

Messner had come to Mengele's attention as he gained prominence as a Nazi youth leader in Koln. Mengele liked him from the moment they met. They came from similar backgrounds, the sons of self-made industrialists. They thought alike. Mengele was even more pleased to discover Hans was a brilliant student in Mengele's own fields, medicine and anthropology. It was just like his relationship with von Verschuer, only he was the mentor, not the protégé. It gave him a great sense of power. When Mengele was appointed *Lagerartz* at Auschwitz, he authorized Messner to direct the research on *Die Wunderkinder*. The appointment elevated Messner from protégé to colleague, an equal, though still technically under Mengele's supervision.

Hans was difficult to supervise. He had arrogance to match his brilliance. He was only twenty-four, but acted two decades older. Because he was himself an ideal specimen for the master race, Mengele had tried to persuade him to spend time at one of Himmler's camps where ideal young men and women bred ideal babies.

But Hans would have none of that. His interest in women did not extend beyond that of a scientist in the laboratory. Nor was he interested in boys, to Mengele's immense relief, for homosexuality could be a one-way ticket to an execution, depending upon a superior officer's mood. Since Messner's work on *Die Wunderkinder* was so important, Mengele did not push him about the camps.

Periodically, Hans came to Auschwitz to help Mengele in his selections and experiments. He spent most of his time bent over petri dishes and test tubes in the underground lab. He had made incredible advances in genetics. He was taking research intended for producing better livestock, fruits and vegetables and was applying it to humans.

Thank God for the KZs, the death camps, thought Mengele. The camps had ensured a steady supply of test subjects for experiments and surgeries. Risky techniques were tried out first on the prisoners, who were doomed to death anyway; also, the Nazis had to find out what made inferiors inferior. From prisoners, they had obtained samples of all parts of the human reproductive systems, as well as human embyros and fetuses in various stages of development. The data were fascinating.

But now the wonderful experimenatation was over, because Himmler had ordered it terminated.

As the car rolled slowly along the bumpy road, Mengele chose his moment. The reactions of his colleague were often unpredictable. Josef spoke in a low voice, leaning close to Messner so his words would not be heard by the driver up front. "Hans, we must talk about an emergency plan—in the unlikely case that Germany goes down in the war."

"But Germany will not go down! Germany will win! We will triumph!" In the darkness, Messner's horrified expression was visible.

"Of course," Mengele agreed, acutely aware of the need to maintain patriotic appearances. "But it is only common sense to have a safety plan. Der führer has ordered it," he added. It was a lie. Der führer wasn't ordering much of anything.

Messner grunted acknowledgment. "Josef, the fortress is impenetrable. We are well below the surface, protected by granite and a glacial wall. What could happen? No enemies know we're here."

"Then you must take this on faith. If anything happens to the Reich, or we can no longer pursue our work in Germany, we must have an organized plan for carrying on our work somewhere else." Mengele folded his hands together on his lap and nervously unlocked and locked his fingers repeatedly. "I have given thought to this, and written down instructions, in case we are separated and unable to communicate. I have left them in an envelope in the file room safe in the laboratory. You *must* follow the instructions, for the work on *Die Wunderkinder* must survive at all costs."

Messner seemed to sense the seriousness of Mengele's concerns, and it sobered him slightly. "Of course, Josef. I will obey—you know that."

Mengele nodded. "Good." He said no more for the rest of the journey.

The tiny airstrip was camouflaged during the day and used only at night. It was far from any villages, though most peasants would have the sense not to say anything if they had any inkling of it. The entire area was saturated with SS patrols.

The pilot was waiting inside the little plane as the car approached. The driver halted the car, and Mengele and Messner got out.

Josef held out his hand and took Messner's large, bony hand in a firm grip. "I'm going to Frankfurt—there are records of Otmar's that must be saved." He pulled Messner out of earshot range of the guard. "Hans, the Reich is in much worse shape than you can imagine. You must get ready to evacuate. Read my instructions. I will return as soon as possible. I don't know exactly when, for transport is becoming increasingly difficult."

Mengele could feel Messner's icy eyes piercing him as the young man said, "There is nothing to worry about here, Josef."

Josef wished he could be so confident. He turned away; there was nothing more to say. He climbed aboard the plane and leaned out the side as he remembered a final thought. "Hans, I want the American shot. *Tonight*."

CHAPTER Two

Hans Messner watched Mengele's plane taxi down the short airstrip and pull up sharply for its ascent. He had enormous respect for Josef and the work he was doing for the Reich, but sometimes his superior struck him as paranoid. Germany would not fall; the setbacks were temporary.

I am the wolf and this is my den. Isn't that what der führer was fond of saying? Hans shared Hitler's awe of wolves. Like them, he was lean and cunning, and he would survive in his lair, shielded by granite and glacier. *Mein Wolfsschanze*, he thought.

The sound of the plane engines died away. Messner got back in the Mercedes. He forgot about Mengele's fears. He was abosrbed once again in the work ahead of him.

Back underground, Messner went directly to the test room, where he found the American flier flipping aimlessly through the Zener cards while the pock-faced Gruber labored over a notebook. Too bad Ryan couldn't be run through a few more tests, but orders were orders. It would be just like Josef to demand to see the log book when he returned to the fortress. A few hours of an American's life were not worth an argument. The log book would show truthfully that the

American was executed upon Messner's return from the airstrip.

As Messner entered the card test room, Ryan stood up from the table and looked into his eyes. The American's shoulders dropped slightly.

Messner gave him an emotionless smile. A man always knows when his death is imminent. He took the notebook from Gruber and scanned the results. "I see you have tested well with the cards."

Ryan looked flustered. "This guessing game doesn't make any sense to me. What does it prove?"

Messner handed the notebook back to Gruber. "Such a shame I can't keep you for our real work."

"What's that?"

"Such a guileless question. While it is doubtful you could escape us, we can't take that chance and have you free in the world, knowing about us. You must die to preserve our secret."

Ryan pushed the cards into a neat stack. "It's customary to grant a dying man a last favor."

"So?"

"So, I want to know what's really going on here. If I'm going to die, it won't matter. What's the reason for all the fancy equipment you've got, and why are so many of the women I've seen pregnant? What's in those canisters in that purple room? And—" he picked up a card printed with wavy lines—"what are these hieroglyphics supposed to prove?"

Messner laughed. "You ask a favor I can't grant, Lieutenant Ryan, for obvious reasons of state security." A snap of his fingers summoned two guards. They grabbed Ryan roughly, one of them tearing the cigarette from his mouth as they pulled him to his feet.

"Easy does it, Fritz!" Ryan objected. The guards paid no attention and shackled his legs together. The short chain gave him enough room to walk a hobbling gait, but not to run.

Messner exited the test room at a brisk pace, leaving the

American to stumble along behind him. Messner knew the guards would see that he kept up.

Ryan shouted at his back, "I have a right to know where you're taking me, *Herr* Messner!"

Messner didn't answer. *You have no rights, American*, he thought. He would have the guards shoot him up on the surface, where they could throw the body in the woods for the mountain wolves. He considered dispatching them with execution orders so that he could return to more important tasks, then decided to witness the execution himself to make sure it was done properly. Since taking over the underground lab, he had not had the responsibility of disposing of an enemy soldier. What a nuisance.

Messner quickened his step. Behind him, Ryan yelped as the guards whacked him with the butts of their Maschinenpistole submachine guns. People coming from the opposite direction made way for Messner, as they always did. Turning around a bend in the corridor, he noted that several light bulbs above were burned out. He came to an abrupt halt and frowned. Was the lab short of light bulbs, or was this just gross negligence?

He motioned to a brunette woman with a clipboard, who jumped to obey his signal with eyes lowered in deference. He made her look at the burned out bulbs and gave her a stinging dressing down for allowing such a thing to happen. "Vigilance!" he shouted at her. "We must all maintain vigilance to keep the Reich running in perfect order."

As the chastened woman departed, the American sputtered a giggly laugh. "Keep the Reich running in perfect order?" he said in English. "That's gotta be the best joke I've heard since I fell into this hellhole. The war is almost over for you guys, Messner. We're blowing you away up on the surface. A few bombs will turn *this* place into a tomb."

Messner ignored him and resumed his journey toward the main rail lift. To his annoyance, the American would not keep quiet.

"I'm talking *big* bombs, pal," Ryan shrieked as his leg

chains clanked. "Us and the Brits aren't dropping the little thousand pounders anymore. We're dropping eight- , ten-thousand-pound bombs, some as much as twenty-two thousand pounds. That's a lot of blasting power—"

Messner twisted around and roared, "Silence!"

One of the guards raised his gun butt and gave Ryan a swift crack on the forehead, sending the American reeling against a cold granite wall. The guard raised his gun again, but Messner shook his head. The loudmouthed American might deserve a beating, but if he couldn't walk on his own, it would only delay the execution.

Ryan staggered along. At least now the donkey had quit braying. Messner cast another glance at him. The blow had broken skin, and blood trickled down into his right eyebrow and down the bridge of his nose. Ryan wiped at it with his cuffed hands.

Twenty-two thousand pounds, Messner wondered. He had never heard of such a bomb. The American had to be lying. Even so, he was confident there was nothing to worry about. The fortress, under a hundred meters of granite and glacial ice, was built to withstand bomb blasts. There were enough supplies to live on for a year, should it become necessary to seal off the fortress from the outside. *Die Wunderkinder* was safe.

They approached a metal catwalk that passed the observation room of the nursery. To go through the observation room was the shortest path; to avoid it meant taking a circuitous route. Messner was impatient. It wouldn't matter if the American saw the nursery room—what could he deduce from that? It would be amusing to see his bewilderment.

He passed through a wide door into a long, narrow room with a low ceiling and windows along one side. He looked down. Below was a large, open room, well lit and comfortably appointed with furniture, beds and cribs. Babies slept in some of the cribs; toddlers played with toys on thick, wooly rugs. Fine Aryan specimen, he thought. He was proud of them and of the role he had played to bring them into the world.

"Holy Toledo," muttered Ryan, still wiping at a thin stream of blood. "What in the devil is this?"

Messner stopped and turned. The American was gaping through the windows. He followed Ryan's gaze to the buxom young mothers, naked to the waist, who were nursing infants. Once again, it confirmed his view that all Americans were obsessed with sex. Personally, he was not aroused by the sight of infants sucking at ample breasts. Women were specimen, to be graded and used or discarded.

"Is this how you guys get your rocks off?" Ryan wanted to know. "Put these girls on display?"

Messner was not familiar with the colloquialism, but Ryan's tone conveyed his meaning.

"Sex as you know it is not allowed here," he said tersely.

"What? No sex?" Ryan's face screwed into a puzzled expression. He looked at Messner and then back down at the girls. "Those babies didn't come out of thin air."

"They were bred from the finest men and women Germany has to offer."

One of the girls, a blond with long, braided hair, looked up to the observation window while an infant suckled at her breast. Her eyes were large and icy blue. Her expression was blank, as if she saw nothing before her.

"She gives me the creeps," said Ryan. "She looks like a zombie."

"She is trying to tell you something without speaking, Lieutenant. If you listen in your mind, maybe you will hear her thoughts and—" Messner stopped short. In his pride, he had said too much. Well, the American would soon be dead.

Ryan shook his head. "*Hear her thoughts*? What in the hell are you talking about?"

Messner motioned to the guards, and they pulled Ryan away from the window. Messner was now having serious doubts about ever incorporating Americans into the Project. If Ryan was a typical specimen, Americans would have to be lumped in with Jews, gypsies and other asocials. What had he expected from such a mongrelized nation as the United States? At least Americans, once they fell under Germany's domination, would make interesting experimental subjects, to be sacrificed in the name of science.

Messner reached one of the main lifts and was about to open the cage door when a dark-haired woman in white called to him from the intersection of two tunnels. He recognized Dr. Helga Kraus, one of his chief assistants. She looked anxious and hurried in his direction.

"What is it, Dr. Kraus?" he said impatiently. "I'm busy."

She waited until she was close enough to speak in a low voice. "I've been looking all over for you. Have you forgotten? It's time for the Schueller woman—she is prepared and waiting in the operating room. The temperature controls—" her voice trailed off.

Messner consulted his watch and swore to himself. He was so absorbed with the American that he had indeed forgotten. It was not like him, and he was loath to admit mistakes, especially in front of his subordinates.

"Of course not," he snapped. "It will have to wait."

"But everything is ready. The ova have been warmed." She dropped her eyes. "All in accordance with your instructions, Dr. Messner."

Once again, Messner cursed silently. The fertilized ova were two years old. Unfrozen, they had a limited life span. If they had been warmed already, he would have to perform the insertion now, before they became nonviable structures. No one else was permitted to do impregnation insertions.

He looked at the empty lift cage and then at Ryan and the guards. He shrugged off his overcoat and handed it to Helga. "I'll be there immediately." She nodded and hurried off.

Messner addressed the American. "A break for you, Lieutenant Ryan. A short stay in your execution."

Ryan's face lit up. "What's happening?"

Without answering, Messner went on down the hallway and through swinging doors that led to a brightly lit white room filled with doctor's instruments. The guards hesitated, then pulled Ryan behind him. He could not keep pace with their fast gait, and Messner heard the lieutenant's feet dragging on the concrete.

Messner entered the white room. Helga was already busy with instruments. She helped Messner into a white gown and tied it in the back. He scrubbed at a deep, stainless steel sink. The guards positioned Ryan along one wall. "If you don't stay quiet, I will put you on the operating table instead," Messner said over his shoulder. To his mild surprise, the American made no retort.

While Messner consulted data on a clipboard, Helga left and reentered with a metal tray covered with a white cloth. On the cloth were a long and slender glass catheter, and a speculum.

"What are you going to do to her?" Ryan said, an edginess in his voice.

Messner held up the catheter, filled with a clear fluid. "I am going to do something the likes of which your scientists only dream of doing," he announced. "I am going to create life."

Ryan snorted. "Sure. Sounds like Frankenstein."

Messner was unruffled as he checked over his data. "Have you ever heard of genetics, Lieutenant Ryan?"

"Mom and Dad have blue eyes, the kid has blue eyes."

"An elementary analogy, but essentially accurate. Have you ever heard of eugenics?"

"Eugenics? Nope."

"Eugenics and genetics go hand in hand. Eugenics, the improvement of the human race through selective breeding, which is genetics."

"What's that got to do with whatever act of barbarism you're going to perform here?" Ryan was getting recklessly sarcastic again.

"You are witnessing eugenics in action. Selective breeding. I want this woman to carry a child. Not hers, someone else's."

"I thought that sort of thing was done only to cattle and sheep."

Messner laughed. "You are talking about artificial insemination, and what I am doing is much more complicated than that. But the principle works for animals. Why not humans?" He held up the catheter for his inspection.

The swinging doors parted as Helga wheeled in a stretcher. On top was a woman covered with a white sheet. Her long blond hair was pinned into a loose knot on top of her head. She had been sedated but was not unconscious. Her head lolled and her eyes were glazed.

Messner lifted the sheet and pulled the woman's feet into metal stirrups. He spread her legs wide and inserted the speculum in her vagina.

"You can't do this to her," Ryan protested. "You're treating her like an animal!"

"I assure you, she has looked forward to this."

A low boom sounded in the distance, and the floor beneath them vibrated. Some glass instruments sitting on a counter rattled. Messner hesitated a moment, then continued.

Ryan cheered. "That was a concussion! Bombers, not far off."

Messner scowled at him. "It's not the first time stray bombs have fallen in the vicinity. Whenever the Luftwaffe shoots down your planes, the pilots drop their bombs in a futile effort to do some damage before they crash."

"There ain't no Luftwaffe up there. Just us and the Brits."

Another boom sounded, louder and stronger, and then another. The floor shook. Ryan laughed. "Those were closer!"

"We are built to withstand bombs."

"One or two lucky hits—that's all it might take."

"Be quiet!" Messner turned back to the woman and reached inside her to feel for the opening of her cervix. Then he withdrew his hand and picked up the catheter. Carefully, he began sliding it up her vagina into her womb.

A deafening explosion threw Messner to the floor. Around

him, glass shattered and loose objects crashed to the floor. Dust and rubble fell down from the granite ceiling and obscured the air with a milky haze.

Messner lay dazed on the floor for a moment. What was that? What happened? The emergency klaxon horn was going off, and the lights were flickering. Screams sounded in the distance.

He started to rise, and a sharp pain made him look at his right hand. It was covered with blood, and still clutched the jagged half of the glass catheter. He let go of it and got to his knees, holding his injured hand before him. The woman was on the floor near him. She was twisted in the sheet, barely conscious and moaning, bleeding from between her legs. Messner got to his feet, looking for the guards and the American. He heard a low, whistling noise, and then another concussion knocked him down again and sent a shower of wet, rocky rubble on top of him. He groaned. Water! Good God, had the glacier and granite been breached? How could it happen?

Electricity shorted in a shower of sparks and the room was plunged into darkness. Messner heard a struggle going on toward one side of the room; near him, the woman still moaned. Shouts of panic and people running came from beyond the doors.

Messner cursed. They *were* sustaining direct bomb hits. The whole place was vibrating, rumbling and shuddering. What had gone wrong? Where was the Luftwaffe? Had the Allies discovered the fortress, or were the bombs aimed at something else? It didn't matter—the damage was being done.

The lights flickered back on as the emergency generator cut in. Now Messner saw one of the guards lying on the floor, his chest concave. Chunks of granite the size of the man's head lay nearby.

The other guard was wrestling with the American, who was straining for a Luger pistol held aloft by the German. The guard managed to twist the Luger inward and squeeze off a point-blank shot into Ryan's side. The American cried out but kept struggling.

The granite wall nearest Messner began to split open, and water from the underground glacial springs spurted in. Messner shot to his feet. There was no time to think. If the fortress was collapsing, he had to get away before he was buried alive.

The letter.... Mengele's letter of instruction, in case of emergency. He had to retrieve the letter from its safe, then escape. He knew a special way out, if he could reach it in time—if the containment doors hadn't already locked shut to seal off damaged portions of the fortress.

To hell with the American! To hell with the others!

Messner sprinted through the swinging doors just as the wall of the white operating room collapsed inward and the roof began to cave in. He didn't look back. Everyone left in there had to be buried alive.

He ran through corridors filled with choking dust and smoke from scattered fires. It was difficult to get his bearings. The corridors were clogged with people screaming and clawing at each other, running madly. Messner pushed and shoved violently. Concussions continued to send shock waves through the walls and floor. Messner was knocked down. He got up and threw himself through the crowd with renewed ferocity.

He squeezed through an intersecting corridor and stopped as he saw knee-deep water pouring at him from the opposite direction. He ran back out and tried another direction.

A baby's high wail floated above the noise. A man staggered by with a blood-covered head and an arm missing, and collapsed heavily into Messner. He pushed the body away vehemently—and gasped when he recognized who it was: Gruber, his card tester. The man was dead.

Messner let Gruber's body fall into a heap behind him. He struggled into a main corridor. A woman clutched at his arm. "Please," she begged, "help me—" He left her behind without hesitation. A long way ahead, he saw one of the containment doors starting to close, to seal off this part of the fortress. He ran like mad.

As Lieutenant James Ryan came to, he wondered why his side was on fire and why his eyes hurt. At first he thought he was back in his saggy double bed in Akron, with his wife, Rachel, asleep on the other side. He had just dreamed a nightmare that he was impaled on a stick and someone was shaking the bed and poking at his eyes.

Then he realized that he wasn't back in Akron, but still in the war, and still in Germany. A prisoner about to be executed—except a bomb had hit somewhere above them.

He blinked in the darkness. Agony. His eyes were full of grit. He was laying on his side, twisted in an odd position. He moved slightly, and pain shot up and down his entire right side. His thoughts swam. Then he remembered struggling with the guard after the concussion threw them to the floor, and the gun going off. He grabbed at his side with his left hand, and felt a mass of sticky, wet flesh. The bullet had grazed him at a shallow angle, otherwise his guts would be decorating the walls. It still hurt like hell, but that was a good sign, for a truly grievous wound would have been numb.

Another concussion shook the floor beneath him. Now he was aware of the cacophony around him—shouts and screaming. He had to get out.

He was in a pile of granite rubble that apparently had cascaded from one side of the room, judging from the slope he felt in the darkness. He sat up and almost passed out again. He must have been hit on the head, because a good portion of his skull hurt like the blazes.

If any bones were broken, he wasn't aware of it. He couldn't see a thing but a tiny thread of light on another side of the room. His hands and legs were still cuffed but free— the chains had been severed by the cave-in. He got up, groaning and clutching at his side. There were no sounds from within the room. He listened for a moment. He seemed to be the only survivor—Messner, his assistant, the woman, the guards—they must be dead.

He laughed out loud, but pain cut him off. So much for you, Messner, and the rest of your Nazi bastards.

And him, too, unless he got the hell out of here somehow.

Slowly, Ryan felt his way through the rubble toward the thread of light. He was winded after a few steps, and it hurt to breathe. He hoped to God the cave-in hadn't trapped him.

He reached the thread of light. It shone through what had been the double doors of the room. Tons of granite had pushed the doors open and jammed them, and then filled most of the gap in between. He clawed at the rubble, but some of the chunks were too heavy to budge. He shouted to the voices on the opposite side, but if his shouts were heard, they were ignored.

Fresh shock waves tore through the rock and concrete. Ryan attacked the pile barring his way with renewed frenzy. He threw himself into the crack where the doors met, trying to widen it enough to push himself through. He kept clawing and pushing, until at last he had an opening just wide enough to force himself through to the other side.

He stumbled free with a gasp. The overhead lights were on in the corridors around him, probably thanks to an emergency generator. Men and women, some of them wounded and some with their dusty clothes in shreds, struggled past. No one paid any attention to him. He paused long enough to squint at his wounded side, but could judge little from the mess of split flesh and blood-soaked, torn clothing. His entire side, from his armpit to his knee, was wet and red from a spreading blood stain. He covered his wound with his left hand as best as he could and staggered into the corridor, letting himself be swept along in the crowd. He had no idea where he was or where he was going. He hoped those around him did, and were not running in blind panic.

Ryan saw a faint purple glow ahead and, as he drew nearer, recognized the room that held the icy metal canisters. The door had been twisted off its hinges. He paused in the ragged opening and looked in. The glass partition was gone, reduced to shards. All but two of the violet lights were out.

The frosty metal canisters were scattered through the wreckage—some had even rolled out into the corridor. A few had been ruptured, and their thick, chalky contents oozed across the floor. The puddles looked like—

—God, he *knew* what the stuff was. A thought flashed into Ryan's head that he should take a canister with him. The Allies would need it. He grabbed the nearest one with his right hand, and cried out as he realized his mistake. The cold and ice instantly froze his hand to the metal. He pried his fingers off, leaving bits of flesh stuck behind.

Forget it, he thought, balling his injured hand into a fist. Just get out of here in one piece.

The lights blinked off and on, and that spurred him on. In the dark, he'd be a dead man for sure.

Hans Messner focussed on the closing containment door and pushed himself to run faster. *I must get the letter*, he repeated to himself over and over again.

The closing door had cut off all but a slice of the corridor. Messner threw himself at it and scraped through. Triumph! He would not die, trapped like an animal.

He heard grunts behind him and turned to see a guard close on his heels. The man was reaching out with his right hand as the iron door slammed shut on it. The man screamed. All Messner could see was the hand clawing at him. Then, severed, it fell to the floor.

Messner turned and kept going. Here there seemed to be fewer people. He had been cut off from the masses trying to get out. *They* were trapped, but he would escape!

He knew where he was now. He dodged down a smoky side corridor, coughing and covering his mouth with his sleeve. Then he took another to the right. He passed the nursery—a pile of stones and boulders. Screams and baby cries were coming from the women's dormitory. He didn't stop.

At last he made it to the file room and fell upon the gray safe. He spun the dial and yanked open its thick, heavy door. Mengele's brown, letter-size envelope lay inside. He folded it crookedly and stuffed it into his shirt pocket, buttoning down the flap. He grabbed a manila folder on the bottom of the safe. It contained enough research information so that he could rebuild *Die Wunderkinder*.

Now to get out. As if in answer, the fortress rumbled and shook with a new violence. He would not try the tram tunnel—if that had not collapsed, it would be packed with others. He would escape instead through one of the ventilation shafts to the outside. The narrow vents were constructed with internal ladder footholds, so that repairmen could access the entire shafts. It was a one-hundred-meter climb to the surface, but he could make it easily.

As he exited the room, Messner was shocked to see how much smoke had filled the air in a matter of minutes, and how many people had fled into the corridor. The lights were flickering as though the emergency generator was about to go. He *had* to find a vent before the lights went. His chances of making it in pitch dark would be slim.

Long ago, Messner had memorized a map of the mazes of the fortress. He summoned the picture to his mind. There should be a vent not far away—first left, then second right. He joined the surge of panicked survivors in the corridor, pushing with all his might through the writhing bodies going in the opposite direction. He was pushed and grabbed in return. Someone tore the left sleeve off his shirt. Messner was yanked from behind so forcefully that he tumbled backward, knocking down two others. The crowd surged over him, painfully digging boots and heels into his body. Someone kicked him in the head, and he saw stars. He put his hands and arms over his neck and head, and struggled to his feet again.

Fools, he thought as he staggered on toward the vent. They all go to their deaths!

When he reached the shaft, he discovered a clever Death's

Head guard had the same idea, and was trying to pry the shaft cover loose. It was intended to be removed only when repairs were necessary, and was screwed firmly into the granite. The guard had managed to pry loose one corner of the rectangle.

"Get away from there!" Messner shouted. "I order you to get away!"

The Totenkopf paid no attention to him. Messner was just about to lunge at him when he saw a familiar figure weaving at him from the other direction. It was the American! He should be dead! But here he was, staggering around with half his body bathed in blood, and the look of a demon in his eye. Some of the containment doors must have failed to close, and Ryan had stumbled around through the labyrinth of corridors to come around to this spot from the opposite side.

The sight of the wounded American distracted Messner for only a few seconds. He grabbed the Totenkopf from behind. "Get away!"

The guard was a huge man, far bulkier than Messner, and he wrenched free easily. With a back swipe of his meaty arm, he sent Messner crashing back against the granite face of the corridor. His Luger fell out of his holster and slid across on the floor.

Messner's breath was knocked from him. He sucked in several gulps of air and sprang again. This time the guard let go of the vent cover and turned on him with a savage grunt, smashing his fist into Messner's face.

Messner crumpled to the floor. Before he could get up, he heard an animal howl of rage, and then the American was on top of him, kicking and flailing.

Messner rolled away and tried to get up, but Ryan—who outweighed him considerably—had a hammerlock on him that he could not shake off. The guard ignored them both and bashed away at the vent cover.

Messner saw the Luger and struggled on his stomach to

reach it. The American was punching him, screaming at him unintelligibly. The blows hurt but lacked a stunning force.

He's weak from blood loss. Thank God! The gun—get the gun—

Messner reached the gun with his fingertips and clawed it into his grasp. He rolled over and twisted up, jamming the barrel into Ryan's solar plexus. He squeezed the trigger.

Nothing happened.

The Luger was jammed.

Messner threw it away in disgust. The American jabbed at his eyes. Messner put his knee into Ryan's chest and gained enough leverage to push him off.

Ryan was slow to react. Messner seized the opportunity and sprang up. He took Ryan by the shoulders and shoved his head back into the granite as hard as he could. Ryan groaned.

Messner smashed Ryan's head again and again until Ryan quit groaning and moving, and blood ran out of his ear. The whites of his eyes rolled up.

Messner heard the vent cover shear away as the Death's Head guard finally pried it loose with his brute strength. He let go of the American. The guard began to scramble up the ladder.

"No!" Messner screamed. "I will go first!" He grabbed the man around the ankles. The guard howled in rage and kicked at him, hanging on tenaciously with his hands. Messner shouted, "No! I will not be defeated! *Not—be—defeated!*" He started to climb up over the guard, turning his face to avoid savage kicks. When he was able to reach the man's face, he stabbed his fingers into his eyes.

The guard yelped and let go with one hand. Messner pried his other hand loose. He hung onto the ladder rungs and swung with his feet, toppling the guard and stuffing him towards the bottom of the vent.

Another explosion shook the fortress. Dust and debris fell into Messner's face, making him choke and cough. He felt warm liquid running down one cheek and realized he was cut. His right hand was bleeding badly, and the blood ran into his sleeve and down into his armpit.

He couldn't breathe.

Air—he must have air—

The lights flickered for the last time, and then he was lost in a sea of blackness. Gasping, he grabbed blindly for a rung. He seized one and pulled himself up. Then again and again. Below him, smoke was pouring into the chute. It wafted upward, cutting into his lungs like razors.

Faster, faster.

He heaved himself up. His cut hand was numb, but somehow he forced it to grip the rungs. His feet slipped repeatedly. He nearly lost his balance and fell off.

Higher, higher.

How far had he climbed? How many more meters to freedom? He went up and up, and gradually the sounds of chaos from below began to recede. He was alone, twisting in the darkness.

Then he saw—or thought he saw—a tiny sliver of light shining above him like a crescent moon. He stared at it as he struggled upward. Were his eyes playing tricks on him, or was it the door at the surface? Messner pushed himself harder. He *had* to reach freedom. Pain wracked his chest with every gasp.

Sounds from the exterior world reached him now—the explosions of flak shells.

He reached the trap door. It was jammed. He shoved but couldn't budge it. He put his shoulder up to it and strained with all his might. He cried with pain as he dislocated his shoulder, but still he pushed.

Below him came a tremendous blast, then orange light. He looked down. Coming up the chute at him with lighting speed was a gigantic fireball. He would be incinerated in seconds.

He summoned all of his remaining strength and pushed again on the door. It burst open to a night sky lit up with white bursts of fire. Cold air rushed into his lungs. He heaved himself up over the side of the opening just as the fireball hit and flamed through the opening with the fury of a giant blow torch. A shower of burning debris cascaded down around him, sizzling as it hit the snow.

Messner flung himself onto the snow. He lay sprawled, his limbs leaden. He dragged his bloody right hand to his chest pocket, feeling for Mengele's envelope. It was still there. But the manila folder... he had no idea what happened to it.

Suddenly he was aware that his clothing was on fire—he was burning up. Frantic, he tried to roll in the snow, but his body seemed agonizingly slow to respond.

I will not die.
I will not die!
Then vertigo and blackness enveloped him.

CHAPTER Three

New York City, April 1973.

Rainer Stern crumpled his twin brother's suicide note in his hand. He clenched his fist tighter and tighter, as if he could compress all of his grief and rage into a hard, small knot in his palm. He raised his fist slowly and brought it to his chest. His eyes, the color of amber topaz, glistened with emotion. His throat was thick and words would not come out, only sounds, like an animal in pain. Leon was dead, and with him a part of Rainer had died as well.

Rainer stood in front of the bay window of his brother's neat brownstone apartment in the Borough Park section of Brooklyn, his eyes unseeing of the overcoated figures who strolled the street below, tucked and bent against a cold spring wind.

The last time he had been here to visit Leon, this room had seemed warm and cozy, for the first time in years. Copies of cheerful paintings were hung on the walls; in one corner sat a dark mahogany Steinway, its stand holding sheet music by Mozart and Beethoven. The neighborhood was comfortable and predictable. Rainer had thought, here we are in our mid-thirties, and at last Leon is getting on with his life. The Holocaust and the camps are finally behind us.

But today, this apartment felt like a tomb. Leon was dead and Rainer felt buried alive. In the room behind Stern, friends made ready for the post-burial mourning feast, but he didn't hear them. He wasn't interested in their condolences or in their heavy, filling food.

The sounds in his throat at last took shape into words. "Leon," he whispered, "why did you do it?"

The ball of paper fell from his fist to the beige and maroon Oriental carpet. He opened his hands and lowered his head into them, his fingers tearing at his thick, curly dark hair. He wanted to scream and cry at the same time, but he held himself in check. *I will not let go, I will not let go.* He rocked back and forth on his feet.

A hand fell lightly on his shoulder. "Rainer, it's ready—the meal of comfort. Everyone is waiting for you."

Stern raised his head and looked out the window, not at the friend who stood beside him. "I can't, Ben. I'm sorry."

"Rainer, you must. Your brother is in the ground now, and *shiva* has begun. It's the custom," his friend reminded him gently. "You must do the proper thing for him."

"Proper?" Stern cleared the thickness in his throat. His tone was derisive. "Was his death 'proper'? Was it just? He didn't kill himself, Ben, *they* killed him. They planted a time bomb in him and after thirty years, it went off. If it hadn't been for *them*—" Stern broke off. Jaws clenched, he turned away from Benjamin Goldman. The tears that had formed in his eyes felt like they had hardened to ice.

Goldman started pulling him toward the dining alcove where two Formica-topped tables were pushed together, covered with a white cloth, and laden with food. "Don't talk like that now, Rainer. We'll talk about it later, if you want. Now you should eat a little, feel better. It's time for us to remember Leon as he was."

Stern nodded and let himself be led. The modest apartment, with its floral wallpaper and mahogany trim, engulfed him. Around the tables, a ring of eight faces loomed at him. Like Goldman, they were friends of his and of Leon's. There were no relatives or spouses. All of the Stern brothers' immediate family, including their parents, had perished in the camps in Germany.

Dark eyes tracked him with concern as he came closer. He moved as if he were sleepwalking. After sitting, he bent down and untied the laces of his black wing tips and stepped out of them. He put on the pair of canvas slippers under the table. Mourner's slippers. Mourners must not wear shoes, not during *shiva*. Rainer was not a particularly religious man, not as much as his brother had been, but following the old customs seemed appropriate in the face of death.

The Nazis tried to take our ways from us and failed, Stern thought. But the thought was not much comfort. Leon's religion had not saved him.

The food on the tables looked unreal. Hard-boiled eggs the roundness of which symbolized the continuity of life, sat in their bowl like unappetizing blobs. Bile rose in the back of Stern's throat, but he sat, his lips stretched like wire in an effort to smile.

The stool beneath him felt hard and strange. One by one, the guests lowered themselves to their own stools. According to Jewish tradition, the stools had replaced the dining chairs. The low height of the seats made everyone look out of proportion—small children seated around a grown-ups' table. It felt odd to be eating a meal of comfort in Leon's home instead of somewhere else, but Rainer was certain his brother would have wanted it.

Stern moved mechanically through the meal. These people were here for him; he must do his part for them. But the eggs stuck in his dry throat, and he gulped red wine to clear it. He pushed a sausage and potato casserole around on his plate. What little conversation arose was exchanged in murmurs, for the meal of comfort is a time for solemn contemplation of the dead.

Stern lost all perspective of the time. For him, the clock

had stopped less than twenty-four hours before. Since then he had relived *the moment* over and over again, the tape replaying in his head without control.

Yesterday. Leon calls him at his Manhattan law office and asks him to come by. There is something he wants to talk about, but not on the phone. His brother sounds in good spirits—a respite from the emotional roller coaster and continuing illnesses that had plagued his life. Rainer is relieved; for days he has suffered an oppressive foreboding concerning Leon.

He arrives between six and six-thirty in the evening. As usual, his spirits lift as he walks through the streets of his former neighborhood of Borough Park—he lived a few blocks away until he moved to Manhattan. It's a community where traditional values of hard work and family are emphasized. He nods to a few Hasidic Jews he passes, men with earlocks dressed in black caftans and hats. Some respond and some don't.

He bounces up the stairs, savoring odors of hot oil and dinners cooking. He hears a baby crying. He knocks on Leon's door. No one answers. He knocks again. Did Leon forget? Did he have to leave unexpectedly? Should Rainer wait?

He tries the door; it is unlocked. Something's wrong, he thinks, unless Leon has lost his memory again. He pushes the door open. In another apartment, the baby sounds strained and frantic, like an infant left unattended. "Leon," he calls, stepping inside and shutting the door behind him. "It's me."

There is no answer.

"Leon?"

He goes through the rooms, looking for his brother.

Until he finds him sprawled in an awkward position across the beige chenille spread of his bed. His face is up and his eyes open. His lips are blue and his skin a ghastly gray. Rainer looks at himself in death. Leon's arms, flung out from his sides, are covered in streams of darkened blood from slashes on his wrist. The room reeks with the fetid smell of stale blood. Rainer sees blood everywhere—the carpet, the walls. He staggers against the door, the wind knocked from him by shock, his mouth open in a soundless howl, and then follows the trail of dried blood to the bathroom. The white porcelain sink is filled with red water. A razor blade lays on the floor.

Then he rushes back to the bedroom and falls on the floor, clutching the cold, stiff hand, begging his brother to come back to life, smearing his face with Leon's blood.

In the adjacent apartment, the infant continues to scream.

"More, Rainer?" A serving dish swam into focus. The tape inside Stern's head shut off.

More food? He swallowed a growl. How could anyone think about putting food in his belly when he had just buried his brother, his only family left on the entire planet? Who gives a damn about *tradition?* He wanted to smash his plate into the wall.

"No, thank you, Elise." His voice was gentle; he tried to smile at his brother's neighbor. She did not withdraw the dish, but held it in front of him. "All right," he agreed. He couldn't fight her. He let a small portion of chopped liver join the rest of his uneaten food.

Elise smiled.

The tape in his head resumed, leaping forward in time.

No autopsy, there will be no autopsy in accordance to our customs, Rabbi Levine insists, and the medical examiner's office backs off. Who needs an autopsy, anyway? The gashes in Leon's wrists leave no doubt about the cause of death. His note leaves no doubt about his reasons. Nearly thirty years after the war, the Nazis finally claim him as their victim.

There will be no embalming, no embalming, the rabbi says. His blood is part of his body and must go with him to the grave.

Fast forward, next morning. Leon, washed clean of blood, in his white robe shroud. The casket lid comes down. The ceremony at the synagogue, a blur of faces. The mourners recite the Kaddish. "... May His great name be blessed for ever and ever ... Amen." The earth absorbs the casket. Stern turns from the grave, opens his overcoat into the cold and rends his starched white shirt, the symbol of grief he will wear for shiva, the seven days of mourning.

Then suddenly he is here, in his brother's home that is no longer a home, chasing unwanted food with his fork.

"Rainer?" Goldman's voice called at him from a distance. Stern's head snapped up.

"I said, Rainer, if you're finished, would you like to go into the living room?"

Stern nodded. He knew what would come next. They would take their little stools and sit around and reminisce about Leon. He wanted them to go so that he could begin going through Leon's belongings in privacy. He wanted to be alone with his grief. He did not need grieving friends and relatives telling stories about his dead brother. Only *he* knew what pain and torment he had suffered.

And Rainer knew he had to let them stay and talk. He sighed. It was *tradition*. This was how they worked out their sorrow. They believed one should not bottle it up.

Why did he want to bottle it up?

Revenge.

He wanted to bottle up his grief in order to keep the fires of revenge burning. Because without the desire for revenge, he could not go on living.

While the others shared their stories about Leon, Stern's attention drifted in and out. He watched the tape again in his mind, seeing, hearing and smelling every detail. Then he went back and forth to different memories: The day he and Leon arrived at Idlewild International Airport, teenagers on their own and in rags ... Finishing school ... Rainer working long days as a law clerk, then studying endless nights for the New York State bar exam ... Passing the exam and launching a promising career with one of the most prestigious law firms in New York ... Advancing to full partner

of the renamed firm, Goldman, Schoenberg, Larkin & Stern
... And on the dark side, Leon's inability to recover from
the scars of the camps, both physically and mentally ...
Leon's unending string of odd jobs, health problems, financial troubles and broken relationships ... The war.

Ah, the war. It stood like a gulf between him and Leon,
despite the fact that they were twins and part of each other's
souls. He kept trying to bridge that gulf, right up to the day
Leon took his own life.

"Excuse me," he said. The voices around him went silent.
He looked at the faces as though seeing them for the first time.
"I would like to speak." He stood up, a little stiffly. His torn
white shirt fluttered from the movement. He tugged on his
brown cashmere cardigan, pulling it tighter around his trim
waist.

"I want to talk about Leon," he began. His voice was
smooth, bold, confident, the way he talked when it came to
matters of law. There was barely a trace of his native German tongue, an accent he had worked diligently to eradicate.
"I wasn't sure I wanted to talk about him at all. I'm going to
tell you a lot of things you already know. I hope you don't
mind. Lawyers need to make a summation in order to put
things in perspective. Bear with me, please." He paced
about the living room, head down, hands in his pockets,
while he thought for a moment.

His guests shifted on their stools in discomfort. Only
chubby Rose Weiss, who lived downstairs, looked at Stern
expectantly. Jacob Krantz was scowling—his normal at-rest
expression. Goldman looked like he did in the courtroom
when the opposing attorney is speaking: intense, attentive.

"It was the war that did this to Leon," Rainer said. "More
specifically, it was *them*. The Nazis. They killed Leon the
same as if they'd put the blade to him themselves." The faces
around him were combinations of grim and sad. "You all know
what I'm talking about," he said, "because there isn't a single
one of you whose life hasn't been affected by what the Nazis
did to our people. That's why some of you are here in America,

why *I'm* here, trying to pick up the tiny little pieces and glue them back together in order to be whole again.

"Except Leon never could feel whole. I don't think he ever felt whole in his entire life, because he never had the chance. We were only five when, on April 7, 1944, the Gestapo came in the middle of one night and raided the home in Munich where we were being hidden. Our parents, you see, had refused to get out of the country, and after 1942, it was too late to leave. The Nazis found us and shipped us to Auschwitz."

Stern, moving slowly around the apartment as he talked, stopped by a photo in a tin frame on the fireplace mantel. It was the only surviving photo of life before the war, fuzzy, faded and dog-eared—him and Leon posing with their arms entwined, thin but handsome little boys whose large eyes stood out from their faces, each the mirror image of the other. He picked it up and looked at it, and then put it down and moved on. "Hitler was only a vague name to Leon and me, but there were others we would come to know quite well, and to loathe and fear."

Krantz rose, his palm held up in protest. "Rainer, perhaps you—"

"I'm fine," snapped Stern. "Sit down and listen!"

Krantz slumped down, astonished at Stern's unbecoming behavior for *shiva*.

Stern resumed. "Leon and I were separated from our family in the first selection. Josef Mengele himself made the choices. To the left, to the right . . . we were marched past him while he decided who would live and who would die. He was so imperious. He stood there in his dark green uniform, jackboots spread, waving his whip at us. Leon and I could sense how frightened the adults were, and that in turn frightened us even more. I remember Mengele's eyes. They were black coals, like devil's eyes. No feeling, no human emotion in them at all. Dead eyes. *Zwillinge*, he kept shouting at us. Twins, he wanted. Our mother shoved us forward, screaming, 'Here! Twins! Twins!' I'm sure she thought she was saving us.

Perhaps, if she had known what was in store for twins, she would not have been so anxious to point us out. I suppose it's moot; identical twins are impossible to overlook.

"Leon and I were sent to the right. So was our father. Mengele spared us while sending our mother and many of the others who came with us straight to be gassed. There was death all around us. Even as we were being spared, others were dying. We kept hearing bursts of machine gun fire, and the screams of the dying and the wailing prayers of those who were made to watch. But from a child's viewpoint, the horror had a feeling of make believe. It wasn't until years later that the horror imploded on us, and especially on Leon."

Stern fell silent, lost in thought. "Anyway," he resumed, "Leon and I were sent to a special twins' quarters, and our father was sent to hard labor. We saw our father only twice more, as he dug burial pits, before he, too, was gassed—"

"For God's sakes, stop." Ben Goldman stood up and looked at the guests. "We don't need to hear this, especially today." Goldman reached out to his friend, but Stern flinched away.

Rainer said, "I told you, you *must* listen. Because what you don't want to hear is the truth of why Leon is in his grave."

Ben sat down, chagrined.

Stern ignored his annoyance and began again. "Leon and I learned quickly why we had been spared—we were to participate in 'experiments.' Mengele, the lying bastard, always assured us nothing would hurt, nothing bad would happen—and then we would be in excruciating pain for days on end. We never knew exactly what was being done to us. We were smeared with chemicals that burned our skin, injected with solutions that made our heads and limbs swell, plunged into freezing baths, shocked with electricity, drained of endless samples of blood. Some of us were operated upon—limbs were amputated and then grafted to the other twin. An operation was as good as a death sentence. We didn't dare cry. Sometimes, we were made to play strange games, guessing the color or number or word that someone was thinking. Correct responses were rewarded with praise; errors punished with injections.

"Every day, Mengele made the selections 'to go to the infirmary.' Sometimes it was his assistant. We tried to be invisible, not look them in the eye, praying that we would be passed over. I don't know who frightened me more—they were both gods of terror. At least Mengele tried to reassure us with lies, telling us an injection would not hurt when in fact it brought excruciating pain. His assistant never did. He was cold through and through. An ice lord, yet he made us call him 'Dr. Hans' as if he were a kindly uncle. Fortunately, he was gone a good deal of the time. We dreaded his appearances.

"For some reason, Leon was chosen to bear the worst. They did that with all the twins—subjected one to more brutal treatment. Many times, Leon was taken away to the infirmary and I was left behind in the barracks. My heart went with him all the way, and I never ceased to feel his suffering.

"When the Allies came and liberated us from our hell, we were 'relocated' to a series of foster parents in Stuttgart, Bern and Zurich. We were rootless, blown about like chaff on the wind. Then we made our way here, on our own, looking for a clean slate, a new beginning. Time would heal. For Leon, it never did—the Nazis had trampled all over his soul. When we finally understood that we had been used as guinea pigs in the Nazis' experiments for their so-called 'master race,' he became worse. He felt haunted, tainted. Unclean. Mengele had permanently poisoned him. The internal suffering lasted his entire life."

Stern's voice dropped. "Even now, though his body be gone, his spirit is still with me, and I feel his torment more than ever." He looked away, a vessel suddenly empty.

The guests stirred. Scowling at him, Mrs. Weiss struggled up off the stool. One by one, they all murmured their parting condolences, and filed out the door.

"Hamakom y'nahaim etkhem shar availai tziyon veeyeru-

shalayim," said Elise, the neighbor. *May the Lord comfort you with all the mourners of Zion and Jerusalem.*

Finally, the only one left with Stern was his friend and law partner, Ben Goldman. "Stay awhile, Ben," Stern said. "Only let's sit on something more comfortable." He indicated the overstuffed sofa and armchairs. They each took an armchair.

Goldman adjusted his round, wire-rimmed spectacles. At forty-five, he was paunchy, with a fondness for well-cut, dark three-piece suits. He was married, a family man, successful and highly respected as one of the best corporate lawyers in New York. "Why don't you take some time off, Rainer? I know you may find this hard to believe, but the firm can get along without you for a couple of weeks—or more."

Stern shook his head. "I don't need rest." He sighed; his shoulders dropped. "I tried to save him, Ben, I really did. All those years, I did everything I could. Nothing worked for very long. Then he seemed to snap out of it on his own. Yesterday, he sounded so good on the phone, like the sun had just come out after years of rain."

"He had made his decision," Goldman said gently. "He felt he had solved his problems."

"I didn't do *enough*!"

"You did more than enough. We may be charged with being our brother's keeper, but only to a point. In the final analysis, each man must be master of his own fate. You cannot be responsible for your brother taking his life."

Stern's eyes had a far-away look. "It took him nearly thirty years to die," he whispered. "Bit by bit. Perhaps I shouldn't blame him for wanting to end the dying."

"I think there is much guilt in your grief. It's only natural. You came out of the camps relatively unscathed, and built a normal life. You became very successful, while Leon did nothing but struggle from one failure to another."

"It's true. All these years I've wondered, why me? Why was I the one to be spared the worst, not Leon? Was he weaker than me? Was there something in him that made him break under the strain? Could I have endured the worst better than him?"

"You are torturing yourself with questions that cannot be answered. What is, is. You can't go back in time and change what happened."

"If I only could."

Goldman leaned forward, elbows and forearms on his knees. "I don't mean to sound unkind, but you are not the only one who suffers. Millions of us were affected by the war. I was never in the camps, but I lost a brother to the Nazis. And a sister as well."

"It's different with twins. Twins share their souls, forever. I can feel Leon in me, speaking to me from beyond the grave."

"And what does he say, Rainer?" Goldman asked quietly.

"That there is unfinished business. Justice to be rendered."

Goldman considered this. "You are not thinking of joining the Nazi hunters, are you, Rainer? This is 1973, and there aren't many left to track down."

Stern shrugged with a wan smile. "The two gods of terror, Mengele and his assistant, Dr Hans Messner, have yet to account for their crimes. Now they have another upon their heads."

Goldman looked down at his shoes. The Biedermier clock on the wall chimed the half hour. "You'd waste yourself. Leave the Nazi-hunting to Weisenthal or the Mossad. You will have your justice if you carry on with your life and your work. The Nazis sought to wipe out our race. What better justice than to survive and prosper? To *live for the future*—not the past? Find yourself a bride and carry on the bloodline."

Stern smiled weakly. There were two reasons why he had not married. One, he had put all his energy into his law career. And two, he was afraid to love yet another person he might somehow lose. "My head tells me you're right, but not my heart," he confessed.

Goldman chuckled. "Your head will prevail. You've got one of the sharpest, most logical minds I've ever seen." He stood up. "I must get back to the children. Ruth is still away, you know. She sends her love and sympathy."

"You've told me already."

"So, I tell you again."

Rainer took Goldman's black wool overcoat out of the foyer closet and held it for him. As Goldman opened the door, Stern said, "I would never dream of hurting another human being. But the way I feel now, if you were Mengele or Messner, I would put a bullet in your head as calmly as I would shake a hand." He swallowed. "That frightens me, Ben."

Goldman's dark eyes searched his face. "And a bullet would solve nothing. You're only reacting to your grief. I know you well, Rainer, and you are not capable of killing." He put a hand on his partner's shoulder. "I don't want to see you in the office for at least the rest of the week. But if you feel a need to talk, call anytime—you know that."

"Thanks, Ben."

Goldman said, in Yiddish, "May the Lord comfort you with all the mourners of Zion and Jerusalem."

When Ben was gone, Stern cast his eye around Leon's apartment, at all the belongings that would have to be judged for salvation or disposal. A crushing loneliness fell upon him.

CHAPTER Four

The sign on the door read, "Park Avenue Family Planning Center." With a smile of pride, Dr. Edward Reston pushed it open and entered.

Inside was a small but comfortably appointed anteroom that looked more like the sitting room of an elegant home than the waiting room of a medical clinic. It was decorated in coordinated earth tone colors of brown, beige, rust and sienna, with a splash here and there of burnt orange. The beige carpet was thick and plush; the expensive overstuffed armchairs comfortable and inviting. A painting on the wall was done in free-form shapes and designs in the same color theme, nondescript but pleasing to the eye.

It was a room designed to put anxious men and women at ease. And, since the clinic had opened two years earlier, it was almost always occupied.

This morning, fifteen minutes before office hours officially began, Reston already had a patient—a young, tastefully dressed brunette woman who sat stiffly in one armchair, eyes on a magazine open on her lap, but not reading. She looked up with a start as Reston came in; he smiled and nodded, and proceeded briskly to the door that led to his private office and examination rooms.

"Good morning, doctor." Nancy DeWitt, Reston's attractive blond nurse, already had coffee perking in the kitchenette and was laying out the files for the day's patients on one side of the doctor's big mahogany desk.

"Sandra already called and will be late this morning," Nancy said. "She has to take her son to the dentist. I'll have to get the phone and fill in out front." Nurse DeWitt clearly was not pleased with the situation as she crowded the files together. "It's going to be a busy day—but I suppose I'll manage."

Reston took off his Burberry and gave it to Nancy to hang in the closet. "Of course you'll manage," he said good-naturedly. "You're one of the most efficient nurses in New York. That's one of two reasons why I hired you."

She gave him a quick smile as she shut the closet door and handed him his white coat. "And the second reason?"

"If I told you, you'd ask for a raise."

Nancy disappeared down the hallway; Reston heard her in the kitchenette, pouring his coffee. He stood at the side of his desk and glanced over the files. He recognized most of the names—they belonged to prominent, wealthy people from all over the world, business tycoons, social gods and goddesses, a film celebrity from the Coast, a European baroness. The names gave Reston a huge feeling of satisfaction. His reputation was spreading—the high and mighty of the world were coming to *him* for the one thing they wanted more than anything else, more than life itself.

DeWitt returned with a mug of black coffee.

"Which one is the woman out there?" Reston asked.

"None—she's a walk-in. She was waiting at the door when I got here."

Reston frowned. He did not like to see walk-ins. Even if his schedule was not full, he preferred advance appointments to maintain the appearance of being in high demand. Appearances were crucial to the high fees he charged.

"She says it's urgent, but I made no promises, doctor. Just

a moment, I'll get the form she filled out." Nancy disappeared again, this time to the reception area, and came back with a newly made file. The label read: "Evered, Alice and Arthur Brandon."

Reston set his mug down on the desk blotter and opened the file. "Evered—*the* Arthur Evered?"

Nancy allowed a tight smile. "That's right."

"Arthur Brandon Evered, chief executive officer of Thorson Industries, one of the largest industrial conglomerates in the world? That's some walk-in."

"You want to see her now? The baroness isn't due for half an hour. If she shows up early, I can always put the phone on the answering service and take her downstairs for coffee. She *hates* to be left alone in the examining room for more than a minute or two." Privacy and confidentiality were strictly observed at the Park Avenue Family Planning Center. Patients were scheduled so that appointments did not overlap and risk embarrassment to prominent people. That was why the waiting room was so small. Usually patients could be shuffled expertly between the waiting room, examining room and Reston's office, but some demanded special hand-holding—like the temperamental baroness.

"Give me five minutes." Reston gulped his coffee and handed the mug back to DeWitt, who left. He sat down in his leather chair to read the vita on the Evereds.

In precisely five minutes, DeWitt opened the door to his office and announced Alice Evered.

Mrs. Evered slipped in, nervous and apologetic. "I'm sorry to come without an appointment—"

"Nonsense. I'm delighted to meet you, Mrs. Evered," Reston said reassuringly, standing and proferring his hand. "Luckily, we had a last-minute cancellation this morning. Won't you please sit down and make yourself comfortable? Would you like coffee?"

The young Mrs. Evered demurred as she sat delicately in the armchair in front of Reston's desk. She was wearing an expensive, well-tailored suit of light blue wool that complemented her fair complexion. The skirt was fashionably short, and, to Reston's appreciation, showed her trim legs to good advantage.

Mrs. Evered's gaze drifted around Reston's office, to the built-in bookcase full of medical texts, and lingered on the diplomas and photographs framed and hung on the walls. "Forgive me, Dr. Reston—I thought you'd be . . . older."

Reston did not reply directly to the remark. His youthful appearance was somewhat of a sore point with him. He'd just turned thirty-five but looked at least five years younger than that. He was exceptionally qualified for what he was doing at his clinic, but a little premature gray would go a long way with his patients. Unfortunately, nature had not been obliging.

"How may I help you, Mrs. Evered?"

She twisted her hands nervously on the looped handles of her navy handbag. "I want a baby, doctor. As soon as possible."

He nodded. "Yes, of course, that's why couples come to me, Mrs. Evered—when they have problems conceiving on their own. But according to the questionnaire you filled out, neither you nor your husband have had any preliminary fertility tests. Perhaps Nurse DeWitt did not explain that I require—"

Alice Evered was already shaking her head. "I don't have time for tests, Dr. Reston. They're useless, anyway. I want to be pregnant *now*—before it's too late."

It was not unusual for his clients to be anxious. By the time most of them sought his services, they'd exhausted every hope of having their own children. But there was an urgency to Mrs. Evered that went beyond mere time. According to the information she'd provided, she was only twenty-nine, and her husband forty-seven. There was plenty of biological time for her to conceive and bear a child. He had a minimum six months' waiting list for his artificial inseminations. But, she was Mrs. Arthur Evered . . .

He leaned back in his chair. "Perhaps you'd better start at the beginning, Mrs. Evered."

Alice organized her thoughts. She gave every appearance of being a well-bred young woman whose upbringing went against the grain of "letting it all hang out," which was the vogue of the middle class. For a woman like Alice, discussing private matters came with difficulty, even if the confidant was a doctor.

"You see," she began, "Arthur and I—we have no children, even though we've been married three years."

"At three years, you're still newlyweds," he said, attempting to put his patient more at ease with a little humor. "But please go on."

Her smile was fleeting. "I'm his *second* wife, Dr. Reston."

"At the risk of seeming impertinent, Mrs. Evered, I'm aware of that."

"Of course. The publicity surrounding his divorce was rather extensive—and dreadfully tacky, I might add. The grounds for the divorce—nothing of the sort was true, but you know the divorce laws in New York State. The real reason was Emily's failure to provide him with an heir." Alice took a deep breath. "Arthur wants a son very badly, an heir to take over Thorson someday, the way he took over from his own father. He left Emily because she never got pregnant, and he felt time was beginning to run out on him."

Reston remembered the highly publicized divorce trial. After a lot of dirty linen had been aired in public, Emily settled out of court, meaning Arthur must have made a hell of a monetary concession. Rich men did not shed their wives without paying through the nose.

"—and in three years, I haven't gotten pregnant, either, doctor," Alice was saying. "It isn't for lack of trying. And I know the problem isn't me. It's Arthur, and he won't admit it."

"How do you know where the problem is, Mrs. Evered, when neither one of you has had the proper tests?"

She shrugged uneasily. "It seems to me that two wives couldn't be barren. It's too coincidental."

"Perhaps. Even if the difficulty is at his end, he may not be sterile. He may simply suffer from oligospermia."

"What's that?"

"Oligospermia is low sperm count."

"To him, it would be the same as sterility. Unthinkable."

Reston nodded. He pulled a gold-plated Cross fountain pen from his coat pocket and jotted some notes on his pad of paper.

"This *is* confidential, isn't it, doctor?"

"Scrupulously so. I must take notes if I am to give you the best service possible. Don't worry, the records are locked, and no one ever sees them but me and Nurse DeWitt, and you may trust her thoroughly. Now, have you ever discussed this with Mr. Evered?"

"I've tried to bring it up. He refuses to talk about it. He —has quite a temper."

It was a familiar story. The husband always had a hard time facing up to a potency problem. It destroyed their self-image of power and virility. And the more dynamic the man in his position in the world, the more disbelieving he was at his inability to sire a child. Reston could well imagine how a man like Arthur Brandon Evered would react. His temper was legendary. The man was a tyrant, named one of the ten worst bosses by *Fortune* magazine. Employees went in and out of Thorson like they were in a revolving door. He would not take kindly to his wife suggesting he was unable to sire his own heir.

But it was Reston's policy that both husband and wife be involved in and agree to an artifical insemination. Perhaps Evered would agree to an "experiment" with the Park Avenue Family Planning Center, one that would not call his virility into question. Reston had used that ploy successfully with other couples.

"It would be preferable, Mrs. Evered, if you could schedule a return appointment with your husband—or schedule one for him alone. Then we could conduct tests and discuss all considerations—"

"I'm afraid that's impossible, Dr. Reston. For various reasons, I cannot broach the subject again. And I certainly cannot tell him I've been *here*. He'd reject any child he knew wasn't his. I don't care how much it costs—I've got to have a baby!" She looked away from Reston, to the wall on the side. Her hands twisted nervously. "I found out he's been—seeing someone."

"I'm sorry," murmured Reston. The barriers of reserve were breaking down.

"I suppose I shouldn't be surprised," Alice said with a false smile. "Arthur is very good looking, and he *is* one of the wealthiest men in the country. If I thought this was just a fling, I would look the other way. But this is how *we* started, doctor, Arthur and I. I'm worried. I don't want to be divorcée number two." She was silent a moment. "I thought about having an affair myself, just to get pregnant. I know a lot of people are pretty casual about sex these days, but I'm not."

What an extraordinary confession. What an extraordinary woman!

Mrs. Evered looked at Reston with pleading eyes. "You've got to help me save my marriage, doctor!"

Reston put his elbows on his desk and made a tent with his fingers. He studied Mrs. Evered. Her long dark blond hair was perfectly curled at her shoulders; her makeup was tasteful. She would have no trouble remarrying should Arthur Evered decide to exchange her for yet another wife, especially with the money she'd get from him. She must really love the man. Well, it wasn't his business, anyway.

"I have in the past assisted women who did not want their husbands to know what they were doing, for similar reasons," he acknowledged. "But there are serious ramifications that must be acknowledged."

"What do you mean?"

"Technically, a matter of legitimacy. Let's say you kept this knowledge from your husband, and he eventually found out and was angry about it. He could claim the child was illegitimate, and disinherit him."

"I hadn't thought of that," said Alice, quite upset to hear this. "The courts would rule that way?"

"I don't know. The law is very vague, mainly because this field is so new and untested. That is why I insist both parents be involved and fully consenting. If you still wish to proceed without your husband, then you must sign a waiver. But I urge you to give it a lot of thought before you do." He paused. "There's something else you might consider. I mentioned your husband may suffer from oligospermia. He still may be able to father a child. I can collect semen over a period of time, you see, and preserve it by freezing. Then I concentrate the sperm and inject it artificially into the womb."

Alice brightened, but the hope didn't last. "What if he's tested and finds out the worst—that he's sterile?"

"That's the risk you must take."

"I can't."

"Then the situation is back to square one."

Alice was lost in thought for a moment. "If I can work it out, how quickly can I become pregnant?"

"My waiting list for an insemination is six to eight months, depending on matching you to the right donor."

"I can't wait six to eight months! Is there any way you could put me first? I'll pay anything!" She added, "I have access to my own funds..."

Reston hmm'd. "I'll see what can be done, Mrs. Evered."

"Perhaps I should go elsewhere..."

"Now, why do that when you've come to the best? The Park Avenue Family Planning Center is the most reputed artificial insemination clinic in the country. I established it myself only two years ago, after spending years practicing at the best advanced labs." Reston pulled a glossy brochure from his center desk drawer. "Here's my vita—Harvard, Massachusetts General, Klein Laboratory of Applied Biogenetics... it's all there. You may look it over at your leisure. I cannot supply patient references because the names of my patients are confidential, but I assure you, they come from all over the world, and they leave satisfied."

"References aren't necessary, doctor. Your reputation by word of mouth speaks for itself."

He smiled at the compliment. "The donors to my sperm bank also remain confidential. I divulge them to *no one*. The donors are thoroughly screened for desirable genetic traits—intelligence, health, longevity, physical beauty—because my patients are most demanding. The donors' family backgrounds also are scrutinized for traits and diseases that may show up every few generations."

"Why is the wait so long?"

"Supply and demand, and the processing that's involved. I take only the highest quality, the very best donor sperm. There are only so many worthy men who meet the genetic qualifications I've established. I go through a rigorous process to match my patients to the most appropriate stock. Some, you see, specify the donor to be a scientist, or a celebrity, or whatever. Then, of course, the inseminations must be done at the right time in the ovulation cycle."

"Can you guarantee me a son?"

Reston shook his head. "I cannot even guarantee that the pregnancy will take, Mrs. Evered. My success rate is quite high, but not one hundred percent. No insemination is guaranteed. There are so many variables, including the physiology and the emotional state of the mother. Nor can I guarantee exactly how the child will turn out. Again, too many variables beyond control. My job is to make the odds as good as possible for a desired outcome."

"But I *must* have a son."

"I can match you to a donor who has fathered mostly males, but beyond that, I have little control." He joked, "If I could, I'd be a very rich man."

She smiled wanly, preoccupied. "Is the procedure—painful? How long does it take?"

"It's as simple as getting a PAP smear. No anesthetic is required. I do it right here at the clinic."

"What if it doesn't take?"

"I'll give you a contract to read that spells out all terms and obligations. The fee includes up to three inseminations. If the first takes, the other two are not performed. If all three fail, then I suggest a patient submit to another battery of tests by various specialists, as there is some underlying reason why her body is rejecting its natural purpose."

"How soon may I have an insemination?" she pressed.

Reston thought a moment. He *could* preempt Mrs. Handley. He could gamble on finding additional sperm stock on short notice, so as not to delay Mrs. Handley so long that he lost her as a patient altogether. "That," he said to Alice, "depends on your cycle, and your fertility. First, we must determine that you are indeed producing healthy ova."

His telephone buzzed and he picked up the receiver. "Yes?" He looked absently at the framed photo of his wife, Gloria, that sat next to the phone.

"Dr. Reston, I'm going downstairs and will put the phone on the service." That was Nurse DeWitt's signal that the baroness had arrived. She would spirit the woman away so that the two patients would not meet in the anteroom. He had about fifteen minutes, twenty tops, to wrap it up with Mrs. Evered.

"Thank you, Miss DeWitt." He replaced the receiver in its cradle and looked at Alice. "I make every effort to accommodate my patients, and your situation certainly demands prompt attention. I'm afraid my daytime calendar is full for the next six months, but I'll be happy to fit you in after hours. If you come back tonight, after the office is closed, I'll do the preliminary fertility test." He stood up and held out his hand. "Please bring back the signed contract. It's for your own protection, you understand."

Mrs. Evered arose from her seat. "Doctor, I don't know how to thank you—"

He waved his hand in a gesture of dismissal. "Don't thank me until your child is born."

"And the fee—"

"Payment is spelled out in the contract. There is a slight surcharge for emergency treatment." He escorted Mrs. Evered out of his inner office to the main door of the clinic. "And don't forget to fill out the form at the back of the contract. It concerns desired genetic characteristics, and it's most important that you answer every question. For example, what color are Arthur's eyes?"

"Blue."

"And so are yours. I don't think you want to try to explain a brown-eyed baby, even though it *could* happen. See what I mean?"

A spark of excitement showed on Alice's face as she began to contemplate a baby as a reality instead of merely a dream. "And he should be athletic—and tall, like Arthur. Arthur played forward in basketball at Princeton, you know. And he should be *very* bright—a good business mind. Shrewd."

Reston opened the main door, trying to encourage Alice to depart without appearing to be rude. "I'm sure you'll think of many traits. I also need to know the general medical histories of both your families. The questions will guide you."

"I'll find a way to get Arthur to come and see you," she promised.

Reston nodded. "Good day, Mrs. Evered, and thank you for coming by. I look forward to working with you and your husband."

He shut the door after her, then turned on his heel and hurried back to his office. The baroness would be arriving in minutes for her initial treatment.

Reston let out the sigh of a perpetually overworked man. His longtime mentor, John Heineman, director of the Klein Laboratory of Applied Biogenetics, certainly had been right. There was more money to be made making rich women pregnant than in being the most glorified heart transplant surgeon. One in seven couples in America was unable to conceive a baby, and a lot of them who rejected adoption were willing to pay almost anything to find a solution to their problem. Artificial insemination wasn't the answer for all of them, but it helped quite a few. Reston could barely keep up with demand. His tenure as senior staff scientist at Klein had convinced him infertility therapy was the way of the future.

Plus, it was only a matter of time before man figured out how to control genes, and that had enormous implications for the fertility field. And when that happened, Reston intended to be well established as the premier authority in the world.

If Gloria didn't drive him to bankruptcy first.

CHAPTER Five

"Would you like to see the day's mail?" Nurse Nancy DeWitt stood in the doorway of Reston's private office, holding a handful of letters and bills.

Reston checked his watch. Six P.M. and the last patient had departed only moments before. Mrs. Evered was due at six-thirty. In front of him on his desk was a stack of patient files awaiting his reports. He had had no time to dictate a word all day due to the steady stream of patients.

He gestured impatiently. "Put it in the basket, Nancy, and I'll get to it when I can. Is there anything I should know about now?"

"I'm afraid very little of it's good, if you want my opinion. I've taken care of a few items, but there is some... personal mail that requires your attention."

"All right, all right." Reston's attention was half on the file in front of him.

"I've ordered sandwiches from the deli."

"Thank you," Edward said absently. He realized he was famished. He had not stopped for lunch.

After DeWitt closed the door, Reston found himself unable to concentrate on his reports. The stack of mail sat in his basket like an oppressive presence. Very little of it good, Nancy had said, and he had a feeling he knew what was there—more bills. Gloria had a master's degree in shopping, and was hard at work on a doctorate.

At last he put down the file and picked up the mail. Nancy had arranged the items in order, with least offending ones first. The top few papers pertained to the clinic, which Nancy had marked "FYI" and neatly penned at the bottom that she had taken care of the business. They concerned things that he really didn't need to know—supplies and such—but which Nancy had probably included for the sole reason of cushioning the shock that followed: Gloria's bills.

Reston was staggered. In the year that they had been married, Gloria had run up enormous debts. She had opened charge accounts in his name at every exclusive store in Manhattan, and judging from the bills that rolled in every month, doctors had no credit limits. He riffled through the invoices. Bergdorf's, Saks, Bloomingdale's, Tiffany, Cartier, Ferragamo, Petrovich Furs...

Petrovich Furs! A full-length black mink coat, a white mink jacket, and a red fox walking coat, all silk-lined and monogrammed, with matching hats. Reston groaned. Her taste for the high life was no surprise to him—it was one of the things that had attracted him to her in the first place. But since their marriage, her definition of the high life kept escalating. If she kept up this pace, she would be in furs while he walked around in his underwear.

The rest of the bills blurred. He was tempted to total them on his desk calculator but didn't want to know the damage. He would have to straighten this out with Gloria, a task he didn't relish. He knew how important it was for her to be accepted into certain social circles, and he did not want to admit that he could not afford everything she wanted. He was doing well with his clinic, but he was not John D. Rockefeller.

Reston's eyes fell on the last paper in the stack. It was not a bill, but a letter, poorly typed on a machine with uneven letters and spacing, and a faded ribbon. It was not signed.

"Dr. Reston,
"Have you no moral conscience? Are you trying to play God? You with your filthy practices, upsetting the role of nature. You should not meddle in the process of procreation, Dr. Reston! To do so is a sin against God and His Universe! There are people on this Earth that God meant never to have children. Leave it that way! If you do not stop, God will visit His Wrath upon you! This is a warning! If you do not heed, you deserve what you get!"

Nancy had clipped the envelope the letter came in to the letter itself. There was no name or return address, but the postmark indicated it had been mailed from somewhere in New York City.

Reston separated the letter from the rest of the mail, opened the file drawer in his desk and slipped it in a folder in the rear. It was not the first hate mail he'd received since he opened his clinic. He didn't take the mail seriously, but he saved it—just in case.

The door to his office opened again and DeWitt entered with a take-out supper of a ham sandwich and coffee, which she set down in front of him.

"I'm sorry about that letter, doctor."

"Don't apologize—it's not your fault there are nuts out there." Reston checked his watch again. Six-twenty. He tore off the cellophane and took a huge bite out of the sandwich.

"I don't know what to do with mail like that. If we get any more, do you want me to throw them out?"

He shook his head, swallowing. "Give them to me, but don't let them upset you. Nut cases who write letters seldom take any action. They've already vented their steam."

Nancy crossed her arms. "I don't understand why anyone would object to us. We're enabling childless couples to conceive. We're not taking away life, like abortion clinics."

"I know. I look upon this as a great service to society." Reston took another bite, chewing fast.

"I guess there's always a loony out there who will object to anything."

Nancy DeWitt sat at her desk, back straight, fingers racing over the keyboard of her brand new IBM Correcting Selectric typewriter. She wore a pair of earphones, and her foot operated the pedal of her dictating machine. She was catching up on the previous day's reports.

The Correcting Selectric, with its "golf ball" element instead of key bars, enabled her to type as fast as Reston could dictate. She was proud of her new machine—it was the very latest in leading edge technology, just like everything the clinic itself symbolized. Reston had paid a premium price for it, and she had waited nine months to get it from the factory. The wait and the price had been worth it. Quality first—that was Reston's philosophy. She was proud to be associated with him and his brilliant work.

DeWitt finished the last report, pulled the page from the typewriter and scanned it for missed errors. Satisfied, she inserted it in the patient's file. She took off her headphones and proceeded to clean up and lock up before going home. It was nearly 8 P.M. She had stayed late without being asked to do so; she always did.

Mrs. Evered was still with the doctor. Nancy would depart quietly without disturbing them.

She collected the tapes and files and locked them into their cabinets. She cleared her desk, tidied the magazines in the waiting room, and cleaned the coffee pot and mugs in the kitchen. She made certain the examining room was clean and neat.

Nurse DeWitt had more than great admiration for Dr. Edward Reston. She was rather in love with him. She had met him at Massachusetts General Hospital in Boston, where he'd done his residency in OB/GYN. She had just graduated from college with her R.N. degree. Half the nurses in the entire hospital had a crush on the handsome, ambitious young man, and envied her for being assigned the same shift and floor as him. He dated some of the nurses, but never her, to her heart's despair. Then he met Gloria, the Boston Brahmin debutante, whose entry in *Debrett's* was an encyclopedia unto itself. That was the end of his footloose and fancy-free days. Dr. Edward D. Reston was *taken*.

After Edward left the hospital for the Klein Laboratory of Applied Biogenetics in Purchase, New York, Nancy thought she'd never see him again. But he had called her two years ago when he was setting up the Park Avenue Family Planning Center, offering her a job. He remembered her as one of the most efficient nurses at the hospital. At first, she hoped he'd broken up with Gloria—but no such luck. Gloria had her hooks into him but *good*.

That was the problem with men, Nancy thought as she dusted around the office. Men were the last ones to find out their women were using them as first-class travel tickets. Now that Gloria was Mrs. Edward D. Reston, she seemed bent on putting herself at the top of Manhattan's social ladder. Poor Edward. He needed a wife who would support him in his goals, not drain his wallet.

As far as their relationship went, Reston was thoroughly businesslike, absorbed by his work. Whenever he spoke of his wife, it was always reverentially. He thought Gloria was wonderful.

But if he ever changed his mind, or his marriage fell apart—Nancy vowed to be there.

DeWitt checked the appointment book for the next day. The roster included three new patients. They just kept coming and coming. Dr. Reston was already overworked. He needed to expand, create a staff of doctors.

Nancy did one last thing before leaving—she called the answering service to check for messages. One call had come in after hours. She could leave it until morning, but, just in case it concerned something the doctor should know tonight...

She wrote down the message on a pink memo sheet and left it where she knew Reston would see it before leaving himself. The message was, "John H. called."

* * *

Alice Evered was going through a typical "second thoughts" crisis. It happened to even the most committed, convinced patients.

"There's no danger of contamination or infection, is there, doctor?" she asked in a worried voice as she sat before him in his office.

Reston folded his hands on the shiny mahogany top of his desk. "The risk of infection is extremely small, Mrs. Evered. We do the procedure under sterile conditions, the same as many simple operations done right in a doctor's office." He always used the first person plural when referring to his services. It gave patients a feeling of reassurance.

"I mean, contamination of the donor sperm. How long can it last before it deteriorates?"

"Sperm has an extremely short life—viability, we call it. But you see, we keep it frozen, and it lasts years without loss of motility or quality."

"It's not frozen when you insert it, is it?" She shivered.

Reston chuckled. "Of course not. We follow strict thawing procedures, and check it first to make sure it has not been damaged by the freezing or thawing processes."

"What if something *does* happen, and the sperm is no good? Would I have to make another appointment and come back again?"

"No. You see, it's frozen in small, individual quantities. We always thaw two. They're maintained and tested separately, so that if one should be unacceptable, there will not be a delay for you. The odds of that happening are very small, I might add, and the odds of *both* being unacceptable are negligible."

"But both would come from the same source?"

"Correct. We do not make substitutions of donors."

Alice Evered weighed her considerations. "I just want to be *sure* of everything, doctor."

Reston stood up. "Come with me, Mrs. Evered. Once you see the setup of my facility, you'll feel much better about the entire process." He touched her lightly on the arm to guide her from his office to the other rooms that opened into the short hallway. He stepped to a steel door and put his hand on the knob. "This room is chilly, Mrs. Evered—are you sure you'll be warm enough?"

She nodded, pulling the collar of her wool suit close to her neck. Reston opened the door and ushered her inside.

"It *is* cold. It's like being in a meat locker," she said.

"We keep it at forty-eight degrees. This is where we do the thawing. But first, step up here and look through this window."

Alice did as Reston instructed her, walking to a window set in the back wall. There was another steel door to the right of the window, with two sets of bolts. A sign on the door said, "Caution: do not open or enter without proper attire." Reston flipped a switch and a low-watt light came on in the other side, illuminating a bank of small freezer compartments.

"I store everything on the premises," explained Reston. "That way, I can maintain control. The sperm is prepared for freezing and packed in small vials, which are bundled together and placed in steel canisters. The canisters, which are stored behind those small compartments, contain an envelope of liquid nitrogen, which keeps the sperm at a temperature of minus seventy-five degrees Centigrade."

"That sounds dreadfully cold."

"That's because storage is long term, and we want to preserve as much as possible in pristine condition. It is possible, certainly, for it to survive at much warmer temperatures."

Mrs. Evered seemed entranced by the silvery boxes. "Isn't it risky to keep everything here, especially in the summertime? What if there's a power outage?"

"Wouldn't affect us. If Con Ed goes down, we have our own battery-operated emergency generator that kicks on. The power system is fail-safe." Reston turned off the light. "The samples are removed from the freezer, then brought into this chamber for thawing and testing. That's what these little boxes here are for." He pointed to several steel cubes resting on a stainless steel counter. "These are thermostat controlled—we put the samples in and quickly raise the temperature. The whole process takes but a few minutes."

"How long do you store the, ah, samples? What's the freezer life?"

"Theoretically, indefinitely. Animal semen is stored ten years or more without deterioration. There have been some experiments in which women were successfully impregnated with semen nearly three years old, and bore healthy children. There's no limit, if the storage conditions are proper. In my case, the stock is rarely over six months old, due to supply and demand."

Edward opened the main door and ushered Alice back out. "And over here, you recall, is the examining and operation room. Let's go in and I'll show you how the procedure is done."

Inside, he pulled open drawers and took out the tools and instruments he used in an insemination. "As I told you, it's like having a PAP smear and cervical exam done. You put your feet in the stirrups, I dilate your cervix with a speculum, and insert the sample with a catheter." He held up a long plastic tube about the thickness of a pencil. "You'll experience minor discomfort. If you like, I'll give you a muscle relaxant beforehand."

Alice shook her head. "No drugs of any kind, doctor." She opened her handbag and pulled out Reston's contract and a check. "Here are your signed papers. I trust a personal check is all right."

"By all means, Mrs. Evered. Have you made a decision about your husband?"

"I've spent all day thinking about what you said. I must have a son, and he must be without question the heir to Thorson. Arthur and I are desperate to have a son, obviously for different reasons. I think I can convince him that this is the right thing to do."

"But these papers—he hasn't signed them."

"But I have. My down payment is an indication of the confidence I have."

Reston had to assume Alice knew what she was doing; it was none of his business what she said to her husband. He smiled. "Shall we get started with the first tests, then?"

It was 11:30 P.M. by the time Edward Reston closed up the Park Avenue Family Planning Center and caught a taxi home. Mrs. Evered had left at nine; he had dictated reports and read professional journals for two and a half hours. On the way out, he had seen DeWitt's message that John Heineman had called. He felt a twinge of guilt that he had not called his old mentor himself in a long time. He would return the call in the morning, suggest getting together.

The taxi came to a stop in front of Reston's apartment building on Sutton Place. He tipped generously, got out and murmured greetings to the doorman.

Inside the door of his penthouse apartment, he nearly stumbled over a pile of delivery boxes. Judging from their size, Gloria had been out depriving the rest of New York of either coats or ball gowns—probably the latter. The charity ball season was, regrettably, once again at hand.

"Darling," said Gloria as Reston hung up his own coat. Evidently his wife had sent the maid to her quarters. He turned and saw her standing at the entrance to the living room, wearing her full-length black mink coat. "Like my new coat?" she said breathlessly.

He had to admit, she *did* look smashing in mink, and it was obvious she was thrilled with the coat. Perhaps he shouldn't complain about the bills; after all, whatever made her happy...

"You look gorgeous," he said, and meant it.

"I got it two weeks ago, actually," she said. "I was waiting for the right moment to show you." She did a pirouete, hugging the coat to her body.

Great timing, he thought—the day the bill comes. What

about the other two furs? Would they come out of a closet at "the right time"?

"What else have you bought?"

"Oh, things," she answered vaguely. "Shoes, dresses, bags. You don't want me to bore you with a shopping list." Gloria came up to him and kissed him on the mouth. He took hold of her; the mink felt soft and luxurious.

She took him by the hand and led him into the living room. "Come in and relax. I've got champagne waiting."

"Champagne? What's the occasion?"

"Nothing special. Don't you think you deserve it on general principles?" She peeled off his suit jacket and undid a few buttons of his shirt. His tie was long gone.

Reston was pleased and flattered. Often when he came home late, Gloria had already retired to bed to watch television or read a book. She always seemed to know, however, when to surprise him with a little pampering. He needed it tonight—he was worn to a frazzle.

The curtains were still pulled back from the giant picture windows in the living room, showing the nighttime postcard view of the East River and Queens, and Manhattan to the south. The mass of city lights cast a red glow up into the sky. It was a peaceful view, belying the dirt and crime and maddening congestion at street level.

By the sofa stood a sterling silver ice bucket on a stand, its contents covered with a white linen cloth.

Gloria gazed out the window while Edward opened the bottle of Dom Perignon. "Aren't you hot in that coat?" he asked.

She shrugged, rubbing her right hand up and down one arm. "While I was out today, I looked at some apartments. Just out of curiosity, you know."

Reston, about to pour the first glass of champagne, froze in mid-motion with a pang in his stomach. "Apartments? Where?" He poured the Dom Perignon.

"Suites, actually. And a penthouse. On Park Avenue and along Central Park. They were all wonderful, Edward, with absolutely *stunning* views." She turned from the window and looked at him.

He handed her a flute of champagne. "What's the matter with this view?"

"Nothing, darling, it's lovely. But Park Avenue, Central Park—those *are* the best addresses."

Reston poured champagne for himself. "I wasn't aware that a Sutton Place penthouse had suddenly fallen out of favor as an address."

"Darling, you *know* the crowd we're with."

"We have another year to go on the lease here." He raised his glass and tapped it against hers. "Cheers, sweetheart. Thanks for the champagne."

Gloria took a delicate sip. "We could sublease, darling, and then not renew. These places I looked at today—they're not for lease, but for sale."

Reston paled, a sense of the inevitable sweeping over him. He couldn't deal with it now. "Let's talk about it later." He set his glass down on the marble-topped cocktail table and sprawled on the sofa. "Gloria, would you please take off that coat?"

A mischievous smile crossed her lips and her eyes sparkled. "Thought you'd never ask." She let the coat slip from her shoulders to the floor. She wore nothing underneath.

CHAPTER Six

Rainer Stern came awake in a sweat, not knowing where he was. Slowly, he made sense out of his darkened surroundings. He was in his bed in his apartment on the Upper West Side. Of course. Where else would he be?

He listened, but the voices had faded. They were coming almost every night now. Voices of dead relatives—Leon, his mother, his father, aunts, uncles, cousins, all jabbering at him at once. In his sleep, the voices surrounded him in a semicircle, like a tribe gathered for story telling. But since they all talked at once, he could never make sense out of what they were saying.

Rainer exhaled. The absence of the voices did little to lessen the tension that gripped his body. He turned on the light by the bed and sat up. His clock read five-ten; he might as well get up.

It was October, and Leon had been dead for six months.

Rainer felt like he was cracking up.

It wasn't only because of the voices, which had started shortly after Leon's suicide. Other unnatural things had been happening, with frightening frequency. He had bizarre hallucinations that would come and go so fast he wondered if he imagined them. The telephone would ring and sometimes he would know who was on the other end before he picked up the receiver. He had flashes of premonition that unnerved him so much he had difficulty concentrating at work.

He swung his legs out of bed. He felt cold all over. Whatever was wrong with him, he wanted it to *stop*.

Stern started for the bathroom. An impluse made him halt by his dresser and pull open the top drawer. Beneath the neatly folded clothing lay a photo of Leon. Rainer had taken it shortly before Leon killed himself. He got it out every now and then and looked at it. He pulled it out now.

By the time Leon had reached age twenty-five, Rainer no longer felt like he was looking in a mirror when he saw Leon. Illness and emotional distress had ravaged Leon's good looks and aged him prematurely. In this photograph, taken about a decade later, Leon was gaunt and haggard, gray around the temples, and trying valiantly to smile.

Rainer stared at the photo.

The image of Leon began to move.

Rainer gasped. He tried to drop the photo but couldn't let go.

The photo became a movie. Leon gestured and his lips moved without sound. He was talking, Rainer realized. To *him*.

Impossible.

With a shudder, Stern managed to let go of the photo. It fell to the floor, and he kicked it out of sight beneath the dresser. Shaking, he went into the bathroom. *It didn't happen*, he tried to convince himself. He thought he was going to be sick, but there was nothing in his stomach to throw up. He hadn't eaten dinner the night before.

He looked at himself in the mirror. What was wrong with him?

Arthur Evered looked like the quintessential American executive: tall, sturdily built, steely blue-green eyes, a strong chin, and a leonine mane of hair that was graying in a most distinguished way. He carried an aura of power around him. Others automatically acquiesced to and accommodated him.

"You look like you need a drink," he said, upon seeing Stern.

Rainer smiled wanly and took the cue. "An excellent idea." He went to the walnut cabinet where his stock of liquor and crystal glasses was stored. He poured two neat shots of Evered's preferred brand, Glenlivet, and handed one glass to Evered, who took it to the sofa and sat down. Stern took a sip and felt a little comforted by the burn of the Scotch.

Evered drank from his glass. He said, "Rainer, I'm contemplating getting a divorce."

Stern was startled. He hadn't seen that one coming. "Are you sure?"

"Ninety-nine percent. I would appreciate it if you would not mention this to the other partners at the moment. But I want you to figure out what it's going to cost me."

"Plenty. You were lucky last time around. You won't buy Alice off so easily." *Poor Alice*, Rainer thought.

"Who's side are you on?" It was meant as a joke, but Evered's expression was deadly.

Stern abandoned his Scotch and perched on the edge of his desk, facing Evered. "Just pointing out the facts."

"I don't care what it costs," Evered said tightly, his self-control cracking. He swallowed half the remaining Scotch. "It's not going to work with Alice."

"I'm sorry." Stern made a quick decision not to ask for details. He sensed that Evered was not ready to give them. "I'll start pulling things together."

Evered drained his glass and rose. "Alice doesn't know yet," he said, and left.

Great, thought Stern. *It's going to be one hell of an evening.*

The limousines were stacked like dominoes end to end at the Park Avenue entrance of the Waldorf-Astoria Hotel, disgorging men in tuxedos and women in silk gowns and furs for the annual Foundation for Nervous Disorders benefit dinner and ball. The men and women represented the wealthy upper crust, that part of society that remained a bastion of conservatism in the face of an antiestablishment youth.

In the back seat of a black Lincoln Continental limo, Gloria Reston fretted. "Look at all these cars double-parked! We'll never get close to the front door!"

Edward Reston patted his wife's black silk-covered knee. "Let the driver do the worrying and the jockeying—that's what he's getting paid for. New York will not crumble if we have to walk a few feet to the door."

"You don't understand, Edward. I want to get out of the car and right onto the carpet, beneath the awning. These things are *important*." She rapped her knuckles on the partition; the driver reached behind him and slid it open.

"Yes, Madam?" He listened patiently while Gloria harangued him about getting them directly to the door. "It may take a while, Madam, considering the traffic and the parking situation."

"I don't care."

"Yes, Madam."

Edward looked at his wife. "Don't get yourself all worked up, honey. Next time, we'll leave earlier."

"And risk arriving when the function *starts*? Sometimes I think you have no sense of propriety, Edward."

But I do have common sense, thought Reston. *And getting trussed up for the privilege of eating a five-hundred-dollar-a-plate rubber steak dinner while society hens peck away at you is not my idea of common sense.*

Nevertheless, some of those women were potential clients.

He said, "Did I tell you you look terrific? White mink goes well with your complexion."

"Yes, you've told me a dozen times." She smiled prettily. "But I like hearing it again." She leaned back into the wide leather seat, her manicured hands daintily clasping her black beaded evening bag on her lap. "I tried to join the publicity committee for this event, but that old harpie, Madelyn Fitzsimmons, wouldn't let me do a thing. Honestly!"

"I thought you were on the publicity committee of the ball we went to the other night—that kidney diseases thing at the Pierre."

"I was. But kidney diseases are on their way *out*, Edward. Nervous disorders are in, and in is where the action is."

"I think I understand," he said, not understanding at all the female power politics of volunteerism.

The limousine inched forward. They were still a long shot away from the kind of entrance Gloria wished to make. At last the driver waited for a break in the traffic, got out, and approached the driver of the limo double-parked almost in front of the awning, and began negotiating.

"I've got a great idea," Reston said. "Let's start a new charity ball, and you can be chairwoman and run the whole show."

Gloria was skeptical. "*New* charity? All the diseases and handicaps have been taken—all the good ones, that is."

"The benefit will be for the Park Avenue Family Planning Center. Why shouldn't I be the beneficiary of five-hundred-dollar-a-plate dinners to help more and more couples have children? We'll call it the annual Fertility Dance."

Gloria shot him her best drop-dead look. "*Really*, Edward. I wish you would take these affairs seriously. They're good for your career."

"I do take them seriously."

The driver returned. Negotiation apparently had been successful, for the limo ahead eased out of its spot, and the Restons' car pulled in. A coup for Gloria—and Edward was sure the price had been steep. He would settle with the driver at the end of the evening.

Within minutes, the chauffeur was opening the rear door, and Gloria was making her arrival at the Waldorf-Astoria. She was well practiced at getting into and out of cars and limos with grace and style, her face set with an expression that conveyed that riding around in a limo dressed in silk and fur was a routine part of her royal life. Reston emerged behind her. They were a handsome couple, and drew many stares from the passersby and other couples entering the hotel.

In the anteroom to the Grand Ballroom, the predinner cocktail service was well under way. Elegantly dressed couples crowded together, drinks in hand, some with tiny plates of hors d'oeuvres served from a buffet. Gloria craned her neck. "Brooke Astor is supposed to be here, and so is Walter Cronkite. Look! There's Senator Marsh and his wife. And there are the Waldmans with the senator—let's go say hello." They joined the small group and made introductions.

Evelyn Waldman, a plump brunette in her mid-thirties, said, "Congratulations, Edward. Gloria tells me you're giving up your delightful little place at Sutton and moving to Park Avenue. Things must be going *very* well."

Gloria chirped about her decorating plans and Reston smiled stiffly. He did not want to be reminded of the enormous mortgage he was taking on. He excused himself to go to the bar for drinks, a gin and tonic for his wife and a bourbon on the rocks for himself.

He spotted two couples who were patients of his, and in accordance with his etiquette of confidentiality, pretended not to know them. He left familiarity up to his patients, and took no offense when they ignored him in public, and knew they took no offense when he did the same to them. From past experience, Reston was confident he would not leave the Waldorf without some discreet introductions from patients who had interested friends. Although he generally did not enjoy attending such events, it was money in the bank to make himself visible. Occasionally someone wanted to engage him in a debate about the morals and ethics of artificial insemination, but he was adept at discouraging arguments.

Reston was on his way back to his wife, jostling through the crowd, when a hand clapped solidly on his right shoulder and he stopped and turned. He looked up into a lean, craggy face, punctuated by deep-set, clear blue eyes.

"John! For God's sake!" Reston grinned, then turned red with embarrassment. "I never returned your call. I'm dreadfully sorry—" He felt terrible. He had not made much effort in the last year or so to stay in touch with Dr. John Heineman, the brilliant scientist who had been his mentor and who had shaped his career, the director of the Klein Laboratory of Applied Biogenetics in Purchase, Westchester County.

Heineman smiled and dismissed the apology with a short wave of his hand. "I hear you are quite busy these days," he said in a low-register voice with a German accent. "It is good to see you so successful, *mein Sohn*. You are a pioneer."

Reston suddenly felt awkward, holding a drink in each hand. "I'd shake hands, but I don't have a third one. I never thought I'd run into you at one of these bashes. I didn't know you were doing the charity circuit."

"I'm often invited but seldom attend. But Klein has a vested interest in hereditary nervous disorders, wouldn't you say?"

"Quite logical." Reston held up his drinks. "Come say hi to Gloria. She's right over there. Aren't you drinking anything?"

Heineman shook his head.

"Still the disciplined health fanatic, eh?" Reston appraised his mentor's appearance and they edged their way through the crush of people. Heineman had to be in his mid-fifties, but scarcely looked it. He was tall and graceful with a lean and muscular build. He still had most of his hair, a generous crop of it, and a beard trimmed neat and short. The blond had faded from its original luster when Reston first met Heineman, and it was sprinkled with gray. Heineman's blue eyes held depth—of intelligence, of energy.

"I keep to my health routine," Heineman answered. "Five miles a day on those back Westchester County roads. You must come up to the lab sometime, Edward. We have expanded the facilities. Purchase is only an hour's drive away."

"Of course." Guilt flooded over Reston again. He had not been to the Klein compound, where he trained under Heineman, since he left to open the Park Avenue Family Planning Center. Some grateful protégé was he. "Your call—"

"It was only to say hello, see how you were doing."

"Business is sensational. I can hardly keep up with the demand."

"And you are selective about those you serve?"

"Definitely. I get inquiries from all over the world, and take only the most prestigious. Most of my patients come from the enclave of Eastern Establishment society, however. You'd be surprised how many wealthy people don't have children to carry on the family empires."

"That's my boy. What did I tell you before? Serve the carriage trade and you have no worries." Heineman gave Reston a slap on the back. "I take great pride in your work, Edward. I always did. You carry on for me, yes?"

Reston's guilt worsened. "John, I owe you an apology for going so long without calling—"

"Please. It is moot. I was out of the country for several months, and just returned three weeks ago."

"Really? Where? Doing what?"

"Here and there. England, the Continent. Mostly my old homeland, Austria. I spoke at a symposium in Vienna, and toured laboratories in Austria, Switzerland, and West Germany, where remarkable work is being done in biogenetics and infertility therapy. They talk of in vitro fertilization, and of embryos being implanted in the womb."

"Yes, I've been keeping up with the journals."

"Well, I heard of some fascinating developments while I was in Vienna."

"I'd like to hear the details."

"Then you definitely must come up to Purchase. We will spend the day."

They reached Reston's wife and the small group of conversationalists. Senator and Mrs. Marsh had attracted another couple Reston didn't know; the Waldmans were still there. He handed Gloria her drink. "Look who's here, darling. You remember John."

Gloria had not seen the scientist since her wedding day, and fussed prettily over Heineman and how wonderful he looked. Reston presented him to the group: "Ladies and gentlemen, this is Dr. John Heineman, director of the Klein Laboratory for Applied Biogenetics up in Purchase. I used to work for Dr. Heineman. He is without a doubt one of the most preeminent scientists in his field, and I can say unequivocally that the work he is doing will someday have a profound impact on society."

"I bribed him to say that," Heineman said, and his audience chuckled.

Once the introductions were made, Senator Marsh, a towering teddy bear of a man with black square glasses, addressed the scientist. "Biogenetics, eh? I've been reading about this new field. The theoreticians say that soon we'll be able to program genes—engineer humans the same way we engineer buildings. Is that what you're working on at Klein, doctor?"

John smiled disarmingly. "That's the correct theory, but what is possible in reality is a long way off, Senator Marsh. Biogenetics *is* a new field, evolving from work done for decades on animal and crop breeding. The same principles can be applied to humans. At Klein, we are pursuing research to learn more about genes and how they determine one's inherited characteristics. Eventually, we hope to be able to control the process."

"It sounds so—*clinical*," said Mrs. Waldman.

"Beneficial, Mrs. Waldman. Think of the hereditary diseases that could be eliminated with what we in the field call planned conception. Think of the enhancements to intelligence and physical stamina. To longevity."

"It sounds like what the Nazis tried to create—a master race," said the man whom Reston didn't know, a Mr. Chandler. His wife dug him in the ribs, and Chandler reddened. "I'm sorry, doctor, if I—"

Heineman looked unruffled. "I am not German, Mr. Chandler. I am Austrian. I did not support the Nazis in the war—in fact, I fled them, to come here. To respond to your comment about the so-called 'master race,' that was Hitler's demented dream, but the Nazis had no idea what they were doing. They conducted experiments, yes, but they worked blind."

Chandler, emboldened by Heineman's reply, pursued the matter. "But doesn't this biogenetics amount to the same thing? The idea being to deliberately create a strain of super human beings with programmed characteristics?"

"Not at all, sir," said Heineman patiently. "The Nazis, you see, envisioned an exclusive race that would rule the world. We biogeneticists are far more democratic. We seek improvements for *all* the peoples of the world. And why should your children not enjoy every advantage possible? If you had the choice, Mr. Chandler, would you not want your children to be free of handicaps and diseases? Would you not want them to have the intelligence to excel in life?"

Reston jumped in. "It's probably going to be a long time before parents 'plan' their offspring. But right now, we *can* stack the odds a bit for favorable outcomes."

The overhead lights blinked off and on, signaling the guests that it was time to adjourn to the Grand Ballroom for the sit-down dinner.

Senator Marsh stuck out his hand to Heineman. "Pleasure to meet you, doctor. I'd like to discuss this topic with you in depth sometime."

Heineman smiled wryly. "I'm sure you're well aware, Senator, that the federal government has chosen to take a hands-off position in this area because of the moral issues some people feel are raised. That's unfortunate, because it means no federal funds are available for research. We at Klein are fortunate to have secured generous private funding."

"Perhaps the federal government *should* be involved."

John pulled out an engraved business card. "I'd be delighted, Senator. Call anytime, and I will arrange a tour of our facility."

As the little group dispersed for their assigned banquet tables, Reston said, "Where are you sitting, John? Perhaps we could make a switch."

"I'm not staying, Edward. My business for the evening is done. It was good to see you, *mein Sohn*. Stay in touch, will you?" Heineman gave him a firm handshake and departed.

Reston took Gloria by the arm and steered her into the ballroom. The sixty tables were festooned with centerpieces of fresh red and white flowers and helium-filled red, white, and blue balloons on long ribbons. He pulled out his tickets. "Table three," he said. "I forgot to look at the roster. Do you know who is sitting with us?"

"Mrs. and Mrs. Arthur Evered." Gloria's smile indicated she was pleased with herself. "I may not have gotten on the publicity committee, but I did pull a string with the chairwoman of seating arrangements."

A pang went through Reston. Alice Evered had called him moments before he left the office this evening to tell him Arthur had agreed to meet with him, and would first thing in the morning be satisfactory? He had agreed. He had not met Arthur Evered personally yet, and he would have preferred not to before they had a chance to talk business.

Gloria, of course, did not know about his involvement with the Evereds. He never discussed his patients even with her, for fear of gossip.

"Wonderful," Edward said without enthusiasm. "Who else?"

"The Handleys."

Christ, the Handleys! Another set of clients. To make matters worse, he had just bumped Mrs. Handley in favor of Mrs. Evered. This was awful. What was he going to talk about—the weather?

"And," said Gloria, still oblivious to his dilemma,

"Rainer Stern. That's Rainer Stern *Esquire*, darling—of Goldman, Schoenberg, Larkin & Stern. I think he's coming alone. Isn't that charming? We can watch the ladies fight over him."

Reston grunted.

"Before we sit down, Edward, I think I'll freshen up."

Reston stood off to the side of the ballroom and waited for Gloria to return. She came back all in a huff. "I can't *believe* it!" she said in a low voice.

"Believe what?"

She stood on her tiptoes and pulled on his neck so that she could whisper in his ear. "I just ran into that old harpie, Madelyn Fitzsimmons, Madame Publicity Chairwoman, in the powder room—and she's positively *reeking* of pot! In the *Waldorf*!"

Reston straightened, amused at the notion of the stiff and most proper Mrs. Fitzsimmons trying to be hip by getting stoned. "Are you sure it's not her perfume?"

"Edward, *really*. It's absolutely outrageous, and all you can do is crack a joke. I wish you'd be more serious."

"I *am* serious, sweetheart. I am."

Stern moved through the benefit in a private haze, trying to make the best of it without being boorish. He barely tasted the first three courses of the four-course dinner: salmon terrine, mixed green salad, veal chop with steamed broccoli, and wild rice. The buzz of the conversation in the ballroom coupled with the background music from the band on stage made it difficult—mercifully—to talk to anyone at the table but the person on either side. The man on his left, Dr. Edward Reston, was preoccupied with conversation. The chair on his right was empty. Stern wondered if it was supposed to have been taken by a woman whom Alice wanted him to meet. He had expected that, but he was glad the chair was empty. His well of social conversation had run dry during cocktail hour. It seemed like Alice had an endless parade of young ladies to introduce.

He noticed that, across the table, Arthur Evered appeared strained.

After a dessert of strawberry glaće with petits fours was served and eaten, Gloria Reston excused herself for a trip to the ladies' room. The band conductor grabbed a microphone and shouted, "All right, ladies and gentlemen, we're going to heat up the party with a little Credence Clearwater!" The band immediately launched into a peppy version of "Proud Mary." The Evereds got up and wandered off; the Handleys got up to dance. Stern settled back in his chair and watched the dance floor fill up with couples. He wondered when Arthur was going to broach the subject of divorce with Alice.

Reston tapped the table to the rhythm and looked around the crowd impatiently. "Damn, where's Gloria?"

Stern turned to him. They had barely spoken since sitting down at the start of the evening. "Mind if I smoke?"

"Not at all. In fact, I'll join you." Reston started to pull a cigar out of his breast jacket pocket.

"Here, have one of mine." Rainer got out two cigars and gave one to Reston. They enjoyed the ritual of lighting the cigars in a comradely silence.

Stern broke it, searching for a topic of mutual interest. "I couldn't overhear your conversation earlier, but it seemed that you and Arthur Evered were getting into quite a debate. Politics? Art's got a lot to say about this Watergate situation."

Reston shrugged without comment, preoccupied with his cigar.

Stern let it drop. He had tried to place the doctor's familiar name earlier, when they were introduced, and couldn't. Suddenly it clicked. "Excuse me, I knew I'd seen your name somewhere before—now I remember. It was in the *Times* a few months ago. You run that fertility clinic on Park Avenue, right?"

"The Park Avenue Family Planning Center. I've gotten some unsolicited publicity, though I try to keep a low profile. Confidentiality, you understand, plus the fact that not everyone agrees with what I'm doing. Planned offspring through artificial insemination stirs up almost as much fervor as that new abortion ruling from the Supreme Court. This is superb tobacco, by the way."

"Dunhill. Next best to Havana."

"Really? You have your own humidor there in the back of the shop?"

Stern nodded. He drew in aromatic smoke. "Artificial insemination does pose some interesting ethical and legal questions pertaining to birthright, inheritance, and responsibility for support," mused Stern. "So far, the law really hasn't dealt with it, except in Oklahoma, where artificial insemination for people was officially legalized in 1967.

"I see it is a personal, private matter, not one for the courts. As long as the donor remains anonymous and the parents are consenting adults, then the couple should be allowed to have a child that is at least in part their own.

"I recall a case in Canada recently where the court ruled that such a child was illegitimate, that artificial insemination was essentially adultery."

"A backward mentality," Reston said. "Thank heavens it hasn't happened in the U.S. Those kinds of rulings can't possibly prevail in the long run, anyway. Artificial insemination is part of the growing field of biogenetics—soon it will become commonplace, as people opt to have the best offspring genetically possible."

"I take it Arthur doesn't agree with you."

Reston shrugged. "I don't know what his opinions on the matter are," he said vaguely. He chuckled at a thought. "You should have been around earlier this evening. An associate of mine in the field was here, and someone inasmuch accused him of being on the same level as the Nazis, trying to create a master race. I tell you, there's a lot of ignorance out there."

Stern did not reply. His throat had tightened, his breathing suddenly painful. His left hand, holding the cigar, was hanging in space while he labored for breath. The ballroom before him receded in a cloud of mist, replaced by jagged scenes from a past that he could never forget. His left arm, which beneath his starched white shirt still bore the tattooed number from Auschwitz, throbbed in pain. *He was a small boy behind barbed wire, desperately hungry and thirsty. Water... he must have water...*

Stern thrust his right hand out for the goblet of water in front of him. The mist closed in around him, blotting out Reston, the table, the crowd on the dance floor, the gold decor of the Grand Ballroom. He spun dizzily in the mist, watching himself and Leon get pricked and poked by the cold, efficient hands of Josef Mengele and 'Dr. Hans' Messner, hearing the screams and cries of faceless children in the background.

The shattering of glass snapped him back to the present. He saw he had burst the water goblet in his bare hand. His hand was bloody. A pool of pink water soaked a good portion of the white tablecloth. Still in a daze, Stern stared at his hand, not feeling the pain from the glass cuts.

Reston jumped to his feet and grabbed Stern by the wrist. "Lord, there must have been a flaw in the glass."

Stern looked up at him, but instead of Reston, he saw the face of Dr. Hans leering down. "Let go," he said as he tried to pull back his hand, the pain now beginning to register. He gritted his teeth.

Reston would not let go. "You may have glass embedded." The doctor applied gentle pressure to encourage bleeding. "Let's get you to first aid."

"I can manage!" Stern snapped. He stood up, aware of stares of those around him. He grabbed his linen napkin and wrapped it around his hand. Before Reston could stop him, he lurched away from the table and hurried out of the ballroom. He did not go to the men's room, he did not look for the hotel's first-aid station. He ran blindly down the stairs and through the blue-carpeted lobby, out into the street, pursued by ghosts of Auschwitz. He had to get away from the vision, the screams and crying.

Leon's voice whispered in his ear. *"It isn't over . . . It isn't over."*

Six blocks away, the sounds and images at last faded, he quit running and stopped to catch his breath. No one paid more than fleeting attention to him. The sight of a man in a tuxedo with a bleeding hand scarcely caused a ripple among the crowds in the street; this was Manhattan. Stern was thankful for the anonymity.

He unwrapped his hand. Blood welled up from the cuts.

What wasn't over?

CHAPTER
Seven

The patrician face in front of Reston was hard and unforgiving; the jaw was clenched, the blue-green eyes piercing. Anger rumbled just below the surface.

"Cut the medical mumbo jumbo, Dr. Reston. What you're trying to tell me is that I'm incapable of fathering a child—with any woman."

"I'm afraid so, Mr. Evered. It appears that—"

"The reason doesn't matter. I'm only interested in the net result."

"Then you have it. I'm very sorry." Reston folded his hands on his desk. This was one part of his work he distinctly did not like.

The light from his high-intensity lamp created a bright spill on his desk. It was Friday, seven-thirty in the morning and just barely getting light outside. Reston reflected that if he continued to squeeze in extra patients before and after office hours, he might as well set up a cot in his office and live there.

He still had no idea how Alice had managed to convince her husband to see him. Undoubtedly it had involved some sort of marital blackmail. He did not want to know. After their exchange of unpleasantries the night before at the Waldorf, he wouldn't have put a nickel down on seeing Arthur here this morning.

But the executive arrived promptly at seven, and had produced the semen sample Reston needed. When he looked through the microscope, the doctor's suspicions were confirmed: he would have to be the bearer of bad news.

Evered rose from his chair and paced around the office like a panther, deep in his own thoughts. He was a man making decisions about himself and his marriage. Reston admired his imposing appearance. He was conservative in clothing and hairstyle—no wide, trendy sideburns for this man. He wore a vested pinstripe suit the color of charcoal, with a Princeton tie. Peeking beneath the starched French cuffs of his white shirt was a gold Rolex watch.

In the business world, Evered was reputed to be a cutthroat and a bastard. But he desperately wanted a child—specifically a son—and that made him human to Reston.

"When I'm confronted with a problem, doctor, I expect a solution. You say you can give me and Alice a son."

"A child, yes." Reston proceeded to explain his services and procedures, as he had to Alice, emphasizing that the offspring would bear at least some of the genetic stamp of the Evereds. He also stressed the confidentiality he maintained. "No one need ever know the true origin," he finished. "The birth certificate will register you as the natural father. My donors sign away all rights. They never know who the recipients are, nor will you know the identity of your donor."

"Just a minute, doctor. Are you telling me that I have *no control* over this situation, that *I* cannot choose who will substitute for *me*?" Anger broke through the surface of Evered's composure.

Reston chose his words carefully. "There are a host of legal considerations I'm sure a businessman like you can appreciate. The system works only if there is complete anonymity at both ends. If, for example, you knew the identity of the donor, you might be tempted to contact him sometime in the future. It might create unbearable curiosity for your wife or child. I'm sure you've heard of the lengths some adopted children go to to find their natural parents. It is much better for all parties concerned that these situations do not arise."

"You aren't listening to me, Dr. Reston. I cannot accept those conditions. Alice and the child don't need to know, but *I* do. If I'm going to be responsible for raising the child, I have the right to determine the donor."

"Mr. Evered, these conditions exist for my own protection as well as that of my patients. I'm sorry, but I make no exceptions."

Evered looked stunned for a moment. Reston knew the man was accustomed to people following his orders, not refusing them. He half expected Evered to storm out. It would not be the first time he'd lost a patient because of his conditions.

But Evered didn't storm out, or lose his temper and start shouting. He stabbed his hands into his pockets. Reston read the signals and was silent. The man badly wanted something he could not get himself; Reston had the means.

"I'm forty-eight," Evered said quietly. "I'm running out of time. I want a son, and I want to be alive to see him take over the business."

Reston had been clasping his hands tightly; now he relaxed. Arthur Evered was won over. But Reston still had to get him to face the uncertainty of the infant's sex. "As I explained to Mrs. Evered, I cannot guarantee a boy. The odds are high that she will get pregnant and complete her term with a healthy child, but it may not be male."

Evered gave Reston a professorial look. "I make it my business to be informed, Dr. Reston. Aren't there two kinds of sperm, one that produces males and one that produces females? Why can't you use only the male-producing sperm?"

"You're right about spermatozoa. If an androsperm fertilizes an egg, a male is created; gynosperm creates a female. But it's not so simple. It is extremely difficult to separate one from the other. It can be done by centrifugal force, but the procedure is unreliable and jeopardizes the health of the sperm itself. It's not worth the risk."

"I'll make it worth your while to take the risk."

Reston shook his head. "You would be wasting your money. Up to a certain age, the sex of the embryo is subject to change. The egg could be fertilized a male, and still change to a female. Science has made great advances, but we are still a long way off from completely controlling the creation of life."

"But you *must* give me the best odds possible."

"Certainly. All of the donors to my bank have fathered several children. I will select one who of course meets all other criteria you've established, and who has a family history of predominantly sons." Reston checked his desk calendar and made notes in the Evered file. "As I've already told Mrs. Evered, I can put you on a priority basis. The timing with her ovulation cycle is fortunate. I'll have my nurse make arrangements with your wife for her to come in early next Monday."

"What about your employees? Will they know the identity of the donor?"

Reston shook his head as he jotted. "They know the patients, of course, and the confidence is strictly kept. Patients never see each other. But I am the only one who handles the sperm samples, and I use a code." He smiled. "I'm the only one who will ever know, Mr. Evered, and there are some things I am very good at forgetting."

The last patient departed the clinic by 5:15 P.M. Reston always tried to finish up early on Fridays, usually without much success. Still, five-fifteen was better than six or six-thirty—or later. He leaned back in his leather chair and closed his eyes for a moment. What a day, starting with Arthur Evered. He already had a donor picked; it was an excellent match. Even though he had stressed to the Evereds that he could not guarantee a male child, he could see they were counting on it. He did not want to face Arthur's wrath if Alice produced a girl. Reston would do voodoo dances beneath a full moon if he thought it would help.

And then there was the hate letter that had arrived in the day's mail. It was the third letter from the same individual —the same typewriter and ribbon, the same language, but with escalating threats. He pulled out the unmarked file at the back of his bottom right desk drawer and looked at the letter again.

"God does not want some people to have children, and you are disobeying His wishes! You will PAY for this! You and your evil clinic will be wiped from the face of the Earth!"

The letters made Reston nervous. He had never received more than one letter from a single source. Before he left tonight, he would double-check the security system.

Edward got up and went to the cabinet where he kept a few bottles of liquor. He was free until ten, when he and Gloria had a dinner engagement with another couple at Lutece. But he wasn't all that anxious to go home right away. Lately the Sutton Place penthouse had been turned upside down as Gloria prepared for their move. The apartment was crawling with minions and drones she had commissioned. The move itself was two months away, but Gloria liked to be prepared. This week, she'd had a delicately boned interior decorator and a long-haired architect fluttering around. They were drawing up plans for the Park Avenue place. From the looks of the plans, the co-op was going to be gutted and given a brand new look. Edward was puzzled; he thought she was nuts about it the way it was.

He poured a shot of Wild Turkey neat. Just so long as the furniture was real furniture with arms. He hated giant pillows piled on the floor, and he hated those armless chairs and sofas that designers claimed were all the rage.

The bourbon went down his throat in a pleasant fire. He

poured a bigger shot. Life was great. He lived in a charmed circle untouched by the chaos that gripped the country—the Vietnam fiasco, the drug crisis, the rebellious students, the growing Watergate scandal. The only worry he had was catching up with a debt that was a little too large. But that should be no problem, not with the business his clinic was doing.

By the time Nancy DeWitt opened his door to say good night, Reston was in great spirits. "Would you like a drink, Nancy?" he invited. She accepted with enthusiasm.

Edward felt expansive. He loosened his tie and put his feet up on his desk. They talked like old friends. He appreciated Nancy.

It wasn't until a couple of hours had passed that, with a shock, he discovered her secret desire. He was pouring out two more drinks, joking about the wasp-waisted interior decorator, when she came up to him and slid her hand along his arm. There was electricity in her touch. He broke off talking and looked down into her face; her eyes were full of a wild light. She was not Nurse Nancy DeWitt, but an extremely attractive woman. Why hadn't he noticed before? For a moment, time hung suspended. Then he put down the Wild Turkey and drew her to him and bent down to kiss her. He didn't think about what he was doing or why; it merely seemed right and irresistible for the moment.

Her lips were sweet and urgent, her body soft and yielding. He responded as any red-blooded man would. She offered no resistance to his searching hands.

"Come home with me," she whispered.

Reston fought the impulse to let go of his inhibitions. With great effort, he drew away and gently undid her embrace. "No, Nancy. I'm terribly sorry. I shouldn't have started this."

"Please, it's all right..."

His voice was firm. "It never happened."

* * *

Reston was disturbed all weekend over the incident with Nancy. He was not disturbed that a sexual attraction had blossomed between him and his nurse; he was disturbed about its implications. He had no desire to cheat on his wife, and certainly did not want to jeopardize his marriage. Nor did he want complications at the clinic. He simply couldn't afford them, and if Nancy became a problem—she would have to go. A damn shame, he thought, for she was a fine assistant.

The matter was still on his mind when he arrived at the clinic the following Monday. It was seven-thirty; Nancy and Sandra, the receptionist, would not be in for about another hour. Reston had four inseminations scheduled for the day, including Alice Evered; he wanted to do the preparatory work alone.

He unlocked the main door and flicked on the light inside. Everything looked normal and in place. He pushed through the door that led to the inner clinic, the short hallway of rooms—and stopped.

He felt no chill in the hallway, which customarily emanated from the freezer room. Then he saw that the freezer room door was not completely latched—which meant it was unlocked. He was certain he had locked it and double-checked it before leaving Friday night.

He put out his hand and touched the metal door. It was cool, but not nearly as cold as it should be. With rising dread, he shoved the door open.

He wanted to scream, but the scream refused to come out of his throat.

The anteroom to the freezer was room temperature. He rushed to the thick steel door to the freezer itself; it was warm. It also was unlocked.

He yanked it open and was greeted by his worst fear. The "fail-safe" cooling system had failed.

His throat released an anguished cry. Panicked, he worked

the levers of the individual box compartments. Lot 300-G, the seed of an Olympic gold medalist marathon runner with an IQ of 140, who had died in a plane crash after selling his sperm to Reston. Irreplaceable—and thawed! Lost forever! Lot 42-R, a Nobel prizewinning physicist. Thawed and ruined. Lot 101-B, a Russian ballet star. Thawed. Lot 20-X, a self-made millionaire financier with an IQ of 160, intended for Alice Evered. Thawed.

"Dead! Dead! They're all dead!" he screamed. "It's impossible!"

Reston sagged against the wall, his ragged breath catching in his chest. His entire stock of sperm was destroyed. "Oh, God, I'm ruined," he moaned. "Ruined!"

His mind worked frantically. He would close the clinic for a few days, postpone patients' appointments. Somehow he had to find a way out without losing everything.

CHAPTER
Eight

Edward plodded along the asphalt path, oblivious to the autumn beauty around him. The pastoral grounds of the Klein Laboratory for Applied Biogenetics in Purchase were ablaze with red, gold, and orange trees. A late afternoon sun slanted across the landscape. Dying leaves fell and drifted to the grass in a cool breeze.

Beside Reston walked his former mentor, Dr. John Heineman, calm and deep in thought as they strolled the network of paths around the grounds.

"You are certain nothing can be salvaged, Edward?"

"Nothing. I checked every lot. The power must have gone off sometime Friday night. By the time I got there this morning, it was too late to do anything but weep."

"It's a setback, Edward, but not the end. We will think of something."

Reston glanced appreciatively at Heineman. He was the only person in whom Edward could confide about the disaster. Somehow, his brilliant mentor would have a solution. Upon Reston's frantic telephone call, Heineman responded immediately with an invitation. Reston left his office and rented a car. He kept a Mercedes sedan in the garage at

Sutton Place, but didn't want to take it on the off chance that Gloria would find out, and inquire why he had needed it when he was supposed to be at his clinic. He sped up the Hutchinson Parkway the forty-odd miles to Purchase.

On the way up, he mentally tallied his assets and debts. The balance sheet was heavy on the debit side.

"Edward, I want to get everything straight, have a clear picture in my mind about what happened. Tell me again."

Reston sighed. Retelling his professional and financial ruin was excruciatingly painful. He recounted his path to the freezer room and pulling open every small compartment in the bank. "Then I went straight to the back room supply closet, where the emergency generator is installed. The power cables that go through the wall and into the freezer were in place, but the fan belt was missing, so the generator never kicked on when someone pulled the plug to the main power.

"The generator failure should have triggered an alarm to the building security. They're supposed to call me via my beeper immediately upon an emergency. I never got any such call. I found the alarm disconnected."

"So the man on duty was never aware of your emergency?"

"No. But there *was* an isolated main power failure on two floors at 2 A.M. Saturday—my floor and the one below. Several fuses apparently blew. The power was off for about fifteen minutes."

"What's the significance of that?"

Reston shrugged. "Probably a side effect of someone tampering with my electrical system. He inadvertently blew the fuses."

"And you say the rest of the office had power when you arrived this morning?"

"I opened the door and turned on the lights as I went. Everything seemed normal. Afterward, I checked the rooms. They all had power but the freezer. It was deliberate sabotage, not an accident." His shoulders slumped. "I'd just like to know who did it—and why."

Heineman let out a long breath. "These are troubled times here in America. It seems if someone doesn't like what you are doing, they try to destroy you with violence. It's all the more frightening because it's anonymous. Cowardly."

"A lousy political statement for some hothead activist—and *my* destruction!"

"Do you have any clues?"

"Every now and then, I get an anonymous hate letter in the mail. I avoid publicity, you know, but word gets around. There's always someone who takes biblical affront, says I'm being immoral."

They stopped beneath an oak tree ablaze with color. Heineman had his back to the sun; Reston had to shade his eyes to look at him. The light made the Austrian's blond-gray hair look white. "There's your saboteur, then," said John. "Have you saved the letters? You can give them to the police."

"No! No police. I can't bring them into this, John. That's all I need, is for a report to wind up on the police blotter, and some nosy newspaper reporter to get hold of it and start snooping around. The headlines! My patients would be in total panic. You know how journalists go for the throat these days. They'd *love* to disclose who among the high and mighty came to a sperm bank for their children. God!" Reston was practically beside himself.

"Calm down, Edward." They resumed their walk.

"Publicity would ruin me *forever*, John. I could never recover, even if I went into general practice and did appendectomies for a living. The stigma would be there."

"So, no police. That rules out collecting on insurance."

"Yes," said Reston quietly, "it does. So I'm ruined, no matter what." The wind blew his Burberry back from his shoulders. "Insurance wouldn't help much, anyway. I could only collect on damaged equipment. The sperm samples themselves weren't eligible for coverage. Besides, some of them are irreplaceable."

"You'll get more."

"Not fast enough. I told you that the demand is far greater than the supply. It'll take time—months—for me to collect the same caliber of samples. What will my clients do? Do you know what it's like telling a desperate thirty-eight-year-old woman that she's going to have to wait indefinitely to get pregnant? A lot of these women don't *have* time! I'm wiped out, John. As good as bankrupt. I'm in debt and mortgaged to the hilt. I'll lose everything."

Heineman rubbed his bearded chin. "You could make reasonable substitutions."

Reston halted. "John, I can't believe you'd say that. What, jack off a few medical students for ten bucks each and then pass it off as something else to my patients? That's unethical as hell!"

"It's survival," said Heineman, looking Edward straight in the eye.

The look chilled Reston. Heineman's blue eyes were glacial; his constricted pupils small, hard pin dots. With his lean face and shaggy hair, he had an animalistic look, cold and predatory. It seemed out of character to the warm mentor Reston had known over the years.

"What about informed consent?" said Reston. "I'm obliged to disclose all pertinent facts to my patients. It's fraudulent to do otherwise."

"If you had gone through the war as I did, Edward, you would understand more about survival. It is man's most basic instinct—self-preservation at *all* costs."

"But this isn't war, John. There are ethics—"

"Ethics be damned!" bellowed Heineman. "We are talking about your survival—as a professional, as a man! You think I suggest a drastic solution lightly? So you want to play by a childish set of rules? Then go back to your clinic and close its doors—forever! Stand up and admit to the scientific/medical community that your work is a flop! Go home and tell your pretty little wife the man she married is a failure!"

Reston was silent while he stared off into space. He

thought about the money he still owed on his state-of-the-art lab equipment; the earnest money down on the luxury co-op on Park Avenue; the unpaid balance on the Mercedes; the substantial bills Gloria had charged; the vacations in Europe; the beach house on Martha's Vineyard that he wanted to buy. He thought about his life-style and about his career and reputation, and his youth, and the fact that thirty-three was far too young to be derailed. With an overwhelming feeling of resignation, he said, "What are my options?"

Heineman began walking again. He turned left down an intersecting path, taking them back in the direction of the white lab buildings, which sat in a cluster of cubes in the center of the twenty-acre compound. "First, get rid of the notion of using medical students. They're terrible gossips. I have something else I can give you. I will have to do some clever record keeping, but I'm sure it won't be missed."

Reston was mystified. "What are you talking about?"

"You'll see once we get inside. We'll get you a high security clearance badge. Tell me, what did you say about this to your wife and employees?"

"Nothing. I didn't know what to say, and was too stunned to want to explain. I called the nurse and receptionist at home and told them I had a personal emergency, that the clinic would be closed a few days. I told the receptionist to contact the patients who had appointments, and advise them they would be rescheduled later."

"She would come into the office to do that?"

"Yes. But she would have no reason to try to get into the freezer. I locked everything back up before I left to come here. Sandra is not what I'd call a curious girl. She does her job and goes home."

"And the nurse?"

"More dedicated. Again, if she came to the office, I doubt she would enter the freezer. I don't allow her to handle the samples."

"She would not notice the freezer is off?"

Reston shrugged. "I have no idea. My guess is, she'll take

the time off as an unexpected holiday. She works long hours."

"And your wife?" pursued Heineman.

"I haven't spoken to her all day. As far as she knows, I'm having a normal day at the clinic. The answering service is picking up all calls—they're to beep me if she phones."

The older scientist nodded. "Good."

"Why are you so concerned about them? I'll have to tell them eventually. I was putting it off as long as possible, until I saw you."

"It's wise that you did. The fewer people who know about this substitution, the better, Edward. In fact, it should be our secret. *Unter vier Augen*, just between you and me."

Reston and Heineman walked down a long corridor, through a series of locking doors. Reston had left his overcoat at the reception area, replacing it with a white lab coat like the one worn by Heineman. They both had plastic security identification badges clipped to the lapels.

The facility was much larger than Reston remembered it. Two wings had been added, and he had the impression that the employee population had at least doubled.

At every locked door, Heineman punched in a code on a numeric keypad embedded in the wall. The doors operated like elevator doors, sliding to one side. Between each locked door were clusters of rooms, also locked.

"We are doing much more proprietary and classified research than when you were here, Edward," John explained. "We have been awarded contracts and grants from major corporations and some individual interests. All of them demand secrecy. Consequently, we have segmented the facility and limited the access of employees. Each little bubble cluster we pass through has its own door to the outside. Some employees are restricted to a single cluster. The higher their level of responsibility and work, the more clusters they can access."

"Are you the only one who has access to the entire compound?"

"Not quite. My assistant director does, and so do the members of the board of trustees. Here we are." Heineman stopped and punched open a door that read, "Class 1-A Clearance Only." Inside was a small room filled with stainless steel counters and tables and white plastic laminate cupboards. One employee, a young man, was inside, bent over a microscope. "Leave us," said Heineman. The employee nodded and removed his slide. He quickly put it and a petri dish away in a refrigerator, and walked out.

Heineman looked at Reston. "What I am about to explain to you is classified top secret, Edward. You must give me your word that it remain so."

"By all means, John. You know you can trust me."

"This room, and all the rooms in this cluster, are dedicated to perfecting in vitro fertilization."

Reston nodded. This was not a revelation. In vitro fertilization was a counterpart of artificial insemination, though more complex. The usual procedure was to remove a woman's eggs from her ovaries, fertilize them in a petri dish, and implant them in the womb within two to three days from the time they were removed. If the woman was infertile, the eggs could be taken from a donor source.

Heineman seemed to read his thoughts. "Nothing new, right?"

"I know what you're about to suggest. I'm not experienced in in vitro fertilization, and it's impractical for the clinic."

Heineman held up his right hand. "Not so fast, Edward, you jump the gun. This is more than in vitro fertilization. We have had some success with engineering genes. We have broken some genetic codes, and can duplicate them."

"You're kidding!"

"It's hit and miss, with more misses than hits, but we have crossed the threshold."

Reston was so excited he momentarily forgot his own predicament. The implications dazzled him. "Gene engineering? Do you realize what this means?"

"Of course I do, Edward. Man controls his destiny. *Wahrheit und Dichtung*. Fact and fiction—they become one. We have produced no infants yet. We have yet to do implantations in the wombs of volunteers. That's the next stage."

"Wait a minute. Fertilized eggs have to be implanted within seventy-two hours. You're not growing babies in a *dish* are you?"

"No. We are allowing the eggs to divide up to sixteen cells, then freezing them."

"*Frozen* embryos? John, that's never been done before."

Heineman grinned. "I know."

"This is a major breakthrough!"

"Yes, but it cannot be released to the press or public, for various reasons tied to the sponsoring client."

In his excitement over a scientific breakthrough, Reston momentarily forgot his dilemma. "What's your success rate?"

"In terms of successfully freezing and thawing embryos, reasonable. I am just ready to begin tests implanting them in receptive wombs. As for the success rate in producing healthy infants—I can only speculate."

Reston suddenly saw what his mentor was leading up to. "And you're telling me this because you're going to give some genetically engineered frozen embryos to me."

"That is correct."

Reston was overwhelmed. "I don't know what to say—where to begin. The procedures—"

"—are not much more complicated than artificial insemination."

"But I've never implanted an embryo in a human being."

Heineman shrugged. "Same principles as you follow now, and essentially the same tools. You are a quick study. I will show you how to thaw the embryos, which takes only a minute or two, and separate them from their cryoprotectant.

You insert the fluid the same as you do an insemination or an inovulation."

"All right," said Reston, uncertain. This was a fast turn of events. "And what have you engineered into the genes?"

"Very little. The coloring of eyes and body hair. Density of build, *und so weiter*—and so on."

"And sex."

"Yes, sex. That is a given."

Sex, thought Reston jubilantly. He could implant male-fertilized embryos in his patients who were desperate for sons—like Alice Evered. At that stage, the chances of a sex change in the womb were nominal.

Heineman went on, "The disadvantage for you is the unknown success rate, as opposed to artificial inseminations."

"It's a most acceptable risk. John, this saves me from disaster!"

"Wait. There are conditions: you cannot disclose the substitution. Your patients must continue to believe they are receiving an artificial insemination. I must protect the confidentiality of this project."

"That may be difficult."

"It is paramount. Otherwise, I cannot help you."

Reston hesitated, once again disturbed by ethical questions. But, he realized, he had no choice. It was this or failure. "All right. I'll do whatever you say. It's better that they don't know. It would raise a whole host of questions and objections."

"Exactly. You must keep the secret as long as necessary —years, if required. Do not keep any written records that would jeopardize me. The client who is sponsoring this project retains the exclusive right to disclose the advances we make. I would love the publicity, but those are the terms *I* am bound to." He paused. "The final condition is this: you must make thorough progress reports to me on each implantation."

"But you just said not to keep any records that would indicate your involvement."

"That is correct—no records at your clinic. But you will make reports directly to me, one copy only." John smiled disarmingly. "I still have a vested interest. You will help my research by providing me information—backgrounds of the parents, pregnancy progress, delivery, follow-ups on the children themselves."

"I keep those kinds of records anyway, up to a point. Not much beyond delivery."

"I'm sure you can find ways. For me, you will make the reports as detailed as possible, but the records you keep for yourself will be minimal. Each embryo will be coded. I want to know specifically who receives which one. You understand? I can carry on my project by looking over your shoulder."

"It won't be quite as controlled as laboratory conditions."

"It will be adequate." Heineman went to a locked door within the room. "Behind this door are the embryos. They range from eight to sixteen cells in size and are frozen in an amniotic-nutrient fluid with cryoprotectant. The eggs and sperm come from no medical students or mothers on welfare. Only the best specimen, male and female. The highest intelligence, the brightest minds. The most *powerful* minds. You know my standard on quality—those were *my* conditions." The corner of his mouth turned up in an uneven grin. "The records will show that today there was a mishap in an experiment, which I myself conducted, resulting in the accidental destruction of twenty-six embryos."

Twenty-six, thought Reston. He felt like a man on death row whose sentence is commuted moments before execution. Twenty-six implantations would buy him time to replace enough spermatozoa to keep the clinic going.

"Why are you doing this at all, John? You risk your own job, your professional standing, just to help me out of a jam."

Heineman put his hand on his protégé's shoulder. "Because you are bright and young. Because you do not deserve to suffer. Because I believe in you. Because one day, you may come to my aid in an hour of need. *Nicht wahr?* Am I not right?"

Reston was unable to reply. He was on the verge of tears.

Nancy Dewitt had been startled to get Reston's early morning telephone call, just as she was leaving for the clinic. He had sounded dreadfully upset, but had not elaborated on his "personal emergency" that required closing the clinic for "a few days."

She had asked him, "Are you sure you're all right? Is there anything I can do for you?" But he demurred.

Nancy started to worry. It wasn't an emergency at all—he didn't want to see her because of what had happened between them the Friday before. He wanted to avoid her. Maybe he was actually at the clinic, seeing patients—and interviewing someone to replace her!

Nancy became increasingly upset. Why had she overstepped her bounds like that? Far better to suffer a silent, unrequited love than to be coldly dismissed. By mid-afternoon, she could no longer stand the anxiety. She was certain Reston was at the clinic, and decided to go there herself. They would talk things out. She would do whatever he wanted, as long as she could stay on.

She applied her makeup and combed her hair with extra care. She chided herself for feeling like a nervous schoolgirl, but that didn't lessen the tension. When she arrived at the clinic, she stood for a moment at the door, palms sweaty, and rehearsed her little speech to Reston once again. She took hold of the doorknob.

To her surprise, the door was locked. She got out her keys and opened the door.

The clinic was empty.

Mystified, Nancy hurried to the reception desk and looked at the appointment calendar. There was a memo from Sandra concerning the patients who had been rescheduled, including

Alice Evered. *Sandra must have come in and gone*, Nancy thought. *Edward really has a personal emergency*.

That set off new worries. Nancy went next to Reston's private office. It, too, was empty. What was wrong? A death in the family? Had he been in an accident? Nancy forgot her own anxieties as she imagined all sorts of dreadful things that could have happened to Edward. Had he called her from a hospital?

Nancy's fears went wild. She didn't know what to do. Should she call Reston's home number? What if he would resent her intrusion?

She did the only thing she could think of to take her mind off her fears: she got busy cleaning and straightening up. She pushed papers into neat stacks and sharpened pencils. Back in the reception area, she threw out a used Styrofoam coffee cup and tided up Sandra's notes.

Nancy opened the door to the hallway, intending to give the kitchenette a once-over. She walked by the freezer bank door without looking at it and entered the kitchenette.

As she wiped a damp rag over the sink and counter, she realized that something in the hallway was wrong, but she couldn't put her finger on it. She went to the door of the kitchenette and stood looking back into the hallway, arms akimbo, face in a puzzled scowl, trying to figure it out.

The hallway was *warm*. There was no blast of chilly air opposite the door to the freezer.

Nancy walked back to the door to the freezer room and put her hand on the knob. It was locked, but it, as well as the steel door, was warm. Nancy gasped. Suddenly she knew what Edward had meant by "emergency."

It was 9 P.M. by the time Reston returned the rental car to its Manhattan agency. He had already called Gloria to let her know he would be late coming home; the maid informed him his wife was out for the evening herself, attending one of her numerous charity planning meetings. It was a relief; Reston did not relish carrying out a charade of nonchalance. Gloria never had more than a passing interest in the details of his work, but she did have an incredible ability to know when something was bothering him that he wouldn't admit. And then she was like a terrier, digging at him until the truth came out.

Edward flagged down a taxi and gave the address of his clinic. He had some cleaning up to do in the freezer. Heineman had promised to have the frozen embryos delivered the next day.

Reston unlocked the main door of the clinic and noticed immediately that more lights were on inside than customary. He went straight to his office. To his surprise and instant dismay, he found Nancy seated in his high-backed leather chair behind his desk. Her face wore an intensely serious expression.

"Nancy, what are you doing here? I thought I told you to take the next three days off."

She folded her arms on the blotter on his desk. "I've been waiting for you, Dr. Reston. We have something to talk about. Your *'personal emergency.'*"

The words chilled Reston. Slowly, he peeled off his overcoat. "What are you talking about, Nancy?" he said quietly.

"What I'm talking about is the fact that this clinic may no longer exist as of today." In a calm, matter-of-fact voice, Nancy recounted her discovery of the warm door to the freezer. Even though she had not been able to enter the bank compartment, she said, she had checked the generator and found it malfunctioned. Conclusion: all sperm destroyed by heat.

"So what exactly is going on, Dr. Reston?"

A great weight descended upon Edward, like a giant millstone rolled onto his shoulders. For a long moment, he did not speak. There was no point in denying the disaster. But how much truth should he tell her? How much truth *could* he tell her, given the conditions of confidentiality to which Heineman had bound him? Nancy was smart, and knew a lot about his business. She was well aware of the lack of immediate supply of extraordinary sperm.

He looked at Nancy. Her features had softened. She *did* seem genuinely concerned. She was a good girl, as loyal as they come.

Reston told Nancy the truth. Everything—almost. He acknowledged that his old friend and mentor, John Heineman, was able to help him out of his jam, save him from ruin—and from having to let go of his staff, he pointed out. But he did not say he would be implanting embryos instead of injecting sperm.

It felt good to tell her; it relieved some of the guilt of secrecy. "It goes beyond me and the clinic itself," he explained. "I've set precedents, pushed out the boundaries to the concepts of childbearing. If the clinic goes, all that progress is set back."

Nancy was most sympathetic. "Of course I will keep the strictest confidence of this," she assured him. "You'll need help in smoothing things out with your patients. Sandra—we'll keep her out of this. And I certainly agree with you that you shouldn't tell Mrs. Reston. There's no need to upset her."

"I knew you'd understand, Nancy. I wasn't going to tell you, but I'm glad I did."

DeWitt rose and came around to the other side of the desk. She went behind Reston and began massaging his shoulders. They were tight with tension, and the pressure was painful but welcome. "Poor dear," Nancy cooed. "What a terrible thing to have to deal with."

"It's going to work out. Oh, that hurts, but it feels good."

"Tension, doctor. Listen, don't you worry about cleaning up the freezer. I'll do it myself while no one is here. Tomorrow, I'll tell Sandra to stay home and I'll have an electrician friend fix your generator and reconnect the main and backup wires. He won't have the foggiest idea what goes on here, and he won't need to know."

"Really? Nancy, that's wonderful. You have no idea how

grateful I am. I've been meaning to give you a raise—"

"I don't want a raise, Dr. Reston."

Her statement startled him. "No raise?"

She stopped her massage and stepped to the side so that he could look up at her. "But there's something I'd like in lieu of a raise." She paused to give her next words emphasis. "I want to get to know you better."

Reston saw the look in her eyes and knew exactly what she meant.

CHAPTER Nine

After Reston's departure, Dr. John Heineman retired to his private office, located near the hub of the facility. He put a Do Not Disturb sign on the outside of the door and then locked it after him. He buzzed the night receptionist on the intercom and left instructions that he was not to be interrupted by any callers, with the exception of Dr. Edward Reston.

Finishing that, Heineman opened a wall safe, took out a thick brown envelope of papers, and spread them out on his desk. The documents were written in German, and were in poor condition—the ink had faded and smeared, and many of the papers were torn. That the papers existed at all was miraculous. They had survived an Allied air raid that had dumped hundreds of thousands of tons of explosives over a section of Swabia in April 1945. They had been hand carried out of a collapsing cavern one hundred meters below the surface of the earth. They had survived the postwar chaos and thirty years of being spirited about the world from one hiding place to another.

Heineman leafed through the papers, his elegant, long fingers following the bold script. The information in them was incomplete, but it was enough. Unknown to the rest of the world, the Nazis had been far ahead in genetic research, decades ahead of their time. Everything they knew was embodied in a marvelous project called *Die Wunderkinder*, the drive to create the superior humans who would lead the Master Race. The work came to an end with the war, the knowledge buried, the progress stopped. But it was not over. *Die Wunderkinder* was about to have a resurrection.

In 1950, Hans Messner assumed the identity that would remain with him for the rest of his life. The papers—his entire false background—was forged by a growing underground pro-Nazi network dedicated to protecting the leaders of the Reich from the Nazi hunters. Messner returned to Austria and established himself in Vienna as Dr. Johann Heineman, a senior research scientist for Fruhling, a pharmaceuticals giant. His false identity carried an ironic twist: Dr. Heineman was Jewish, himself a victim and former prisoner of the Nazis.

While he maintained his facade, Messner searched relentlessly for Mengele, intent on carrying out his instructions to the end. The plan to resurrect the destroyed lab, carry on the genetic work, ensure the survival of the fittest of the Reich, was his obsession. Mengele's son, Rolf, refused to believe Messner had been a colleague of his father's and steadfastly denied knowledge of his whereabouts. When rumor had it that Mengele had surfaced in West Germany, Messner tried in vain to find him. He also pursued dead-end leads in Mexico, Argentina, and Brazil. His repeated failures left him bewildered; surely Mengele had received at least one of his coded communiqués. Was his mentor rejecting him? Why?

Messner also tried to excavate the site of the secret laboratory, but for years dared not make such a move. His good salary with Fruhling enabled him to save enough money to buy a plot of land in the Alps not far from the site. The existence of the lab died in secrecy; Messner never found a mention of it in any press reports. For years, he psychologically held his breath, fearing the site would be discovered, the lab unearthed. If anything of value remained, enemies of the Reich would get it.

In 1960, Fruhling opened a plant and administrative center in the United States, near Boston. Messner/Heineman was transferred. In America, Heineman quickly gained a reputation for his brilliant work. He anglicized his first name to John. After a respectable period, he left Fruhling and joined one of the new research labs investigating the frontiers of genetics, where at last he could pick up where he had left off in the war. He was careful not to show his hand, or reveal things he had learned decades before. No one but him, as a representative of the Reich, would have control of the applications made possible by his knowledge. Inwardly, he laughed at the primitive state of the infertility therapy and gene engineering. Men had yet to discover "breakthroughs" that were elementary to him. Heineman did make sufficient "discoveries" that propelled him to celebrity status in his field, and enabled him to patent some processes that earned him a small fortune. He bided his time, waiting for the right moment to put his true knowledge to work.

As the fields of genetics and infertility therapy advanced—with his subtle help—the Klein Laboratory for Applied Biogenetics was established, and Heineman selected as its first director. It was a coveted position, for it gave him power, prestige, and autonomy, a perfect cover for him to carry on his real work, using the most advanced facilities and under the protection of a "proprietary research project" label. The next step in his plan was to acquire a protégé, someone to fill the same shoes he filled for Josef Mengele, someone who would help him rebuild what he had lost in the war.

He found such a person in the young Dr. Edward Reston, whose brilliant record at Harvard and Massachusetts General caught his attention. Reston had just the right mix of ambition and idealism to be pliable, and Heineman wasted no time in recruiting him. His instincts told him to maintain his Austrian Jew cover, to not reveal his secrets to Reston—yet. When the young man expressed a desire to break out on his own, Heineman helped him secure the financing necessary to open his sperm bank. One day, he knew, he would call in his chips.

Since his emigration to the U.S., Heineman regularly returned to Austria, ostensibly on vacation, but in actuality making secret trips into the Bavarian Alps in West Germany, beyond the parcel of land he owned. He discovered the ruins of his laboratory, well hidden by the growth of forest. Over a period of years, he dug, little by little, moving land around painstakingly so as not to call attention to what he was doing, tunneling deep into the earth.

He found nothing but shattered remnants—it was like making an archeological dig of an earthquake site. Most, but not all, of the natural caverns had collapsed in the bombings. The deeper he went, the colder it became; the natural glacial springs were still doing their job. To properly explore some of the narrow tunnels, he had to learn spelunking.

The laboratory had been huge. Heineman knew the odds were small of finding what he wanted—the canisters of meticulously genetically programmed sperm and ova, kept separate, the seed of the leaders of the Master Race. And even if he found them, he knew, the odds were even smaller that any of the contents had survived the collapse and destruction.

He wormed his way through cracks in the rock that were so small he had to crawl on his belly, with barely enough room to clear his backside. The debris he encountered was riddled with the bones of the victims who were trapped the night the bombs fell. As far as he knew, he was the sole survivor of *Die Wunderkinder*.

By some miracle, he found several canisters, three of sperm and one of ova. But his excitement was quickly quashed when he saw that they were all duds, ruined by thawing and contaminated by ruptures in the metal.

And then, in 1973, he found the golden prizes—two canisters, one male and one female, sperm and ova, stuck deep in a formation of ice in a frigid pocket near the underground springs. The canisters were sealed, their skins unruptured.

They were cold enough that possibly—very possibly—their contents might be preserved intact, without deterioration.

"*Mein Gott! Mein Gott!*" he shouted, his words reverberating through the clammy tunnels. "I can't believe it!"

Clutching his prizes, he returned to the surface as fast as possible, his progress made agonizingly slow by the narrow cracks and crevices. He rushed his canisters to a refrigerator. He could not risk freezing with liquid nitrogen until he examined the contents.

Heineman quickly made arrangements with a research lab in Switzerland for confidential access to a workroom. It was a common arrangement in the international scientific community, and Heineman was internationally reknowned and respected. He was barely able to contain his excitement as he prepared his slides for viewing beneath the microscope. He held his breath as he focused first upon the sperm. Movement! Most were still, but some moved, though sluggishly. Heineman was exultant.

His examination of the ova revealed, happily, the same conditions—a high percentage of loss, but enough survival to salvage *Die Wunderkinder*. He screened out the viable sperm and ova, and fertilized the eggs in petri dishes. He let the embryos divide to a few cells, and then froze them in liquid nitrogen. He transported them back to the United States and stored them in a locked freezer at Klein, to which he had the only key. He falsified some documents to create a phony, confidential "project."

When the time was right, he would bring the leaders of the New Reich to life. But he had to be discreet, keeping all links to himself invisible until the resulting children were old enough to command. And, he had to maintain some control.

Heineman knew exactly how he would propagate his race. It would be too risky to try to raise the children himself; there were too many prying eyes these days. Besides, he would need money to finance the new regime. Far better if the children had wealthy parents.

He needed a reliable but unwitting accomplice. Edward Reston would be his Trojan horse.

Smiling, Heineman put his old papers away. It had been a simple matter to sabotage the Park Avenue Family Planning Center. As he had expected, everything was falling neatly into place. Reston was so predictable.

Now would come the most difficult period—the waiting. First, to see how many of the twenty-six embryos went to term. Then, the years of childhood. When the children reached the edge of puberty, he would come for them.

CHAPTER Ten

It was December 5, and snow had come early to Manhattan. Huge, wet flakes of it swirled through the air, sticking to the streets and sidewalks. The first snow of winter always brought an exhilaration—people wanted to walk in it and play in it, revel in its cool, pristine whiteness, the freshness it brought to the otherwise polluted air. Snow was welcome —until it piled high enough, and the traffic and pedestrians turned it to dirty slush. Then it became a nuisance.

In his law office, Stern jotted notes on his yellow legal pad. Before him, his desk was covered with legal briefs, court cases, and documents. He wore a slight frown while he worked, his amber eyes intense, his world narrowed to *Dyson vs. Clements*, a ten-million-dollar patent infringement lawsuit against one of his firm's new clients. If this case didn't give him an ulcer, nothing would. Clements, the client, *was* in a fix, and Stern had a premonition that the plaintiff would not be willing to settle out of court. He reached for his mug of coffee and drank from it, eyes still on the brief in front of him.

Rainer set the mug down. Beyond his huge picture window, the swirling snow caught his eye, and he stopped work to watch it fall. The blizzard of flakes gave the city a fairyland look. And, as always when it snowed, especially for the first time in the season, Stern recalled his childhood, and felt vaguely homesick for a life he barely remembered in another country. The memories brought pain as well as homesickness, for they could not be recalled without the accompanying thoughts of the events that had terminated the childhood happiness, the nightmare of Auschwitz.

This winter, the memories were doubly painful, the thoughts of Leon's suicide still in the forefront of Rainer's mind. He ached; he was hollow inside. Where was his justice? Where was his revenge?

The intercom on Rainer's desk buzzed. The name Arthur Evered floated into his head, though there was no logical reason for it.

"Yes?"

"A call from Arthur Evered," said Connie.

Stern jumped. "Put it through." He picked up the receiver and waited a moment. A female voice came on and said, "Please hold for Arthur Evered." There was another pause, and then Evered's forceful voice boomed in Stern's ear.

"Morning, Rainer."

"Hi, Art. How's the game these days?"

"Good enough to take you on again."

"Let's do it."

"I'll have my girl reserve a court at the club and get back to you. Listen, Rainer, I need some changes in my estate planning."

"Oh?"

What now? Was Arthur reconsidering divorce, after he had told Stern he had changed his mind? But the news was the opposite.

"Alice is going to have a baby next spring," Evered said.

"Congratulations! That *is* good news." Children was another topic Evered seldom discussed, yet Stern had guessed he wanted a son. He had seen the way Evered looked with envy at men with their teenage sons at the club and out on the links.

Evered sighed. "I know it's premature—that anything could happen between now and then—"

"No, it's wise to start the paperwork now. You'll need the will revised, a trust set up, insurance—I'll get in touch with your accountant."

"Rainer, here's how I want to handle the will: I want to draw up a new one, and then add a confidential codicil."

Stern was puzzled. "Why write a new will and add a codicil when we can incorporate everything into the new version at once? It would be stronger."

"For various reasons, that's the way I want it."

What the client wants, the client gets. "All right, Art. No problem. What's the codicil for?"

"It's *completely* confidential, Rainer."

"I can't draft it if I don't know what it is."

"I don't want you to draft it. I've already written it myself, and Alice and I have signed it. I want it sealed and included in the safe deposit box papers. Is there going to be any legal problem?"

"I can't tell you without seeing the language. There's also the matter of witnesses."

"I've taken care of witnesses."

"You're putting me in a bind, Arthur. I can't be responsible for the outcome for something of which I have no knowledge or control. I urge you to reconsider."

"This is the way it's got to be, Rainer."

"Is a sizable sum of money involved?"

"Fairly."

Stern shifted in his chair. "I'll check into it, see if any precedents exist and what potential problems might arise."

"Good." Evered hesitated. "The confidentiality of the codicil *is* necessary, Rainer."

"I understand," Stern replied, though the matter still puzzled him. He couldn't help but feel insulted that Evered wasn't trusting him completely, in light of his outstanding track record servicing the Evered/Thorson account. What did Arthur Evered want to hide?

He would worry about that later. First, he had to wrestle with *Dyson vs. Clements*. He got up and walked out of his office, heading down the hall to the library room. He could have summoned one of the paralegals to fetch the information he wanted, but he felt a need to move around, get away from the snow scene outside his window. If he didn't keep a tight grip on himself, Leon was going to start talking in his ear again, and he didn't want to hear him. His brother's voice, like the voices that came to him in the early morning hours, spoke nonsense most of the time.

The library was small and narrow and filled floor to ceiling with shelves of books. He started moving through the stacks. He thought he was alone.

"Hi, Mr. Stern," said a female voice. Lisa McCauley, one of the firm's newest clerks, appeared in his aisle.

"Hello, Lisa," Stern replied pleasantly. Lisa was attractive. She was fresh out of law school, a pert brunette with a keen mind and a sparkling personality. He had been thinking about asking her out.

"Great day for a sleigh ride, eh?" she said.

He watched her reach for a book, taking in the shapely curves of her bust and hips. Desire swept over him. God, he needed a woman. Not just for bed—he had had his fill of unsatisfying one-night stands. He wanted a woman who could end the ache inside of him.

"Lisa..." he began.

She put the book in the crook of her arm and looked up at him, her pretty face expectant.

Rainer shrank away.

An instant before, he had seen nothing but an attractive young woman. Now the skin of her face was translucent, and he could see the skull beneath. Her entire body was bathed in an aura of gray and a sickly yellow.

This girl is going to die, he thought.

"No," he murmured, shaking his head.

"What's wrong?" She giggled, her teeth clacking inside the death's head skull. "Did I put my lipstick on crooked?"

Stern stumbled backward into a metal rack of books, sending some falling to the floor in a pile. He turned and grabbed for the doorknob.

Back in his office, Stern hugged his middle and shivered. He knew without a doubt that Lisa was doomed, but his rational mind screamed in objection. How could it be possible?

He told himself nothing would happen to her. He was wrong. It was a crazy hallucination.

He went back to work on *Dyson vs. Clements* but couldn't concentrate. He couldn't get the death skull out of his mind.

Finally he decided to see Lisa. At the very least, he owed her an apology for his behavior. And seeing her again, fresh and healthy, would dispel this horrible image from his mind.

Stern went out to the open cluster of desks where the clerks and paralegals worked. Lisa's desk was empty.

"Lisa's gone to lunch," one of her coworkers said. Stern nodded and went back to his office. Everything was going to be all right.

He managed to lose himself in his work, until knuckles rapped on his door and roused him.

His visitor was Ben Goldman.

"Don't you ever eat?" said Ben.

Stern stretched in his chair. "I guess I got lost in *Clements*. It's going to be a bitch, you know."

"I think we'll have to concentrate on containing the damage."

Goldman looked at him quizzically. "I can see you're preoccupied. I'll let you get back to work." He left.

Stern stared out the window. The snow was still coming down.

What about Lisa?

The clock on his desk read 3 P.M. Lisa should be back from lunch by now. He returned to her desk, but it was empty. Maybe she was in the ladies' room . . .

"Mr. Stern." Connie was beside him, touching him on the arm. Her voice was thick, and her eyes were red and puffy.

"I just took a telephone call from the police, Mr. Stern. It's Lisa. She's—she's—A taxi skidded out of control in the snow and hit her. She's dead."

"I must be going crazy," Stern said, his hoarse voice barely under control.

He kept pacing around the musty, gloomy office of Dr. Alexander Neissen, psychiatrist. He had just finished a raving monologue of all the bizarre experiences he had seen and heard since Leon had died.

"I wish you would sit down, Mr. Stern," said Neissen.

"I *can't* sit down." Stern looked at the doctor. He was a small, hunched man of about sixty-five, whose brown eyes were magnified like fly eyes behind thick round spectacles. The backs of his hands were covered with liver spots, and his fingers were short and blunt. Progressive baldness had carved deep triangles at his temples. Stern had never heard of him nor known a thing about him before he called and made the appointment. He had run his finger down the list of psychiatrists in the Yellow Pages until an inner voice stopped him and said, *That's the one*.

"You're not losing your mind, so you might as well relax."

Something in Neissen's voice made Stern obey.

"It's very simple, Mr. Stern. What's happened to you is that you have become psychic."

"*Psychic!*" Stern started up out of his chair, but Neissen waved him back down.

"It's not a disease, Mr. Stern, nor is it terminal."

"But psychic? That's outrageous!"

Neissen's fly eyes studied him. "I have seen it happen in a good number of people. Somehow they seem to find me. It must be my vibrations." He chuckled.

Stern thought, *It's not me who's crazy, it's him*.

"You see, first of all, you had an identical twin. Twins share what we call a sympathetic bond. They feel what's on each other's mind. Am I right?"

Stern thought about it and nodded. "That's true. But that doesn't have anything to do with being psychic."

"Yes, it does. You are reacting to stereotypes—Gypsy women with tea leaves and crystal balls. The condition of being psychic merely means you are receptive to experiences that are beyond the ordinary five senses, and that includes feeling what your twin feels."

"Maybe."

"Then, you see, you suffered a shock. Many shocks throughout your life, but a serious shock with the suicide of your twin. The shock broke down a barrier."

"I don't understand."

"Theoretically, everyone has the potential to be psychic—to see and hear the things you have experienced. Most of us don't because some sort of barrier prevents us from opening our minds and being receptive. Because you are a twin, your barrier is thinner than most. And now, Mr. Stern, it has come down altogether."

"I want it back up again."

"That's unlikely. In cases such as yours, the transition is usually permanent. At best, your experiences may fade over time, become less frequent and intense. But they will never go away."

Stern groaned. "I can't live like this."

Neissen pursed his lips. "You must learn to control it."

"How?"

"I don't know, Mr. Stern. I'm not psychic."

CHAPTER
Eleven

August 18, 1974

The heavy, ivory-colored envelope addressed in a personal hand and marked "Personal" was stuck in Stern's mail among the business letters. He picked it up and examined it, pleased that he had no idea what was inside. For months, he had done his best to systematically shut out the intrusive thoughts, images, voices, and dreams, and had succeeded, he believed, in squelching them through vigorous denial. Dr. Neissen had been wrong. He hadn't had a "flash" in nearly two months. He was normal again.

He put the tip of a silver letter opener under the envelope flap and ripped it open. Inside was a card engraved in an elegant, raised black script that read:

>Mr. and Mrs. Arthur Evered
>are pleased to announce
>the birth of their son
>Brandon Ames Evered
>on
>July 24, 1974
>Weight 9 pounds 2 ounces

So Arthur had his heir at last, and a strapping one at that. Stern rather pitied the child—he would grow up facing some enormous shoes to fill, and a stern father with high expectations.

He buzzed Connie and asked her to send flowers to the Evereds.

He sat back and stared into space, momentarily pulled into other thoughts. They must be happy, Arthur and Alice. No more consideration of divorce. They were a family now, with a son to raise.

The murmur started so low in his ear that he listened for a while without realizing what he was hearing, until suddenly the words registered in hammer blows.

"It isn't over, Rainer..."

CHAPTER
Twelve

New York City, late May 1987

For Arthur Evered, it seemed impossible to get through a meal without arguing with his thirteen-year-old son. "The decision has been made," he repeated firmly.

"I don't care what you say!" Brandon retorted in a voice already deepened by puberty. "I'm *not* going to that dumb boarding school in Switzerland in the fall—or next year or ever!" Brandon glared at Arthur across the glass and brass table in the breakfast nook of the Evereds' luxurious East Side co-op. He clutched his butter knife in his fist, ignoring the plate of hot bran muffins in front of him. His icy blue eyes flashed from beneath strands of blond hair that had been carefully moussed and arranged in the studied disarray preferred by teenagers and abhorred by their parents.

Arthur glared back at his son, struggling to keep a lid on his temper. He was well aware that the teen years were rife with rebellion, but during the last year, Brandon had pushed him to the wall repeatedly. He was a handsome boy, with a lanky build that promised to fill out. And he was smart as a whip. But damn, he was a headstrong kid!

"Brandon, don't wave your butter knife around like that.

Either use it or put it down." Alice, to Arthur's left, spoke as if the three of them were having a pleasant conversation instead of another argument.

Brandon let the knife drop with a clatter on the thick glass tabletop. Alice winced but said nothing.

Arthur put down his coffee cup. The coffee burned in his tight stomach. "Young man, I've had it with your attitude. *Pick that knife up and put it down properly, like you were raised with some manners.*"

Brandon sulked for a moment, then did as Arthur told him. "I'm not going to Switzerland," he repeated, staring at his plate. "Switzerland is for cows."

Arthur started to answer, but his wife put her hand on his arm.

"We've already registered you, dear," she said. "We're sending you to one of the finest prep schools in the world. We only want the best for you."

"How would *you* know what's best for me? You're not me! I'll hate it."

"How do you know? You've never been to Switzerland."

"I just *know*."

"Brandon, we want you to have the best education possible. Believe me, you'll appreciate it when you get older."

"That's forever! It's not *now*."

Arthur intervened, his voice tightly controlled. "I went to the same school, Brandon. You may not understand it at your age, but you make contacts at school that last a lifetime."

"That's right," Alice chimed in. "It's important for you to circulate in the proper circles."

"I don't care about 'proper circles.' I don't want to leave my friends at Winston!"

"You'll make new ones, lots of them. And Switzerland is a beautiful country. You'll be able to travel all over Europe on your breaks."

Brandon folded his arms across his chest and made an animal noise of disgust.

Arthur felt his self-control breaking. One more second and he was going to smack his son. "You are excused from this table, Brandon. I don't want to hear any more about the boarding school. The subject is *closed*."

Brandon looked at Alice. "*Mom...*" He drew out the word in a pleading voice.

"You heard your father, Brandon."

Brandon shoved himself away from the table, his face twisted with anger. "You both hate me, and I hate you back! I'll kill myself before you make me go to Switzerland!" He stomped off.

Arthur and Alice exchanged weary looks.

Alice called after her son. "We don't hate you, Brandon, we *love* you."

"No, you don't," he shouted back. "I hate you, I hate you, I hate you!"

Arthur said in a low voice, "That's it. He's grounded for the rest of the summer."

"Arthur, don't make matters worse. He'll simmer down. I can't take it when the two of you start going at each other." She changed the subject and raised her voice. "Where are you going today, Brandon?"

"Out!"

"That's no answer to your mother," bellowed Arthur, rising from the table. Alice tugged on his shirtsleeve and pulled him back down to his seat.

"Where is 'out'?" called Alice. "Is it too much to ask for a straight answer?"

Brandon's voice came from the hallway. "I'm going to meet Tommy, Jason, and Jeff." The door to the Evered co-op opened and slammed shut.

For a minute, a strained silence reigned at the breakfast table. The housekeeper appeared from the kitchen bearing a silver coffee server, but Arthur waved her away. He was too upset to eat or drink anything more. He pushed away his plate of cold, half-eaten scrambled eggs and toast.

Alice said, "It's not good for you to get all worked up,

Arthur. You know what the doctor said about too much stress and your high blood pressure."

"That kid makes me so damn *mad*!" Arthur made a fist.

"He's just going through a phase. All teenagers fight with their parents." Alice called to the housekeeper. "Maria—you can clear the table now."

Arthur balled his linen napkin and threw it on the table as he rose from his seat. As he walked away, he pulled up on his navy pinstripe trousers. The waistband was getting uncomfortably tight, to his increasing annoyance. He detested getting older, constantly battling middle-age spread and the overall deterioration of the body. The increasing gray in his hair didn't bother him. In fact, gray looked distinguished framing his lean face. But his spreading midriff was something else. Despite what the doctor had told him about taking it easy, he would simply have to step up his gym workouts. He would *not* tolerate a paunch.

"I don't care what kind of phase Brandon is having, I'm sick of it," Arthur said to Alice. "I thought we raised that kid to be more than a typical teenager."

Alice, up from the table, walked to the foyer and collected Arthur's jacket, briefcase, and newspapers. "We did, and it shows. Brandon is consistently at the top of his class. He's so smart, the teachers say they have a hard time keeping up with *him* sometimes." She glanced at her husband. "But he's still a boy trying to grow up. Surely you remember the pain of adolescence."

"When I was a boy, if I talked back to my father, I was horsewhipped in the stables."

"Times change, darling. School discipline isn't what it used to be, either, even though we're sending Brandon to Winston, which you know is the best private school in the city." She handed the jacket, briefcase, and newspapers to Arthur. "Brandon will grow out of it—you've just got to have patience. He'll go to Switzerland and come home on his first break raving about how wonderful it is."

"I wouldn't put money on it. We'll probably get a call from the headmaster informing us he's run away."

"Don't be such a pessimist about your own son!"

Arthur bit back words that rose in his throat. He wanted to say, *He's not my son!* He had said those words before in the past, opening up a vicious battleground between him and Alice. He refrained from it now; one domestic problem was enough.

Alice continued, "We should count our blessings. Brandon is bright with a promising future ahead of him at Thorson, he's not involved in that horrible drug scene, and he chooses nice friends."

"I agree with you on the first two points, but I don't know about the third. Those kids he pals around with are all pretty strange to me."

"You mean the haircuts and the clothes? Those are the latest teen trends."

"No. I mean, they act like they've got some secret sorcery society going. Mumbo jumbo on the telephone."

"You don't understand teenagers, darling. They've got to have their own private little world, you see, something that's *not* adult, and preferably something parents don't approve of."

"*That's* for sure." Arthur sighed, feeling calmness returning. Once again, Alice had talked him down. She was his rock of tranquility, the smooth lagoon in a sea of turbulence. He didn't know what he'd do without her, especially since Brandon had begun to flex his pubescent muscles.

He looked at his Rolex. "Frank should have the car out front by now."

"Don't worry about Brandon, dear. He'll come around." She pecked him on the cheek.

"Alice . . ." he began, hesitating.

"Yes?"

"Do you think Brandon . . . *knows*?"

"Knows? You mean—" She made a gesture.

"Yes."

"I don't see how he could. We've never told anyone. Unless *you* did."

"No, I've kept our promise, Alice, about the Park Avenue Family Planning Center. But I've wondered that Brandon somehow might have found out about the circumstances of his birth, and that's the real reason why he hates us so much."

She laughed delicately. "Don't be silly. All teenagers hate their parents from time to time. It's part of growing up."

"No. I mean, he *really* hates us. At least, he hates me. Sometimes I feel it so strongly, this hate coming straight from his heart. It's almost tangible. I don't know what I've done to deserve it."

"You haven't done anything—it's all in your head. You've been working too hard again. Why don't you take some time off and we'll go somewhere, get out of this hot city?"

"I can't, darling, I told you that. This summer is impossible. But you and Brandon can go. Take him to Europe, or rent a house in the Hamptons. It's not too late to get a place for the rest of the season."

Alice shook her head. "He doesn't want to go anywhere this summer. He says his best friends are staying in town, and besides that, he doesn't want to miss any meetings of the Junior Science Club. He was elected president, you know, just before the end of term." She heaved her shoulders. "I can't budge him."

"Then why were you talking about going away?"

"I meant just the two of us."

"And leave Brandon?"

"He's old enough, Art. He wouldn't be completely alone —there's Maria and Frank. One of the neighbors could look in on him from time to time." She snapped her fingers. "I know, we could ask the Tates if Brandon could stay with them. You know how close he and Jeffrey are."

Arthur shook his head. "I just don't trust Brandon, Alice. I'm sorry. That's one of the reasons why we need to send him to Switzerland, so he gets a good dose of discipline." He opened the door to leave. "Don't wait for me for supper. I'll be late tonight."

Alice nodded with resignation. "As usual."

As Arthur came out of the front of their co-op building on Seventy-ninth Street between Fifth and Madison Avenues, he saw his silver stretch Lincoln limo double-parked and waiting. The driver, Frank, got out and opened the rear door for him. He slid in, still preoccupied with the argument with Brandon.

Every time he and the boy clashed, Arthur resented the fact that Brandon was not his own son, but the product of his wife's artificial union with another man's seed. He had never felt Brandon was really his son, and in times of anger, he couldn't help emotionally disowning him altogether. He often wished he had never consented to his wife's artificial insemination.

Brandon isn't part of me and never will be, he thought as the limo entered the morning rush traffic on Fifth Avenue. *There's something inside of him that I will never be able to understand, let alone control.*

Pains stabbed his chest and ran down his left arm. He coughed and clutched his chest. Frank's alarmed eyes looked at him in the rearview mirror. "Are you all right, sir?"

Evered cleared his throat. "Fine, fine," he said, even though he didn't feel right. He clawed at the pocket of his suit jacket, laying on the seat to his left. He grasped the tiny vial of nitroglycerin pills.

"Do you want me to stop, sir? Go home?"

"No, no." Evered snapped open the vial, shook out a pill and swallowed it. At least he had a boy to call his son, he thought. Not like Rainer Stern, the poor bastard. All that suffering . . .

Evered sank back into the gray leather seat with his eyes closed, breathing hard, and waited for the pain in his chest to subside.

* * *

Brandon stormed out of the co-op building and headed toward the meeting place with his friends. *I hate Mom and Dad, I hate them*, he said silently over and over again. But he couldn't hang on to the anger. It quickly became secondary to the day ahead. There were adventures waiting for him.

The morning sun was bright and the air already thick and hot, heralding an uncharacteristically muggy day for May—a day for moving slowly. Nevertheless, he propelled himself across Fifth Avenue at an awkward lope and headed toward Central Park. His plain, vanilla-colored T-shirt was cut short, exposing his midriff. His faded Levi's hung loosely around his slim waist and hips. He wore a pair of beat-up Reebok running shoes.

A quick, darting movement caught the corner of his eye. He turned his head, caught a glimpse of a tall figure darting into a doorway across the street. He disappeared in the massive Gothic architecture of the Ukrainian Institute of America.

There's that man again, thought Brandon. *That's the third time I've seen him. Who is he?*

He was tempted to change direction and cross the street again to get a better look. He had the feeling the man was interested in him and was watching him, but didn't want to meet. If the stranger didn't want to be seen, he was careless.

Brandon shrugged it off and entered the asphalt pedestrian pathway to Central Park. He headed toward Belvedere Castle and the high rocks. The park was alive with strollers, joggers, and ballplayers in the huge fields. The gray granite castle appeared before him, perched on an outcropping of rock and overlooking a marshy little lake. It was a miniature medieval castle, complete with turrets and watch tower, and was a favorite play area for children. Brandon and his friends liked to meet there and sit on the rocks below the castle walls.

As Brandon drew nearer, he saw that Jeff, Jason, and

Tommy were already waiting for him, leaning against the front of the castle.

Jeffrey Tate, Jason McCord, and Tommy Walker were the same age as he and were in his class at Winston, an exclusive private school on the East Side of town. Jason and Tommy lived on the East Side near Brandon. Jeff lived on Central Park West near the Museum of Natural History, where the Junior Science Club met, the club of which Brandon was president and his friends were members.

The Winston School catered to the affluent WASPs of Manhattan. The small student body of three hundred included a handful of Jewish and Japanese children whose parents wielded enough political or social clout to make up for their non-WASP bloodline. As a matter of principle, the school routinely turned away the applications of oil sheikhs; despite their petro-wealth, no Middle Eastern faces would ever appear in the gold-leafed hallways.

The school had an outstanding reputation for academic excellence and achievement, which, along with the elitism of its name, justified the exorbitant tuition. Even so, most of the parents paid the fees out of their small change accounts. Brandon, like many of the students, rode to school in a chauffeured limousine.

School had just ended for the summer, and Brandon planned to meet his three buddies in the park nearly every day and cook up "adventures."

Brandon saw that Jeff was smoking a cigarette. He looked cool; he was well practiced in the art of inhaling, blowing out smoke through his nostrils, and holding the cigarette in just the right posture. He had taught Brandon how to do it. Jason had laid off smoking because he turned out for wrestling. Tommy thought smoking was dumb, but that was typical of him.

Brandon waved and shouted at the boys, catching their attention. Jeff reached to the breast pocket of his white T-shirt and pulled out a half-filled pack of Marlboros. The blue lettering emblazoned across his chest read, "Bonaire" in large print, and below it, in smaller print, "Skin diving capital of the world." It was a souvenir of his winter scuba vacation.

Brandon broke into a dog trot while Jeff lit a cigarette for him with the glowing tip of his own. When he reached them, Jeff extended his left hand palm side up, and Brandon slapped it in greeting. He took the cigarette Jeff offered him.

Brandon inhaled deeply and blew out the smoke through his nose. "Marlboro. What happened to Benson & Hedges?"

Jeff shrugged, left hand in the front pocket of his white jeans. "Old man quit smoking them."

"Come on," Brandon said. "There's too many little brats here. Let's go for a walk." He headed down the asphalt path going south. Jeff fell in step alongside him, and Tommy and Jason followed. Brandon was the acknowledged and uncontested leader of the four, and of the entire group they hung out with. No one had ever nominated him, nor had he ever proclaimed himself leader. He simply took charge, and everyone else went along with it. The "Two Blondies," as Brandon jokingly called Jeff and Jason, saw to it.

Brandon thought it was right that he should lead, because he was by far the smartest in the clique. Tommy was the only other one who came close to Brandon, in Brandon's opinion, and sometimes that worried him. Smart guys eventually wanted to do things *their* way.

Tommy, however, showed little inclination to take charge. He was a spare, self-absorbed boy with light brown hair and pale skin that couldn't take too much sun. He could never spend his days in the Caribbean sun and acquire a bronze tan like Jeff or Jason, but that was fine by him. He was happier among the book stacks and the science labs than among the beach boys. Mentally he was extremely quick, and had earned the nickname "Brain" at Winston.

Today, like Brandon, Tommy wore Levi's and running shoes. His shirt was a lightweight souvenir baseball jersey with the emblem of the New York Mets on the front and the number 23 on the back.

Brandon spoke up. "Okay, guys, what'll we do today?"

"Let's go down to the lake," suggested Tommy. "We haven't been there in a while."

Brandon vetoed it. "Let's go to the zoo."

"We always go to the zoo," said Tommy. "It's getting boring. Besides, it's hot this morning, and the whole place will smell like shit. The lake will be cool."

"The zoo," said Jeff. "It's more interesting."

"The zoo," agreed Jason.

Brandon grinned. Jeff and Jason always agreed with him, no matter what. He veered down the shortcut path to the New Zoo, on the east side of Central Park near Sixty-fifth Street.

"Your old man still bugging you about going to Switzerland?" Jeff asked Brandon.

"Yeah. He thinks he's going to make me, but I'm not going." Finished with his cigarette, Brandon flicked the lit butt onto the pathway. It rolled to the edge of the grass in front of him, but he didn't bother to step on it to crush it out.

"Switzerland would be *death*," said Jeff. "The end of the earth."

"How're you going to get out of it?" Tommy asked.

Brandon tapped the side of his head. "Smarts."

They swaggered on through the park. Brandon liked the way joggers, skaters, bicyclists, and pedestrians always yielded to their right of way. People seemed to know they were important.

He took several deep breaths of the muggy air and began to put himself in what he called his "space." Other people had to take drugs to get high; he could do it naturally by concentration. It came easily for him; he had been doing it almost ever since he could remember. When he was in his "space," everything around him took on a crystal clarity. Colors were heightened, sounds amplified. He felt extra smart, extra strong. If he was with his friends and they were in their space, they could "do things."

One of the best parts of being in his space was being able

to get into other people's heads. He could look at people and figure out what they were thinking. Not everyone, and not in great detail—usually just moods. He might sense someone was worried, or happy. He could almost always pick up others' reactions to him and his friends, and he liked the uncertainty he and they created. Occasionally he could pick up specific thoughts. They flashed into his head without warning.

Brandon was eight years old when it finally dawned on him that he was different from his parents, and from most other people. When he babbled about his "space," no one knew what he was talking about. His ability to see and hear things that others couldn't earned him his parents' scorn—and sometimes punishment—for his "overactive imagination."

He remembered once telling his mother that he had seen his father hugging and kissing a strange woman; he wanted to know who she was. The image had popped into his head and seemed as real as if his father and the other woman were standing right in front of him.

"That's a lie! You're making that up!" his mother screamed at him. "Stop making up stories!" For that, he had been confined to his room for the rest of the day.

He began to withdraw into a private world that he shared with no one. Until he entered the Winston School, and hit it off with Jeff and Jason, and then Tommy and a few other boys and girls. He was relieved to discover that he was not alone; there were others like him, and they, too, had withdrawn to private worlds because no one understood or accepted them.

Everyone in his little clique was *sympatico*. On the same wavelength. Blood brother and sister. Melissa Holliday, who knew a lot about astrology, said it was because they all had their birthdays close together. Brandon didn't know about that.

What he did know was that when he was with his friends, he felt as though they were one unit, linked together by energy, made strong. Together, they could "do things"; there was a genie inside of them who granted their wishes. Other times, Brandon felt an invisible distance from his friends, as though one or more of them chose to withdraw from the group as a whole; it was as though they pulled down a mental blind. Then it was harder for all of them to "do things." And it was impossible to "do things" alone.

A youth wearing cutoffs, a red tank top, and a Walkman set strapped around his waist came toward them from the opposite direction on roller skates. He made no effort to veer to the side of the boys, who walked three abreast. Brandon snapped out of his space. For a moment, the boys and the skater played chicken, to see who would yield to the other. At the last moment, Brandon and Jeff split and jumped to the sides, allowing the skater to pass between them. The youth's face was haughty.

Brandon whirled and looked at the back of the departing boy. "Let's get that guy," he said, his voice a growl. "I think he should fall on his ass, don't you?"

The boys snickered. Brandon concentrated his gaze upon the retreating skater, who was forcing others to step out of his way instead of weaving around them. Brandon asked the genie inside of him to make the skater fall. He imagined the youth hitting a crack or stone in the asphalt, tripping and losing his balance.

The skater picked up speed with several long strides. He was almost out of sight.

You'll get yours, thought Brandon. He knew the other three were thinking the same thoughts; he felt them.

The skater caught one of his wheels on an unseen object or hole in the path, and pitched over. With a yelp, the rider threw out his arms as he went over forward but couldn't prevent himself from falling. He twisted in the air and landed first on his rear and then cracked his right shoulder, nearly bringing an elderly man down with him.

Brandon and his friends burst into hysterical laughter, holding their sides and pointing at the skater as they hooted.

The youth rolled to his side and groaned, the movement twisting his face with pain. A middle-aged man in a business suit stopped to offer him help, and pulled him to his feet. The man gave a disapproving glance at the boys for their amusement at the skater's misfortune.

"Are you all right?" the boys heard the man ask.

The skater groaned. "Man, I don't know. My back..." he put his left hand to the small of his back and limped to a nearby bench. "I think I'm okay. Thanks, mister."

The businessman left, and several passersby who had stopped to stare resumed their activities. The skater slowly stood up, still obviously in pain.

Brandon cupped his hands around his mouth and shouted. "Way to go, hotshot. Real coordination!" Laughing, the boys turned their backs on the skater and walked on. Jeff got out cigarettes, lit two, and passed one to Brandon.

When they got to the New Zoo, they bought hot pretzels from a vendor and sat down on the grass on a bank near the entrance.

The New Zoo was still undergoing renovation, and parts of it weren't open. Located in a rocky, hilly portion of the park, it comprised several zoned habitats where animals were allowed to roam uncaged. Red brick pavilions with white pillars dotted the zoo. There also was a café, a yellow and green gingerbread information booth, and a huge animal clock cast of bronze called the Delacorte Clock. It was ringed by statues of a bear, a hippopotamus, a goat, and a kangaroo, all holding musical instruments. At the quarter hour, the animals wheeled around the clock while chimes played nursey rhymes.

Among the few species in the small zoo, Brandon favored the arctic foxes and, for their name alone, the poison arrow frogs.

The boys liked to watch people come and go at the zoo and make up nasty stories about them. The people were more interesting than the animals—especially the girls, who would be ranked according to their figures. When the boys were bored with the New Zoo, they sometimes drifted over to the nearby Children's Zoo, a tiny little courtyard of chickens, goats, rabbits, and mice for preschoolers and small children. Sometimes they went deeper into the grassy hills of the park to play war games with an imaginary army.

Brandon watched as a fat woman clutching the hand of a skinny little boy about six years old marched along the path toward the Children's Zoo. The boy's head seemed large for his body, and a pair of glasses in dark frames added to his disproportion. He was conscious of the stares of the three older boys, and squirmed in the grip of the woman.

Jason elbowed Tommy. "Hippo lady brought a chicken for the zoo."

"A pretty scrawny one," said Brandon. "What a reject." He made loud clucking noises. The other boys tittered.

"I'll bet his name is Chuck," said Tommy. "Chuck the Chicken. He lives in a coop instead of a co-op."

"A coo-op," embellished Brandon.

The fat woman chose to ignore them. She tightened her grip on the boy and dragged him on into the zoo.

Much of the day passed in this fashion. Twice Brandon caught a flicker of movement out of the corner of his eye, the same flash of tall and blond-white he had seen near his co-op building. But when he snapped his head around, the image was gone. He sensed a presence; the strange man was somewhere in the surrounding dense foliage, watching.

The second time he glimpsed the strange figure, he prodded Jeff and said, "Did you see that?"

"What?"

"That flash of white. Like someone's hiding in the bushes way over there."

Jeff looked in the direction Brandon indicated. "I don't see anything. Let's go take a look."

Brandon grabbed the back pocket of Jeff's jeans as he started to get up. "Forget it, it's not worth it. I thought I saw this guy who's been hanging around my building lately, but I guess not."

"We've got lots of guys hanging around our building," said Tommy. "They're all panhandling."

"No, this one isn't a bum." Brandon described his sketchy impression of the strange man.

"That sounds like the guy in my dreams," said Tommy.

"What dreams?"

Tommy shrugged. "I keep having dreams about this old geezer like the one you describe. They're bad dreams, actually. Like he's the teacher of a science class I don't want to be in, and he punishes me for failing."

Brandon snickered. "For you, that *is* a nightmare. You ace everything, especially science."

"Maybe this guy's a new teacher for next term, and he's spying on us," Jason suggested.

"How long have you been having these dreams?" Brandon wanted to know.

"A couple of weeks, maybe."

Jeff snapped his fingers. "I know—he's a kidnapper. My old man's always lecturing me about dudes who want to snatch rich kids."

Brandon scowled. "Would you stop with the wise ideas? You're muddying things up here."

"So what's *your* big explanation?"

Brandon shrugged. "I don't know yet." He still felt the unseen presence, but his genie, the voice inside him, told him not to be afraid.

By mid-afternoon, they were tired of playing tricks on people, and turned to the pigeons and squirrels in the park. Brandon nudged Jeff and pointed to a flock of pigeons feeding on bread crumbs someone had scattered. "Are you thinking what I'm thinking?"

Jeff shrugged. "Sure. Why not?"

Brandon closed his eyes briefly and called up the vision of his genie. The vision was always the same: his genie with his own face, big and dominant, in the center of the vision. The genie was flanked by lesser "helper" genies—the magical imps of the friends around him. He directed his genie to scatter the bread.

A sudden dust devil whirled through the hot air, scooping up scraps of paper, twigs, and debris and swirling them into a miniature cyclone. The dust devil hit the crumbs and sucked them up. The pigeons, frightened by the disturbance, flapped away.

The boys laughed. "Pigeons are so dumb," Brandon said. "They're the dumbest birds on the earth."

"They're dirty. They leave pigeon shit all over the place," said Tommy.

"See that one over there, the light gray one? I'll bet I can catch it."

The pigeon Brandon had targeted had realighted on the ground and was weaving and bobbing about. Brandon approached it in a crouch, imagining the pigeon frozen in a cube of ice. In a few seconds, the pigeon stopped moving. He snatched it up in his hands.

The pigeon made no effort to escape his grasp. One eye regarded him with a blank look. He felt the tiny heart thumping in the breast.

"Stupid pigeon!" Brandon exclaimed, suddenly hating the bird for no particular reason beyond its being a pigeon. He seized the little neck and twisted it. The head fell to one side, and the body jerked spasmodically. Brandon dropped the bird on the ground. It lay on its side, wings flapping crazily in the death throes of its nervous system, until at last it lay still. Brandon's stomach felt hollow.

"Gross," said Jason, looking like he had a bad taste in his mouth.

Brandon picked up the corpse by a wing with his thumb and forefinger and heaved it into the bushes.

"You didn't need to do that," protested Tommy.

Brandon shot him a defiant look. "Why not? You a wimp or something?"

"The pigeon didn't do anything to you. It wasn't like that creep on the skates."

Brandon felt himself getting mad. He didn't like to be challenged, particularly when he had to defend an action he didn't fully understand himself. He didn't know why he killed the pigeon. It was an impulse. But he had done it, so therefore it must be right. "I felt like it, okay?"

"Hey! You!" An angry female voice assailed them. Brandon turned to see a woman bearing down on them. She looked like a businesswoman, wearing a black and white dress with a black silk bow at the collar, carrying a wine-colored briefcase. She came right up to Brandon, barely taller than he, and shouted at him.

"Did you kill that bird?"

"No, ma'am."

"What do you mean, no? I saw you pick it up and throw it down."

"It was already dead. That's why I threw it down."

She put her left hand on her hip. "Then why did it keep moving after it hit the ground?"

"I mean, I thought it was dead. It must have been dying." He shot a glance at Jeff and Tommy and Jason, who were staring at the woman with sullen faces.

"I think you deliberately killed that bird. That was cruel, and I should report you to the police." She glowered at him, but he was not chastised and did not drop his eyes in deference. He felt her sense of authority and indignation weaken. "Don't do it again," she said, her voice losing force. "Leave the birds alone."

Brandon nodded, and she continued on her way through the park.

Tommy and Jeff covered their mouths to muffle their laughter. "Way to go, Evered," said Jason. He mimicked Brandon in falsetto: *"No, ma'am. I mean, I thought it was dead."*

Brandon grinned. He looked at the back of the retreating woman. "Does she know she's got runs in her stockings?"

"Great idea," said Jeff.

Brandon looked again at the businesswoman. The backs

of her white pantyhose split with ugly runs. The boys laughed loud enough to attract her attention, and she cast a dark look at them over her shoulder, but kept on going, oblivious to her state.

The boys didn't stay much longer at the zoo area. On the way out of the park, Brandon said, "I've got to split. See you tonight at the club meeting?"

The boys indicated they were coming. Jason said, "But it hasn't been much fun since those four nerds joined."

"I know," said Brandon. "But now that I'm president, I'm going to do something about it."

"What's that? Mr. Finley says anybody can join."

"Mr. Finley's just another stupid adult."

"I think we should drop out and form our own club—without Mr. Finley," said Jeff.

"If we did that, the museum wouldn't let us meet there, and I like the museum," Brandon answered. "We have to have an adult advisor." His lips curled up in a mischievous smile. "But Finley doesn't have to know everything." He outlined some of his ideas for taking care of the "nerds" in the club.

Then he went home for supper. He didn't want to go home, but he knew if he put in an appearance, it would make his mother happy, and she wouldn't hassle him about going out again.

Dusk was settling over the skyline when Brandon re-emerged from his building, on his way to the Junior Science Club meeting at the American Museum of Natural History. As usual, he planned to catch the crosstown bus at the corner of Fifth Avenue and Seventy-ninth Street. The bus cut through Central Park and stopped right in front of the museum on the West Side.

He stepped out onto the sidewalk and was instantly enveloped by the jitters. He felt the presence of the stranger again, unseen but near. Dammit, what *did* the man want? Why was Brandon being singled out?

He ran hot and cold between anger, curiosity, and fright. A lump formed in his throat; he hurried down the sidewalk. The setting sun created a patchwork of shadows among the tall buildings.

A hand reached out from the shadows and grabbed Brandon by the arm, yanking him toward the narrow well of darkness between two buildings.

"Good evening, Brandon," said a deep voice with a foreign accent.

Brandon gasped, twisting in the grasp. The hand was bony and strong. He looked up into a face that was so lean it was almost gaunt. It was the mysterious stranger! A close-trimmed beard ran along his jawline. The man's prominent cheekbones were accented by a thick head of hair that was gray-white. Even in the shadows, his eyes stood out from his face. They were icy and blue, hard and penetrating. For a fleeting moment, Brandon wasn't sure he was looking at an apparition or a man.

The genie inside of him shushed the cry that rose in his throat. *Quiet ... quiet ...* the voice said. *Don't be afraid ...*

The man said, "I'm sorry to frighten you."

"I—I'm not frightened."

"No? That's good." He did not lessen his grip on the boy's arm.

"Why are you following me?"

"Have I been?"

"Yes! I've seen you."

"Have you?"

"What do you *want*?" Brandon tried to pull away but could not.

"I'm looking for my children. I need your help."

"I don't know your children. I don't know you."

"You do know me, in a way, but you don't realize it."

"What are you *talking* about?" The man was crazy—all he did was speak in riddles! The blue eyes bored into Brandon, making him increasingly uncomfortable. "Who *are* you?"

"Someone who will set your imagination free."

Another riddle answer. "I don't understand!"

"If you bring your friends to see me, I will explain everything."

"My friends? Which friends?"

"All the friends who have the magic. You know the ones I mean. Bring them to see me."

"Why? What do you want with us?"

"I am a friend to all of you. A magician, if you will. Do you like games?"

Brandon nodded.

"I have some secret games for you to play, games that no one else in the world can play but you. Will you come?"

The blue eyes were liquid now, soothing, sending a feeling of warmth through Brandon. "What if we don't want to play your games?"

"Then you don't have to. But I think you'll find them fun. Bring your friends to the zoo in the park tomorrow afternoon at two." The man released his hold on Brandon and slid out of the well of shadows, onto the sidewalk.

"Wait! Who are you?"

But the stranger had already turned the corner of the street and was gone.

CHAPTER Thirteen

The American Museum of Natural History was one of Brandon Evered's favorite places in New York City. One of the largest museums in the world, it covered an entire block on the West Side of the city, just off Central Park. It was founded in 1869, and had been added to several times. Most of it looked like a rambling, moody Gothic castle built out of pink granite, surrounded by a black wrought-iron fence.

Inside, spread over four floors, were thirty-eight exhibit halls and galleries, some small and others enormous, some with low ceilings and others with vaulted ceilings up to one hundred feet high. The museum owned more than thirty-five million specimen, many of them on display and some stored away in vaults that were not open to the public.

What intrigued Brandon about the museum was its air of dark mystery. It was the perfect place for the Junior Science Club to meet in the evenings, because after hours the already moody museum took on an added spookiness.

The lighting in most areas was kept to a minimum. Without a map, you could get lost in the halls. The exhibits were set up in many of the chambers so that there was no straight path from one end to the other. You entered and were forced to go either left or right, and wind your way through narrow corridors filled with dioramas along the walls and free-standing display cases in the middle. If you didn't know where you were, you could easily take a turn into a dead end. There were elevators serving the basement and four upper floors, but they were slow. There were several staircases, but not all staircases went to all floors.

Brandon, naturally, had the entire floor plan memorized, including most of the hidden passageways that ran behind the walls, which the staff used for gaining access to the dioramas.

Brandon waited impatiently for Mr. Finley to call the Junior Science Club to order, his impatience aggravated by the inadequate air-conditioning in the stuffy little meeting room inside the museum. The room had no windows and was lit by bright fluorescent lights. It was located on the first floor, off the Northwest Coast Indians hall. Most other school groups had to meet in the basement, where the cafeteria and junior souvenir shop were located. The Junior Science Club was an exception, because the director of Winston School had clout. Many of the parents of Winston students were persuaded to make generous charitable contributions to a school arts fund, which then doled out money to museums and performing arts companies, in exchange for privileges for Winston students, of course.

Brandon twisted in his seat, a school desk chair, and looked around him. The turnout was good tonight—seventeen boys and girls, including the four "nerds." He was determined that tonight was going to be the last for at least two of the outsiders.

The other twelve kids present were Brandon's most important Winston classmates, his blood brothers and sisters who shared the magic. Wrestling in the back of the room were Jeff Tate and Jason McCord, the tough, blond boys who were Brandon's "enforcers." To the side of the room, Tommy Walker was perched on a desk, talking to Lori Gallagher, a sweet-faced girl with long, dusty brown hair. She was too skinny for the likes of Brandon, but Tommy had begun to notice her at the end of spring term, and from the looks of it, was still infatuated. Brandon made a mental note to start giving them a hard time as lovebirds.

A few seats to the rear of Tommy and Lori, Melissa Holliday was gossiping to Sarah Perkins while casting frequent coy glances in Brandon's direction. Melissa, a dark-haired beauty who looked far older than her thirteen years, had a crush on Brandon that had endured weeks of his indifference. He looked Melissa up and down. She wore a peach-colored tank top and tight white designer jeans. He decided he liked the way her figure was changing, the way she was filling out in front. Melissa might be okay after all.

The rest of Brandon's magic circle of thirteen included Michael, Jennifer, Doug, Samantha, Elizabeth, and David. The only one of the group whom Brandon distinctly did not like was David, a boy small for his age, and too timid and whiny for Brandon's tastes. He might be a blood brother, but Brandon had him marked. Sooner or later, he would teach David a lesson or two about being tough.

Brandon shot a look at Mr. Finley, who was squeezed into a desk in the front row, absorbed by a clipboard-full of papers.

Come on, Mr. Didley, let's get going, Brandon thought. *We haven't got all night.* He fidgeted in his chair, thinking of the things he wanted to do this particular evening. He liked to sneak off to more interesting galleries on the floor, like Meteorites, Minerals, and Gems, or off to the Hayden Planetarium, which had a lot of neat space exhibits. Or, better yet, he liked to steal down into the basement and prowl around the off-limits areas where specimens were stored. It was easy to avoid the night guards.

At last Finley consulted his watch and stood up to face the group. "Ladies and gentleman, if we could please be quiet, we'll begin the meeting." He peered owlishly through his dark-rimmed glasses at the boys and girls.

Stan Finley, a science teacher at Winston, was a gawky bachelor of thirty-five whose Adam's apple bobbed in his throat when he talked. He voluntarily served as the advisor to the Junior Science Club, whose membership consisted mostly of Winston students, but technically was open to any child in the city.

Brandon knew that Finley was not thrilled that the boys and girls had insisted on continuing their meetings throughout the summer instead of taking a break, but since he wasn't leaving the city, he had agreed to their pleas.

"Ladies and gentlemen, if we could please begin," he said in a louder voice.

The youngsters gradually quit chattering and settled into their little desks. Finley waited until the last whispering was ended before continuing. He spoke with his hands up and palms out, bobbing them up and down almost in unison with his Adam's apple, his shoulders slightly rounded. "First we'll take attendance, and then I'll turn the meeting over to our president, Brandon."

The advisor checked off names on his clipboard and then went to the back of the room, where he began to set up flip charts and tape posters to the wall. Brandon stood up in front of the club. He liked being leader, having all eyes upon him. There were twelve other genies in the room, and they all supported him. He could draw on their energy, suck it up like a huge battery.

He dispensed with business and the club broke into pairs to work on the current project, making telescopes. Finley was teaching them how to grind the mirrors for four-and-a-quarter-inch reflecting telescopes. The flip charts and posters were step-by-step procedures that supplemented Finley's lectures.

The boys and girls pushed the desks to one side of the room and pulled long tables into the cleared space. They covered the tables with newspaper and got out their kits, which they kept stored in lockers at the museum.

The mirror blanks, disks of Pyrex four and a quarter

inches in diameter, were ground by rubbing carborundum grit and water over them with a disk of plate glass. The children would use finer and finer grit as the mirror blanks became more concave, finishing with emory powder. The mirror blanks would be polished on pitch laps with rouge and water. The whole process would take weeks.

While one youth did the grinding, the other worked on construction of the telescope tube and mount. They traded roles every week.

Finley walked around the room, looking over shoulders, answering questions and correcting grinding techniques. When he was satisfied that everyone was on the proper course, he told Brandon he was going downstairs to "get coffee." Brandon knew he would stay away as long as possible. It was the teacher's usual procedure. He was always nervous and jittery, like he couldn't wait to get away from them.

Brandon waited until Finley had been gone about five minutes. Then it was time to deal with the "nerds." All he had to do was think about it, knowing that Jason and Jeff and usually Tommy would be with him automatically, and the rest of the magic kids would somehow pick it up. They were, after all, blood brothers and sisters.

While everyone else in the club kept busy, Brandon quit grinding and walked over to the nearest "nerd." His name was Gary, and he was fourteen, a big lug of a kid, overweight and sloppy. He had a passion for science, but he wasn't a blood brother—no magic. He had to go.

"Say, Gary, how ya doin'?" Brandon said.

Gary looked up from his telescope mount, pleased to be noticed by the president of the Junior Science Club. "I'm doing all right," he said, grinning self-consciously.

Brandon stuck his hands in the front pockets of his jeans. "Say, Gary, did anyone tell you about the initiation for new members?"

Gary suddenly looked bewildered. "Initiation? No, they didn't." He looked to his teammate, Jason, for an indication of support or reinforcement, but Jason kept his head down at he ground and remained silent.

Brandon hmmm'd. "Well, there is one. You gotta do it if you want to stay in the club."

"Oh. I've never been initiated into anything before."

Brandon smiled. "You'll have fun."

Gary hesitated. "What do I have to do?"

"Come with me."

Gary looked around. "But the telescope—Mr. Finley—"

"Mr. Finley won't be back till it's almost time to go home. Don't worry, he knows about the initiation."

"He does?" The fat boy bit his lower lip. "Is it the same for everyone?"

"Not quite. It depends, you know. But *everyone* has to be initiated."

"Everyone? Even you?"

"That's right," Brandon lied with a straight face, watching Jason crack a smile. "What's the matter? You a wimp or something?"

Gary reddened. "No, I'm *not* a wimp. Okay, let's do it."

"Come on, Jason." Brandon motioned to the fair-haired, muscular boy. "You too, Jeff," he called.

Jason stopped grinding and wiped his hands on his blue jeans. He prodded a scared-looking Gary toward the door. Jeff joined them.

Brandon announced, "Everyone else keep on working." Some of the kids looked up. Those who comprised the clique had knowing expressions on their faces.

Jason, Jeff, and Brandon led Gary toward the heart of the museum. Brandon pointed to a surveillance camera mounted near the ceiling in a corner. "These things are all over the place, and the guards have monitors. So, we've got to watch out for Mr. Inferior."

Gary was bewildered. "Mr. Inferior?"

"You know, the black guy at the main entrance where you

come in after hours. He's supposed to keep an eye on all the monitors. If he sees us, he'll send someone to chase us out."

"Then what are we going to do, if the cameras are everywhere?"

"Simple," said Brandon. He pointed at the monitor above them. It went blank.

Gary gasped. "How did that happen?"

"Magic," said Brandon.

"Did *you* do that?"

Brandon shrugged. Gary looked at him as if he were a ghost.

They wound their way through a maze of corridors, passing through the exhibit gallery of Small Mammals—otter, muskrat, mink, and the like—on into North American Mammals. Mountain lions were positioned in a diorama overlooking the Grand Canyon, while on the other side, the mooselike wapiti foraged in a forest. The hall was dimly lit and somber, with its dominant colors of slate blue, clay red, and beige, and the exhibits were set up to form narrow, winding pathways, so that there was no straight way through the gallery. Some of the dioramas were in the walls while others were free-standing. They passed bighorn sheep, caribou, moose, muskox, and bear.

In one wall case, three snarling wolves ran over a snowpack after an unseen quarry. Gary stopped to gaze at the wolves. The leader's lips were pulled back, baring sharp fangs. Suddenly it was all a blur. He screamed and jumped back as the stuffed animals rose from their poses and smashed into the glass, cracking it.

"What was *that*?" Gary said hoarsely. "They were *moving*. I thought they were going to get us!" He stared in astonishment at the wolves, still in their original poses, but now in a heap in front of the glass, their angry eyes looking at him as if *he* were their prey. Everything was back to normal.

Brandon and Jason exchanged amused glances. Gary was an easy target.

"Are you crazy?" Brandon said. "Stuffed animals can't come to life."

"But I thought they did—just for a moment—it seemed..."

Jason said, "I'll bet it was the ghosts again. The ghosts picked them up and threw them."

Gary looked panicked. "*Ghosts?*"

"This whole place is full of ghosts," Jason said nonchalantly. "Mostly animal ghosts. They're mad because they were killed and stuffed to be put on display."

"That's right," said Brandon. "They'll get you if you don't watch out. They're always smashing and moving things."

"But I've been here a lot and nothing like that has *ever* happened," protested Gary.

"That's because you've been here during the day," Brandon explained. "They only do their tricks at night." He stopped and clapped his palm to his forehead. "We're going in the wrong direction. It's *that* way." He pointed back the way they had come. Jason and Jeff grinned conspiratorially to each other.

"What's that way?" said Gary. "I'm getting confused."

"You'll see," said Brandon.

They retraced their path through the mammals and cut through a corner of the Northwest Coast Indians hall. But instead of going back to the classroom, they turned left down a corridor, then right, heading toward Meteorites, Minerals, and Gems. All along the way, the cameras quit working as they approached. The monitors placed in various locations, which the guards could check on their rounds, blinked off. It was simple. All Brandon and Jason had to do was think them off. Brandon sensed Gary's increasing unease.

They bypassed Mollusks and Mankind and entered a gallery that was used for short-term, special exhibits. Currently on display was a reproduction of Aztec life. Lit only by low lights, the room was dark and shadowy. The gray sculptures that were scale models of the Aztec pyramids, temples, and dwellings stood out in stark contrast from the shadows. Carved stone faces and totems glowered down at the boys from walls.

"This place gives me the creeps," said Gary, rubbing his arms.

"This is where sacrifices are made to the Aztec gods," said Brandon.

"You mean it's a replica of the Aztec temples."

"No, I mean the real thing. There's a secret cult that comes here twice a month in the night, and makes sacrifices to the ghosts to appease them. Sometimes they sacrifice animals, sometimes babies."

"You're making that up."

"Watch who you're calling a liar," Jeff said menacingly, grabbing Gary's pudgy arm.

"I'm sorry, I'm sorry. Okay?"

"Here's the initiation," said Brandon. "The cult is coming tonight. They're going to make their sacrifice in that temple right over there." He pointed to a huge pyramid, taller than the boys, with a small door cut in one side. It looked like a person could enter the model by crouching down. "You have to go in there and wait and offer to take the place of whatever they're going to sacrifice."

"*What?*"

"They won't take you up on it. But you have to convince them that you *really* want to save the sacrifice. It's probably going to be a baby—that's what they've been into lately."

"*Jeeesus!* Are you serious?"

"You want to stay in the club?" asked Jason.

Gary swallowed. "Yes. You're sure about this?"

Brandon nodded. "Once you convince the cult, they'll thank you for being so unselfish and let you go." He scowled. "Look, we've all had to do this. If you're too wimpy..."

Gary shook his head. "No, I'll do whatever you say."

Brandon pointed to the doorway. "You'd better get in there. They'll be here any time."

"What about you? Where will you be?"

"Hiding back here." Brandon pointed to a corner. "Don't worry, we won't leave."

"What do I say to them?"

"That's up to you."

Gary hesitated, then tucked himself into a crouch and squeezed through the opening of the temple model.

Brandon stuck his head in the opening and hissed, "Get ready! They're coming!" He and his two companions backed off. Brandon nodded, and the three of them used their genies to summon forth a huge round ceremonial stone, six feet in diameter, from another part of the exhibit room. The stone rolled on its edge until it covered the doorway to the temple, and then the boys stopped it. Gary was trapped inside.

"Hey!" Gary called, his voice faint. "I can't see in here! Something's blocking the door."

The boys giggled. The next part of the trick on Gary was one of their favorite sports—"making pictures." They had recently discovered that their combined genie magic could create realistic pictures in the minds of others, visions that seemed very real to the victim.

Now they concentrated on pictures for Gary, conjuring up savage Aztecs with knives, who were going to tie Gary down on a stone bed for sacrifice.

When the screams began, they knew they had succeeded.

"Let's get out of here," Brandon said to Jason. "One of the janitors will find him. Or Mr. Inferior."

"Fatso won't tell on us?"

Brandon shook his head. "He's too scared. I bet we don't see him at the next meeting."

The boys returned to the classroom. They had time enough for one more "nerd" before Mr. Inferior could send out the night janitors to repair the cameras and monitors, and before Mr. Finley returned to the club.

They picked on Roger Thibaut, a nine-year-old whiz kid

whose outsize spectacles looked too heavy for his small face and skinny frame. Roger, when he talked about science and astronomy, sounded very grown up. Aside from his outsider status, he had an irritating, uppity bearing that gave Brandon the impression Roger thought he was better than the rest of them. Stupid kid, would he be taught a lesson!

Brandon, Jeff, and Jason went through nearly the same routine about initiation. Roger was annoyed at having to stop work on his telescope, but agreed with an air of "let's get this over with." He pushed his spectacles back on the bridge of his nose, a habit that had gotten under Brandon's skin.

A thought occurred to Brandon that Roger Thibaut was deathly afraid of snakes and reptiles. He glanced at Jeff and Jason and saw that his blood brothers had picked up the same thought. They steered the scrawny Roger up the stairs to the Reptiles and Amphibians hall on the third floor.

"You aren't going to make me break anything, are you?" Roger said, propelling himself awkwardly on his thin legs. "I don't want to do anything against the rules. I don't want to get in trouble."

"Don't worry," Brandon answered.

Reptiles and Amphibians was a short gallery. Foot traffic was steered down the middle, past a gauntlet of free-standing glass display cases that could be viewed from all sides. The first cases were innocuous—frogs, toads, and small lizards. But then Brandon and his friends sensed the younger boy's apprehension rise as they passed snakes—the big Eastern Diamondbacks and the deadly Cottonmouths.

Roger gasped and stopped. "It moved! That snake! Right there." Roger pointed to the Eastern Diamondback, frozen in a coiled, ready-to-strike posture.

"No, it didn't," said Brandon. "Must be the lights playing tricks on your eyes."

After the snakes came a huge case containing three Komodo Dragons, fearsome creatures ten feet long and two hundred pounds, with nasty, hooded eyes, immense hinged jaws, and long forked tongues. In their poses, one of the dragons was feeding on a dead wild pig, while the other two glared out at spectators. The exhibit text said the Komodo Dragon was the largest living lizard in the world, and Roger Thibault didn't doubt it.

He did not want to walk past the dragons, but there was no way to avoid them. Roger looked behind him. "Can we go back out? Isn't there another way to get wherever we're going?"

"Nope." Jason gave him a shove to keep him moving forward until Roger was directly in front of the dragons.

"Stand here," commanded Brandon.

"B-but I don't like these things," said Roger.

"Really? This'll be your initiation, then. Show us you're not afraid."

"Why?"

"Because everybody in the Junior Science Club has to show that they're not chicken." Brandon raised his voice. "*Look* at the dragons!"

Roger, who had dropped his eyes, raised them hesitantly. Jason and Jeff each grabbed one of his arms so that he could not run off.

Roger screamed. "They're moving!"

Brandon laughed, knowing that to Roger, the dragons were indeed coming to life, snapping their jaws and whipping their tails as they moved toward him. "Don't be stupid. They're dead, dummy—they're *stuffed*."

"No, they're alive! They're gonna get out! Let me out of here! Let go!" He struggled futilely in Jason's strong grip.

Jason said, "Look, chicken, if you fail the initiation, you can't stay in the club. That's the *rule*."

"I don't care!" Roger started to cry.

Just ahead of the dragons were two long and low cases, one containing an alligator and one containing a crocodile. Now these creatures seemed to come alive, snapping their huge jaws and sliding forward on their bellies and stubby legs. Their snouts hit the cases again and again, as if they were determined to break out.

Roger screamed again. "They're going to get me!" His panic escalated. "They're coming out of the case! Do something! Help!" He tried to run away, but Jason and Jeff kept a strong grip on him.

"Shut up!" Brandon yelled. "You wimp! You want to get us all in trouble?"

A masculine voice echoed through the corridors, words lost in the reverberations.

"It's one of the night crew," Brandon hissed. "Dump him, and let's get out of here."

The boys let go of Roger, who collapsed in a heap on the floor, still crying his lungs out. The three dashed out of sight, entering a doorway along one wall that was supposed to be locked but never was, which opened to a passageway behind the exhibit cases. It was used by the museum employees when exhibits were changed or serviced. They ran through the narrow, dark passage, hands touching the wall for guidance, until they came out in a far corridor of the museum.

They fell out into the corridor, breathless, filled with laughter. Brandon quickly got his bearings, and steered them back toward the Junior Science Club meeting room.

"We never left the meeting room, got it?"

"Got it," said Jason.

"Copy," said Jeff.

They stopped to catch their breaths, and then returned to the club room. Half the children were working on their telescopes, the other half were goofing off. There was immediate, silent communication among the thirteen blood brothers and sisters; everyone understood what had taken place, and what to say should an adult ask questions. The two remaining outsiders kept their heads down, casting sideways glances out of the corners of their eyes, understanding their place in the pecking order of the group—which meant "hear no evil, see no evil, speak no evil."

Mr. Finley stormed in minutes later in a fit of uncharacteristic bravado. "What is the meaning of this?" he demanded of Brandon. "What is Roger doing out in the reptile section terrified out of his wits? One of the security men came downstairs and told me he found Roger crying about the snakes coming out of the cases to get him."

Brandon shrugged and looked respectful. "Don't ask me, Mr. Finley. He said he was going to go home early, and left."

"I've just put him in a cab to go home. He says you and Jason and Jeff played some sort of nasty trick on him." Finley narrowed his eyes.

"I don't know why he'd tell a lie like that," said Brandon. "We've been right here."

Finley looked around the room, trying to read the faces of the other children for clues. He found nothing. Then he realized a face was missing. "Where's Gary?"

Again Brandon shrugged. "He got bored and wanted to look around. I think he went over to the Aztec exhibit. Can we go now, Mr. Finley? It's almost time for the meeting to be over."

CHAPTER Fourteen

The afternoon sun over Manhattan was scorching; the air thick and humid. Every living creature, people and animals alike, moved slowly. At the Children's Zoo and New Zoo in Central Park, cross parents struggled to manage children made even crosser by the stifling heat.

Outside the main entrance to the zoo waited a group of thirteen children, seven boys and six girls, all twelve or thirteen years of age. To the passerby, there was nothing remarkable about them, except perhaps that they were all handsome children. Nor was it evident that they were all part of a group. They were scattered in small clusters and were engaged in different activities. Some drew pictures with sticks in the dirt; some tossed pebbles; some seemed lost in thought.

But to one man in particular, they stood out as exceptional children.

Dr. Hans Messner watched them from a distance, knowing they could not see him but were aware of his presence. He watched, absorbed by curiosity, filled with pride.

Off to one side, partially hidden by shrubbery, four of the boys engaged themselves against a squirrel. Messner recognized each one by name—Brandon Evered, Jeffrey Tate, Jason McCord, and Michael Larsen. With fascination, he saw the squirrel freeze as though immobilized, while the boys pulled on its tail and poked it. Then Brandon produced a small rectangular flask and sprayed a liquid over the squirrel. Just as Messner realized it was lighter fluid, Jason produced a match and set the squirrel into a tiny bonfire. Released from its immobilization, the hapless animal dashed frantically in circles before toppling over and thrashing until it was dead. If it had screamed, Messner hadn't heard it.

The boys watched the dying squirrel with impassive, almost bored faces.

Messner knew how they had frozen the squirrel. They had done it with their minds. He knew what no one else in the world knew about these children, what the children themselves were only beginning to discover: that they possessed exceptional psychic powers.

He had looked forward to this day for a long time. Now *Die Wunderkinder* was finally realized, and his creations were old enough for him to claim. He would lead them, teach them, shape them, hone their powers—and through them, create more of them.

Victory at last!

He looked at his watch. It was the appointed time to show himself. The children were waiting. *His* wonderful children. He no longer had to hide beneath the mask of John Heineman; he could be his real self again at last.

Messner stepped forward, his footing sure, his gaze steady under the brilliant sun. *The Reich shall rise again,* he thought. *The Master Race is born.*

He approached the children in measured footsteps. They anticipated him; they ceased their activities and looked up to regard him. He exulted in their confidence and composure. *See how courageous they are,* he thought. *They look up to me; they know I have come to teach them.*

By the time he reached them, they had collected into a single group. What fine faces they had! With one or two exceptions, they exhibited the ideal Aryan features, but even the exceptions would be tolerated, since he had had limited control over their parentage. The most important attribute was their *minds*. The power that shone forth from their eyes was awesome.

He stopped before them and waited a moment before speaking. Then he said, "Hello, children. I am Hans Messner, and you know why I have come."

His confident smile fell as he was struck by a wave of hostility from the children. The feeling was incredible, as though their thoughts had substance. For a split second, he couldn't believe it. His heart quickened. They had developed far more than he'd dared to dream.

"You're mistaken," he said, putting up his hands, palms out toward the children. "I'm your *friend*. I'm not like other adults who don't understand you."

"But you're not one of us," said Brandon. "So why should we listen to you?"

"*You're* a bold one." Messner regarded Brandon, then each of the children individually. Had he waited too many years to approach them? Long before, he had considered and rejected kidnapping. He had waited until at least some of the children were old enough to grasp the significance of their uniqueness, and would come with him willingly—and stay with him. He said, "It's good that you're bold, for only the bold survive and succeed. You must listen to me because there are many things you must learn, and only I can teach them to you."

"We don't like teachers," said Brandon.

"You misunderstand. You were born to fulfill a purpose, a destiny. Like children born to grow up to be kings and queens."

"We know," Brandon answered coldly. "That's why we stick together. *No* outsiders."

"But I'm not an outsider. I helped bring you into the world. In a sense, I'm your father—rather, your godfather."

"If that's so," said Jeff, "then where've you been all these years? In a nursing home?"

The children snickered.

Messner was chagrined. "I've been waiting for you to grow up. I know all about you and your families."

"That sounds like garbage to me," said Jason. "We can tell if you're lying."

Messner's head suddenly felt full, as if his brain were swelling and pressing against his skull to the bursting point. Spears of pain shot through his temples. Instantly he knew what caused it—he was being probed psychically. He could feel the collected mental energy from all thirteen children coalesce into a single beam of incredible power. His skin prickled with fear. How had they learned, on their own, to combine their psychic energy like this? It was far more powerful and sophisticated than tormenting animals. It was frightening.

The pain in Messner's head stopped as Brandon broke the silence. "You're just like every other grown-up—you want to give us orders, make us do things we'll hate."

"No, you don't understand. It is *you* who will give the orders someday—to everyone in the world. But first you must learn from me. I will help you become kings and queens."

A small boy on the side of the group spoke up. Messner recognized the one named David, and remembered he had evaluated him as one of lesser potential. The boy said, "I don't understand what he means by this 'master race' stuff. And what does World War II have to do with it? That's ancient history."

Messner gasped. He hadn't said a word about World War II or the Reich's blueprint for the Master Race. The children had picked it up from his thoughts! He opened his mouth to explain, but Brandon cut him off.

"It doesn't mean anything, David. He's crazy."

"He thinks he's God," said the girl named Melissa. "He

believes he created us!" A scornful laugh rose among the children.

Brandon pointed to the boy Messner knew as Tommy Walker. "Is this the man from your dreams?"

"Yes. He wants to lock us up in a special school, and punish us a lot."

"No—"

Brandon said, "You're a creep. We don't need you. We don't *like* you."

Another wave of hostility from all the children flooded over Messner, so strong that he took half a step backward. The children's eyes were big and radiant. Astonished, he said, "Why not?"

"Because you want to take us away and make us prisoners," Brandon said.

"I want you to come with me, yes. You must run away. But I don't want to make you prisoners. And I have no intention of punishing you for anything."

"Yes, you do! We can tell—you can't hide it from us. You want to keep us in a jail and do nasty things to us, like the rats in science class."

Messner shook his head, struggling to keep cool. It was true that he intended to take the children away and not let them leave him. He had everything ready to go, waiting in his van, parked off Fifth Avenue. He had his most important papers with him, tucked on his person for safekeeping. But the children had seen the wrong picture. "No, no. Not a jail. I have a big home, out in the woods, where nobody will find us and bother us. We'll play games. War games, just like you do here in the park."

"Liar!" Brandon exclaimed. "Liar, liar!"

"Liar!" joined in Jeff. Jason joined in, and then several others, until the entire group of children was chanting, "*Liar, liar!*" Pedestrians turned their heads and stopped to stare.

"Hush!" Messner waved his hands at them, trying to get them to stop. "You're attracting too much attention!"

The children kept chanting, stepping closer and closer to Messner. Suddenly he lost his temper and roared, *"Be quiet! I order you to be quiet!"*

The chanting stopped abruptly, but hostility still radiated from the thirteen pairs of eyes. Messner returned their stares and said loudly, "That was very good, children. You will all do well in the play tomorrow." He smiled at the onlookers, for whose benefit he had made up the line about a play. The onlookers drifted away. Messner lowered his voice and said to the kids, "I've had enough of this! You will do as I say! We will leave the park now, and go to a van that is waiting for us off Fifth Avenue. You will not go home. Everything you need is at my home in the woods. You have a new life to begin."

Brandon balled his fists at his side. "You're not going to tell us what to do!"

Messner glared at Brandon. He knew from his secret observations that the boy was headstrong, but he had run out of patience. How *dare* these children defy him, when he had dedicated his entire life to bringing them into the world. How *dare* they speak back to him. He would teach them discipline! He was not afraid of them. He reached out with his right hand and grabbed Brandon by the arm. "The first thing you will learn is not to speak back to me! Go!" He jabbed his left index finger in the direction of Fifth Avenue.

"Let go of me!" Brandon yelled, twisting in the German's grasp.

Without warning, pain shot through Messner's head and down into his entire body. He gasped and released Brandon, who leaped away from him. Messner's vision clouded over. He struggled to focus on the children. The source of pain energy shot out from *them*—he could sense it, almost see flashing sparks of it. Their faces were screwed up in hate, directed at him.

"No," he protested. "You don't understand! Stop!"

"We want you to go away," said Brandon. "We hate you! Leave us alone! Come on, everybody. We hate him!"

The pain escalated. Messner's chest felt like it was bound by iron bands, and his throat felt like it was plugged with a stone. He choked. "Don't! You don't know what you're doing!" He looked wildly around him, but no one seemed to be paying attention to them.

"Leave us alone!" Brandon said.

Messner staggered backward, dizzy, his cloudy field of vision narrowed to a tunnel by edges of darkness. He put his hands to his head in a futile effort to stop the excruciating pain that made his skull feel like it was about to explode. "Please... stop... you're killing me... you don't understand what you can do..." He closed his eyes and swayed.

"We don't ever want to see you again!" Brandon's voice shrieked at him. "Don't follow us or spy on us—*ever*!"

Messner was incapable of answering. His breath came in ragged, pain-wracked heaves. He could see nothing but black shot with bolts of red. A thought floated in the back of his mind that he was dying. *Impossible*, he thought. *I cannot die. I survived before. My work isn't done. I've got to live!"*

He couldn't feel his legs anymore and lost his balance. It seemed to take forever to hit the ground. The blow was cushioned by the fact that his consciousness was no longer in his body, but floating away into space.

Brandon watched the white-haired man crumple to the ground with a moan. The body twitched and then was still. The eyes stayed open, staring sightlessly up into the sky, then rolling up into the head until nothing but the whites showed. Brandon's breath caught in his throat.

"He's *dead*!" exclaimed Jason. "We went too far!"

A woman screamed. Two men and a woman rushed to Messner and huddled over him, shaking him and shouting, "Hey! Are you all right? What happened?"

Within moments, a panicked crowd converged on the stricken man. "Get back!" a man shouted. "Give him air!"

"Is he dead?" asked an anxious woman. "I saw him just stagger and fall over."

"I don't know," answered the man who had shouted for air. "Somebody call an ambulance!"

"Heart attack," a heavyset man muttered. "It's this heat. Same thing happened to a guy in my building yesterday. Collapsed and was gone, just like that." He snapped his fingers.

"This man is dead," a woman asserted. "Look at him—he's not breathing!"

"Will somebody *please* get an ambulance! Everybody, get back!"

Brandon stood rigid, uncertain what to do. Was Hans Messner *really* dead? He had meant only to scare the man away. His eye was caught by a bulge in one of Messner's rear pockets. A thought flashed into his head that he should have whatever was in that pocket.

Around him, he felt fright rising among some of the other children. He was beginning to panic himself but knew he couldn't lose control in front of the others. They had to get out of sight, but slowly, quietly, without attracting attention. Fortunately, the adults hovering over Messner were too preoccupied to notice what was going on around them. Brandon flicked his thumb at his group, accompanying the signal with a silent command to slip away. A few steps at a time, they slipped into the shrubbery.

Brandon was the last to leave. Before doing so, he squeezed into the crowd around Messner. The bulge in Messner's pocket was starting to show as a thick envelope. Brandon got close and deftly removed it. He shoved it down into his jeans and bolted away.

As he was vanishing into the bushes, an adult female voice near Messner said, "Wasn't this man with a group of kids? I thought I saw him talking to a bunch of boys and girls, but I don't see any of them now."

"Maybe he was a *molester*," another female voice suggested.

"Yeah," a man said. "They're all over the park."

Free of the scene, Brandon pumped his legs in an all-out

run, followed closely by Jeff and Jason, with the rest of the group strung out behind. He tore through the park, cutting across asphalt paths and plunging into bushes, ripping past startled strollers, until he was deep in the vast park, and he had to stop because his lungs were near bursting.

Brandon dropped onto the grass, his chest heaving as he caught his breath. Jeff and Jason were close behind, followed by Tommy and Michael. The remaining children straggled up. Lori was crying; tears streamed down her face. As soon as she sat down and caught her breath, she began bawling.

Brandon jumped to his feet. "Shut up, Lori! Quit acting like a baby!"

"But he's dead," she whimpered. "That man is *dead*. Now they're going to come and get us."

"*Who's* going to get us? Nobody knows we were there. Didn't you hear that lady—she only *thought* he was talking to kids."

"That could mean any kids, not us," said Jeff. "We're in the clear."

"Did we really do that to him?" piped up David.

"Of course we did, stupid," Brandon said.

"But we *killed* him, Brandon," said Samantha, who was becoming affected by Lori's tears. "What are we going to do now?"

"I don't want to play like this anymore," said David.

Jason said, "I'm *glad* we got him. He was a jerk and a liar."

"Jason's right," Jeff said. "He deserved it. He was going to take us prisoners."

Samantha said, "I'm with David. You guys have gone too far. I'm going home and I'm not telling *anybody* what happened. And if anybody rats, they'll be sorry!"

Brandon folded his arms across his chest. The argument was getting out of hand. "Everybody shut up and sit down. Nobody goes home. That goes double for you, Samantha."

The others obeyed, settling onto the grass around Brandon, who remained standing. "Let's take a vote. How many didn't like him?"

All the hands went up.

"How many wanted to go with him?"

No hands went up.

"Then we're all in agreement. We solved the problem, so there's nothing to be upset about."

"Wait a minute, Brandon—"

"*I'm* doing the talking, Tommy." Brandon looked around at the twelve faces. "We're all going to stick together. If we don't, it's going to split us up, and you all know what *that* means. It means no more magic tricks. Anyone who wants to split up and lose magic, raise a hand."

The children looked at each other. No hands went up.

"Good," said Brandon. He smiled coldly. "I think we just found a way to solve a lot of other problems—without anyone knowing what we're doing." He let his words sink in, pleased at the response he sensed in his thoughts. There was a spot of reluctance here and there, but overall acceptance. He could tell David was going to be a problem, but he knew how to push David around. Samantha, who had agreed with David, would have to be watched. And Lori might be a problem—she was so flighty and emotional. Jason and Jeff were rock solid. He was uncertain about Tommy, who usually went along with him but sometimes could get up on a high horse. The rest of them—Elizabeth, Melissa, Jennifer, Michael, Doug, and Sarah—fell into line.

Brandon went on, "Grown-ups are the enemy, right?"

"Right!" the children answered in unison.

"So are kids who are different from us."

"Right!"

"We know what's best."

"Right!"

"We're going to do what we want, and nobody's going to stop us."

"Right!"

"Here's the plan," said Brandon. "From now on, we're a secret society. *Totally* secret. Our purpose will be to help each other solve problems."

"That's a great idea!" enthused Jeff. "How fast can we start working on parents? I'm tired of studying every night."

There was scattered applause.

"We'll have regular meetings," said Brandon. "We'll discuss problems and plan *solutions*."

Samantha said, "What'll we call ourselves? We've got to be more than the Junior Science Club."

"Right," said Mike, "because the society should be limited to the thirteen of us."

Brandon, recalling a lesson from a social studies class, said, "I've got it: 'The Secret Society of Loki.'"

"Who's Loki?" said Melissa.

"Remember from Mrs. Harwood's class? Loki is a god from Norse and German mythology who was sneaky and clever. That'll be our trademark."

"Sounds great," said Jason. "All in favor, say aye."

"Aye!"

Sarah raised her hand to speak. "I think Tommy ought to be president of the Secret Society of Loki. Brandon is already president of the Junior Science Club."

Brandon tensed, anger rising in his throat. He waited for Tommy to speak, but the boy remained silent, his face impassive and his thoughts shrouded. "It's my idea," Brandon said flatly. "*I'm* going to be president."

Silence fell; there were no challenges.

"We'll seal the society with a blood oath," Brandon said. He reached into his jeans and drew out a pocket knife. "Everybody stick out their thumbs."

The thirteen children formed a circle. One by one, each pledged a blood oath of lifelong loyalty and secrecy, using Brandon's knife to cut a slit on their right thumbs.

While the impromptu ceremony took place, Brandon's

thoughts wandered. The thick envelope in his pocket burned like a hot coal. He couldn't wait to get home and read in secrecy what was inside. He had a feeling the tall, gaunt stranger had possessed some very interesting information—about them.

CHAPTER
Fifteen

"No, no, Brandon, like *this*." Arthur Evered held out his racquetball racket for his son to see the proper grip. "See where I've got my fingers wrapped around the handle? Then bring the racket back like this—"Evered demonstrated—"and snap your wrist just as you make contact with the ball. The snap is what gives the ball power."

Brandon looked bored, and it annoyed Arthur. Dammit, he was trying to teach the boy a good sport. His son stood with one hip thrust to the side, his long legs looking coltish in his red gym shorts. His downturned mouth gave him a sullen look. But what disturbed Arthur the most was the hostility in the boy's icy blue eyes. *If looks could kill* was the thought that kept running through Evered's mind.

Arthur glanced out the Plexiglas partition. The back wall of the racquetball court at the Manhattan Royal Athletic Club was Plexiglas, in order to allow onlookers to watch games. At the moment, the Evereds had no audience.

He wiped his brow of sweat. In the summertime, the overtaxed air-conditioning was never adequate for the heat generated in these courts.

"Why aren't you paying attention to me, Brandon?"

Brandon shrugged. "I don't see what good it is to learn how to play racquetball. I bet they don't play it in *Switzerland*." He gave the last word sarcastic emphasis.

Evered shook his racket at his son. "I told you, Brandon, I'll have no more pouting about your going to Switzerland."

"You and Mom just want to get rid of me. You don't care about *me* and what *I* want to do." Brandon hit the small blue ball toward the floor and as it rose, batted it down again. "This is a stupid game."

For a moment, Arthur was tempted to strike his son across the face. He wanted to wipe away the defiance in the eyes and in the set of the mouth. He was mad because he had left work early to play racquetball with his son, in an effort to improve the father-son relationship. But it seemed that every time the two of them were in the same room, hostility erupted and ruined his intentions.

Arthur controlled his anger. "You insult me when you call racquetball a 'stupid game.' I enjoy playing it, and I'd hoped you would enjoy it, too."

Brandon didn't respond. A movement beyond the Plexiglas caught Arthur's eye. Brandon turned, and he followed his son's gaze. He was startled to see that a group of six teenagers, four boys and two girls, had materialized on the other side of the glass wall. Brandon grinned and waved at them, and they waved back with a solemn air.

"Who are these kids?" Arthur wanted to know. He didn't like the looks of them. They had the same hostile, intense light in their eyes that Brandon did, and the same sullen expression.

"Some friends of mine."

"What friends? Who?"

"You wouldn't know, Dad. You never pay any attention to my friends."

The remark set Arthur's teeth on edge again. He swallowed the irritation. He looked at the kids and smiled hesitantly. He didn't recognize any of them, but that didn't mean he had never seen any of them before. He had never paid much attention to Brandon's friends; they all made him uneasy. Two of the boys were blond and muscular; the third was thin and brown-haired. One of the girls had a thick mane of dark hair, tied back by a barrette, and the other had long blond hair. They appeared to be about Brandon's age.

"Are they from school, Brandon?"

"Uh-hunh. And the Science Club."

"How did they get in here, past the desk?"

"I arranged it."

"You didn't tell me."

Brandon bunched his shoulders. "I wasn't sure they were coming." He faced the far court wall and swung his racket in a windmill fashion. "Come on, Dad, we got an audience, let's play."

Evered glanced again at the children, suppressing a chill that ran through him. "All right, son. You can introduce me when we're done, if they're still here."

"They'll be here."

There was an implication, a tone, in Brandon's voice that made Arthur's stomach tighten. He pushed the feeling away, and pulled up on his white cotton gym shorts. He positioned himself to rally for the serve.

Arthur won the first serve handily. He decided he would not pull back in order to make Brandon look better to his friends. His son had made little effort to learn the mechanics and techniques of the game. Maybe some embarrassment would teach him a lesson.

Evered went full out, putting all his strength into hitting the ball, aiming his shots strategically to make it as difficult as possible for Brandon to return them. To his surprise, Brandon rose extremely well to the challenge, and played much harder and better than Arthur expected. The elder Evered was pleased. Maybe he and Brandon would establish a rapport after all.

Arthur had to work hard for his first point. He served again, and the rally went on and on. At last he missed, and Brandon got the serve.

Whack! Whack! They exchanged volleys. Evered was high on a rush of adrenalin and concentration, making agile turns, reaching, twisting, and jumping. He pushed himself harder, feeling sweat sting his eyes. His face felt flushed and hot. He wished the club would improve the air-conditioning.

He slammed a shot low into the far wall, one of his best techniques. When done properly, the ball rebounded by skimming close to the floor, virtually impossible for an opponent to return. But as Arthur positioned himself for the shot, Brandon maneuvered himself to catch the ball close to the wall, before it skimmed out over the floor. Jesus! It was as though Brandon had *anticipated* him in advance, known the shot he was going to use.

Brandon's return caused Arthur to dash back and to the left, twisting his body to catch the ball just as it ricocheted off the left wall. The rally continued, until Arthur was panting for breath. He was in good shape, but a middle-aged body was no match for the energy of a teenager. Brandon showed no signs of tiring.

Damn, he was not going to fag out in front of Brandon's friends like a worn-out old man! He'd show them all who was master of the game!

Arthur pushed himself harder.

He wasn't sure at what point he became aware that something was wrong, terribly wrong. The warm air inside the court got hotter and thicker, until suddenly he felt as though he were swimming through water. He didn't slacken. Then his vision grayed around the edges, narrowing on him like a tunnel.

The bolt of pain stopped him in mid-swing, dropping him to his knees. An invisible sledgehammer hit him again center in the chest, paralyzing him. He couldn't breathe in or out, or reach for the little tin of nitroglycerin pills buttoned in the back pocket of his shorts.

He went from his knees to his back, rolling on the wooden floor of the court, clutching his chest with his left hand and reaching toward Brandon with his right. His mind screamed, *Brandon, help me! The pills!* but no words came out.

Brandon stared down at him, unmoving, a slight smile playing on his lips. His eyes were strangely radiant. Arthur glimpsed the six children on the other side of the glass. They were staring at him, too, not moving. For God's sake, why weren't they helping him?

An odd, stray thought surfaced through the haze of pain. *My God, they want me to die!*

The sledgehammer came down on Arthur's chest again. He gasped, and knew it was his final breath. A dark curtain of nothingness descended around him.

Alice Evered hurried along the crowded sidewalks of midtown Manhattan. The thick, muggy air magnified the hassles of maneuvering through the throngs of people, and intensified the stench of garbage and pollution. She should have followed her own instincts and cleared out of the city, at least for a few weeks.

Alice had put her slim little Gucci purse around her neck and one shoulder so that it hung crosswise on her body, freeing her to clutch three shopping bags from Bergdorf Goodman, Saks, and Henri Bendel. She had dallied in her shopping more than she'd planned, and now she was stuck in evening rush hour congestion, making her way up and across town from Henri Bendel's to their East Side co-op. There was not a free taxi to be seen, and the buses were jammed. Alice *never* rode the subway.

She checked her watch. She would have to hurry. It was cook's day off, and she wanted to have supper ready for Brandon and Arthur when they returned from their racquetball game at the club.

Alice considered stopping at a pay phone and calling for the limo, but by the time Frank reached her in the slow-moving traffic, she could be home on foot. Thank goodness she had worn flats.

The heat was wilting. Her collar-length hair, fashionably

pulled back from her face and clipped on each side with barrettes, hung limply. Her peach-colored cotton dress was shapeless and wrinkled, and damp with perspiration.

Alice hoped Arthur and Brandon were getting along at the club. The tension between the two had reached unbearable levels in the past few days. Alice had begun to think perhaps she and Arthur should relent and not send Brandon to Switzerland. The boy hated the idea so much she feared it would do more harm than good.

Brandon's thirteenth birthday was coming up next week. Uncharacteristically, he hadn't been pestering them about gifts. She still didn't know what to buy him—his likes and dislikes came and went so fast she could scarcely keep up with them.

Alice stopped for a traffic light. A group of kids came up and stood beside her, laughing and talking. She glanced at them. They appeared to be about Brandon's age, on the edge of puberty. Four girls, giggling and poking each other. Alice turned slightly and noticed two teenage boys behind the girls. There seemed to be some flirting going on.

She smiled to herself. What a silly age.

Alice caught the eye of one of the girls. Goose bumps prickled her skin, despite the heat. The girl was pretty, with blond hair cut short on the top and sides and long in the back—a trendy haircut—and luminous blue eyes. It was the eyes that disturbed Alice. There was a heavy presence in them than was incongruous with the rest of the girl's sweet features.

She shivered again and averted her gaze. The walk signal flashed on. Alice hesitated, intending to let the girls go ahead of her. But they lingered, whispering to each other. The boys also hung back, waiting for the girls.

Alice stepped off the curb, forgetting about the kids by the time she was across the street. She pushed her way through the oncoming wave of pedestrians.

She was halfway through the next block when Alice got the feeling she was being followed. *Why, that's ridiculous,* she told herself. She rationalized that she was tired and irritated from the heat and humidity, exacerbated by the fact that she was caught in rush hour.

Nevertheless, the feeling persisted. Alice kept walking but turned her head to glance behind her. A few paces behind was the group of girls, followed by the boys. Nothing unusual about that; hadn't they all been headed in the same direction as she?

Still, Alice could not shrug off a growing sense of foreboding. She kept telling herself nothing was wrong, her imagination had gone haywire from heat and fatigue. Nevertheless, at the next corner she impulsively turned left instead of heading straight on. She told herself it was because the sidewalk ahead of her had looked too crowded.

The block Alice chose was torn up with the construction of a high-rise tower. Part of the sidewalk was closed off, and a narrow pedestrian path had been fashioned with sheets of plywood. A plywood wall ringed the construction pit, and a plywood roof covered the pedestrian walkway.

Construction work was still going on, and the noise of jackhammers and heavy machinery jangled her nerves. Men were operating cranes, swinging heavy loads. Steel girders rose some twenty stories in the air, and sounds of riveting and hammering drifted down to the street level.

Alice hated construction sites and generally avoided them. She always had the paranoid fear that something would fall on her head. She turned to retreat to the corner. She did a sharp intake of breath. The group of teenagers was not far behind her. They, too, had turned left.

They're following me! Alice thought, then immediately rejected the idea as absurd. It was nothing more than coincidence that they were taking the same route. At some point, they would go separate ways.

Alice hesitated. For a reason she could not identify, she did not want to walk back and pass the teenagers. She spun on her heel and walked rapidly toward the construction zone. Her shopping bags dragged on her arms.

She squeezed through the walkway by turning sideways and holding one arm out in front of her and one behind. The construction noise seemed magnified, ringing in her ears. By the time she reached the end of the covered walkway, she realized she had been holding her breath, and let it out in a big sigh.

Alice glanced to the rear. The teenagers trailed her. Her heart began to thump in her chest. She wanted to confront them and shout, "Why are you following me?" But it was irrational. Crazy.

The covered walkway did not extend to the end of the construction zone. Alice quickened her pace. The plywood wall ended and was replaced by a chicken-wire fence. Out of the left corner of her eye, Alice was aware of men and machinery moving. The dust in the air clogged her lungs.

Alice did not know that twenty floors above her, a heavy steel wrench lay on an I-beam, carelessly left behind by a worker who had gone off shift. None of the remaining workers noticed it, or realized how the vibrations of their work was causing the wrench to slip closer to the edge of the beam.

The wrench slipped closer, until it teetered for a split second. It plummeted to the ground. It struck Alice just left of the center of her skull, killing her instantly.

Not far away from the construction site, Brandon impassively watched horrified employees of the Manhattan Royal Athletic Club try in vain to revive his father while they waited for an ambulance to plow through traffic. His friends had disappeared in the commotion, according to plan.

Brandon's head buzzed and he felt slow and groggy. A man pumped his father's chest and administered mouth-to-mouth resuscitation. Brandon knew it would do no good. But let them find out for themselves.

He knew the instant his mother died.

A voice said, "Oh my God, help him. Help that poor boy! He's in shock."

Someone rushed to his side as he fainted.

CHAPTER Sixteen

Stern looked up as his secretary opened the door to his office. Her name was Judy. Connie had long since gone on to other jobs, and Judy was the latest in the line of successors. Good secretaries were getting harder and harder to find and keep.

Judy said, "Mr. and Mrs. Tate are here with Brandon Evered."

"Have the Tates wait in the conference room. I want to see Brandon first, alone. Give me about five minutes before you bring him in."

Judy nodded and closed the door. Stern shuffled through the papers before him on the desk. They related to the Evered estate. The will had already been read; Brandon stood to be a rich young man in a few years.

Small consolation, Stern thought, for a thirteen-year-old boy whose parents are dead, and who witnessed the death of his father.

But not his real father. Rainer wondered if the boy had ever suspected the truth—that he was, well, sort of "adopted," that his mother was natural, and his real father was a faceless, nameless entity out of a test tube. Stern picked out the envelope that had contained the sealed and secret codicil to the Evereds' will. He reexperienced the cold shock that had run through him the first time he had read it, on the day of the Evereds' deaths, and he had learned of their decision to seek the services of the Park Avenue Family Planning Center. Brandon was never to know. Privately, Stern questioned the wisdom of this, and also the practicality of it. But, those were the wishes of his deceased clients, and he had to honor them.

The door opened and Judy ushered in a tall, lean blond-haired boy, and introduced the two of them. *My God, he's striking*, Stern thought. He had met Brandon only once before, when he was much younger and smaller. Arthur had seldom talked about him, but that was characteristic of the privacy of the man.

He wondered, *if I had a son, would he be so striking?* He caught himself. There were no sons, no daughters, no wife, and there never would be. Family was not meant to be part of his life. He was forty-nine. Women still considered him attractive, but his relationships were transitory. He had devoted fourteen years to getting the demons out of him.

He had to maintain *control*, and it took every ounce of his energy. The voices were at bay at last, and he was determined they were going to stay that way.

Rainer rose and stepped around his desk to extend his hand to Brandon, and offered him a seat on the white leather sofa in his office. Stern chose a matching armchair at right angles to the sofa. He wanted this talk to be friendly and informal.

"You've changed a lot since I last saw you," he began. "You probably don't remember, but I met you once before, when you were about six." Stern smiled.

"I don't remember," Brandon said coldly. He did not smile.

Stern was taken aback at the boy's icy demeanor. His blue eyes held a hostility that seemed uncharacteristic for a teenager. Perhaps it was the migraine headaches. Stern had heard the boy had suffered a lot of them since the deaths. He said, "I'm sorry about your parents."

"I'm not. They hated me." Brandon looked at the emerald-colored pile carpet.

Stern suddenly felt out of his depth. He had no idea how to respond. He decided to move on quickly. "I want to talk to you, Brandon, as one man to another about your future. You know, of course, that your parents were quite wealthy, and left you a great deal of money. Some of it is in trust to provide for your care and schooling now. The rest will be held in trust until you reach twenty-one, when it will be turned over to you."

"I already know that," Brandon snapped.

"Of course. I just wanted to reiterate that your future is secure."

"I'm not a dummy. I understand all that trust stuff. What do you want from me?"

Stern crossed his legs. He reminded himself that Brandon had a genius I.Q., and he should not be surprised at precocious behavior. Still, the boy's coldness was unsettling. Since a "brotherly chat" approach wasn't working, he decided to be more "lawyerly."

"What I want from you is honesty about guardianship. Because you are not old enough to live on your own, you are a ward of the court. You must have a guardian."

A great, impatient sigh escaped Brandon. "Can't anybody understand that I'm going to live with Mr. and Mrs. Tate? Jeff Tate is my best friend."

"Brandon, there are certain legal procedures that must be followed in a case like this. Mr. and Mrs. Tate *have* applied to be your guardians. So has your uncle, your mother's brother, who lives in Minnesota."

"*No!* Not him! Never!"

"As a blood relative, I'm afraid his right to guardianship supersedes the Tates', and a judge is likely to rule in his favor."

"I'll run away first! He'll send me away, just like Mom and Dad were going to do."

"What do you mean, send you away?"

"They were going to send me to Switzerland this fall, to go to some yucky boarding school. I *hate* Switzerland! I'm *glad* they're dead, so I don't have to go!"

Stern had difficulty controlling his reaction to such unbridled hate. He put on his courtroom face. "I see. Well, I don't see any reason to pursue those plans if you feel so strongly."

Brandon slumped into the sofa in relief.

"You *do* want to live with the Tates? If you wish, I can appeal to the court to appoint someone else as your guardian."

"It's got to be the Tates," Brandon insisted. "I won't be separated from my best friend. I want to stay at Winston."

Poor kid, thought Stern. *He's clinging to whatever he can. No wonder he's lashing out.* He said, "Then I will help you do that." He stood up.

Brandon jumped to his feet. "I won't have to go to my creepy uncle's?"

"We'll try to persuade him that you'll be better off with the Tates. No promises, though. Thank you for coming today, Brandon. I'll be seeing you again soon."

After Brandon left, Stern waited a few minutes before calling in the Tates to discuss court procedures for guardianship. The presence of the boy lingered in his office like a bad aftertaste.

He went back to his desk, where his attention returned to the Evered codicil. Dr. Edward Reston didn't know it yet, but he, also, was about to become rich.

The small waiting room of the Park Avenue Family Planning Center was empty when Stern pushed open the door at 6 P.M. A rush of cold air greeted him; the air-conditioning was turned up higher than in the rest of the building. It made him shiver, but it was a welcome respite from the thick summer heat in the streets.

He took in the decor. At first glance, it looked neat and tasteful; then he noticed that the furniture was a bit worn, the white carpet rather gray, the lampshades in need of replacement.

Stern went to the reception window, where a grim-faced woman in a white nurse's uniform stood, awaiting him. Her name tag read "N. DeWitt." It was hard to judge her age. Her hands and body said late thirties, but her face looked much older, as though years of problems and worries had eroded the flesh and carved in lines and wrinkles.

"Mr. Stern?" Her eyes were hard and suspicious.

"Yes." He wondered if this were the same woman who had given him such a difficult time on the telephone, when he was trying to set up an appointment with Reston. His secretary had been unable to get beyond explaining that he was an attorney who had business with the doctor, before the receiver was slammed in her ear. Stern himself hadn't fared much better, until he finally convinced the woman on the other end of the line that his business was urgent—but confidential.

DeWitt's lips thinned to a mean line. She seemed to be struggling with something inside. She blurted, "You're not Gloria's lawyer, are you? I've not heard of you, but she's always hiring somebody new, and I'm *not* going to allow you to harass the doctor!"

"Gloria?"

"*You* know—Mrs. Reston. Or should I say, the ex-Mrs. Reston?" DeWitt's voice was full of contempt.

Stern vaguely remembered meeting a Mrs. Reston at a charity dinner. Thirteen or fourteen years ago, wasn't it? So the marriage had hit the skids, which meant Reston probably was in financial trouble. Stern said, "No, I'm not representing Mrs. Reston."

DeWitt looked at him as if he were lying. "Just the same,

the doctor's got enough problems. I won't let you see him if you're here to give him another one."

The door to the waiting room opened. Stern recognized Edward Reston, considerably grayer and aged since that long-ago charity bash at the Waldorf. He wondered if he had aged as much himself. He didn't want to think so.

"It's all right, Nancy," Reston said. "Come in to my office, Mr. Stern."

Stern looked around Reston's office as he settled himself into a chair in front of the doctor's desk. The obligatory diplomas were hung on one wall, along with a collection of photographs, apparently of the doctor in younger days, posed in what appeared to be laboratory settings. His bookshelf was full of leather-bound medical and scientific volumes. The doctor himself seemed much grimmer than the jaunty, irreverent man Stern remembered, and Rainer had the impression the demeanor was not temporary, but an accumulation over the years.

Stern said, "You may not recall, doctor, but we met some years ago at a charity dinner at the Waldorf."

Reston looked blankly at him for a moment, then recognition spread over his features. "Of course. Your name and face seemed so familiar—I was trying to place them..." His voice trailed off. He sat down with a weariness. "I'm sorry if Nancy gave you a bad time. She's very—" he finished the sentence with a gesture that Stern could interpret however he wanted. "Would you like a drink, Mr. Stern? Coffee?"

Stern shook his head. "I'll get right to the point. I'm here on behalf of my deceased clients, Arthur and Alice Evered."

A look of panic seized Reston. His eyes widened and he gripped the edge of his desk. He stammered, "I—I read about their deaths. But there must be some mistake—"

"No mistake." Stern put his attaché case on his lap and opened it. "I understand you maintain strict confidentiality about your clients, and I will honor that. But the Evereds left behind documentation of their, er, treatment here in 1973."

He glanced over the top of his raised attaché lid. Reston still looked panicked. "I'm not here to cause you concern, doctor. In fact, I'm sure you'll like what I have to say."

Stern extracted a legal-size manila folder with a sheaf of papers held inside by a metal clip. He shut his case. "You may recall that the Evereds are survived by a son, Brandon, age thirteen. They were always extremely grateful that you enabled them to have a son. They provided for you in their will, out of that gratitude."

Reston seemed to have difficulty absorbing the words. "They—*provided* for me?"

Stern opened the manila folder and flipped through the papers. "You are to receive a lump sum of one million dollars from their estate. There—"

Reston interrupted. "*One million dollars?*" The panic had changed to shock.

"That's right. There are conditions, of course. The money is to be used to create a foundation for research in fertility. Everything is spelled out here." He held out the folder. "I suggest you read over this at your leisure."

Reston was still stuck on the revelation of money. "*One million dollars? Lord!*"

Stern wondered if the man had slipped his gears over the years. He seemed out of touch.

Reston jabbed his finger toward the door of his office. "Don't tell *her*," he whispered.

Stern blinked and placed the folder on top of his attaché. "My involvement is strictly between the two of us. What you tell anyone else is your own business."

Reston nodded. "Good, good." He rose from his chair and went to a cupboard, which he opened to reveal a liquor stash. "Scotch, Rainer?" Suddenly they were buddies. Reston's hands shook as he took out a glass and a decanter.

Stern relented. "A shot, neat."

"Must... *all* of the money go to this foundation?" Reston kept his eyes on the liquor as he poured.

Stern knew immediately what the doctor meant. He also

knew that a sharp attorney could find loopholes in the Evereds' conditions to avert the funds to other uses. But that was Reston's affair. He said, "I can only advise you of the terms established by my late clients."

Reston handed him a glass of Scotch. Stern put his attaché on the floor and rose to his feet.

The doctor licked his lips. "The reason I ask—you see, my wife and I—Nancy and I—"

I already got the picture. Affair with nurse breaks up marriage; vengeful wife takes husband to cleaners.

"—I'm in a tight spot at the moment," finished Reston.

"I suggest you obtain your own counsel before you sign the papers," answered Stern.

Reston's head bobbed nervously. "Absolutely, absolutely." He took a deep breath. "Well, this certainly is good news." He clinked glasses with Stern. "Cheers." He took a swallow, then his face clouded. "Of course, I'm dreadfully sorry about the Evereds. I remember them as fine people. And so generous. I never dreamed..."

Stuff it, you insincere bastard, thought Stern. He suddenly disliked Edward Reston. He was a changed man, changed from an idealistic pioneer of science and medicine to a grasping, self-centered paranoiac.

Stern turned away from the doctor to hide his feelings, and walked to the wall of framed diplomas and photographs. He looked at them absently, his thoughts elsewhere.

Suddenly he realized his eyes were held by a black-and-white photograph of Reston and an older man. Judging from the youth on Reston's face, the photo must have been taken about fifteen to twenty years earlier. The two men were dressed in white lab coats and stood, beaming, with arms linked around each other's back. The older man was tall and lean, almost gaunt, with a thick shock of light hair, and a neatly trimmed full beard. His eyes were sharp and intense, and very unsettling. They seemed to hold Stern in a spell. He shivered.

"That's the man who's really responsible for the existence of this clinic," said Reston, coming up behind Stern.

"Who is he? He looks familiar."

"Dr. John Heineman. The pioneer of biogenetic engineering."

Stern mulled the name. "Heineman? No, I don't believe I know him. He must look like someone I've met before."

"Heineman used to be director of the Klein Laboratory of Applied Biogenetics, up in Purchase."

"Used to be? Where is he now?"

"I don't know." The doctor seemed embarrassed.

Stern said, "He established your clinic?"

"No, I did. But I couldn't have done it without John. He was my mentor. Pulled me out of Massachusetts General and steered me into biogenetics and fertility. He trained me, gave me inspiration. If you ever had a mentor, Rainer, I'm sure you know what I mean."

Stern was silent. *I, too, have had inspiration*, he thought. The tattoo from Auschwitz burned on his wrist. *My inspiration is a line of tombstones stretching to infinity.*

"Heineman's background is interesting," Reston volunteered chattily. "He's from Austria. Lived through the Holocaust. He's Jewish, you see."

Rainer held his breath. Was that why the man seemed so familiar? Had his face registered on the memory of a small boy in a concentration camp?

"He was never imprisoned in one of the big concentration camps, but he did spend years in hiding." Reston shook his head. "John's story sounds like something straight out of a movie."

"Amazing," murmured Stern.

Reston looked at him. "You've got a bit of an accent. Similar to John's but not nearly as pronounced."

"I was born in Germany." Stern offered no more. He stared at the photo of Heineman. There was an arrogance in the man's countenance. Perhaps it was arrogance at not having had to suffer. Stern was certain that John Heineman was a man he would not like.

While Stern was meeting with Reston, "Mr. Inferior" braced himself at the American Museum of Natural History for the weekly onslaught of the Junior Science Club.

"Mr. Inferior" was actually Rupert Baines, a big, lumbering black man of fifty-five who worked as a night security guard at the museum. He was easygoing with most people, with one notable exception—the members of the Junior Science Club.

The kids were monsters, pure and simple. When they came through the entrance where he was stationed, they made cutting racial remarks. If that weren't enough, their presence in the museum made him nervous. It was like some dark energy had invaded the place.

The nastiest of the bunch was the one who had dubbed him "Mr. Inferior." The kid was tall and gangly with short blond hair, and he usually showed up with two other blond boys who looked like thugs.

Baines glanced out the open door of his post. *Speak of the whitey devil.* Bearing down on him was Gangly and his two bullies. Rupert tensed. Maybe this time they would blast on in without insulting him.

Gangly was wearing a white T-shirt with a slogan printed across the chest: "Beam me up, Scotty, there's no intelligent life down here." The two bullies were dressed like twins in faded blue jeans and plain yellow T-shirts that had been ripped of their sleeves and collars.

For a moment, Baines thought his prayer would be answered, and the kids would ignore him. His hopes were dashed. Gangly and his bullies halted in front of him.

Gangly pointed to the slogan on his shirt. "Hey, Mr. Inferior, I wore this just for you. You can read, can't you?" The bullies snickered.

Baines squirmed. If he answered them, he would suffer

more humiliation. If he ignored them, they would heckle him until he answered them. If he got angry, they might get violent, and if he got in a fight with kids—even if he didn't start it—he would lose his job. They would run home to Rich and Powerful Daddy and Mommy, and phone calls would be made to the director of the museum, and his ass would be in a red-hot sling.

Any way he cut it, Rupert Baines came out the loser. He said nothing.

"Whatsa matter, Mr. Inferior?" prodded Gangly. "You deaf as well as dumb?" The bullies snickered again.

A knot of rage grew in Rupert's stomach. What this kid needed was a good thrashing. He bottled his rage and stood up. His physical presence was imposing. "I haven't done anything to you kids. Why don't you run along to your club meeting?"

The boys stared up at him, not in the least intimidated. God, they had wicked eyes! If Rupert's mother were alive, she'd say the devil owned those eyes.

The tension between Baines and the boys was thick and heavy. Rupert's temples throbbed. With a shock, he realized that he was *afraid* of them.

The telephone on his desk shrilled. Baines jumped and answered it, trying not to shake. It was a guard from another post in the museum, doing a routine check. He listened with only part of his attention.

Gangly looked more malevolent than ever. Baines feared they would wait for him to get off the phone, and mumbled into the receiver to prolong the conversation.

Then Gangly made a signal and the boys departed, heading for their meeting room. Baines ended the conversation and replaced the receiver with an enormous sigh of relief. His hand trembled, and his stomach fluttered. Fury and humiliation mixed and boiled within him.

Rich whitey snot-nosed brats.

* * *

"The meeting of the Secret Society of Loki will come to order."

Brandon stood at the head of the classroom near the Hayden Planetarium, flanked by Jeff and Jason. Mr. Finley had just fled to the basement for his two-hour cup of coffee, and the thirteen members of the secret society were ready to get down to business. To Finley and the outside world, they were still the Junior Science Club, but there were no outsiders among the ranks anymore. All four nerds had been "encouraged" to drop out. Brandon had seen to that.

Brandon examined each of the faces in the room, probing for the thoughts behind them. He was getting better at that, since he had discovered for himself he could do it alone, and then had taught himself how to slowly strengthen the ability. It gave him a power above the others in the group. He still could not "read" thoughts per se, but he could sense attitudes and feelings, like when someone disagreed with him but said the opposite. His ability worked best on his blood brothers and sisters, and only when he was near them. He couldn't sit in his room at the Tates' co-op on the West Side and figure out what Tommy was thinking across town—though Brandon wished he could. Ever since the "eliminations" had started, Tommy was causing a lot of trouble. Even now, with Tommy not more than six feet away from him, Brandon was having difficulty getting a fix on his thoughts.

"This is the first meeting since Operation Freedom," Brandon said, referring to the elimination of his parents. "Does anyone have any trouble to report?"

The members of Loki were silent.

"Then we got away with it," Brandon concluded, smiling. "Simple. Does anyone have any problems that need solutions?"

The twelve followers glanced at one another.

"Melissa," Brandon said. She had not said a word or given any signal; he had sensed her thoughts.

She looked uncomfortable.

"I know you don't feel ready to talk about it, but let's get it into the open," Brandon said. "We can help you."

Melissa's pretty porcelain features twisted; she looked about ready to cry. "Mom's going to move," she blurted. "She's taking a job in California, and she says I have to go with her."

Several of the children hissed in disapproval.

"We can't have that," said Brandon. "We have to stick together. She won't let you go live with your dad?"

Melissa shook her head. "Dad doesn't want me. But even if he did, Mom wouldn't allow it. They've hated each other since the divorce. I've tried *everything*, but she says I absolutely have to go."

"Run away," suggested Tommy. "We'll hide you."

Brandon glared at Tommy. "Running away is no solution! Mrs. Holliday would send out the police and everyone else she could think of. If we're going to solve the problem, we have to solve it for *good*."

"Elimination," said Jason. "I vote for elimination."

"Aye," said Michael. "Elimination."

"Look," said Tommy. "That sort of stuff is going to get us into trouble sooner or later. Besides, it's . . . not right."

Brandon was pleased with the swell of opposition that arose from the others. "Seems everyone else feels differently, Tommy. You got anything else brilliant to say?"

Tommy shrugged.

Brandon called for a vote. "All those in favor of eliminating Mrs. Holliday, signify by raising their right hand."

Ten hands shot up. Hesitantly, Tommy raised his.

Brandon added his own assenting vote. "Melissa?"

Eyes downcast, she twiddled her thumbs and chewed on her lower lip. "She's a bitch," she said. "I hate her." She raised her hand.

Brandon nodded. "Okay, we'll work up an action plan. Now, there's one other item of business. Remember that old guy nut case who met us in the park? Well, I stole some papers off him. It seems there is another man in town who knows about us—someone he told. A doctor Edward Reston."

"So?" said Elizabeth.

"So, we find out about this doctor and keep an eye on him. If he makes trouble for us—" Brandon drew his index finger across his throat. "I appoint a committee to spy on him. Let's see..." His eyes scanned the group. "Mike. Samantha. And Tommy." Brandon grinned.

"What else was in the papers?" Tommy asked.

"Nothing much. Junk." Brandon looked at his watch. "Before Mr. Finley comes back, we've got to do our mind exercises, and then get some work done on the telescopes. Everybody break up into their teams. Tonight let's practice the magic carpet linkup."

The twelve mixed and divided into four groups of three. They moved chairs to the sides and sat on the floor in little triangles.

The magic carpet linkup was an exercise developed and led by Brandon. Before confronting Hans Messner, he already had realized the pranks they played on others could be taken one step further. The papers he had stolen from the German had proved to be fascinating, describing latent "psychic powers" he and his friends were supposed to have been born with. The papers did not describe how this came to be—why them and not others—but that wasn't important. The papers included a plan for developing these powers over a period of years. Brandon was fascinated to learn how they could improve their powers with exercises. It was a great idea, and he adopted it. The magic genie was out. That was kid stuff. Laser beams of thought energy were in.

Brandon did not share Messner's information with the group, except for mentioning the connection to Dr. Edward Reston. He elected to use the information to improve his own powers first, so that he would always be ahead of everyone else. He would lead them through psychokinesis, the moving of objects, which he preferred to call "magic carpet" because it sounded less threatening. He would refine their telepathy and learn how to control the violent energy none of them understood, the killing force.

Brandon had liked Messner's goals of establishing them as a ruling class. But he would do it himself, his own way, without outside interference. Already, his exercises had brought progress. Patterns were emerging. Together, the children could be very powerful; individually less so. Generally, it took a minimum of three to do "heavy duty" acts such as moving large objects. At least six had to be together to accomplish an "elimination."

Thought communication came more easily and was more accurate, though for some peculiar reason, distance was still a limiting factor. According to what Brandon had read about telepathy, it should be possible no matter what distance separated those who were linked. But for the members of the Secret Society of Loki, the power diminished with distance.

And, each child still possessed the ability to shut the others out with a mental "shield." Happily for Brandon, shields were temporary, for they required energy to maintain. Brandon was no longer worried about Tommy because he knew the potential rival could not keep up his privacy forever. Tommy's shield waxed and waned, and when his resistance was low and Brandon was near enough, he picked up on Tommy's feelings. Tommy was merely apathetic to a lot of Brandon's plans. No threat there.

It was Brandon's goal to be able to do everything himself without having to rely on the others. He was practicing on his own, and growing in strength daily.

He looked at the groups and said, "Okay, is everybody ready for magic carpet? We'll do chairs tonight. Let's try to keep movement smoother, and not smash them up." He watched while they began concentrating. They were his army, an army that needed no weapons. An army of invisible soldiers.

Brandon liked being in charge. He liked having power. No one was going to stop him from getting more of it.

CHAPTER Seventeen

About two weeks after his meeting with Brandon Evered, Stern was having lunch at 21 with a client. They were down to coffee. The woman excused herself for a few minutes.

Stern leaned back in his chair. The restaurant was abuzz with the talk of its well-dressed, well-heeled patrons. He let the surrounding activity enter his sphere of awareness. During lunch, his attention had been focused completely on his client and the business they were discussing, and he had shut out everything else.

He took a sip of coffee. Two women at a table near him were involved in an animated, gossipy conversation. He glanced at them and then looked away. One of them, dressed in a bright yellow silk dress, had a strong, nasal voice that rose above the rest of the noise. Without consciously eavesdropping, he zeroed in on what she was saying.

"—and now poor little Melissa is a virtual orphan." Stern thought of Brandon Evered, and his attention was piqued.

"Her father doesn't want her?" the woman's companion said. Her voice was lower, and he had difficulty hearing her.

"What, George Holliday take on responsibility? All he ever wanted was Marilyn's money. It's a good thing she divorced him. He hardly got a dime, you know. She had a sharp attorney."

"Maybe George sabotaged her car for revenge."

"That's stretching it," said the woman in the silk dress. "She was caught in the middle of that seven-car pileup on the West Side Highway. Just one of those things."

"So what's going to happen to Melissa?"

"Well, with all those millions in trust, she's set for life. But I understand that the parents of one of her friends are going to seek custody."

"Who's that?"

"Perkins. Taylor and Lee Perkins. Their daughter attends the same school as Melissa."

"I don't think I know them," the companion said.

"You know what?" The woman in yellow lowered her voice conspiratorially. Out of the corner of his eye, Stern could see her lean across the table. He strained to hear the words. "I heard that George may not really be the father of Melissa."

"You're kidding! Who is?"

"I don't know, and I would just die to find out. But Roberta told me that Marilyn confided in her once that she was having difficulty getting pregnant and was thinking of adopting."

"But she *had* Melissa."

"Exactly," said yellow dress with a triumphant note.

"So? It still could have been George. Maybe it just took a while."

"Well! George never did pay much attention to the poor child. And now she's thirteen and her mother's gone, and he won't have anything to do with her. That says a lot."

"I wonder if it was Greg Kennedy? I always thought Marilyn had a thing for him," mused the companion.

"If you ask me, Melissa doesn't look much like either George *or* Marilyn," scoffed yellow dress. The two women laughed.

Stern saw his client making her way back to the table. He tuned out and stood up.

A teenage heiress taken in by her friend's family. He wouldn't have thought much of it, if he hadn't recently handled the Evered case. But the snatch of conversation had left a vivid impression upon him.

The headline in the morning *Times* a few days later leaped out at Stern like a neon sign. The wording was understated in typical *Times* fashion. But it wasn't the wording that stunned him, it was the news itself—and the "coincidence."

> *John A. McCord Dies;*
> *Chief of Barstar Corp.*

It was one of the lead articles on the obituary page. For a moment, Stern's eyes were riveted to the headline, unable to move below to the text. Barstar was one of his firm's major clients.

He turned his gaze out the smoked glass window of his limousine, at the cityscape moving past him. It was 6:30 A.M., too early for the rush hour throngs, but not too early for the fast trackers heading for the financial district in lower Manhattan. He had an urgent desire to speak, to exclaim over the obit and wave it in the air, but there was no one else in the black leather back seat of the Lincoln stretch, and only his driver in the front.

It can't be, Stern whispered to himself. John McCord is —was—only forty-seven.

He read the obit. John A. McCord, chief executive officer and president of Barstar Corp., a multinational conglomerate, had collapsed of a heart attack the day before and died instantly.

At the time of the attack, McCord had been at home with his family. He was pronounced dead at the scene. He was survived by a wife, Carol, thirty-nine, and a thirteen-year-old son, Jason.

For some reason, the news rattled Stern more than it should have. The Barstar account was handled by Ben Goldman. Stern had met McCord but a few times in the past several years. He recalled McCord as an autocratic, overbearing man, typical of that breed of hyper-driven executive who sacrifices all for his career—a lot like the late Arthur Evered. Sensitivity to others was not one of his strong suits. Perhaps it wasn't so surprising that he drove himself into a fatal heart attack by age forty-seven.

Stern thought about it all the way to the office, and when he saw Goldman, he brought it up.

"Such a shame, such a shame," said Goldman, shaking his head and clucking his tongue. "I got the call about it last night." He rummaged through his desk. "A man at the peak of his powers. Apparently he had a heart condition that didn't manifest itself with warning signs until it was too late."

Stern shifted his weight against the doorjamb of Goldman's office. "How's Mrs. McCord holding up?"

"In shock and under sedation, of course. But I feel worse for the boy." Goldman found a clean handkerchief in a middle drawer. He took off his wire-rimmed glasses and cleaned them. He never used the handkerchief that he kept in the breast pocket of his suit.

"It's always hardest on the children," Stern said.

"They didn't get along, he and his son, Jason. But what parent does with a teenager?" Ben sighed. "I should know. I have two myself."

"I imagine Jason will have to come to terms with a lot of guilt over his father dying while they were angry with one another."

"Right, and no trust fund will heal that. The shock in this case had to be particularly severe. The young fellow was having a party at home when it happened, right in front of his friends. You can imagine what that did to all of them."

A shudder went through Stern. "Just like Brandon," he murmured. *Brandon Evered again.*

"What?"

"I'm reminded of Arthur Evered. He collapsed and died while he and his son were on the racquetball court. I believe some of Brandon's friends were watching."

Goldman nodded solemnly. "What a tragedy that was, too. You know, I believe Jason McCord attends the same school as that Evered boy. Winston?"

"Yes," Stern said, surprised. "Winston."

Goldman inspected his glasses and then put them back on. "Well, teenage boys tend to bottle everything inside them, but perhaps those two will find a way to lean on each other."

Stern went to his own office with a hollowness growing in his stomach. What a strange coincidence, that three parents of two boys who attended the same small, exclusive school should die so close together.

...their daughter attends the same school as Melissa.... No, thought Stern, that would be too bizarre for the girl he had heard about in 21 to also be a student at Winston.

...she was caught in the middle of that seven-car pileup on the West Side Highway...

Arthur Evered, dead of a heart attack...

John A. McCord, dead of a heart attack...

Alice Evered, killed in a construction accident...

Rainer, you're imagining connections that are preposterous. You have more important business to worry about, like Dyson versus Clements.

A buzzing started in his head, voices clamoring to get closer. Stern pushed them back. *I will not listen*, he said to himself, repeating the words over and over again until the buzzing faded away.

The funeral service for John A. McCord took place three days later, at the flower-filled High Ridge Presbyterian Church in Greenwich, Connecticut, where the McCords maintained a weekend estate. Stern was present, along with Ben Goldman, and Allen Larkin, another partner in the law firm. The guests numbered about one hundred; John McCord had wielded a far and powerful reach in his business and community.

The day was gray and drizzly. It had rained on the day of the Evereds' service, too. Stern was getting to feel an old hand at funerals. He hated them.

The memory of Leon's austere service kept rising up within him, fresh and sharp as though it had happened yesterday instead of more than a decade before.

Throughout the service and eulogy, Stern's attention wandered, drifting back in time to black images when he and Leon were subjected to the cruelties of the young Nazi named "Dr. Hans." Death always made him think of the camps, for the camps *were* death. Living death.

Approximately two dozen of the guests went on to the graveside for the interment. The three attorneys had not planned to be among them, but Carol McCord insisted. Her husband had known Ben Goldman for a long time.

A green canopy was erected over the grave to protect against the rain, but it wasn't large enough to accommodate everyone, and some of the guests had to huddle under umbrellas, outside the canopy.

It wasn't until Stern was standing in the ring around the grave that he noticed Brandon Evered with a raven-haired girl about his age. He hadn't seen them at the church; they must have been sitting behind him. But now they joined the boy he recognized as Jason McCord, their eyes solemn, faces like masks. He caught Brandon's eye and gave him a nod and hesitant smile, but he and the other two looked through him, as though he were glass.

He felt cold again. They were such odd children.

Then Rainer noticed three more children, two boys and a girl, who appeared at the side of Brandon, Jason, and the dark-haired girl. They whispered among each other, the six of them. He wondered if the three kids, plus Brandon and the girl, were at Jason's party the night his father died.

Stern had an instinctive dislike for the unknown children,

even though he had never before seen them. There was something familiar about all of them, a look in the eye, a... *presence*. That's what it was, a presence. A negative presence.

Now they were all looking at him, as if he had waved to get their attention. Or were they? They were staring in his direction, he thought, but maybe they were looking at something else.

Their gaze made him extremely uncomfortable.

They are of one mind.

What an odd thought to spring up. Stern shook his head slightly.

The minister was offering a final prayer, committing the body to the earth, ashes to ashes, dust to dust. The coffin was lowered into the ground. Carol McCord stepped forward and tossed after it a handful of dirt and a single white rose. Sobbing quietly, she stepped back.

Jason didn't move. He wasn't looking at the grave, or at his mother. He was still looking at Rainer Stern. It wasn't a friendly look at all.

Jason turned his gaze to Brandon and began walking away from the grave. Brandon shot Stern a final, cold look and then took the girl's hand. "Come on, Melissa," he said.

Melissa!

Stern did not sleep most of the night. His mind clicked through scenarios in which a group of teenagers—perhaps all students of Winston School—methodically murdered their parents. None of his scenarios stood up to scrutiny. All four deaths, the Evereds, McCord, and Mrs. Holliday, had been either accidental or of natural causes, beyond doubt. Stern didn't think any teenagers, no matter how clever, could plot four deaths like that and carry them off without making mistakes. And if they had committed murder and covered it up, they wouldn't be able to maintain their cool for long. Someone would break down and confess.

Stern decided it was a freak string of events that had no connection to one another. *Forget it*, he kept telling himself.

But the children had disturbed him, and his thoughts would not rest. When at last he dozed off, just before dawn, he was roused by a noise in the room. He opened his eyes and saw, in the half light of early morning, Leon standing over him. Leon was dressed in the same shirt and trousers he had worn on the last day of his life, only there was no blood on them. They were clean and neat, and Leon looked in the peak of health, and it seemed like the most natural thing for him to be standing there. He appeared from time to time in Rainer's dreams, for that was one of the ways Stern had managed to contain his "experiences." Dreams were okay. Visions were not.

Stern sat up and said, "Leon, what is it?"

Leon did not reply but kept looking to the side of Stern. Puzzled, Stern followed his gaze and then noticed that the clock on his nighstand said one o'clock, and that was impossible because it was much later than that. He reached out and touched the plastic case, and then looked back at Leon, but Leon was gone.

With a start, Stern realized he had *not* been dreaming. He was fully awake. He had been roused by a noise and had looked up to see Leon, who looked at his broken clock and disappeared. Stern felt his stomach drop, and he started to shiver. He had not had a vision in years.

But he was more upset over the clock. He had looked at it many times during his fitful night, and he would have noticed if it had stopped. How had the hands gone back to one o'clock?

I don't want to know why this happened, he thought, his throat tight and dry. *I don't want to think about it. I never saw Leon*.

The light coming through the blind slats was growing brighter. It had to be at least 5 or 6 A.M. *If I get dressed and go to work, I'll forget about this*, he thought.

Stern got up and went to his dresser. He picked up his watch, a gold Baum & Mercier.

The hands said one o'clock.

Stunned, Rainer put the watch down. He rubbed a hand across his bare chest. *It's like a message. But what on earth is the significance of one o'clock?*

He didn't have the vaguest idea. He got into the shower and turned the water on cold. He didn't want to think about anything but the spray hitting him like ice needles.

When he got out, part of the answer came to him.

The service for John McCord had started at one o'clock in the afternoon.

But there was some other significance about one o'clock, if he could only think of it. With shaky hands, he reset his watch. He went back to the bedside clock and reset that.

The clocks in the kitchen and living room also had stopped at one o'clock. Stern adjusted them, and checked the twenty-four-hour digital clock on his videocassette recorder. It was frozen at 13:00. As soon as he saw it, he had the rest of the answer to the significance of the time. It was the number thirteen.

Brandon Evered was thirteen. So was Jason McCord. And Stern bet Melissa Holliday also was thirteen.

Whatever was going on, he had to get to the bottom of it.

At the office, Stern set aside the stack of work awaiting him and told Judy to hold all calls. He shut his door, always a sign to his colleagues that he did not want to be disturbed.

He called Winston School and asked if a Melissa Holliday was registered as a student. An indignant female voice on the other end informed him that information was not given out over the telephone, and hung up.

Next he tried to locate George Holliday, but there was no such listing under any of three different spellings he tried of the last name. George had probably left town and gone on to greener pastures. It probably wouldn't be difficult to track him down in a day or two, but Stern was in a fever to get answers *now* to the questions burning inside him.

He buzzed Judy. "Cancel all my appointments for the rest of the day. Something has come up." Within minutes, he was out the door, leaving the bewildered secretary stewing over his calendar.

Stern headed for the New York County Courthouse, located in Foley Square in lower Manhattan, not far from his office. He went straight to the basement room where the county clerk kept the records of divorces filed in Manhattan in the State Supreme Court.

He remembered the words of the woman in yellow at 21. *. . . he hardly got a dime, you know, she had a sharp attorney.*

Stern searched the index book for the case number of the divorce. Holiday, Halliday, and Holliday. There were rows of the names in all three spellings. Then he found the one he was looking for: Marilyn Sims Holliday versus George Evan Holliday. The first two numbers told him the suit had been filed in 1981. He copied the names and number onto a small piece of paper. He looked over the file clerks on duty and picked one, a pretty young woman with an open face.

"Hello," he said cordially, handing her the piece of paper and his business card. "I'm interested in this file."

The young woman was impressed by the name she recognized on the business card. She was used to dealing with lowly law clerks who did the grunt work. She beamed a radiant smile at Stern and bustled off.

She returned quickly, her face clouded over. "I—I'm sorry, Mr. Stern," she stammered, ill at ease at having to refuse an important person. "But without notarized authorization from the parties involved, I can't give you the file. They're sealed, you know, to everyone but. . ." her voice dropped off as she realized she, a mere file clerk, was telling a lawyer his business. Her cheeks turned red.

Stern nodded understandingly. "I'm well aware of that, Miss—?"

"Kurtz. Amy Kurtz."

"Amy Kurtz," he repeated pleasantly. "Have you been working here long? You don't look familiar." In truth, Stern hadn't been to Room 103 in the County Courthouse in a couple of years.

"About two months," Amy answered.

"Two months. You like it?"

She nodded vigorously.

"I imagine there's a lot to learn about what goes on around here."

"It's incredible," she enthused. Stern saw her glance at his left hand. There was no wedding band; no rings at all, in fact.

"Amy," he said, leaning closer. He put his hand on her arm and gently drew her off to one side. "I just need a quick and very small favor."

Amy's smile froze on her face. Her eyes darted back and forth. "I can't give you the file," she said helplessly.

"I don't want the file."

"I don't understand, then."

"I only want the name of the attorney for the plaintiff."

"But I'm not allowed—"

"It will take you less than a minute to go back and check."

Amy nodded slowly, then had second thoughts. "I'd better ask first."

Stern tightened his grip on her arm. "Please don't. I'm in a hurry. It's a very small personal favor, and I always remember people who do me favors, no matter how small."

Her eyes searched his face for a moment. "All right," she said, and left.

She returned and gave Stern the name: Barry Langford III.

Stern had to agree with the gossip's assessment of Barry Langford III—he was a sharp attorney. Langford specialized in matrimonial law, relieving wealthy clients of unwanted spouses, along with a good chunk of their money. An adolescent in his forties, he liked high-profile living and fancied flashy cars and anorexic-looking models. Stern and Langford had met periodically over the years. As an attorney, Stern had grudging respect for Langford. As a man, he had no use for him whatsoever. He did not relish the thought of approaching him about Marilyn Holliday. It was a safe bet that if Langford had handled her divorce, he would be probating her will and making custody arrangements for her daughter.

Stern knew where he could probably find Langford, and have a casual conversation that would avoid the formal overtones of a call to the man's office. At lunchtime, he dropped by the exclusive New York Horizon Club, located in the financial district on the forty-fourth floor of an office building. Stern maintained several club memberships, and this was one of them. They served their purpose for business.

Sure enough, Langford was perched at the clubby bar, his back to the windows that afforded a spectacular view of Manhattan. He was talking to a man Stern did not recognize. Almost as soon as Stern entered the bar, the man got up, slapped Langford on the shoulder, and left.

Stern filled the void and took the empty stool. "Good afternoon, Mr. Langford." He signaled the bartender and ordered a Scotch neat.

"Well, Rainer Stern," Langford said lazily, puffing on his cigarette. He indicated another round for himself, bourbon and water on the rocks. "Haven't seen you around town much lately. Mergers and acquisitions been keeping you busy, eh?"

"Somewhat."

Langford had gained weight since the last time Stern had seen him. He had a puffy, bloated look. His neck bulged over the tight, starched collar of his white shirt. Stern noticed the diamond ring on his right little finger.

Stern skipped the small talk and said, "I wanted to ask

you something about your deceased client, Marilyn Holliday."

Langford nodded and put out his cigarette. He reached out to the box of cigarettes in front of him and lit another. "What do you want, Stern?"

"Actually, information about Melissa, the daughter."

"What for?"

"Something that may concern clients of mine." *Even if they are dead.*

Langford gave a short, harsh laugh. "Mucking around in family court, are you? Isn't that a bit out of your territory?"

"Business clients have private lives. I understand an interested third party wants to take custody of the daughter."

"Whoa. Are you telling me you've dug up some long-lost, fortune-hunting, twice-removed aunt who's going to contest? If you are, you can forget it right now."

The drinks arrived, and Stern took a swallow of his. "My clients have two main concerns. If the answers are satisfactory, I think I can assure you they won't trouble you."

"And they are?"

"One, that Melissa continue to be given the best possible education."

Langford snorted. "For Chrissakes, she's enrolled at Winston. After that, she'll be able to attend any university in the world."

"That's a few years off. Melissa is only . . . er, fourteen?"

"Thirteen," corrected Langford condescendingly.

Stern nodded, absorbing this. "Two, that there be no possibility of George Holliday trying to take custody."

"These birds of yours are easy. You can tell them that as far as Melissa goes, George Holliday has dropped off the face of the earth."

Stern raised his eyebrows. "The father has no interest in the child?"

"You got it in spades, baby."

"Fathers have been known to change their minds."

"Not this one. He isn't the girl's father, anyway."

Stern feigned surprise.

Langford looked irritated. "Come on, Stern, if you'd done your homework, you'd know that."

"How so?" asked Rainer, thinking of the gossips at 21, who were dubious but not certain of Melissa's parentage.

"It came out in the divorce. Very messy in the family."

"As you know, I haven't asked you for permission to review the divorce file, so fill me in."

"Melissa's natural father is an A.D.—anonymous donor, from a sperm bank. It was Marilyn's idea. George was against it from the beginning, but she convinced him to go along with it."

Stern's eyes widened and he looked away. "Really?" he said, trying to keep his voice down to mild interest. "You mean that sperm bank on Park Avenue?"

"There's only one, jocko."

Stern abandoned his drink and stood up. "Thanks, Langford, you've been a big help."

"I take it I won't be hearing from you on behalf of these clients of yours."

"I don't think so."

Langford chuckled. "Sorry to kill your big fee," he said, obviously not sorry at all.

Stern walked out. The information about Melissa Holliday was exactly what he had not wanted to hear.

CHAPTER
Eighteen

"This is a special emergency meeting of the Secret Society of Loki," announced Brandon. He felt extraordinarily tense as he stood before his twelve followers in the stuffy classroom at the American Museum of Natural History. As usual, Mr. Finley had excused himself for his customary "cup of coffee" downstairs.

Brandon was aware that his tension flowed out to the others. They absorbed it and then reflected it back to him, creating a stress that virtually made the air hum.

"Are we in trouble over Mr. McCord?" asked David.

"No and yes," answered Brandon. "No one suspects what really happened, and there's no way to prove it even if they did. But those of us who went to the funeral noticed a man who is forming bad thoughts in his head. His name is Rainer Stern, and he's an attorney. He's got some involvement with my dad's business, and with Jason's dad, and Melissa's mom.

"He's wondering how we're all connected," Brandon went on. "If he gets too curious, he might discover our secrets."

"So what are you saying, Brandon?" asked Lori.

"Anyone who finds out about us has to go, the same way

as the parents and that Messner guy in the park. Period. Otherwise, we'll be separated. What is it, Tommy? Something's bothering you."

Tommy said, "Mr. Stern knows Dr. Reston."

Several of the children whispered among themselves.

"Then he does know about us for sure," said Jason. "They're probably plotting against us."

"Maybe they've already gone to the police," said Jennifer.

Brandon silenced the group with a wave of his hand. "Tell us what you know, Tommy."

"Mr. Stern has been to see Dr. Reston at his office, when I was on spy watch. I saw him go in once, just after the clinic closed. When he came out, there wasn't anything else to do, so I followed him back to his office and found out who he was."

"You're sure it's the same man?"

"Yes. From Goldman, Schoenberg, Larkin, & Stern, right?"

"Right." Brandon squared his shoulders. "It's time for the Invisible Warriors to go into action again."

"You mean we've got to get rid of *both* of them?" said Mike.

"As soon as possible."

"Are we going to sock it to them? Do a big accident in the streets?" Doug rubbed his hands in gleeful anticipation.

"No, dummy, we're not," snapped Brandon. "I said Invisible Warriors. We're going to do it carefully and quietly, and not attract attention."

Lori grimaced. "I don't want to do it anymore."

"You'll do what I tell you to, Lori. Because if you don't, *all* of us will be hurt. Let's vote on it."

Five hands shot up immediately. Jason, Jeff, Melissa, Sarah, and Michael. One by one, the rest of the group added their votes in affirmation. Edward Reston, doctor, and Rainer Stern, lawyer, would have to die.

* * *

The door to the Park Avenue Family Planning Center burst open with such force that it hit the wall and reverberated back. Two girls, dressed in shorts, T-shirts, and sneakers, dashed into the waiting room and tore through the inner door and down the hall. They were laughing and shrieking, one obviously chasing the other in some kind of game.

"You're gonna be It! You're gonna be It!" shouted the one with long blond pigtails.

"No, I'm not," shouted the dark-haired girl in front of her. "Gonna have to catch me first!"

Nancy DeWitt, at the file cabinet, slammed the drawer shut. She shot a look at the receptionist, who was open-mouthed in astonishment at her window. The intrusion had happened so fast, neither knew what to do or say for a moment.

Nancy's face creased in anger. "What in the..." she muttered to herself as she strode out of the office into the hallway. "Girls! Girls! Get out of here at once!"

The girls ignored her. Screaming with laughter, they raced in and out of the clinic's rooms down the hall. The dark-haired girl grabbed the handle of the freezer room, but it was locked. She ran on.

"What are you doing in here?" screeched Nancy, on their heels. "This is a private doctor's clinic! Get out of here immediately!"

The girls plunged into an examination room. Nancy was horrified to hear an adult female scream. Just as she reached the door, the girls bolted out, pushing past her. "I'm sorry, Mrs. Krenfield," Nancy said, looking in on the patient who was waiting for Dr. Reston to see her. "Are you all right?"

"What in the blazes is going on?" the woman answered hotly, thrashing about on the examining table under her sheet.

A male voice bellowed, "For God's sake, what's all the commotion about?"

"Dr. Reston," said Nancy, as the doctor emerged from his private office, where he'd been reviewing the file of Mrs. Krenfield, "I don't—they just ran in—I can't—"

The girls plowed into Reston, making him stumble backward into his office. They chased each other around his desk.

"I've got you now!" shouted the blond girl.

"No, you haven't!"

Reston recovered his balance and marched over to the girls, catching them both by the arm. Nancy and the receptionist stood out of the way. Nancy crossed her arms over her chest as she watched the girls struggle in the doctor's grasp.

"Ow! Hey, mister, we're just playing a game!" protested the dark-haired girl.

"Play it somewhere else!" bellowed Reston. "Get out of here before I call the police!"

The girls, out of breath, looked solemnly at each other. Reston released them. They ran out of the clinic, their giggles drifting after them.

Reston looked at Nancy for explanation. She had none.

Stern's yellow cab crawled up Park Avenue in heavy traffic. The cab was not air-conditioned, and the four open windows did nothing to relieve the stifling heat. Beneath his white cotton shirt, beads of sweat rolled down his stomach. Why hadn't he gotten the hell out of this miserable city for the summer? New York was a pollution-filled steam bath this time of year.

The lanes of traffic inched along. The pace was uncharacteristically slow for 11 A.M.—yet a midday traffic jam was never unusual in Manhattan. Given the incredible density of people and vehicles, it was a wonder the city functioned at all.

Stern glanced out the back window. A teenage boy on a

ten-speed bicycle cut expertly through the cars and passed the cab on the right. The kid looked just like a bicyclist he had seen out the cab down in lower Manhattan. He wore the same outfit—a backward Met cap, red T-shirt, and cutoffs. Well, it couldn't be the same kid.

Stern tracked the bicycle as it weaved through the traffic up ahead. It must be miserable to ride a bike in this heat, but at least the kid was getting somewhere. And he wasn't.

He said out loud, "Driver, I'll get out here."

The taxi was still blocks away from his destination, the Park Avenue Family Planning Center, but Stern had lost patience with the traffic. The driver, a sullen Middle Eastern type who spoke little English, didn't object. He pulled over to the curb.

Stern paid the driver and began walking at a brisk pace. On foot, he made faster progress up the avenue than did the vehicles. He carried only his oyster-colored suit jacket; he had left his attaché back at the office.

He was paying a surprise visit to Dr. Edward Reston.

And he was an angry man.

The sidewalks reflected heat like a furnace. Stern loosened his maize foulard tie. The discomfort of the heat only added to his anger. Edward Reston had a lot of truth to tell.

Just about an hour earlier, Stern had finished inspecting private papers belonging to Mr. and Mrs. John McCord. The papers had been locked in a safety deposit box, and Mrs. McCord had given the law firm permission to access the box. Stern had been looking for one paper in particular, a contract for certain services rendered about fourteen years ago. And he had found it.

He decided immediately to see Reston.

Stern was so intent on the purpose of his visit that he blocked out his surroundings. As he neared the doctor's building, deep in the uptown fashionable residential district of the avenue, he did not notice a boy and a girl on the sidewalk on the opposite side of the street.

But the children noticed him.

The brown-haired boy idly maneuvered a skateboard. The dark-haired girl was perched on a low ledge bordering the sidewalk, sipping a soda and watching the boy.

Michael and Melissa were ready for the arrival of Rainer Stern.

Jason and Jeff, their lookouts posted outside Stern's office building, had reported his departure, communicating silently via their steadily improving mental telepathy. Tommy, on his bicycle, had followed Stern's taxi; the slow pace of the traffic had made it easy for him to keep up.

As Stern got out of the taxi, Tommy signaled to Michael, the mission squad leader, that the lawyer was nearly there. Tommy had completed his assigned role in the mission, and headed away on his bicycle.

Michael stepped off his skateboard as he watched Stern approach on the other side of the street. "Damn! Where's everybody else? They should be here by now. We can't do it without them."

Stern paused outside the building entrance and wiped his brow. He opened the door and went in.

Melissa said, "Don't worry, they'll come. Should we wait out here or go in?"

"We'll wait here for now," Michael answered. He was extremely uptight. Brandon had put him in charge and would hold him responsible for anything that went wrong.

CHAPTER Nineteen

As soon as he entered Reston's clinic, Stern knew he was about as welcome as a carrier of the plague.

The startled receptionist began to say, "Can I help—" and was cut off by Reston's nasty-tempered nurse, who stepped to the reception window.

"The doctor is *busy*."

Was she always this grouchy? For the moment, Stern didn't care as he luxuriated in the air-conditioning. He gave her his firm, not-to-be-refused lawyerly smile. "It's urgent. I'll wait."

Nurse DeWitt was not to be put off either. "He's with a patient. And he has a *full* day. You'll have to make an appointment to come back, Mr. Stern."

She's lying.

"As I said, Miss DeWitt, it's urgent. And personal. I'll wait." He locked his jaws in his not-to-be-refused smile.

The nurse scowled. "If you could tell me what your business is, I'll ask—"

"We seem to be having trouble communicating. Let me repeat two words: 'urgent' and 'personal.'"

Nancy looked uncertain for a moment, and Stern knew he had won.

"He *does* have a few moments free before the next patient," she admitted.

"Fine." Stern waited while Nancy disappeared into the doctor's inner sanctum. He began to feel uncomfortable. A dark foreboding crept over him that made him shiver. The office suddenly felt small and claustrophobic. He tried without success to shrug the feeling off.

Nancy returned and ushered him into Reston's private office.

Reston, his expression harried, rose from behind his desk and extended his hand. "Mr. Stern," he said, his voice flat and insincere. "How nice to see you again."

Stern shook his hand. It was limp. His feeling of foreboding increased. He blinked in the glare of the overhead fluorescent lights. There was a pounding on the ceiling and he looked up.

"There's some remodeling being done upstairs," Reston said. "Heck of a racket. Nancy, no interruptions, please."

When Nancy had gone and shut the door, Reston sat down on the chair behind his desk. Stern took a nearby straight-backed, armless chair and pulled it up to the side of the desk.

The lawyer got right to the point. "I'm here about three former clients of yours: Evered, McCord, and—Holliday. Do you remember them?"

The names had the effect of a bomb blast on Reston. His face blanched and his eyes widened. He quickly recovered, and folded his hands across his stomach. "Of course I remember the Evereds and their generous grant to me. Let me see . . . Holliday and McCord . . . if they were patients of mine, it must have been quite some time ago." He bunched his shoulders disarmingly. "I've treated hundreds of people over the years—I can't remember each one."

"I'll help you, then. They all contracted for your services about fourteen years ago. They all had children—only children—two boys, one girl, who are now thirteen. By a remarkable coincidence, the children are all friends and attend the same exclusive private school. Like most teenagers, they haven't gotten along with their parents. And now Mr. and Mrs. Evered, Mrs. Holliday, and Mr. McCord are dead."

Stern watched Reston closely. The doctor swallowed and averted his vision.

"Really, Mr. Stern, this is all very interesting, but I don't see what the connection is to me..."

"There's something else that's very peculiar about these children. It's in their eyes."

"Their eyes?"

"These three children apparently are not related by blood, yet they share a common trait. It shows in the eyes. This same trait is shared by several other of their friends I've seen. They're related to each other, and I believe their relation to each other has something to do with the fact that four adults are dead." Reston's unease increased. Stern leaned forward. "I have three questions, doctor: What is the connection between these children? How many more like them are there? And why are some of their parents dead?"

"I think you're mad."

"I know what I'm talking about."

"First of all, the children are not related to each other. That's impossible. Yes, the Evereds, Hollidays, and McCords came to me for help. They conceived artificially, and I used different sources for each one."

"That's interesting, Dr. Reston. A moment ago you barely remembered the names. Now you say you remember clearly what you did fourteen years ago to three women."

Reston flushed. "If you're sniffing around for a lawsuit, perhaps I should have my own attorney present before I answer anymore questions."

My, thought Stern, *how quickly he's forgotten the one million dollars I arranged for him from the Evered estate. And the fact that I have never required him to account for how it's being spent.* He said, "I'm here on personal business."

"Well, what *do* you want?" Reston said testily.

"I'm curious, Dr. Reston. Lawyers don't believe in coincidences, you know. So, I'm wondering why four adults are dead. Funny thing, they all had only children who were artificially conceived on your premises, and at about the same time. Funny thing, they all sort of look like each other, in an odd way. Funny thing, they all inherit a lot of money. And one more funny thing, doctor—so did you."

Reston sputtered. "This is an outrage, Mr. Stern. How dare you—"

"Dr. Reston," Stern interrupted, "it has been my experience in the law profession that whenever people are outraged, they have something to hide."

"And what do you think I might be hiding?"

"I have no idea. That's why I thought I'd drop in for a friendly chat."

"If you'll excuse me now, I'm quite busy—"

"Premeditated murder."

Reston's already pale face went one more shade whiter. *"What?"*

"You heard what I said, Dr. Reston. Premeditated murder. These children are killing their parents, and somehow they're making it look accidental."

Reston stared down at his bandaged hand. It shook. "Come now, Mr. Stern—"

"Think, doctor, because my...intuition tells me I'm right. If so, then other parents who were patients of yours might die."

Reston swiveled his chair away from Stern. He stared at his photograph- and certificate-covered wall. His voice was barely a whisper. "I was worried about them from the beginning..."

At last, thought Stern. A crack in the dam. The rest would come gushing forth. Stern leaned back in his chair, neutral and receptive, the concerned friend. "Tell me about it."

Reston looked over his shoulder at the lawyer. His eyes were wide. "I can't. It's private...confidential..."

Stern's voice was soft and soothing. "Then at least tell me how I can prevent more deaths. There *will* be more. Won't there?"

"I don't know. Nor do I know if what you claim is true—about the Evereds and the others."

"But you think it *might* be true."

Slowly, Reston rose from his chair. "It was 1973. In the fall."

Michael was growing increasingly worried. The minutes dragged, and still no sign of Doug, David, and Sarah. They had all been notified; where were they? Why wasn't Brandon doing this himself?

Melissa slurped noisily on her straw as she reached the bottom of the can.

"Stop it," Michael said.

"Touchy, touchy."

"You don't suppose they chickened out?"

"David would, but not Doug or Sarah."

"We're running out of time," Michael fumed. "We'll have to go inside and get into position."

Sarah came dashing around the corner, out of breath. "My bus got stuck in traffic. I ran all the way for four blocks," she gasped.

"What about David and Doug?"

Sarah shrugged. "I haven't seen them."

Michael cursed and looked at his black Swatch. "We don't know how long the lawyer is going to be in there, so we'd better move. We'll go upstairs to the clinic floor and wait in the stairwell for David and Doug. That's the fallback plan, so they should know where to find us." He pushed back an unruly lock of brown hair that kept falling across his forehead. "Let's go."

October 1973. God, could he ever forget? Reston paced back and forth. Evered, Holliday, and McCord. He knew the names well. They had been burned into his brain forever, along with ten other names.

He stopped before the photographs that were framed and hung on the wall. He stared at an old black-and-white photo of himself and Dr. John Heineman. Heineman, the man who had helped him set up his clinic, and who had rescued him from disaster that terrible weekend when the electricity was sabotaged.

Even as desperate as he was back then, he'd had a bad feeling about substituting the embryos. Fourteen years had gone by, and at last he had felt safe from repercussions. But the past was coming back like a boomerang.

"What happened in the fall of 1973?" Stern asked, prodding Reston out of his thoughts.

Reston glanced up at the ceiling as the pounding took on new force. Then he turned to face Stern. "The truth is, I can't tell you the genetic sources of those children."

"Why not? Didn't you keep records?"

"Yes, but they were... extraordinary cases."

"How many children are we talking about, Dr. Reston?"

"Thirteen." He glanced anxiously at the lawyer but could read nothing from his face.

Stern said, "I see. Then there is a connection among them."

"Yes."

"Let's go back to the beginning. The fall of 1973."

Reston reluctantly summarized the disaster that had struck and ruined his sperm stock, and how his old mentor, Heineman, had come to his aid. Without that, he pointed out to Stern, he would have been ruined financially.

The lawyer listened with his brow furrowed in concentration. When Reston was finished, Stern said, "So you implanted embryos, which he supplied. And you knew nothing about where exactly they came from?"

Reston was embarrassed. "You must understand, Stern, I wasn't in a position to ask. I was desperate. I trusted him implicitly."

"What were his conditions?"

"His conditions?"

"Surely he wanted something from you in return."

Reston's humiliation deepened. "I was not to disclose the nature or source of the implantations. My patients believed they were being inseminated with sperm."

"And—?"

"And, I was to give him the names of the pregnancies that took." He added in self-defense, "There was nothing unusual about either request."

Stern's eyes were half-closed. "Maybe not. What else?"

Reston sighed. "He wanted periodic reports on the health of the children."

"How did you do that?"

"I obtained their pediatric records."

"How so, doctor? Aren't those confidential?"

"Yes," said Reston, lowering his eyes, embarrassed again by his violation of professional ethics. "It was complicated in a few cases. Some of the doctors owed me favors. Others —well, they all had low-paid staff."

Stern nodded. "I get the picture. Did you do the bribes yourself?"

"Of course not."

"How many implantations did you perform?"

"Twenty-six. Only thirteen went to term."

"So it is quite likely, indeed, that these thirteen children *are* related to each other from previous generations."

"Perhaps."

"And what do you think Dr. Heineman's motive was in giving them to you?"

"Nothing."

"Nothing at all?"

"We had been friends a long time. I needed help. Fortunately, John was involved in a genetics research program involving frozen embryos."

"What kind of research?"

"I'm sorry, it's classified," Reston replied automatically.

The soft, relaxed expression on Stern's face hardened, and his eyes opened wider. "I don't think confidentiality is an issue any longer. Exactly what kind of research?"

Reston fidgeted. "It had to do with programming heredity to improve factors such as stamina, resistance to disease, longevity, and intelligence. John always considered the human body and mind as machines that could be improved by retooling the genetic codes that are stamped at birth." Reston thought he detected a tensing in Stern.

"And what kind of superhumans were these embryos he gave you supposed to be?" the lawyer asked.

"Not superhumans, Mr. Stern. This isn't science fiction."

"What did he have to say about your thirteen children as they grew older?"

"Nothing." Reston looked at one of the photographs of Heineman smiling into the camera. "The subject never came up. About a year ago, he told me to quit sending reports."

"Why?"

The questions were beginning to irritate Reston. "He said he was satisfied with the results."

"Would he mind answering some questions now?"

"He's no longer at the Klein Laboratory in Purchase. I don't know where he is."

"Why not? I thought he was your good friend."

Reston squirmed. After he had unethically implanted the embryos, he had started avoiding Heineman, sending his reports by courier and doing nothing else. "I've lost touch with him. I did hear recently that he suffered a heart attack, or stroke. I don't even know if he's still alive."

Stern rose from his chair and came to stand next to Reston, looking at the photo that the doctor was staring at absently. "I remember this photo from my last visit. Something familiar about him . . . *Oh, my God*."

He was five years old and sitting on a cold steel table while Dr. Hans ran bony fingers over him, pulled up and down on his eyelids, and probed through his mouth. The tall, thin man turned and bent over an assortment of frightening needles and syringes, which Rainer knew would bring him incredible pain and suffering. He looked past Dr. Hans to the wall in front of him. Even, neat rows of human eyeballs were pinned to a board like butterflies. There were brown ones, blue ones, green ones, and gray ones. No two eyeballs were the same. They stared sightlessly at him like a gallery of grotesque marbles. He shivered and tried not to cry.

Rainer glanced to his left. On another small steel table lay the bloated corpse of a boy. The seven-year-old had swelled up like a sausage after getting an injection the day before, and minutes before had been alive. Rainer knew he was dead because Dr. Mengele, standing over the boy, had pronounced him so, and Dr. Hans had shrugged and said, "I'll do the autopsy," and Dr. Mengele had answered, "No, I'll do it, you finish with them," and Dr. Hans had said, "All right, but these two must be my last today because I have to get back to the laboratory."

Rainer looked to his right. On yet another small steel table sat his brother, Leon, waiting, his face a mirror of Rainer's own terror. They tried to comfort each other in their thoughts. Don't be afraid...

The scene dissolved to another.

Leon's head was swollen to nearly twice its normal size, his thin arms and legs were puffed like balloons, his eyes were sunken pockets of black and blue. He lay upon a thin blanket on the concrete floor of their dormitory, mute and numb in an ocean of pain. Rainer lay next to him, shivering, unable to sleep, acutely aware of his brother's agony and the fact that he had not had the same reaction to the shots. He desperately wanted their mother, whom they had not seen in months. He felt guilty about not being sick like Leon, and about being powerless to ease his brother's distress. Don't die... don't die... he kept praying silently. He knew what happened at the camp when one twin died. The other was killed so that Mengele could cut them both open and compare. He had seen it happen.

Stern snapped back into the present and found himself staring at the aged face of Dr. Hans Messner, alias John Heineman. With trembling hands, he took the photo down from the wall, scarcely believing what he was seeing. "It's *him*."

"Who? What?"

"This man." Stern pointed at the photo of Heineman. "He's a . . . *Nazi*." He shook the photo at Reston. "Goddamn it, didn't you *know*?" He looked again at the likeness, half afraid he would see it begin to move and speak, like the photographs of Leon once did. The figure in the photo remained motionless, but that did not still the growing, staggering horror inside of him.

"I don't know what you're talking about," Reston protested, his voice sounding distant. "You've got John mistaken with someone else."

"There's no mistake. It's *him*. 'Dr. Hans' we called him at Auschwitz. Hans Messner."

"*Auschwitz?* You were— ?" Reston left the question unfinished.

Stern looked up from the photo. He was being swept away by an avalanche of emotions. He was on a thin edge of losing control, and if he lost it, the emotions and unbidden voices would smother him. He struggled to keep from going under in the avalanche. The implications . . . The pieces were falling into place . . . the genetics, the children's eyes, the deaths, the connections . . .

He said, "My God, those children. Those children, Dr. Reston—they have got to be destroyed!"

Reston took two steps away from him, moving toward the center of the office. "Have you gone out of your mind?"

"Those embryo children Heineman—Hans Messner—gave you are the products of *evil*."

"This is lunacy—"

"They are part of a Nazi genetics blueprint that's still alive. Don't you see?"

"Really! I won't listen to such nonsense."

Stern's horror was turning to anger. It was as though all the pain in his life had accumulated in one gigantic boil, and the boil had burst. How could this have happened? How could Reston have been so stupid? His temples pounded as he tried to keep his voice steady. "Hans Messner was a Nazi doctor who sometimes came to Auschwitz to help Josef Mengele mutilate people in the name of science. In the name of perfecting genetics to create a 'master race.' That's the man you know."

Reston shook his head in steadfast denial. "Impossible."

Stern set the photo on top of a file cabinet and stepped closer to Reston, clenching his fists at his side. "I know what I'm talking about, doctor, because I was *there*. The Nazis prized *zwillinge*—twins—for their genetics experiments, and my twin brother and I were put in their program. Our parents and other relatives were gassed." Stern lowered his voice. "They liked to cut up the Jews, you see, to find out what made us 'inferior.' I survived, but my brother died later of... complications." He took a deep breath. "So the bastard Messner lived, and has continued his genetics work as John Heineman, still trying to create the perfect, master race. And he has succeeded, thanks to you, doctor. Do you know what this means?"

"It means nothing. Why, I've known John for years—"

"You've known a *lie*."

"A Nazi would be in hiding..."

"Sometimes the best way to hide is in plain sight." Stern narrowed his eyes as a thought occurred to him. He said, "You've become Messner's accomplice, his front man."

"This is outrageous," Reston said hotly, raising his voice above the racket going on upstairs. "I will not be treated like this!"

"You helped him create thirteen little monsters—programmed assassins! For what? To murder rich people for their money to finance a new Reich? Where does the murder stop, Dr. Reston?"

Reston shrank backward again, farther into the center of the office.

Stern followed. "Isn't that right?"

"No!"

"Where *is* Messner?"

"I told you I don't know where John is, and I don't want anything to do with this, or with you. This is slander!"

"Why are you protecting him? How much inheritance money did *you* expect to get out of the deal?"

"You'll regret this, Stern—" Reston said through clenched teeth.

Stern grabbed Reston by the front of his white doctor's coat. "This man is a murderer! The blood is on your hands, too, Reston."

Reston tried to pry Stern's fingers loose, but Rainer's grip was like iron. Reston sputtered, "If you don't get out of here, I'll call the police—"

Stern shook him. "You listen to me, doctor, because you're responsible for opening up one hell of a Pandora's box. The new children of the Reich are thirteen years old and committing murder. Four people are dead and it's not going to stop there. What are you going to do about it?"

Reston pulled himself loose with a violent jerk. "Get out!" he screamed. "Get out!"

From their place in the stairwell, Michael, Melissa, and Sarah waited for Doug and David. They heard the elevator open and rapid footsteps approach the stairwell. Michael breathed an enormous sigh of relief as the two boys opened the door. They were going to succeed in their mission after all.

"Okay," Michael said. "Does everybody remember the layout of the place?" They nodded. "Let's join hands and concentrate. As soon as it's done, we split."

* * *

Stern went after Reston and grabbed him again by the arm. The whole room seemed to shake with the pounding going on upstairs. He felt choked, claustrophobic again. Then something odd began to happen, as though he had been transported into a time warp. The surroundings continued to shake and then began to distort in shimmering waves, as though he were looking through a fish-eye lens. He squinted. The room, and now the doctor, distorted further. He saw Reston's lips move, but the words were drowned in a supernatural roaring.

A piece of the room began to separate and vibrate violently on its own. Up above. Stern looked up into the glare of the huge, long fluorescent lights hanging from the ceiling, directly over him and Reston.

A crack split the roaring. The large metal light fixture broke loose from the ceiling and fell.

Stern hunched over and slammed himself into Reston, who gasped as the wind was knocked from him. The impact sent the doctor hurtling backward and to the side. The two men crashed to the floor and rolled over each other before hitting the wall.

The fluorescent light fixture smashed down in an explosion of popping tubes, electrical shorts, crunching metal, and flying glass fragments.

Grunting, Stern rolled over and sat up. He was dazed. The doctor was on his back, groaning. At the spot on the floor where they'd stood just seconds before, the ruined light fixture lay twisted and smoking in a tangle of ripped wires. It had nearly killed them.

"What do you *mean*, you failed!"

Brandon was livid. He glared at Michael and shouted again, "How could you possibly fail? You stupid *idiots!*"

It was dusk in Central Park. The thirteen members of the Secret Society of Loki had convened in an isolated spot near the lake deep in the park's center, well hidden by vegetation, to hear the report from the mission squad. Brandon had sensed immediately that the mission against the doctor and lawyer had not succeeded, and "wrong number" phone calls to the offices had verified his suspicion. But he kept his anger in check pending an explanation from Michael.

Apprehension rose from the other kids as Brandon confronted Michael. They sat cross-legged on the ground, aimlessly pulling up tufts of grass, waiting for Brandon to provide the cue for group action.

"I should have done it myself!" Brandon said contemptuously.

Michael, who was the only one standing besides Brandon, looked around the group for support. To Brandon's satisfaction, he got none, not even from the other members of his mission team. Michael was on his own. Nobody liked to be the object of Brandon's temper.

"It was a fluke," Michael said defensively.

"A fluke. More like a pile of mistakes. You should have verified it at the scene, instead of leaving immediately. Hit-and-run cowards." He scrutinized Michael in failing light, probing for his thoughts. He said, "But you ran away because you were all frightened." He strode to Michael and gave him a shove on the shoulder. "There's no room for cowards in my group!"

"It's not *your* group, it's *our* group," Michael said in a low voice, eyes to the ground.

"Oh yeah? *I* give the orders around here, and I'll fight anybody who wants to disagree. Any takers?" Nobody spoke or moved. "Come on, Mike, you shot off your mouth. Let's see you back it up with some muscle."

Michael folded his arms across his chest, but Brandon knew better. The boy was scared stiff.

Michael said, "Cool off, Brandon."

"Take it back. What you said about me not being the leader."

"I didn't quite say that—"

"Take it back!"

Michael raised his hands, palms out. "Okay, okay."

"Say it!"

Michael's lips thinned. "This is—your group."

The admission failed to subdue Brandon's boiling anger. He was going to force Michael to repeat the words louder, then changed his mind. He was wasting time; there was an example to set.

Michael spoke again. "So we made a mistake. Nobody's perfect, Brandon. We'll get them the next time we try."

Brandon gave him a cruel smile. "What makes you think there's going to be a next time for you?"

Michael's jaw dropped. Collectively, the group held its breath.

Michael sputtered. "But we have to get them."

"We—the group—will. But maybe not you." Beside him, at his feet, Brandon felt Jason and Jeff stir as they picked up his thoughts that were intended only for them. The guard dogs were ready to do their master's bidding, their hackles rising at the scent of a prey.

Michael took a hesitant step backward. "What are you talking about?"

"You blew it. Why should the rest of us trust you again to do the job right?"

"Okay, so put someone else in charge."

"I will. But that's not enough."

"What do you mean?" Michael could not keep his voice from cracking.

"When you do something wrong, you should get punished."

"But I—we—didn't do anything wrong. We just made a mistake!"

"Same thing in my book. The group charged you with a mission, and you failed."

"I wasn't the only one!"

"Trying to blame the others? As squad leader, you were responsible."

Michael was slowly walking backward, away from the

group, shaking his head. "Don't," he pleaded. "It's not my fault."

Brandon laughed. Michael was scared stiff that something horrible was going to happen to him.

Brandon whirled and turned his back on Michael, who still kept retreating by small paces. "Stand up, David!"

A shock rippled through the other children. David looked around him for support, but no one would meet his eyes.

"Stand up, I said!"

David awkwardly rose. He shifted his weight from one foot to another in silence. Brandon let him squirm. What a pathetic kid. Small for his age. So spindly, so weak physically. Barely able to keep his emotions under control. And *no* stomach for dirty work. Heck, some of the *girls* were better soldiers than he! He had purposefully assigned David to the mission squad to toughen him up. But it was obvious now that David was a throwback, a reject. Defective. He would never be anything but a drag, a liability, to the Secret Society of Loki.

Brandon closed the distance between them, until he was a few inches from David, looking down upon him. "You've been letting Mike take the rap, David. That's very cowardly of you."

"I don't know what you're talking about." David's voice quavered.

"*You're* the real weak link in the chain. You always have been."

David's face crumpled. It was obvious he was striving mightily to keep the tears at bay. "That's not so."

"It is, David, and everybody here knows it. We've all had to make excuses for you and carry your load."

"It's true," shrilled Michael. "He cried! He ruined the mission! If it hadn't been for him, we would have succeeded."

"Yeah, I'm not surprised," said Brandon. "I'm sick of you, David, and I'm not going to put up with you anymore."

"I haven't done anything wrong!"

"Everything you do is wrong. You've got a bad attitude and it's bad for the rest of us. I'm kicking you out of the club."

Two fat tears welled out of David's eyes and rolled down his hollow cheeks. The moisture was barely visible in the failing light. He stared at Brandon for a moment and then turned to go. *He looks like a whipped puppy*, thought Brandon with satisfaction.

Brandon let David get a few feet away from the group. Just as he sensed David was about to break into a run, he called out, "Not so fast."

David froze.

"Aren't you forgetting something, David?"

"Wh-what?"

"The oath we all took when we formed the Secret Society of Loki? That none of us would ever leave the group except by death?"

David gasped. The group tensed, and waited.

Brandon said, "What do you think that means, David?"

Tommy interrupted. "I think we all assumed that the oath meant we were lifelong members, Brandon."

Brandon shot him a hostile look. Tommy was interfering in business too often lately. "You're technically correct, Tommy. As long as we're alive, we're members."

"B-but you've just kicked me out," said David.

"So I have."

Then it dawned on David what Brandon meant by reminding him of the oath. "No!" he cried. "You can't do that!"

"It's the law of the group," Brandon said coolly.

None of the other children moved or spoke. Brandon sensed uncertainty among some of them.

"Why?" screamed David. "I haven't done anything!"

"We can't take the risk that you'd tell our secrets."

"I won't! I promise!"

"David," Brandon said mockingly, "you know you'd tell, if someone so much as threatened to take away your allowance. Then we'd *all* be in trouble." He sensed group opinion coalescing against the boy.

"I won't tell anyone! Never!"

Tommy got to his feet and stepped up to Brandon. "Let him stay in the group. He just won't be trusted to do important stuff."

"You shut up!" Brandon shouted at Tommy. "How come you're spouting off so often? Maybe I ought to kick you out, too."

Tommy said, "You set David up to punish him."

"Mr. Tough Guy. Why are you sticking up for that little runt? Nobody else is."

"Let's be fair, Brandon."

Brandon drew his fist back and smashed Tommy in the face. Tommy toppled backward as blood sprayed out of his nose. As soon as he hit the ground, Jeff and Jason were on top of him, pinning him down.

David seized the moment of distraction and started to run.

"Stop him!" Brandon ordered. Jeff and Jason let go of Tommy and scrambled after David. Brandon focused a beam of thought, white and sharp like a laser beam, and summoned forth collective energy from the group. The energy was hot and sharp and lethal, and he turned it on the fleeing boy.

David went down like a deer felled by a rifle shot. He lay on the ground, sobbing, trying to get up but unable to rise. "No, no!" he kept screaming. "Let me go!"

"Shut him up, or we'll attract attention," said Brandon.

The group responded, and instantly David's vocal cords were cut. He kept opening his mouth, shaping words, but no more sounds came out.

The words formed in Brandon's mind: *David is a pigeon. Roast the pigeon.*

In the darkness, David rolled on the grass, his mouth stretched open in a soundless howl. His hands clawed at the air. As the temperature of his body soared, a thin gray cloud of smoke began to rise from him.

Brandon forced him to roll toward the lake, faster and faster, like a runaway log plunging down a hill. The water hissed and steamed as the flailing David rolled in and submerged.

David is heavy, very heavy. Not a pigeon anymore, but a chunk of iron. Down, down, down he goes, deep into the mud at the bottom of the lake, never to rise again.

With a final, wild thrash, David sank beneath the black surface of the water. Within seconds, the bubbles of air escaping from his lungs were gone; within minutes, the ripples had dispersed. Brandon walked slowly to the lake's edge. The water was smooth.

The group was silent, including Tommy, who kept wiping at his bloodstained face. Brandon knew none of them wanted the same fate, and they would do nothing to provoke him.

"When the grown-ups ask, tell them David ran away," he said. "We don't know where he went. We'll lay low and not have any meetings for a while." He looked back at the lake. "They'll never find him."

CHAPTER Twenty

"Listen to this," Stern said.

Rainer held up the hardcover book he had been reading. Over the top of it, he eyed Reston, who was sunk into the broken-down cushions of his sofa, engrossed in another book. Around them, Reston's modest Murray Hill apartment was dark, save for pools of light cast over their shoulders from a beige pottery table lamp and a brass pole lamp.

Two weeks had gone by since the light fixture "accident" in Reston's clinic. Stern had passed much of the time buried in more research on psychic phenomena and on the Nazis' eugenics program, letting his casework slide to the point where Ben Goldman had pointedly asked him if he intended to leave the firm. Without explaining, Stern had promised to catch up.

What he had unearthed and put together disturbed him greatly. More things about his past were falling into place—like the flashcard mind-guessing games Mengele had made all the twins play. The conclusions he had reached about Reston's embryo children were devasting. They had been born with highly developed extrasensory ability, which they had learned to use in ways that most people would not believe: using the power of their thought to move objects, and, perhaps, even to kill. Stern himself would find it hard to believe, had he not experienced supernatural phenomena himself.

The power to kill by thought, he had read, was theoretical and had never been proven.

Until now.

He had called Reston early that morning. "I have some material that will interest you."

"All right," the doctor had said in a grudging voice. He gave a time and the address of his apartment and then hung up. Stern had showed up with an armload of books. The address and the furnishings belied the doctor's deteriorated financial state. There were signs of a woman's presence. The yellow and blue kitchenette was too clean and decorated for a single man, and there were copies of *McCall's* and *Vogue* scattered about. Stern guessed the woman was Nancy DeWitt, though she was not present and Reston made no reference to her.

Now, several hours later, Stern could see that Reston remained unconvinced of his theories and his assertion that John Heineman was Hans Messner. Still, he had agreed to meet, and that was a sign of doubt in the doctor's mind.

"Are you listening?" Stern said.

Reston looked up, his face registering weariness and skepticism.

The title of the book Stern held was *Breakthroughs of the Mind*. He quoted from a page:

"'The Russians, as well as the Americans, have done a great deal of testing of the mind-body link, and the transference of sympathetic emotion. As early as 1958, experiments reportedly showed that intense concentration on the part of one test subject raised the blood pressure of the second test subject, who was positioned fifty miles away.'"

Stern paused and glanced at Reston. The doctor was scowling. He continued:

"'Perhaps the best-documented and best-known study was

conducted in 1979 by Dr. Ivan Riminsky, with two test subjects, one stationed in Moscow and the second in Leningrad. Both subjects had demonstrated an ability in transmitting and receiving information by telepathy in other controlled experiments. Dr. Riminsky had the sender, in Moscow, create a mental image of sneezing, coughing, and choking, and concentrate on sending this image to the receiver in Leningrad. At precisely the time of the telepathic transmission, the receiver began to complain he couldn't breathe well, and started to cough. His nose and eyes ran as though he had suffered a fit of sneezing. The attack ceased at the moment the sender stopped transmitting his image.'"

Reston said, "You expect me to believe the *Russians*? That's a pack of propaganda lies."

"I'm not finished yet." Stern flipped back to another page. "'While much folklore and myth have surrounded supernormal powers of the mind for centuries...'" His voice trailed off as he zoomed his finger through the text, rising as he found the material he was seeking.

"'Among the first thoroughly documented studies in the twentieth century was the work of Dr. Karl Schmidt of Frankfurt, Germany. Schmidt's research into sympathetic thought transmission was coupled with his belief that the predisposition to such supernormal ability was inherited. In the 1930s, his work attracted the attention of Otmar von Verscheur, the director of the Kaiser Wilhelm Institute of Human Genetics and Eugenics in Berlin. Apparently nothing ever came of Schmidt's research, and he ceased work on his project during World War II. No documents of his exist beyond 1940.'"

Stern's eyes flashed, but the import of the information was lost on Reston, who said, "So?"

"Otmar von Verscheur was a flag-waving Nazi, one of the Third Reich's most influential citizens. He provided a lot of the inspiration for Hitler's racial supremacy program, and whipped up public sentiment in favor of it. Göring, Himmler, and Heydrich didn't come up with the *final solu-*

tion by themselves—they had plenty of help from cretins like von Verscheur." Stern's voice escalated. "It just so happens that one Josef Mengele was a student of von Verscheur's at the University of Frankfurt, and von Verscheur lit the fire for the need for a 'master race' under him, too. *That's* how Mengele got so fascinated with heredity and with twins—so fascinated that when he was named *Lagerarzt* at Auschwitz, he turned part of it into a laboratory in which he and Hans Messner carried out their unspeakable experiments upon living subjects. Us! The Jews! The 'dregs of Europe'! *Judenrein, Judenrein*! All of Europe, the whole world, had to be *Judenrein*! We would be replaced by this abominable super race—thanks to Mengele and Messner!"

Stern stopped, flushed. He had been shouting.

Reston gave him a cold look. "I guess I don't know my history that well, Stern. At least not as you present it. I'm not a Jew."

For a moment, Stern wanted to rip Reston's icy WASP features apart. Instead, he thrust out his left arm into a pool of lamplight, unbuttoned his sleeve, and shoved it up. His identification tattoo from Auschwitz, faded and distorted but still unmistakable for what it was, spread across his inner forearm above the wrist bone.

"Do you have one of these, Reston?"

Reston stared at the tattoo, then looked away, refusing to meet Stern's gaze. He crossed his arms over his chest. "That book doesn't say anything about either Mengele or Messner actually being involved in Schmidt's work. It only says Schmidt attracted von Verscheur's attention. You are drawing a conclusion based on a circumstantial association." He added under his breath, "I thought *you* were the lawyer."

"I am," said Stern, catching the last remark. "And as a lawyer, I look for associations and relationships that lead to conclusions."

"So what do you infer?"

"That Schmidt's program was *not* abandoned during the

war. It was absorbed into Hitler's racial eugenics machine, without Schmidt, and was turned over to Mengele and Messner, who worked hellbent to program pyschic ability into the genes of their master race."

"I'll go along with that for the moment. And—?"

"We know that Himmler operated breeding farms in an attempt to produce 'pure' Aryan babies, but that was slow and inefficient, and took manpower away from the fronts." Stern tucked his hands into his hip pockets and walked into the shadows of Reston's living room. His shoes made scuffing noises on the worn carpet as he paced back and forth. He had covered this ground before with Reston, but obviously he would have to cover it again. "Let's hypothesize that the Nazis did succeed in making enormous breakthroughs in genetics programming, which were to be implemented through selective artificial insemination and impregnation. A man's sperm could be preserved and turned into dozens of babies while he was away fighting. A woman's eggs could be implanted in carrier mothers who weren't fit to provide genes themselves. Since psychic ability is rare, that would enable the Nazis to make the most of the individuals in Schmidt's old program."

"There's no such documentation of any artificial conception being done by the Nazis, nor of any breakthroughs in genetics. They would have had to be decades ahead of science elsewhere."

"Exactly, doctor. They were. And there's no documentation because the work would have been top secret, and I pose to you that the documentation was destroyed—accidentally or deliberately."

Reston sighed. "All right, then what?"

"Maybe some of the sperm and eggs developed by the Nazis survived the war."

Reston laughed. "For thirty years? That's ridiculous."

"I thought the potential lifespan was indefinite."

"Technically, yes, if kept cold enough, but—"

"I know—the bombings, the destruction, the disruption.

How could the right storage conditions possibly be maintained? It doesn't matter. It only matters that it happened."

"You're saying that in 1973 John gave me embryos created from thirty-year-old Nazi eggs and sperm?" Reston said, incredulous.

"Correction. Hans Messner gave them to you."

"I still don't believe that. If this wild scenario of yours did indeed happen, John was unwitting in his role. Besides, there are big holes in this theory. Why wait thirty years? And why use an outside party like me?"

"I'm sure there are good answers, and Messner will have to provide them, when we find him. He's around. He would not abandon his children of the new Reich."

"Children of the New Reich," scoffed Reston. "No matter what their genetic origin, these kids have been raised Americans. Hitler and the Third Reich are nothing more to them than blurry pictures in boring history books. That's why your theory doesn't hold up, Mr. Stern. If a Nazi wanted to ressurrect work on the 'master race,' he would be raising his children himself in secrecy."

"Like I said before, sometimes the best strategy is to hide in plain sight. The children know they possess special abilities, and they stick together in a group. Now some parents have died mysteriously and several of them stand to inherit a lot of money in a few years. Messner could make good use of them and their money."

Reston put his head back against the sofa and closed his eyes. "I don't know why I agreed to see you. You're wasting my time."

"Those kids are going to try to kill *us*," Stern said. "They know we're on to them, and so does Messner."

"Are you saying *John* is trying to kill *me*?"

Stern didn't answer directly. "I've told you, the falling light was no accident. That failed, and they'll try again. It will look like an accident."

"I find that theory to be the most implausible of all. That

falling light fixture *was* an accident. The remodeling upstairs jarred it loose."

Stern threw up his hands in exasperation. "Okay. I'll pursue this on my own." He picked up his books. "I've done some checking. 'John Heineman' suffered a heart attack, recovered, and was released from the hospital. He paid his bill, quit his job, and left no forwarding address. He's controlling these little monsters. I'll find him no matter what it takes."

Reston opened his eyes. "Are you going to the authorities?"

"Who'd believe me? I have no tangible proof." Stern shook his head. "Even if I did have proof, I wouldn't. You probably don't understand, Dr. Reston, but this comes down to a very personal matter."

"It sounds to me like you're on a witchhunt for a Nazi, and John is going to be your fall guy. Look, the war has been over for more than forty years. Don't you Jews ever *forget?*"

Stern's eyes were steely and bright. "No. Never." He turned on his heel and stormed out of the apartment, leaving the books behind.

Goddamn Reston, he swore to himself as he bolted down the stairs. Goddamn that son of a bitch WASP doctor! The world was full of Restons, soft, privileged, and apathetic. No wonder the Holocaust had been permitted to happen.

Reston sat in the dark for a long time after Stern left. He was thinking about what the lawyer had said, and about the events in his own life since 1973. Everything turned on that horrible day when he had discovered the electricity failure. Greed and fear of professional failure certainly had taken him down a pretty path. An affair, a disastrous divorce, a falling off of his practice . . . Even the grant money from the Evereds' estate had been gobbled up to pay debts.

And look at this place. Reston cast his eyes around the apartment, seeing shapes in the darkness beyond the twin pools of light. From a penthouse on Park Avenue to a one-bedroom flat in Murray Hill, and an unhappy mistress to boot. He looked at his watch. Nancy should be home any minute.

Thinking of Nancy made him feel guilty. He knew she genuinely loved him, and he knew he could never return more than affection. He just wanted Gloria back, despite what she'd done to him in the divorce.

He got up and went into the kitchen to fix a Scotch on the rocks. One thing *was* certain: he didn't need a crazy Jew like Stern mucking up his life as well. He was acutely aware that the thirteen "embryo children" were odd kids, but Stern's tale was fantastic beyond belief. And John Heineman was a moral, honest man, not a Nazi named Hans Messner.

He had been worried that Stern was going to make legal trouble for him over his unethical and possibly illegal use of the embryos, but he could see that wasn't the case. The lawyer was tilting at bizarre windmills. He could relax. To hell with Rainer Stern.

Edward had just finished pouring out a generous drink when a thought struck him like a thunderbolt. Just before Stern had arrived on the day the light fixture fell, two teenage girls had burst into his office. He—and Nancy—had thought they were playing a game. They were in and out so fast he didn't get a clear look at them, but it wouldn't have mattered. He had no photos of the embryo children.

Stern claimed the light fixture was no accident.

Maybe the girls weren't playing a game.

Maybe they had done a reconnaissance.

Stern felt the eyes upon him as soon as he hit the street outside Reston's apartment. He couldn't see them, but he could feel them—several pair of watchful, unfriendly eyes. *The children*, he thought. Chills ran up and down him, even though the night was warm and humid. He hurried down the sidewalk, not paying attention to where he was going, dodging pedestrians, his mind still going over the conversation in Reston's shabby apartment.

He passed Thirty-fourth Street and Third Avenue, and saw a line of people queued at a movie theater. The brightly lit marquee proclaimed the latest summer horror film. The next showing was in fifteen minutes, at a quarter past ten.

Horror, he thought. *That's what my life is.*

The invisible eyes went with him. He kept turning quickly and looking over his shoulder, seeing no children, at least none that he recognized. None who would send a shudder of fear down his spine.

They're following me. They know where I work, where I live, where I go. They're going to try to kill me, and I don't even know what most of them look like.

He walked faster, uncharacteristically shoving at those he passed, unmindful of the contemptuous looks and occasional insults. His heart was racing, his mind galloping with imagined threats. What were they going to try to do to him? How many children were out there hiding in the night? Dammit, how could they follow him and not be seen? He didn't know what to do.

Rainer whipped around a corner, heading west toward Park Avenue and the center of midtown. Mistake! There were few pedestrians and virtually no traffic on the narrow one-way street. He started to go back but had the feeling that would be an even greater mistake. He turned around again and headed down the street.

Would they try to kill him now? Focus their thoughts on him, "think" him dead? Was that how they did it? Would they raise his blood pressure to dangerous levels? Make him have a heart attack?

The thought made him stop in his tracks, the world spinning around him and his ears humming with voices that threatened to override his control. He momentarily lost his balance and zigzagged on the pavement, causing two Oriental men coming toward him from the opposite direction to step hastily off the curb and cross the street.

His heartbeat hammered against his ribs. He walked faster, feeling the invisible eyes boring into him. His own eyes searched the shadowy nooks and crannies along the street. Where were they hiding?

He passed a big metal garbage bin stinking of garbage rotting in the summer heat. *Goddamn you,* he thought. *I want to see you.*

Ahead of him, a young woman smoked a cigarette beneath an awning. He couldn't tell how old she was. One of their lookouts? He held his breath and scrutinized her as he approached. She looked at him warily. The expression on her face told him she was equally leery of him.

Rainer passed her and stopped. Her footsteps already were receding in the opposite direction; she was walking away. He suddenly realized he was in the middle of a very long and deserted block.

Pain spread through his chest. He didn't know if it was from tension—or from *them.* He started walking again, fast, wishing a taxi would turn down the street. None did. Then he laughed out loud. What good was a taxi against thought?

Two bodies sprang at him from a darkened doorway. They were young and male—teenagers—and they seized him and pinned him with expert strength against a wall in the shadows. Rainer struggled against his assailants, not believing the invisible eyes had caught him. Then he was staring at the shiny steel shaft of a switchblade held inches from his face, and he quit resisting.

"We just want your wallet, man. And the watch. Nice and easy."

It took Stern a moment to realize that the two boys were not from the group of Messner's children, but were ordinary street punks, and he was being mugged.

The steel blade waved in Stern's face. The second boy, who now had Stern gripped from behind, tightened his grip. The knife wielder said, "We don't want to cut you, man, unless we have to. Hurry up!"

The knife wielder had the face of a pit bull. The lips were

stretched back over the teeth in an ugly grin. Stern shook off his paralysis. He reached slowly to his back pocket with his right hand. "I haven't got much money on me..."

"Just gimme the wallet! Jimmy, get his watch."

The second boy seized Stern's left wrist and yanked impatiently on the clasp of the watchband, pulling the Baum & Mercier watch roughly off him. Rainer didn't look at him but heard the satisfaction in the boy's voice. "It ain't a Rolex, but it's a beaut."

"C'mon, c'mon, the *wallet*, jack!"

The sound of a fast-approaching car froze them. The knife wielder turned his body away from the street, shielding the blade.

The second boy hissed. "Shit, it's the fuzz!"

With a soft click, the switchblade disappeared and was palmed. The teenage assailants took off.

Stern gasped and leaned back against the wall.

The patrol car slowed and halted abreast of Stern. The driver leaned out the window. "Is everything okay?"

The boys had vanished. Stern started to say, "yes," then changed his mind. He said, "I've been robbed."

CHAPTER
Twenty-One

After Stern's departure, Reston grew restless and decided to go to the only refuge he had these days, his office in his clinic. He was upset, and did not want to see Nancy or endure her questions about Stern. He had refused to tell her the reason why Stern was back in his life again. Confiding in Nancy once before had not solved problems, but created new ones. She was not happy with his silence.

He looked around him. The shabby Murray Hill apartment was unbearably depressing.

While he worked at the clinic, Reston kept glancing nervously at the new fluorescent light fixture in his ceiling. The electrician had insisted the fixture was so secure that a major earthquake wouldn't jar it loose, but Reston wasn't so sure. He had moved his desk well out from under the light, and he no longer closed his door when he worked, in case he had to make a speedy exit.

He attempted to do his regular work, but without success. He had brought with him the books Stern had left behind in his apartment, and felt an irresistible urge to open them, despite his opinion that this psychic stuff was nonsense.

At last Reston gave in to the urge and began leafing through the books, reviewing the information Stern had pointed out on the experiments to transfer pain and discomfort by thought. It seemed so wild, so like science fiction—yet here were documented studies by supposedly rational men that demonstrated just that.

The idea was frightening.

Reston picked up a thin volume entitled *Mind Warfare*.

This has really got to be science fiction, he thought. He skimmed the table of contents and then the text itself. The focus of the book was on psychokinesis, the influence of the mind over matter, which some scientists believed could be harnessed to move objects and cripple or even kill other humans. The book reported on alleged work by the military in both the United States and Russia. PK, as it was called, was viewed by the brass as a possible godsend in fighting. Armies trained in PK theoretically could deflect missiles, guide missiles, disarm artillery, scramble radio signals—even kill enemy soldiers without ever getting within firing range.

Preposterous!

Or was it?

Take a group of children, bred from meticulously selected genes developed over generations to produce certain characteristics—such as psychic ability. The children, created in a close environment, could discover their affinity for one another and gravitate together. At a certain age they would discover, probably accidentally, that they can do things with their minds that other people can't ... that they can combine their mental energies to produce a magnified effect. Then, as they grow older, they enter their confrontational teen years—and realize they have a perfect solution for dealing with problems. They make the sources of the problems *go away*.

Reston swallowed hard. If that was true, then what would these children do as adults?

Ed, you've been working too hard. You're going off the deep end here.

He drummed his fingers on the desktop. He looked again at the light. Maybe he had been too hasty writing off Stern. As improbable as it sounded, perhaps the lawyer *was* on to something.

But the only person who knew the truth was the man he knew as John Heineman, whom Stern insisted was a Nazi criminal—and who, if indeed he were still alive, could be anywhere on the planet.

The sound of shattering glass made Reston stiffen. It was the sound of small, thin pieces of glass breaking, and it was muffled. It seemed to come from within his clinic. He jumped to his feet, his stomach a ball of ice. No one could have possibly entered. The main door was double-locked and the alarm system was activated.

Then why did he feel an invisible presence?

The shattering sound was followed by an eerie silence. Reston found his voice. "Hello? Is someone there?"

There was no answer. Faintly, he could hear another sound, a crackling noise, like someone crumpling a sheet of brittle plastic wrap into a ball.

Reston's whole body trembled as he went to the door of his office and looked out down the hall of the clinic. The crackling noise, louder now, seemed to be coming from the freezer room. He cast his eyes around but saw no one. Hesitantly, he walked to the freezer room and turned the handle of the door.

At the twist of the knob, the door exploded open on him, knocking him back against the opposite wall of the hallway. Black, acrid smoke billowed out. Small flames crept up the sides of the room from the floor.

Reston backed away, choking, throwing up his arm in a futile attempt to ward off the heat and smoke. What happened to the fire alarm? It was heat sensitive, and should have gone off long before flames erupted. But the bell remained silent.

Reston grabbed the door and tried to slam it shut. It was warped and wouldn't latch, but at least it provided a barrier. Smoke and tongues of flame erupted around its edges.

He dashed down the hallway to the waiting room, where he tugged at the knob on the main door. The key! He needed his key to unlock the dead bolt. He dug in his pocket for his ring of keys, and jammed a key in the dead bolt.

The key broke in the lock.

Reston pulled the stub of key out and stared at it in amazement. He yanked on the handle, but the dead bolt was still locked with the broken key stuck in it, and there was nothing he could do about it.

He dropped the rest of his keys on the floor and ran to the receptionist's telephone.

The phone line was dead.

Reston punched madly at the buttons on the cradle but got no response. He stabbed zero, hoping that by some miracle he could raise the operator. Nothing happened.

With a shout, Reston picked up the dead telephone and hurled it against the wall. The smoke was seeping into the front of the clinic, stinging his eyes and making him cough.

Of course, the fire extinguisher! It was mounted on a wall near the freezer. He ran back into the hall, but fire had already claimed the back wall, and there was no way he could reach the extinguisher.

A fit of coughing racked his chest. The increasing smoke cut his throat and lungs. Little balls of fire were growing into big ones. He had to get out before the clinic became an inferno.

He ran back to his office and pounded on the window. He was ten stories above the street, with no fire escape. "Somebody, help!" He looked out, and what he saw horrified him more than the fire consuming his surroundings. Far below, on the other side of the street, illuminated by the yellow glow of street lamps, a group of youths looked up toward his window, watching.

Reston recoiled from the window. He coughed and shut his eyes against the stinging smoke. He was trapped, and he was going to die if he didn't think of something fast.

On his hands and knees, Reston crawled along the floor, disoriented and sweating, his vision obscured by smoke. His hand struck warm metal, something square and compact and tall. His fingers groped upward and found glass. The water cooler! He was in the receptionist area.

He clawed his way up the stand, using it to steady himself as he got to his feet. He fumbled for the lever and felt tepid water splash into his waiting palm. Water! He tried to shout in jubilation, but the sound that came out was a cracked, hysterical giggle. Water could give him precious seconds to live.

He cupped his hands beneath the spigot, cursing the slow flow that was designed for tiny paper cups, and when his hands were full, he dashed the liquid against his face and into his burning eyes. Again and again he filled his hands, drinking some and splashing some, gasping in relief. He started to fill his hands one more time, then stopped. He just thought of something that could help get him out of here alive—a storage credenza in the next room, where Nancy kept miscellaneous supplies.

He tore off his shirt, ripping the buttons out of the cotton, and held it beneath the spigot. The water trickled out. It seemed to take forever for the shirt to get soaked. When it was, he ripped out an arm and tied it in a mask around his nose and mouth. Then he put the soaked shirt, minus the sleeve, back on.

It was minimally effective but might be enough to do the job. Dimly he remembered what he had once learned about fires a long time ago in school, and kept low to the floor, where he could breathe the unconsumed oxygen. He prayed it would make a difference, for his chest was already a mass of pain from smoke inhalation.

Reston scrambled out toward the adjacent room where the credenza was located. He couldn't see well and operated by internal bearings.

His heart sank at the extent of the fire that greeted him in the hallway. The rooms at the end of the hall were fully involved, and flames roared out the destroyed doorways. He would have to act fast, for the fire was spreading quickly toward him.

He plunged out into the hallway, hugging the wall until he found a doorway, and threw himself against it. He tumbled into one of his examination rooms. He was lucky to find the credenza right away, saving more precious seconds. The metal was hot but not untouchable. He yanked it open and made an animal noise of triumph when his hand grabbed what he had hoped would still be there—a jar of first aid burn cream.

Clutching the jar, he rose into a low crouch and turned to the examining table that was mounted on a pedestal in the center of the room. Yanking the white linen off the top of the table, he bunched it and tucked it against his middle. He then spun around and, still crouching low, dashed back out through the hall to the reception area.

When he reached the water cooler, he was choking badly from smoke inhalation and felt dizzy, on the verge of passing out. He splashed more water on his face mask and willed himself to keep moving.

Reston smeared the cream over his exposed flesh and his lower legs. It wouldn't prevent him from being burned, but it might make a crucial difference in severity.

The cuffs of his pants were already singed. He wadded up the linen and held it under the spigot. He turned the lever. Goddamn it, the water was so slow! He'd be dead by the time the cloth was soaked.

With an angry grunt, he stood and gave the water cooler a

mighty shove. It toppled over to the left, and the heavy glass smashed and water spilled out over the floor.

Reston hastily mopped up the puddles with the linen, and then took the soaked cloth and wrapped himself completely up in it. He bowed his head and raced out toward the waiting room. Part of the wall around the door was shimmering with low orange and red flames.

For a moment, he thought he could not go on, and he would have to perish. He braced himself for one last effort and flung himself toward the frame of the dead-bolted front door, leading with his right shoulder. He felt the damaged frame give way a little, but not enough. He drew back and hit it again, but the wood didn't yield. He prepared to hit the door a third time, but when he took a breath, no oxygen reached his lungs. He choked and doubled over in a paroxysm of coughing. He gasped for air and collapsed on the floor.

At the moment when Reston was breaking the water cooler, Stern was getting out of a taxi on the Madison Avenue side of Reston's building.

After he had given the details of his mugging to the police, the officers had offered to take him home. He accepted; the invisible eyes were vanquished. Except, he had asked to be dropped off at Reston's apartment building instead.

No one was home, and Stern was immediately worried. There was no logical reason that Reston would have gone to his clinic, but Stern knew he was there. He felt compelled to go there.

This is ridiculous; it's got to be nearly midnight, he estimated, looking up at the huge red brick building with its white concrete cornices. *Forget it and call him in the morning*.

An inner force refused to let him leave.

He headed for the front entrance. It would be locked, but he would buzz the clinic. He stopped. That wasn't the right thing to do. He didn't fully understand why, but he turned and walked around the block to the opposite side of the building to an unmarked steel door. It was a fire stairwell and was supposed to be locked on the outside but wasn't.

Stern opened the door and peeked in.

From the outside came a boom and the sound of window glass breaking. A funnel of orange blossomed out overhead against the yellow-white glow of city lights.

Reston!

Stern took the stairs two and three at a time, up the ten flights to the Park Avenue Family Planning Center floor. When he got there, he found the corridors filling up with a haze of smoke. Tiny flames were shooting out around the door frame to the clinic. It was eerie, for no fire bells were ringing.

Without thinking, Stern tried to open the door. The metal handle was hot, and he yelped as he let go. At the end of the corridor, he spotted a firebox with an extinguisher and ax. He broke the glass and grabbed the ax.

Rainer ran back to the clinic door and started chopping. He broke out an opening between the door and the frame, and squeezed through.

The smoke was thick. He pressed his sleeve against his mouth.

He saw the huddle of white on the floor.

"Reston!"

Stern lifted up the doctor in a bear hug and dragged him out into the corridor. He tore off the sheet and the shirtsleeve face mask and slapped the doctor's cheeks. "Reston!"

The doctor was alive but unconscious. Miraculously, he didn't seem to have suffered severe burns.

Over the roar of the fire, Stern heard approaching sirens and horns. Once again, an inner force prompted Stern. *No authorities.* They had to get out before they were found.

But Reston needed immediate medical treatment.

The sirens and horns grew louder. Stern knew that police

would arrive in moments, along with the fire crews, and cordon off the area.

Stern lifted Reston up and supported him against his body as he half carried him, half dragged him toward the stairwell. "Hang on," he said. "We're getting out of here."

CHAPTER
Twenty-Two

Melissa, Michael, Doug, Elizabeth, Samantha, and Sarah stormed out of the subway station at West Eighty-first Street and Central Park, each trying to prepare an explanation for Brandon as to why they had failed in a second mission to get the attorney, Rainer Stern. Melissa chewed on her lower lip, ravaging the tender pink flesh. She could not erase from her mind the look on David's face as he sank below the lake waters to his death. That was the price for incurring Brandon's wrath, and surely he would be furious at their news— if he didn't know already. Brandon's powers seemed to be getting stronger and stronger.

Melissa concentrated on blocking herself off mentally from the rest of her group. She wanted to be left alone.

The five headed for the Bannerford building where the Tates lived in their magnificent co-op. Brandon had ordered a council meeting following the missions against Stern and Reston. Melissa hoped Brandon's team wouldn't be back yet.

At the imposing entrance of the Bannerford, the doorman, a young man with a tight-fitting maroon and gold uniform, rushed to open the heavy brass and glass door for the children. He bowed and kept his eyes down. He no longer asked them their names, or ordered them to wait while he phoned the Tates' penthouse suite. He had learned the hard way, by a tongue-lashing from Master Jeffrey Tate, that his friends were to be admitted immediately at all hours. He *did* want the Tates' generous Christmas bonus, didn't he?

Melissa felt the doorman's eyes on their backs as they sailed through the marble foyer to the bank of elevators. She caught his thoughts, and they didn't match his bowing and scraping: *"Rich little fuckers... I hope the elevator cable breaks..."*

She whirled around, catching the scowl on his face turn to a forced grin. *Choke on it*, she thought, and turned around to catch up with the others. Doug punched the button for the elevator that went straight to the penthouse kitchen, the entrance they preferred to the formal one.

Behind them came a gagging sound. They looked. The doorman was frantically trying to undo the collar of his uniform. Melissa put her hand to her mouth and giggled.

The ornate brass-plated door of the elevator opened and they stepped inside. As soon as the door closed, the six of them burst into laughter at the plight of the doorman, easing the tension that was building up among them.

"I'll handle it with Brandon," Melissa announced.

"You're not the mission captain," said Michael. "I am."

"But he likes me, dummy. I'll kiss him. *You* want to kiss him?"

Michael shot her a disdainful look that said *girls*. He made no further effort to dissuade her from assuming the burden of dealing with Brandon.

They were barely at the kitchen entrance to the suite when the door was opened by Harwood Kendall, the Tates' butler. He must have spotted them on the video camera installed in the elevator. Harwood was British, of course, and his sharp English features were frozen in a constant imperious expression. To the children, he seemed to be suffering from a permanent condition of constipation. When Jeff's parents were gone—as they were now at the Riviera—Harwood was at the mercy of Masters Jeff and Brandon, who kept him up until all odd hours of the night with their demands to be waited upon.

"Hiya, Harwood," greeted Michael as the six barged past him. "Hope we didn't interrupt you screwing the cook." The stunned butler, whom the kids knew *was* having an affair with the cook, coughed and fumbled for words.

"Er, Master Jeffrey and Master Brandon are—"

"In Jeff's room," finished Melissa. "Don't you think we know that?" As they swept past a Louis XIV settee, Melissa added, "And bring us some Cokes, Harwood. Remember, I want mine with no ice."

The door to Jeff's enormous room was slightly ajar. Melissa took a deep breath. She felt like they were going into a courtroom.

The other seven members of the Secret Society of Loki were there, awaiting the arrival of the lawyer mission team. Jeff and Brandon were bent over a partially assembled plastic model of an F-14 fighter jet. Jason lounged on the bed, wearing earphones. Tommy and Lori were playing an obviously uninteresting game of hearts. Jennifer was absorbed in a teen fan magazine.

Here goes, thought Melissa as she and the other five members of her team slid into the room.

Brandon looked up at them. A thin curl of smoke from the cigarette in his hand drifted up toward the ceiling. His blue eyes were large and burning with displeasure. Melissa's throat went dry. With a suddenness that made her jump, the door to Jeff's room slammed shut.

Yikes, thought Melissa, did Brandon do that *by himself*?

She didn't have time to speculate on whether or not Brandon had learned to use yet more power independently of the group. She was too busy defending herself.

"So you dumb shits blew it again." Brandon raised the cigarette to his lips and took a long drag. He let the smoke out through his nostrils, keeping his eyes riveted on Melissa. "And you're the one who's gonna tell me about it."

Melissa, aware that everyone was staring at her, bit her lip. Jason sat up but left his headphones on. Tommy and Lori put down their cards, while Jennifer set aside her magazine. Jeff stood by Brandon like a soldier.

"It wasn't our fault," said Michael.

Brandon glared at him. "No one asked you, pantywaist." While Michael reddened, Brandon took another drag and stabbed out the cigarette in the Baccarat crystal ashtray near the jet model. "I call this meeting of the Secret Society of Loki to order. All members are present. The first report is from the doctor mission team. As captain of the team, I will deliver the report. Mission accomplished." He drew a finger across his throat as his eyes scanned the room. "End of report. Next we will hear from the Target Lawyer mission team, which screwed up again. *Captain*—" the word was twisted with sarcasm—"Michael has appointed Melissa to make excuses for him."

"That's not fair, Brandon," Melissa protested.

"I decide what's fair. Well? We're waiting, Melissa. What's the matter? You never shut up in school, not even when Mrs. Bagley sends you to detention. So talk."

Before Melissa could begin, a rapping sounded on the door.

Brandon looked annoyed. "What is it?"

"The soft drinks ordered by Miss Melissa, Master Brandon," came Harwood's voice from the other side of the door.

Melissa batted her eyes coquettishly. "I thought you might like a Coke, Brandon."

Brandon plainly did *not*, but he allowed Harwood to enter. "Just hurry it up."

Harwood brought tall glasses filled with ice and Coca-Cola, save for Melissa's glass, which had no ice. He jittered around the room in a haste to deliver the drinks and get out. "Will there be anything else, Master Jeffrey or Master Brandon?"

Brandon answered. "Beat it." As Harwood's ramrod stiff body was exiting the room, Brandon threw out a thought laser and gave the servant a goose. Harwood danced a little jig but never looked back. He squared his shoulders and shut the door behind him.

Brandon's amusement faded rapidly. "So spit it out, Melissa. We haven't got all night."

Melissa steeled herself and told the story of how they had difficulty following Stern, and then were forced to abandon him when the police arrived. "They were looking for the muggers," she ended defensively. "We couldn't stay around."

Brandon picked up the F-14 model and threw it at the wall. Broken plastic fragments showered to the floor. "Hey," said Jeff, "that was one of my best kits—" His protest died in his throat. Brandon was in a fury.

"Dopes! Can't you do anything right? What are you, a whole bunch of Davids?"

Melissa paled at the mention of the executed boy. Once Brandon's temper let loose . . .

"You should all be punished for this!"

"Brandon—"

Brandon cut her off. "Why is it the only way I can count on something is to do it myself? *My* team didn't fail!"

"That's right, Brandon." Tommy spoke up coolly. "We got the most important guy—the doctor with all the records. The lawyer isn't that big a deal. Without the doctor, he's nothing."

Melissa let out a small sigh and mentally thanked Tommy for coming to her defense.

Brandon would not be placated. "We have to get them both, jerk. Just like that crazy old man."

"I think you're exaggerating. When he finds out the doctor is dead, the lawyer will give up."

Jeff hooked his thumbs in his jeans pocket. "I'm with Brandon. We should go after him again, until we get him."

Jason suddenly threw up his arms and clasped the headphones to his ears. "Wait a minute, everyone!" He listened, astonishment on his face. "It's on the news—the clinic fire." He listened again. The others watched him with expectation. Jason's perfect mouth fell open and then formed a single word.

"*Shit!*"

"What is it?" Brandon said. "What's the matter?" He strode over to the bed and yanked the headphones off Jason's head.

"Ow!" Jason rubbed his right ear. "You could have asked first, Brandon."

Brandon ignored him and held the headset to one ear. After a few seconds, he threw the headphones back at Jason. "I missed it. What did they say? Did they find the body?"

Jason looked grim. "They said the clinic was destroyed all right, and investigators are searching for clues as to what started the fire—"

"The body, dimwit! What about Dr. Reston?"

"There wasn't any body. They said luckily no one was injured in the fire, that the clinic was empty."

Brandon let loose a shriek of rage. "*Impossible!*"

Jennifer ventured, "Maybe he burned up to ashes and they wouldn't be able to tell."

Jason shook his head. "Naw, there would be a bone or something left. Those fire guys are smart. A building can be burned to a pile of sticks, and they can still find victims."

"What *else* did the news say?" Brandon demanded.

Jason shrugged. "That the owner of the clinic, Dr. Reston, could not be reached."

"*What!*"

"But he was in there," said Jeff. "We saw him go in, and he never came out."

"Right, but we left just before the fire trucks arrived," chimed in Tommy. "So how do we know he didn't escape?"

"Because nobody could survive a fire in a locked room," Jeff argued back. "We stayed long enough to make certain he was trapped."

"Since when are you the big expert on fires, Jeff?"

"I know more than you do, Tommy."

"Shut up, you guys," snapped Brandon. "Everybody shut up and listen." He looked around the room, meeting everyone's gaze one at a time. "Wipe that smart ass smile off your face, Melissa. You and your team are still in trouble." He stabbed a finger at Lori. "What's *your* problem?"

Lori had drawn her thin arms tightly across her chest, and was shaking violently. Tommy scooted over to her and put an arm around her shoulder. "She's just upset about the fire. She doesn't like to hurt people."

"I asked her, not you, Romeo."

"I—I'm sorry, Brandon," Lori said in a small voice. "I'll be all right." She shivered again and Tommy gave her a hug. He picked up her glass of Coke and held it up to her mouth, encouraging her to drink. She took a small sip.

Brandon clasped his hands behind his back and paced about the room. "Okay, there are two possibilities. The first is that the newscast is inaccurate. That happens a lot with the first reports of disasters. Maybe they'll find Reston's body in a thorough search." He paused and then went on, "The second possibility is Dr. Reston managed to survive. If so, we've got to find him right away and finish the mission."

Elizabeth raised her hand. "If he survived, he must have been hurt. He might be in a hospital."

Brandon shook his head. "That would be on the news."

"Maybe Reston—or someone else—didn't want anyone to know he's helpless in a hospital," suggested Jason.

"I doubt it, but we'll play it safe and call the ones in the city. Jennifer, you and Elizabeth are in charge. Go into the master bedroom and start phoning now. Make sure that idiot Harwood doesn't know what you're doing."

Jennifer and Elizabeth got up and left.

Brandon unclasped his hands and reached into his shirt pocket for his pack of cigarettes. He pulled out a long Benson & Hedges menthol and lit it. His lips curved into a wicked smile. "Maybe we're overlooking the obvious. He might be back at home."

Out on the dark street, Brandon led his eleven followers toward the subway. He still seethed at the failure of the two missions. The doctor and the lawyer were the only two people standing in his way of proceeding with a plan he had mapped out for the group. He could see it would not be good to gradually get rid of the rest of the parents. That was too risky. He had another, better idea, and it hinged on no one knowing their secrets.

A thought about his dead mother entered his mind from nowhere. Since she had died, she was always in the background, disapproving of what Brandon did, just like when she had been living. He could hear her nagging at him, and it made him angry. A headache began to form at the back of his head, arcing bolts of pain up over the top of his skull to his forehead. He tried to deny the pain, but it kept increasing.

Brandon started to lope, and the rest followed in a tight little pack. The exertion eased the intensity of the headache, and Brandon shut out Alice's ghostly voice until he couldn't hear it anymore.

The Murray Hill apartment that Reston and Nancy shared was on the fifth floor of a brownstone erected in the 1930s. The features of the twin lion-headed demons that guarded the ornate entrance were almost always covered with soot. The structure was christened "The Valhalla," in accordance with the original landlord's fantasy, but the modest apartments fell far short of the halls of the gods. Living here was a bitter pill for Nancy. It was just her luck that Edward Reston would run out of money when he turned to her for solace. The ex-Mrs. Reston, meanwhile, continued to live in high style on her divorce settlement.

Nancy sat curled in a brown overstuffed armchair, sipping on a glass of Dry Sack sherry, depressed about her deteriorating relationship with Edward. They hardly spoke to one another anymore, and hadn't made love in two weeks. It was that lawyer Stern's fault. Edward wouldn't tell her why the attorney had been to see him, but she just knew it was causing trouble.

They'd had tickets to a Mostly Mozart concert at Avery Fisher Hall tonight, but Edward had announced at the last minute that he wasn't going. He had work to catch up on. What work? He had few patients these days.

Nancy had gone by herself, determined not to let Edward spoil the evening. But the concert hadn't been much fun, and Nancy hardly listened to the music. She decided that she would try to make up with Edward when she got home.

But she was greeted by a dark and empty apartment, and a terse note from Reston that he had gone to the clinic to work in the office.

The clinic, the clinic! Always the clinic.

She had called him there several times, but he had taken the phone off the hook. She resolved to wait up for him, no matter how late he came home.

She picked up the bottle of sherry and examined the little bit that was left. She would have a hangover later but didn't care. She poured the contents into her glass and drained the sweet liquor in one gulp. There.

The apartment was not air-conditioned, and the air was still stuffy with lingering summer heat, despite the late hour and the open windows. The sherry and the stuffiness made her drowsy. Nancy turned off the lights and dozed off in the chair. She dreamed someone had broken into the apartment and was tiptoeing around while she slept. She snapped awake. She heard a scrabbling sound at the door and froze.

Then she let out her breath. It was only Edward, home at last.

But the scrabbling sound continued, and she heard no key turn in the lock.

She got up and went to the door. "Edward?"

There was no response. It wasn't Edward after all. Perhaps it was the neighbor's cat prowling around the halls.

Nancy yawned. She ached from sleeping in the chair, and decided to give up her living room vigil and go to bed. She walked into the bedroom and sat down on the edge of the bed for a moment before she got undressed.

A hand whipped out from under the bed and grabbed her by the ankle.

Nancy shrieked. She leaped away from the bed, wrenching free of the hand. She turned and looked down where the sheet met the floor, but there was no hand. For a fleeting moment, Nancy thought she'd imagined it.

To her horror, she realized she didn't imagine it. Muffled giggles came from under the bed.

Her breath caught in her throat. She said, "Who's there? What do you want?"

More giggles floated out. Nancy's heart began to beat fast. "Who *is* it? How did you get in here? What do you want? *Answer me!*"

The snickering stopped. Drawn as though mesmerized, Nancy slowly stooped down and peered under the bed, scared half to death at what she might find.

Eyes glinted at her in the darkness. The underside of her bed seemed filled with eyes and shadowy shapes.

Nancy snapped upright with a sharp cry.

A pubescent male voice said, "Hi. I'm Brandon."

Nancy tried to scream, but her vocal chords refused to function, and the sound strangled deep in her throat. She took a step backward.

Three forms slithered out from under the bed, rising up like sea monsters out of dark depths until they stood over her, slightly taller than she. They were teenage boys, and their pale skin and light hair stood out against the semidarkness of the room. One, the tallest, was lean, and had the cruelest eyes Nancy had ever seen. The other two, stockier, flanked him like guard dogs.

"Who are you?" she whimpered, pulling her arms tightly around her. "Why are you here?"

In answer, a flashlight flicked on, the beam directed at her face. It came from one of the stockier boys. Nancy squinted and turned her face.

The boy with the cruel eyes said, "Let the rest of the group in now, Jeff. Jason, cut the light."

The flashlight went off. Nancy heard the dead bolt on the front door click open, yet none of the boys had moved. Was someone else in the living room? She wanted to turn to look, but an invisible force held her frozen in place. She swallowed hard in a dry throat. She wanted to speak, but her lips were stuck together.

The door to the apartment opened and the soft sounds of feet moving in sneakers sounded behind her. The door closed. Muffled voices murmured. How many of them were there? It sounded like an army. She had to try to escape.

Nancy gave a muted cry and twisted away from the three boys in front of her, but her feet would not perform. She glimpsed a group of boys and girls clustered in the doorway of the bedroom.

Her head was snapped back by an incredible force. She tried to raise her arms, but they were lead weights. Before her, the drawers of her dresser opened and objects and clothing began flying out and sailing around the room, as though whipped up by some demon force. Invisible hands yanked her arms behind her back. A pair of white pantyhose circled her head and then wrapped quickly around her wrists, binding her hands. Another pair spun around her ankles. Then she was lifted by the same unseen force and pushed backward onto her bed.

The boy named Brandon stepped up and leaned over her. Now she could see his face clearly, the outline of his high cheekbones, the fullness of his lips, the sharp ridge of his nose—and the glittering coldness of his eyes. She wanted to look away but couldn't.

The boy said, "Where's Dr. Reston?"

Nancy's eyes widened. Her vocal chords worked again, but her voice was raspy. "Edward? How do you know him? What do you want?"

"That's none of your business."

Who *were* these monsters? Where had they come from? She had never seen these boys before in her life. What was Edward mixed up in? "I—don't know where he is."

"Liar."

Nancy felt an enormous wave of violent hostility pour out from the boy. He would savage her in an instant. She bit her lower lip as tears squeezed out of the corners of her eyes.

The boys named Jason and Jeff floated into view, flanking Brandon. "You'd better tell us," said Jeff.

If she didn't, would they kill her? If she did, would they kill her anyway?

"I told you, I don't know."

Brandon's hand lashed out and stung her cheek. "We can do a lot worse, Miss DeWitt."

Oh, God, they knew who she was, too. She was doomed. Nancy rolled her head from side to side. "Don't..." A fullness in her throat choked her, like someone had thick fingers wrapped around her neck, though none were there. She gasped.

"Let go of her throat, Jeff, you dumb shit. How can you expect her to talk like that?"

The choking sensation eased.

"Let's just probe," said Jason.

Probe? What were they talking about? Rape? The panic inside of Nancy mounted.

"I don't want to waste the energy on a probe, 'cause we're gonna need it when we find the doctor," said Brandon. "She'll talk." He bent down so close to her face that she could feel his hot breath. "Won't you, Miss DeWitt?"

"I don't *know* where he is."

"Sure you do." Brandon's face got very ugly. "Tell us."

Nancy sobbed. They would kill her—she could see it in Brandon's cruel eyes. She tried to think fast, holding onto hope that she would survive this terrible ordeal. She could tell them... and they would leave... and she would call the police.

She spoke in a small voice. "He's at his clinic, on Park Avenue."

Brandon's ugly expression got even darker. "No, he's not, you liar."

"He is, I swear it."

"I'm warning you."

In desperation, Nancy said, "If he's not at the clinic, then I don't know where he is!"

Brandon gritted his teeth and clenched a fist. The lamp by the side of the bed shattered without being touched. Nancy's heart skipped a beat and she braced for the blow, but none came.

Instead, she felt internal pain, an excruciating headache. Her vision turned red and she cried out in anguish. Just when she thought she could not endure the pain another second, it stopped. Her mind went blank. She could hear and see and feel, but couldn't form words or thoughts. She felt dopey, like she'd had too much gas at the dentist's.

"What a fucking waste of energy," said Brandon. "She really thinks he's at the clinic."

"Let's get out of here," said Jason.

"We can't just leave her," objected Jeff. "She knows about us now."

"Leave," Brandon commanded. He stepped back. The pantyhose wrapped and tied tightly around Nancy's wrists and ankles unwound and fell loose on the sheets. Hesitantly, Nancy lifted out her arms. They were numb, and flopped awkwardly. Needles of pain shot through them as the circulation came back. She stared at them stupidly.

The children started out. The apartment door opened of its own volition. Brandon gave Nancy one last wicked smile before he walked out. "Good night, Miss DeWitt."

As soon as the door closed behind Brandon, she scrambled up from the bed, moving like a toy gone out of order, her limbs not coordinating with one another. Her head felt like a cotton ball.

First she stumbled to the door, intending to throw the dead bolt and put up the chain to keep the monsters from returning. But the chain was up and the dead bolt was locked.

She had no time to try to comprehend. She had to reach the police. Edward was in danger! She stumbled back to the bedroom and picked up the white receiver. The line was dead.

She threw down the receiver and went to the beige phone in the living room. It was dead, too.

Nancy staggered to one of the open double-sashed windows in the living room, leaning out into the night. But instead of a scream, only a low wail came out of her throat. Five stories below, the street was empty.

A knife of pain slashed through her brain, worse than the previous attack. Globes of light exploded before her eyes. Another wave of pain hit. Nancy moaned.

A voice broke through the pain, and she heard a word in her mind.

Jump.

Other voices joined in, united in a singsong chant. *Jump . . . jump . . . jump . . . jump . . .*

Nancy moaned again, staring down at the street, getting dizzy. "I don't want to die!"

Jump . . . jump . . . jump . . .

She couldn't think straight. The street called out to her, begging her to come to its embrace. She felt she was being pulled out of the window by the same invisible force that had seized her in the bedroom and frozen her feet. Resisting the force brought on waves of unbearable pain.

With great effort, Nancy backed a few inches away from the window. Then the force took over again and sent her in lurching steps to the telephone table, where she kept a pencil and small notepad. She seized the pencil and began to write, horrified at the words that appeared in a crude version of her own neat handwriting.

She was composing her own suicide note.

Tears streamed down her face and stained the paper, but she could not stop writing. When the terse note was finished, the pencil flew out of her grasp.

Nancy began to walk back to the window in slow, jerky steps. The compelling force was overwhelming and victorious. She was going to die, and an odd peace settled over her.

She put one knee up on the windowsill. She looked out. Below, on the other side of the street, a group of children clustered in the shadows and watched in silence. She put the other knee up. A warm breeze ruffled her hair.

Nancy jumped.

CHAPTER
Twenty-Three

A cool breeze swept in off Long Island Sound to the shore of the north fork of Long Island, rustling the bullrushes. The sand beneath Stern's sneakers was moist from a recent rain, and crunched as he walked. The sky was overcast. He looked out over the white-capped gray water. In the distance, on the other side of the Sound, he could make out the long, dark shore of Connecticut.

In the past, he had come here to Oyster Point to relax and reflect in the haven of an isolated cottage. This time, Oyster Point was more than a refuge from the workaday life.

Behind him Reston said, "I never loved her the way she deserved to be loved."

Stern kept plodding along the sand, breathing deeply the invigorating tonic of rain-washed salt air. They were less than a quarter of a mile from the silvery cedar-shingle cottage where they had been staying, located on a solitary stretch of coast. He said, "Do you want to keep going, or do you want to go back to the house?"

"I can go a little farther," said Reston. "I'm feeling much better. That was some witch doctor you took me to."

"No witch doctor. Just a regular M.D. who lives in my apartment building."

"You're sure he won't make a report? The police are still looking for me."

"He's solid. I suspect he has mob connections. I performed a quick legal service for him once on the Q.T. Believe me, he was glad to return the favor and balance the debt." Stern turned and glanced at Reston over his shoulder. "He's probably used to stitching up nine-millimeter bullet holes in his back room. You were easy. Smoke inhalation and a few first-degree burns."

Reston wheezed. "I guess I haven't got my wind back yet."

Stern pointed to a log up ahead. "Let's sit down there."

The log was damp from the earlier rain, but they sat anyway.

Reston said in a tight voice, "I still can't believe Nancy is ... gone."

Stern dropped his eyes to the sand. He felt sorry for the tragedies but was unable to express himself. He had been drained of emotion long ago. He said quietly, "I don't know how the kids killed her, but they did. We've got to stop them, Edward. They're monsters."

Reston put his head in his hands. "I don't know. I wish I knew for sure about Nancy. The papers said suicide ... she left a note ..."

"Don't believe it. You know Nancy would never have jumped out of the window by her own choice."

"I wish I could talk to the police. They must know more than they're telling the press."

"You know that's impossible. If we get involved with the police, our hands will be tied. We have got to see this through on our own."

"You're right, you're right." Reston looked out across the water. A solitary gull floated on the air currents overhead. "How long have we been here?"

"Eight days." Stern worried about his law practice. He'd

been forced to abandon his cases, including the sensitive, ten-million-dollar lawsuit against the firm's client, Clements. He had logged in a lot of hours on the case, all his investigation for naught.

But this was more important.

Reston said, "It doesn't seem like eight days. I guess I've lost track of time."

"You were out of it for a while. I've got news for you—it's going to take a lot longer for your eyebrows to grow back." He smiled.

Reston felt the singed stubs of hair that were his eyebrows. "Oh, well. I don't have to worry about my looks, do I?" His attempt to be lighthearted failed. He buried his head in his hands again and shook with dry sobs. Stern put a hand on his shoulder.

A few minutes passed, and then Reston rubbed his eyes and lifted his face. "Look at me, acting like a baby."

"Grief," said Stern. "You're suffering."

"What do I know about suffering? You've been through more pain than I could endure in ten lifetimes. How have you stayed sane?"

Stern made a wry smile. "That's a matter of judgment."

"How do you keep going?"

"I suppose I haven't yet fulfilled my purpose on this planet." Voices murmured in Stern's ear, but he kept them back. He would not let them speak.

What would he do with Hans Messner when he found him? He was a lawyer, sworn to uphold the tenets of justice, the right of every man to be held innocent until proven guilty in a court of law.

But he would not turn Hans Messner over to a court of law, not even an Israeli court, and surrender his right to satisfaction.

Hans Messner was *his*.

As if guessing his thoughts, Reston said, "You're looking for revenge, aren't you? For the Holocaust." When Stern did not reply immediately, Reston hurried on, "I don't blame you. But you're still wrong about John Heineman."

"Am I? What's your theory then?"

"I think the children were created out of a grotesque experiment that went off course."

Stern watched the gull hang suspended in the air. "Indeed they are grotesque, doctor. Indeed they are."

The conversation had taken an awkward turn. Reston changed the subject. "You're sure we're safe here?"

"Reasonably. I'm officially on personal leave from the firm, and no one knows where I've gone." Stern thought, *Thank God Ben was so understanding*.

"So here we are at Oyster Point. Rather godforsaken."

"Exactly. Oyster Point is an ugly little place that doesn't attract tourists—they all go south to the glitzy Hamptons. I've been out here before when I wanted to make a clean break from civilization. And it's far enough away from Manhattan and the kids so that we're out of immediate danger."

"You still believe that distance makes a difference with those kids? Weakens their power?"

"Yes. It's not logical, if there's any logic at all to extrasensory phenomena, but it's the only explanation for the fact that they were always nearby when one of their disasters occurred." Stern bent down and picked up a shard of mussel shell that had been polished by the surf.

"Maybe they were morbidly fascinated."

"If I were one of them, I would want to be as far away from the scene as possible. It's instinctive among children to not want to be caught doing something wrong."

Reston kicked at the sand. "I have a hard time believing mere children are capable of plotting murder."

"I'm positive they're being controlled by Heineman." For Reston's benefit, he referred to Messner by his alias. The truth would come out, but for now, it caused needless friction. "Heineman has gone into hiding, and we have to find him first before we can deal with the children."

"John wouldn't want to kill me."

"I'm afraid you were marked from the beginning because you knew the truth about the children's origin."

"But John could have taken the kids anywhere and I wouldn't have known or cared."

"You still posed a potential problem. The smoking gun."

"So where do we go from here?"

"Now that you're functional again, we can find a phone. I'm sure you've got contacts who might have information about Mes—er, Heineman."

Reston considered this. "I'll give it a shot. What about you?"

"I'm going back to the city for a few days."

"*What?*"

Stern grinned. "Don't worry, I'll keep a low profile. I can't afford a run-in with the police, but they aren't actively looking for me like they are you. And today is the first day of school, so our little friends will be busy. I hope." He explained his idea.

Brandon squirmed in his hard, uncomfortable school seat, his arms spread out across the little desk, his fingers clutching the desk's edge. First period science this year, what a drag. Mr. Finley droned on, outlining the subjects that would be covered in the weeks ahead. Brandon didn't listen.

He hated having to come back to school, hated his uniform of tan slacks with navy blue wool blazer, decorated with the Winston School crest. He hated having to sit here and be bored stiff by stupid adults who knew less than he did. He hated everything.

The only good thing was his seat. As usual, the students were arranged alphabetically, and in this class Brandon was in the far left row toward the end. It afforded him a good view of the rest of the class without twisting.

Some of his Loki followers also were stuck with Mr. Finley for home period. Jason slouched way down in his seat, arms folded across his chest. The back of his head bristled with short blond hairs. Near Jason sat Michael, who was equally bored, judging from his posture.

On the other side of the classroom, Jennifer sat up straight, hands folded neatly on her desk, feet planted on the floor. Brandon could envision the expression on her face: rapt attention. Almost directly across from him by several rows, Tommy leaned forward on his desk. He looked like he was actually interested in what Finley Fudley had to say. So typical of Tommy.

The fact that they were sitting here in class instead of hunting down their quarry was chiefly Tommy's fault. Brandon's thoughts grew dark. He'd advocated skipping school for as long as necessary until they found the doctor and the lawyer. The two birds had flown their coops.

Tommy had objected to the plan. That in itself didn't surprise Brandon because Tommy was getting to be more and more troublesome. He didn't count him a friend anymore. If Tommy weren't so strong in his own power, Brandon would do a David number on him.

Tommy argued for going back to school, claiming that their collective absence would cause trouble. Even several of them cutting out would be bad—reports would go out to parents, questions would be asked that none of the Loki wanted to answer.

Brandon realized that but felt the adults could be handled. Nothing was more important than getting the enemy, as he put it. To his shock, a majority of the Loki members sided with Tommy. Though his own powers were growing, he was not strong enough to impose his will on the entire group.

Not yet.

Well, perhaps things would turn out all right. Once he put his own plan into action, the doctor and lawyer might no longer matter.

So here he sat in school, bored and angry, already impatient for the school day to end so that his real work could begin.

"Brandon? Will you answer the question please?" Mr. Finley's voice cut through his reverie.

He hadn't heard the question, and his cheeks turned crimson as others in the class turned to look at him. Finley had asked him on purpose, of course, seeing that he wasn't paying attention. Brandon knew the teacher expected to make an example out of him to admonish everyone else to pay attention.

Finley had chalked an equation on the blackboard. There was a blank spot after the equal sign. Brandon didn't have the slightest idea what the equation related to. A few students who didn't like Brandon snickered.

Finley turned to the blackboard and raised his arm to tap his piece of chalk at the equation. Just as his arm went up, the sleeve of his suit jacket ripped open at the shoulder. Flustered, he dropped his arm. The class burst into giggles.

Brandon leaned back in his seat and laughed.

Back in Manhattan on the chic East Side, Stern hurried along the sidewalk with a newly purchased portfolio in one hand and a hat pulled down to partially hide his face. Until they found Messner, he had one last desperate idea for getting at least a few of the "embryo children" off the streets. It was a longshot, but that was all he had left.

In the portfolio was a list that Reston had made out with the names and addresses of all thirteen children. Stern had thought it most interesting that Reston had memorized the information, but he had not commented upon it.

The first name on his list was Elizabeth Rankin, who lived on East Seventy-first. Stern talked his way past the doorman of the swank building. As soon as the Rankins' door was opened by a maid, he launched into his line.

"Hello, I'm Richard Sobel from the Winston School counseling staff, and I'd like to see Mrs. or Mr. Rankin about their daughter, Elizabeth—"

The maid looked surprised.

Stern said, "This *is* the Rankin residence, isn't it?"

"Yes, bu' neither the Mister nor Missus is home," the maid answered in a heavy Jamaican accent. "What yo' want?"

"When can I call again?"

"They won't be back till this evening, after work."

Stern was chagrined. That meant the daughter would probably be home, too. If both Mr. and Mrs. Rankin worked, they would be a bad bet for him. He said, "I'm terribly sorry to have disturbed you."

"You don't want to come back?"

"It won't be necessary."

"Leave a message?"

"No, thank you. It's a small matter, I can contact them by phone." He turned to go and then thought of something. He stopped the maid from closing the door. "I'm not sure when I will phone, so I would appreciate it if you would not mention my coming by today."

The maid nodded dully.

Stern looked at his list. The second name was David Martin.

"David's been missing for over three weeks now, Mr. Sobel. Didn't they tell you that at Winston?" A nervous Mrs. Martin twisted her hands together as they stood in the marbled foyer of the Martin co-op. She was a tiny, birdlike woman who looked severely stressed.

"No, I'm sorry, madam, I was going by last term's records. I'd hoped to get your cooperation for a new counseling program. David had been exhibiting behavioral problems, you see." *In other words, let's get him sequestered and under observation until this whole thing is explained and under control.*

"Well, there's nothing wrong with David!" she snapped. "He's a model student, straight A's, and has *never* given us a problem. He's our only child, and we've absolutely devoted ourselves to him. I was hoping you could tell me news about him—" Her voice faltered.

"I'm afraid not, Mrs. Martin."

She chewed on a knuckle. "He just vanished. The police keep telling us he probably ran away. We've got a private detective working on it. I can't believe David would do that." She squinted at Stern. "I thought I knew all the administrators at Winston, but your name is not familiar."

Stern reached out to the brass doorknob. "I must be going, Mrs. Martin, or I'll be late for an appointment. I hope you hear about your son soon. My apologies for intruding."

With any luck, Stern thought as he exited the building, David Martin will be dead. Eleven to go.

He looked at his watch. It was an inexpensive Seiko he had purchased earlier in the day in a tourist trap on Fifth Avenue, one of those shops that is perpetually "going out of business" and "slashing prices." It was almost time for school to be out for the day. He would take no chances.

Stern spent the night in the Rexford Hotel, a shabby place in Hell's Kitchen where none of the help asked questions or gave a damn about anything beyond getting meager tips. He insisted on a room on the second floor directly across from the stairwell. Paranoia was setting in.

The following day, he resumed his work. The third name on the list was Michael Stewart. Much to Stern's surprise, it was the father who was home during the day, not the mother.

Jack Stewart was a strapping fellow who could have passed for a stevedore or wrestler. When they shook hands, Stewart's beefy paw swallowed Stern's hand like a whale swallowing a tuna. His expression seemed set in a permanent glower. *He must have made his money in professional sports*, thought Stern. *He certainly doesn't look like the typical affluent executive who sends his kid to Winston.*

"You come to tell me there's a problem with my kid, Mr. Sobel?" he said in a rough Bronx accent.

"It has come to my attention that Michael would benefit from some immediate counseling, Mr. Stewart. We would like to place him—"

"Yeah? Sounds like you're the one with the problem. There's nothing wrong with *my* kid. We done the best for him, got him inta de best school."

This is getting to be a familiar litany, thought Stern. *No parent wants to think his child is anything less than angelic*.

Stewart went on, "The only problem Mike's got is his mother."

"His mother?"

"She flipped out. Dopey dame. She's been saying for months that Mike was trying to eat her brain out because he hated her. Can you imagine that?" Stewart snorted. "So one night she went bonkers and tore after him with a butcher knife. Damn near killed the poor kid—would have, if I hadn't been home. I pushed her face in pretty good, and then I had her committed upstate. She agreed. It was either that or a messy deal with the police."

Shocked, Stern tried to keep an impassive face. "A trauma like that is all the more reason to place Michael in a special counseling program. Perhaps you would consider—"

Stewart stepped forward. "The only thing I'm gonna consider, mac, is giving you ten seconds to get outta my sight."

Rainer stood in front of the apartment building where Tommy Myers lived. His first three visits had turned up nothing useful. One more, he decided, and if this one turned up bust, he would think of some other tactic. He steeled himself.

As soon as the Myers' apartment door opened, a mustiness assaulted Stern's nostrils. It was the smell of stale air, illness, and medication. He wrinkled his nose.

"May I help you?" said the woman in the door. She was dressed in a white nurse's uniform. Behind her, Stern glimpsed the apartment. It was semi-dark, as though all the curtains and blinds were pulled.

"Richard Sobel," he said. "I'm here to see Mrs. Myers."

"Is she expecting you?"

"I'm from the Winston School—"

The nurse looked puzzled. "I don't recall her setting up an appointment. Wait a moment." She shut the door. Stern fidgeted for several minutes before the door was reopened. "You may come in, Mr. Sobel, but you may stay only a few minutes."

As soon as Stern was fully inside the dark, cavernous apartment, he saw the reason for the nurse, and for the time limitation of his visit. Mrs. Myers was confined to a wheelchair, her shriveled and distorted body the victim of some deteriorating disease. It was impossible to tell her age. She looked ancient, but Stern guessed she was much younger. She had beady eyes and a hawklike nose, and she peered at him with distrust. His heart sank.

With the nurse hovering over Mrs. Myers, he went through his spiel.

With great effort, the ill woman tried to respond, but she had little control over her facial muscles and vocal cords. The only sounds that came out of her contorting mouth were unintelligible.

"What is she saying?" Stern asked the nurse.

"I'm not sure, but it's something about Tommy being unhappy."

"Why don't you ask me yourself?"

The adolescent voice came from behind Stern. He turned and saw a slender, brown-haired boy with the beginnings of a handsome face, staring at him with the most intense eyes Rainer had ever seen, eyes that made him extremely uneasy. He recognized the boy from John McCord's funeral. He tensed.

"Tommy!" the nurse exclaimed. "Where've you been? I thought you went to school."

The boy shrugged. He came closer. He was tall for his age, Stern thought. "I didn't feel like going today. I've been in my room."

His mother squirmed in her wheelchair, making animal noises.

"It's all right, Mother," the boy said, laying a slender

hand on her shoulder. "I'm keeping up with my studies. I'm home more than you realize."

Stern was trapped. He had not intended to run face to face into one of the children. He was doomed.

"Don't worry," Tommy said to him, as if sensing his thoughts. "I can answer your questions." He addressed his mother again: "I'll handle this, Mother." He took hold of Stern's hand, sending a strange electricity of strength and power through Rainer, making him shiver.

Tommy said, "Let's go outside."

Neither spoke again until they were out in the sunshine. The streets of the East Side neighborhood were quiet and clean, a respectable area populated by well-to-do families.

I don't believe it, thought Stern, struggling to control the panic that threatened to grab hold of him. *It's a trap*. The voices inside began humming again, incoherent, yet strangely calming. He said to himself, *I'm going to be okay*.

He felt as though he were in a dream. Tommy steered him to a corner street vendor selling Dove Bar ice cream bars. Stern bought one for the boy, but declined to join him. He was struck by the incredible irony of him buying an ice cream bar for a child he had told Reston had to be "destroyed." He still wondered if Tommy meant to lead him into a trap. Perhaps the others were not in school, either, but were hiding, waiting for him. Yet, he felt compelled to do as this child said. They left the vendor and strolled down the street.

Once again, Tommy anticipated his thoughts. "I'm alone, Mr. Stern—that *is* your real name, isn't it, not Sobel? I stayed home from school today because I had a feeling you would come." Tommy took a large bite out of the fat bar, splintering the hard chocolate coating. Beneath was chocolate ice cream.

Stern stopped and grabbed the boy's shoulder, spinning him around. "Who are you kids? Why are you killing innocent people?"

Tommy blinked, unperturbed. He shrugged off Stern's

grasp and continued down the sidewalk. "We're different from you and everyone else, Mr. Stern. It's not our fault."

"I know. I know more than you think."

"And *I* know what you understand. We're better, you see. We found each other, and we stick together. We can do things you only dream of. We think, and it comes true."

"But why hurt others? What have they done to you?"

"It wasn't my idea. It started with Brandon."

"Brandon Evered?"

"He's the leader."

"It sounds like some of you don't like what you're doing."

"Maybe."

"Why don't you leave your group?"

"You can't leave Brandon," said Tommy. "He hurts people who disagree with him."

"So the deaths of his parents were deliberate, not accidental."

"They were going to send Brandon to a Swiss boarding school, and he didn't want to go."

"And the other parents—Holliday and McCord?"

"The same."

"How did you do it? I think I know how, but tell me. The deaths appeared to be accidents or natural causes."

"It's complicated to explain, Mr. Stern."

Rainer hesitated. "And your mother, Tommy?"

"I—we—didn't do that. She has multiple sclerosis, and it's been coming on for years."

"Where's your father?"

"He divorced Mom a long time ago. I don't know where he is. Probably sailing in the Aegean."

"You're practically alone, then."

Tommy was silent.

A thought occurred to Stern. "David Martin—his mother told me he's disappeared and may have run away."

"Nope. He drowned in the lake at Central Park. Brandon never liked David and blamed him for some mistakes. He made us do that to him. Except I didn't participate."

Stern felt clammy. How could this boy eat ice cream and calmly talk about killing people? He stopped and looked around them, half expecting to see a band of wild teenagers come charging at him. "Why are you telling me this, Tommy?"

"Because I don't like Brandon anymore, and neither do some of the others. I don't like hurting people. Maybe you can help, since you already know about us." He finished off the last of his Dove Bar. "Are you hungry, Mr. Stern? I could go for something else."

Rainer let Tommy steer him to a Greek café called the Apollo. They went to the rear and slid into a red vinyl booth, facing each other across a Formica tabletop that was supposed to imitate marble. A fat waiter in a food-stained white apron came over with large red menus, but Tommy waved them aside. "I'll have a double cheeseburger with fries and a chocolate soda."

Stern ordered black coffee. When the waiter had gone, he looked around the café nervously.

"Quit worrying," the boy said. "The others aren't around."

They are of one mind, Stern reminded himself. He said, "If you share your thoughts, why don't Brandon and the others know you are here, talking to me?"

"It doesn't work like that. First of all, you have to make an effort to share, or to take. Works both ways. We can keep each other out, for a while. We call it the mind shield. It's like a barrier we throw up. The only thing Brandon knows right now is that he can't reach me. It makes him mad when any of us do that, but he can't stop us."

"You just said he could hurt you."

Tommy shrugged. "That takes energy. He can't hurt all of us all the time, or he wouldn't have any energy left."

For a split second—perhaps it was the earnest expression on Tommy's face—Stern softened toward the boy and thought of him in terms of being someone's son. It was irrational, but he couldn't help himself. "Did you ever think about becoming a lawyer, Tommy? You've got a very sharp, logical mind."

Tommy grinned. "I'd like to be a lawyer. Lawyers run the world."

"They run America," Stern conceded. "Sometimes not for the best. But that's a topic for another time. Tell me more about this mind shield of yours." He thought of the mental bond between himself and his dead brother. They too, he remembered, had had their little techniques for shutting the other out.

"It's like a TV blackout—you know, when they black out the broadcast of a big football game in the home town. You can't tune in with your own TV set. But it takes a lot of energy to keep the shield going, so it's only temporary."

"How much longer will yours last?" Stern asked, worried.

"Who knows. Incidentally, I've got you shielded as well, so it's hard to estimate."

"Me?" Stern looked around him, almost expecting to see an energy force field. There was nothing. Nothing visible, that is. Yet he realized he did feel differently, a trifle electrified. "Are you kids able to *read my thoughts?*"

"Not very well because you're not blood."

"Blood?"

"One of us. We sealed ourselves with a blood oath."

The waiter brought Stern's coffee and Tommy's soda.

"You planned to meet me, didn't you?" Stern said.

"Sort of. I felt you coming yesterday. I knew you would come to my apartment. That's why I stayed home from school."

Stern remembered his words to Reston: *"Those children have got to be destroyed... They're monsters."* They had killed four adults and had tried twice to kill Reston and himself. They were bad seed born under a bad sign. Unsalvageable.

Except, perhaps, this boy. He was, after all, still a child.

Stern folded his hands on the Formica. "You have very

unusual abilities, Tommy. You can't expect to keep that a secret forever. Would you volunteer for scientific research?"

"I'm not a freak, Mr. Stern," said Tommy, bringing his fist down on the table. "I don't want to be a guinea pig."

The boy's words struck home. Stern was immediately transported back in time some forty years, to a dirty, cold "hospital" in the Polish woods, where unspeakable horrors took place every day, and human medical "mistakes" were burned to ashes in the ovens. "I know the feeling," he said softly.

"Besides," Tommy went on, "we don't want adults to learn what we know. Adults go around making a mess of the world."

Stern's smile held no humor. "You've got an excellent point. But have you made the world better by killing people?"

Tommy swirled his straw through the soda. "Without Brandon, things would be a lot different."

The waiter returned with Tommy's double cheeseburger and fries. Tommy reached for the ketchup bottle and splatted a huge glob onto the side of the platter. "Want some?" he asked Stern, pointing to the fries.

Stern shook his head. "What is it you hope I can do? I seem to be at a distinct disadvantage against your combined abilities."

"You're more like us than you think. You'll find a way."

He recalled the visions, the dreams, the voices... the psychiatrist named Neissen... all stuffed away in the back of his mind and thoroughly denied. Stern was going to ask Tommy to explain exactly what he meant, then decided against it. He wasn't sure he wanted to find out.

Tommy was going on, "—at least half of the group—there are twelve of us left, you know—supports Brandon. Two of us are firmly opposed, and three or four others might be waffling. They would take some persuading."

"Two of you? Who is the second?"

"Lori Gallagher. Would you like to meet her?"

"Yes. When? After school?"

"Right now." Tommy took a huge bite out of his cheeseburger.

A cool, small hand touched Stern on the back of the neck. His hair stood on end and his flesh prickled. He twisted in his seat. On the other side of the booth, on her knees and looking over the top of the seat at him, was a girl about Tommy's age, with long, dusty-brown hair, milky-pale skin, and luminescent blue eyes that were too big for her thin face.

"How long have you been here?" Stern asked in astonishment.

"A few minutes." She came around and slid onto the seat next to Tommy.

"Lori had a test fourth period, so she couldn't cut the whole day," Tommy explained.

Lori helped herself to one of Tommy's fries.

Stern was suddenly very nervous and wished for a cigar, though he had given up smoking years ago. He looked at the children, who were momentarily absorbed in the greasy food. They looked so... *normal*. What was he going to do with them? He said, "Why do you need me?"

"Because you've got the solution to our problem," Lori said.

"No, I don't."

"Then you just don't know it, yet."

Stern rubbed his brow. "I see. All right, if I help you, will you help me?"

They nodded without speaking, busy chewing.

"You will never again use your abilities to hurt anyone, or for a bad purpose."

Tommy and Lori looked at each other. Tommy said, "Sure."

Stern leaned back in the booth. "Okay, Tommy, isn't it about time you told me about your real leader?"

Tommy frowned. "Who's that?"

"The man who organized you and gives you your instructions. Hans Messner."

"Who?" said Lori.

"Hans Messner," Tommy said. "He means that old guy in the park."

Stern's anticipation rose. "Where is he?"

"He's dead."

"*Dead?* No, he's not."

Tommy mopped up a blob of ketchup with a French fry. He told Stern about the encounter between his group and the man who wanted them to go away with him. "He was crazy," Tommy finished. "Nobody believed him. And Brandon would never let someone else step in and take over as leader. No way."

"You didn't kill him," said Stern, not knowing how he knew what he now knew. "He suffered a heart attack but recovered. You have had no contact with him since that happened?"

"Nope."

Rainer's stomach tightened. All along he had assumed the children's attacks had been orchestrated by Hans Messner. Now he learned they were acting on their own. Which made them more deadly than ever.

Stern and the two children parted company about an hour later. Tommy was worried about being able to maintain his protective mental screen much longer. He was getting tired, he explained to Stern. They agreed to meet again the following day, after school so that Tommy and Lori would not have to skip classes again.

"We have club meetings every week at the American Museum of Natural History," Tommy said. "If you want to catch everyone at once, that would be the best time to do it."

"We'll see," Stern said.

When the children were out of sight, Stern headed for the garage where he had parked his silver BMW. He would return to Oyster Point and get Reston, and they would come back to the city together to meet again with Tommy and Lori.

Stern paid no attention to the street activity going on around him. He was a block from the garage when his thoughts were shattered. A black sedan came tearing toward him, traveling on the wrong side of the street, out of control.

People on the sidewalk screamed and scrambled to get out of the way. On the driver's side, a terrified woman spun the useless wheel and shouted through her open window, "I can't stop! Oh, God, I can't stop!"

Stern stood frozen in horror as the car lurched and struck an elderly woman with a cane, pulling her beneath the wheels, crushing her and dragging her along the street. The car headed straight for him. At the last moment, he twisted his body and dove to the left, rolling along the sidewalk. Pain shot up his left leg. He forced himself to keep rolling, past a fire hydrant, bracing himself for the end.

The car slammed into the fire hydrant and rose up on its rear wheels like some great metal beast before descending with a gigantic explosion of breaking glass and popping tires. The hydrant burst open, spewing water over the sidewalk and street.

The door of the sedan sprang open, and the woman driver flew through the air like a rag doll and hit the side of a building with a thud.

Water mixed with blood and ran a wide pink river down the asphalt. Bystanders screamed and shouted, dashing to the scene to help the victims. Two were beyond help.

Stern, trying to get to his feet in a daze, was pulled up by a strong pair of arms. "You all right, mister?"

He nodded woozily, testing his injured leg, not knowing whether the pain meant it was broken or just severely bruised. He gazed stupidly at the car. The heap of smashed metal groaned and shifted, crushing down on the lifeless body of the old woman, who was still pinned beneath.

The acrid-sweet smell of gasoline wafted out, mixing with the smells of smoke, burned rubber, dirt, and blood.

"Get back!" someone shouted. "The gas tank might blow!"

The crowd of bystanders pushed back in unison.

I have to get away, Stern told himself. *No police . . . no police . . .* He put weight on his leg. The pain was bad but not unbearable; the leg was not broken. He shrugged himself away from the man who'd pulled him to his feet, and began to stagger off down the street.

"Hey, mister," the man called after him. "You gotta stay here! Someone has called the ambulance. You might need help!"

Rainer turned. "Kids," he said. "Did you see any kids?"

The man looked puzzled. "No. Are yours missing?"

Stern didn't answer and resumed his jerky walk. No one came after him or tried to stop him. They were too engrossed in the grisly scene of the accident.

Had he been betrayed? The inner voices rose up inside of him, and he was powerless to stop them.

Two teenagers lured you into a trap, lied to you, and left you to be killed.

No, another voice within him argued. *That's not how it is. This was not their doing.*

The argument went back and forth until the voices blended into each other and the words were indistinguishable.

Stern collected his BMW and sped back to Oyster Point, half afraid he would find Edward Reston dead in a pool of blood. He kept telling himself the fear was groundless, reminding himself what Tommy had told him, confirming his speculation that the children's power decreased in proportion to distance. The closer they were and the more of them there were, the stronger the power. Oyster Point was too far away, accessible only by car. Unless, he thought, they had found a way to make the trip in a group.

The Secret Society of Loki. That's what they called themselves, Tommy had said. Stern turned the name over and over in his mind. The Loki children. It had a nasty sound.

He burst into the cottage and found Reston gone. His few belongings were scattered about. Frantic, Stern ran out into the low dunes along the beach. The loose sand slowed his progress until he got out of the dunes and onto the rocky, tide-hardened sand. The beach was empty.

CHAPTER Twenty-Four

Edward Reston was exhausted, but he kept his hands on the wheel and his foot pressed down on the gas pedal. The lingering effects of smoke inhalation made him tire easily and labor for breath. He was getting better, but sometimes his lungs felt like pieces of corrugated meat. He was in a little Toyota, speeding along the Long Island Expressway west toward the Throg's Neck Bridge, and Westchester County.

He reflected that he could have waited for Stern to come back, but there was no telling when that would be—if he came back at all. So Edward had elected to take action on his own. Besides, he was about to go stir-crazy in Oyster Point.

The phone calls he had made concerning John Heineman had led nowhere. The man had severed all his ties in the medical/scientific communities and vanished. There was only one last thing Reston could think of: Heineman's home. Like Stern's idea to visit the children's parents, it was a long shot, but long shots were all they had.

Reston hadn't been to Heineman's home in Purchase in years. He wasn't certain the man still lived in the same place. He had kept the same unlisted telephone number over the years but could have changed his address. Reston wasn't sure what visiting a vacant home would turn up. He only knew he had to do it.

The Oyster Point cottage was in a secluded location, and Reston had walked several miles down a sandy dirt road to get to another country road with promising traffic. He had hitched a ride to Riverhead with a potato farmer driving a pickup truck. He supposed he could have hitched all the way to Westchester, if he hadn't been concerned about time. The obliging farmer knew of a car rental agency in Riverhead, and dropped him off. Reston had gotten out of the clinic fire with his wallet intact. Thank God for plastic credit.

He checked the dashboard digital clock. He would reach Purchase before noon. Good.

The dappled sunlight filtering through enormous oaks and sycamores made the winding roads around Purchase charming and picturesque. Gracious homes were set far back from the road, protected from sightseers by wooded lots or lawns with tree screens.

The scene was the epitome of serenity, but Reston felt far from relaxed. Once he left the Hutchinson Parkway, he drove by rote, old memories coming back to prompt him which ways to turn.

The home where Heineman had lived enjoyed good privacy. Characteristically, it was more a compound than a home. The main house was a stately Normandy with white brick walls and a black-shingled roof that reigned on a hillock over three acres. There was a detached garage, which Reston remembered had been converted into a private little lab. Heineman was always at work on a string of projects of his own.

Reston pulled in the long and circular gravel driveway and stopped at the front door. The house didn't appear vacant. Curtains still hung in the windows; orange and yellow chrysanthemums bloomed in beds cut out in the lawn. Then he noticed that the garden beds, obviously once carefully cultivated, had grown sloppy with creeping weeds.

He rang the doorbell, not expecting an answer. He jiggled the door. It was, of course, locked. The curtains were drawn back from some of the windows. Reston stepped around to them, shaded his eyes against the glare reflected in the panes, and looked in. Judging from the living room, the furniture had been left with the house. The room looked set up, waiting for its owner to return.

Reston went around to the back of the house to look in the rear windows. He had just pulled himself up on a window ledge to get a better view when a hostile masculine voice startled him.

"Can I help you?"

Reston dropped back to the ground. The owner of the voice, a tall man dressed in corduroys and a crew shirt, stood about twenty feet off. Next to him stood a muscular Doberman, eyeing Reston with an aggressive, cross-eyed look. The dog was not leashed. Reston decided he would make no sudden movements.

"You startled me," he said, striving to sound casual. "I didn't hear you."

The man's eyes flitted back to the front lawn. Reston guessed he had come up the grass instead of the gravel drive.

"You looking for something?" The hostility was still there.

Reston was flustered. "Is—the house for sale?"

The man's eyes narrowed. He reached down and stroked the dog's head. "As far as I know. You'd have to ask Lois Harkens about that."

"Lois Harkens?"

"Down at Country Realty."

"Thanks. I will."

Very slowly, Reston brushed off his hands.

"Is that what you're here for?" asked the man.

Reston decided to embroider on the lie. "Maybe. I'm in

the market for something around here, and a friend told me about this place..." His voice trailed off.

The man stepped closer. The Doberman stuck to his side.

Reston blurted, "Are you watching the property?"

"Sort of. I live down the road. I saw you drive in. We've been having a lot of break-ins around here lately."

Edward wished his eyebrows had grown back. "Sorry to worry you. I was only curious. Do you know what happened to the owner? I mean, I like to know why houses are on the market. At today's prices, you don't want to buy someone's plumbing problems." He smiled disarmingly, but the man did not smile back.

"I can't answer that. A single man lived here. Quiet fellow. Stuck to himself."

"Well. I guess I'll pay a visit to Lois Harkens. Thanks for the information." Reston started to edge away, looking questioningly at the dog.

"Maxwell won't hurt you," the man said. But Reston did not turn his back all the way back to his car.

Lois Harkens was a spare, tough woman made out of steel cable. In a market where houses routinely sold for three-quarters-of-a-million dollars and up, she was accustomed to driving big deals.

She had perfected a superficial, honeyed manner for prospective clients and had a permanent smile. "The Heineman property," she enthused, when Reston presented himself at the Country Realty office as Bill Edwards. "What a charming, *delightful* place. You certainly have good taste, Mr. Edwards." She went through the ploy of checking her calendar. "Why, your timing is perfect. I can take you out there right now."

Reston insisted on driving his own car instead of allowing Harkens to chauffeur him in her Jaguar. "I'll have to leave right from there," he explained, alluding to pressing business.

He followed Harkens. While she drove up to the front

door, he parked the car at the entrance to the drive. She looked at him quizzically for explanation, but he offered none.

The air inside the house was stale. Reston interrupted Harkens' spiel about the genuine quarry tile hand-laid in the foyer. "How long has this house been on the market?"

She took his question to mean, *Is there a problem why this house hasn't sold by now*, and said, "Not long, Mr. Edwards. Houses like these don't attract your average buyer, you understand."

"How long?"

"Well, since earlier this summer," she said reluctantly. "Now, if you'll look over here, we have a living room of lovely proportions, with a cathedral ceiling and a beautiful fireplace framed in imported Italian tiles . . ."

Reston nodded and murmured through the tour. The house was much the same as he remembered it, strongly masculine in flavor, with minimal, functional furnishings. So typical of Heineman. There was no sign of a woman's presence. Reston wondered why Heineman had never married. He was certain it wasn't that John preferred men.

"Why is the owner selling?" he asked.

"I understand he moved," said Harkens, sweeping on to a kitchen that was half the size of Reston's entire Murray Hill apartment. A woman would have considered it a dream kitchen and hung up copper pots and pans, and bunches of dried herbs. In its present state, the kitchen looked neglected. The real estate agent babbled on about cupboard space and the state-of-the-art appliances. He wished she would get on with it. He had not yet seen what he was looking for.

"Do you know where the owner went?" Reston broke in.

Harkens clearly disliked being interrupted. "I don't, Mr. Edwards."

"Then how can we close a deal? He would have to sign the papers."

She brightened. "Banks and attorneys can handle that, Mr. Edwards. You like what you've seen so far?"

"I'm impressed."

"Before we go upstairs to the bedrooms, there's one last room to see in the rear of the main floor. It's my favorite room in this house, and I know you're just going to love it." Harkens ushered Reston into a study. It was dark and private with walnut paneling, and brass lamps with forest green shades. One wall was given over to floor-to-ceiling walnut bookshelves, crammed with hardbound books. The center attraction in the room was a massive mahogany desk and padded brown leather swivel chair. "As I said, Mr. Edwards, all the furnishings come with the house."

Reston went to the desk and admired it, pulling open the center drawer. "Beautiful." He winced. He put his hand to his chest and groaned.

"What is it, Mr. Edwards?" Harkens asked anxiously, coming quickly to his side.

Reston sank down in the leather chair, still pressing his chest. "I'm sorry... I've been ill..."

"Is there anything I can do? A glass of water? Would you like to lie down?"

Reston closed his eyes. "I'll be all right if I can rest a moment." His breathing was labored.

"Oh, dear!"

He opened his eyes and fumbled in the pocket of his trousers. "Actually, if you wouldn't mind, Mrs. Harkens—"

"Of course not. What do you need?"

"I seem to have left my pills out in the car. In the glove compartment."

"I'll get them right away, Mr. Edwards!" Lois Harkens sped out of the study.

Reston waited until she was out of earshot and then began tearing through the contents of the desk drawers. Most of the papers were related to business of the Klein laboratory. Reston hastily scanned them. Perhaps there was a telephone number, an address, a memo—anything with a clue to Heineman's present whereabouts.

He found nothing in the desk and went quickly to a file cabinet. It wasn't locked. The drawers were jammed with folders labeled according to various research projects, the dates going back years. He pawed through them.

Nothing!

He went back to the desk for one more search. He was flipping through papers when a name caught his attention. The Martell Institute. The document was a research paper written by the director of the institute, Dr. Mikhail B. Cernak.

Reston started to look through it when he heard footsteps running toward the study. He shut the drawers and folded up the report, stuffing it into his pocket. He slumped back in the chair and closed his eyes. He didn't have to fake rapid breathing.

"Mr. Edwards, I can't find your pills! I looked everywhere."

Reston struggled to sit up. "It's all right," he said, his words punctuated with gasps. "I'm—feeling better. It passed. I must have—left them at home. Foolish of me."

Harkens was clearly relieved that Reston was not going to suffer a medical emergency on her. "Perhaps we should see the rest of the house another time," she said, wringing her hands.

"I think you're right." Reston slowly got to his feet. "Thank you, Mrs. Harkens. I'll be in touch."

Reston sat in his car in the Purchase post office parking lot and scanned Cernak's paper. There would be no need to try to pry information out of a suspicious banker or attorney in charge of handling a house transaction. Reston was certain he now knew where to find John Heineman.

He was filled with relief. They were one step away from bringing the children under control. And John Heineman could clear his name of Stern's Nazi allegations.

He checked the dashboard clock. Time to head back to Oyster Point.

Early the next day, Stern and Reston were on their way to the Martell Institute, near Los Angeles.

Their Boeing 747 lifted smoothly off the runway at John F. Kennedy International Airport. The morning was glorious, perfect for flying, Stern thought, looking out the window from his seat in the first-class cabin. The sky was a crystal azure blue dotted with little puffs of white clouds. Long Island and Manhattan dropped away beneath the climbing jet. He hoped he would see the view again—by coming home. He glanced at Reston in the seat next to him. The doctor had his eyes closed.

Stern leaned forward and reached under the seat in front of him, pulling out his portfolio and opening it to take out the research paper by Dr. Mikhail Cernak, director of the Martell Institute. The manuscript was entitled, "Identification and Manipulation of Psychic Broadcast Frequencies."

"Was this ever published?" asked Stern.

"Beats me," answered Reston, opening his eyes. "I don't read those kinds of journals. How many times are you going to read that paper?"

"As often as necessary. Tell me again about this Martell Institute."

"I've heard of it before, but I don't know a great deal about it. It's small, one of those offbeat places that specialize in pyschic research. It's located up in the north hills. It's mostly privately funded, but I understand that the federal government has underwritten work there from time to time."

"And Cernak?"

"Czechoslovakian. He defected to the West, about ten years ago, I believe."

"Interesting," mused Stern. "The Russians and the East Europeans have invested a lot of time and money in psychic research. In fact, it was the Czechs who coined the term 'psychotronics,' the study of how man-made devices could harness natural psychic energy to perform paranormal activities like telepathy and telekinesis. A Czech inventor named Robert Pavlita claimed to invent what he called a 'psychotronic generator' back in the sixties."

"What did it do?"

"Pavlita said it could draw out psychic energy from humans and store it. Then the energy could be deployed to move objects. He claimed to be able to generate electricity to run machines, and to be able to kill insects and small animals, speed up plant growth, magnetize objects—a whole supermarket of things. None of it was ever proved conclusively to Western scientists."

"What was this generator made of?"

"Metals. Copper, iron, gold. I have no idea how it was constructed, or how it operated, except that it was small. Pavlita said the stronger the psychic energy of the source, the greater the power of the generator. So, it's plausible that Cernak has been elaborating on Pavlita's work." The no smoking/fasten seat belt sign flashed off. Stern undid his and tilted his seat back. "I think it's significant that Cernak is no longer at the Martell Institute."

"That's not quite right," corrected Reston, who undid his own seat belt. "Remember, when I called to verify that John was there, I asked to speak to Cernak and was told he was out of the country on an extended leave."

"Same thing. Mark my words."

"I still think I should have spoken to John, let him know we were coming."

Stern shook his head. "We'll learn a lot more from a surprise visit." He started to reread Cernak's paper.

Reston spoke up. "What makes you so sure we can trust those two kids, Tommy and Lori? It seems obvious you were set up for that car accident."

"I can't explain the accident, though it did seem deliberate. But I believe the kids were telling me the truth. Some of them want out of this rolling death machine."

Reston was skeptical. "No one would ever believe us if we had to explain ourselves."

"That's why we're not telling anyone."

A flight attendant rolled up a linen-covered beverage cart and offered them drinks. Reston took a Bloody Mary. Stern said, "Just coffee, please."

Rainer hoped Tommy and Lori would be safe, now that they had made contact with him. Before leaving for the airport, he had called Tommy at home. Without elaborating, he had told the boy he and Reston would be gone for up to several days. He had urged Tommy to make sure he and Lori kept up their mind shields as best as they could. He would contact the boy again when he returned.

Tommy had not been happy to hear the news. Brandon, he had said, was growing suspicious that Tommy and Lori were up to something he wouldn't like. Tommy swore he and the girl had had nothing to do with the car accident. "Hurry back, Mr. Stern," he had pleaded.

Brandon sauntered into the novelty store at Columbus Avenue and West Eighty-seventh Street. Ordinarily, Harwood the butler or one of the maids would have been dispatched on this shopping errand, but he didn't want to entrust it to anyone. He had cut class in order to do the shopping himself for the party goods for the next club meeting. Everything had to be *perfect*, and only he could make certain of that.

He had decided to throw a party, and he had two good reasons for doing so. One, a party would celebrate the big announcement he was going to make at the next meeting of the Secret Society of Loki. Two, he had never really gotten to celebrate his birthday during the summer because of the deaths of his parents. He felt cheated.

He knew the rest of the group would love a party, except perhaps for Tommy and Lori, the spoilsports. They were still withdrawn into their private little shells and avoiding him at school. Brandon was determined to put a stop to their behavior at the next meeting, even if it meant kicking them out of the club.

The novelty store proprietor was a small, foreign-looking man whose pointed beard exaggerated an already pointed chin. He reminded Brandon of a photo of Lenin he'd seen in one of his history books. Brandon was even more amused when the man opened his mouth and spoke with a stilted Russian accent.

"Yes, may I help you?" The man's unfriendly tone did not match his words.

He thinks I'm here to shoplift, thought Brandon. *He hates kids. He'll probably follow me all over. What a jerk.* He said, "I need stuff for a party. Paper plates, hats, napkins. The works."

"I see. How many guests?"

"Twelve of us." Brandon's sharp blue eyes scanned the small shop. "I want something expensive," he added.

The man's huge brown eyes lit up with dollar signs. "I have wide range of goods I am sure you like." He steered Brandon to a rack of items whose designs were aimed at the adolescent market—Masters of the Universe, Inhumanoids, Gremlins, and Cabbage Patch Kids. Brandon was immediately attracted to a parody of Mickey Mouse called Meanie Mouse—a nasty-looking, rat-faced creature dressed in black leather and studs. But he passed it over in favor of Masters of the Universe. He had a whole set of the toys back home.

The proprietor beamed. "Excellent." He pulled out packages of plastic-laminated paper plates and a set of napkins. Brandon picked up on his thoughts. The markup on Masters of the Universe was the highest of anything in the store.

Next Brandon selected red and black crepe paper streamers—his favorite colors—and the most expensive red plastic eating utensils, and a huge roll of Scotch Magic Transparent Tape.

Soon the proprietor had accumulated quite a stack of party goods on the counter. "Ah, how you wish to pay...?"

"Cash."

The proprietor's smile broadened. Rich kids with cash were welcome any time. "Will there be anything else?"

Brandon's eye caught a big plastic package containing a two-foot-high Go-Bot. A perfect fit with Masters of the Universe. It looked neat. "Is that a centerpiece?"

"Yes. It opens like accordion. You want to see?" The Russian hurried over to the decoration and snatched it off its hook.

"Nope. I'll take it."

The Russian moved back behind the sales counter. Let's see . . ." He had an ancient cash register, but he did not use the machine to tally up the total. Instead, he used a worn and soiled wooden abacus that he had brought with him from his native country. He spun the beads back and forth, his lips moving silently.

Brandon added everything up in his head. He reached the total before the proprietor did.

"Forty-four seventy-five," the man said.

What a cheat! The Russian had added in an extra four dollars. *He probably thinks I'd never know the difference*, thought Brandon, suppressing his anger. *Well, it doesn't matter—I hadn't planned on paying full price, anyway.*

Brandon gave the man three tens and concentrated on a spot in the middle of the man's hairy brows.

"Out of sixty," said the proprietor. He stabbed a key on the cash register and the money drawer opened. He counted out the change of fifteen dollars and twenty-five cents into Brandon's palm. He bagged the goods and handed two plastic sacks to Brandon with a beaming smile. "Thank you, thank you, young man. Do come in again."

Brandon walked out with a triumphant grin. Not a bad deal, all this stuff for just under fifteen bucks. A thrill ran through him. It wasn't the money he'd saved that excited him, it was making people do what he wanted.

I oughta be a stockbroker. I could make a fortune in nothing flat. I could make or break whole industries! Whole countries! His mind soared with the fantasy. Brandon Evered, Ruler of the World.

He headed south toward West Seventy-ninth, where the Tate home was located.

Most of the neighborhood around him had long since been gentrified from a slum into pricey shops, trendy restaurants, and expensive apartments and co-ops. Small, seedy pockets still existed, however, blemishes in the fresh complexion of the area.

In the lower Eighties, Brandon passed one of these little pockets, a narrow, run-down building that had once been a single-room-occupancy flophouse, and now was vacant. In the doorway, a derelict squatted with a bottle in a brown bag. He put his hand out as Brandon went by. "Spare any change?"

Brandon glared at the man. He hated the weak and the poor. They were pathetic. He'd have to do something about this—this insect. He concentrated.

The wino's hands began to tremble violently. Brandon strode on. Behind him, he heard the bottle smash to the sidewalk. He smiled. The old guy shouldn't be drinking like that, anyway.

He turned and saw the derelict weep as he tried to salvage some of the wine dripping out of the soaked paper bag.

This time, Brandon's sense of triumph was cut short. A headache came on suddenly and in full force, sending spears of pain shooting through his entire cranium. God, it was awful! Unbearable! *Mother, quit doing this to me*, he shouted silently. *I hate you!* He bit his tongue. He had to get home as fast as possible.

Within five minutes, he was sweeping into the entrance of the Bannerford building, oblivious to everything but the pulsating pain inside his head. The young doorman leaped to open the door for him. "Good day, Brandon."

Brandon hurt too much to respond with one of his customary caustic remarks. He stumbled toward the elevators.

"Do you need help, sir?" the doorman called after him.

"No!"

Luckily, there was an elevator car at ground level, and the door opened as soon as Brandon punched the button. As he got in, he felt a wave of hatred from the doorman. The politeness was all an act. Deep down, the doorman despised every fiber in Brandon's being and wished he would burn in hell.

The image made him choke. He couldn't shut it off. He didn't know why—maybe it was because of the pain. The image of him burning alive was searing right into his brain.

Inside the Tate penthouse, Brandon dashed into his room and slammed the door. With a groan, he dropped his sacks of party goods and buried his head in his hands, rocking back and forth on his feet. Still the pain and the hellish image refused to be vanquished.

Dizzy, he staggered to his dresser and groped through a messy drawer of underwear for the vial of prescription painkillers he kept hidden. He had conned a pharmacist out of them at a late-night drugstore. They were megadoses of Darvon, virtual horse pills in size. At first, one had been enough to kill the wracking pain of his headaches. Now it took three.

His hands shaking, he tapped out three caplets and swallowed them. He collapsed onto his bed, shaking, at the mercy of the Darvon.

He had to do something about these headaches. They were getting worse. But what could he do? He couldn't confide in any of the others, not even Jeff or Jason. They would think he was getting weak, and he would lose control of the group. They would vote him out of the presidency, and turn it over to somebody like Tommy.

He couldn't bear the thought of that. Better the pain. He clutched the bedspread in his fists and stifled a scream.

CHAPTER
Twenty-Five

Los Angeles baked and sparkled under a hot, late-morning sun.

Stern and Reston climbed into a taxi and gave the address of the Martell Institute. The taxi, which did not seem to be in peak running condition, chugged out on the San Diego Freeway going north. The meter clicked away furiously as the fare mounted. L.A. taxis, Stern decided, must charge by the foot.

They passed Westwood, and got off onto Hollywood Boulevard going east.

"Nichols Canyon isn't much farther," the driver assured them. Stern was not accustomed to polite cab drivers. The last time he had ridden in a New York City taxi, the driver had looked at the tip and said, "Fuck you," but took the tip, just the same.

They turned off Hollywood Boulevard and turned north, entering the hills that ringed the Los Angeles basin. Ahead of them, they could see homes carved into the steep hillsides. As they got deeper into Nichols Canyon and higher up, the homes became fewer and farther apart, and the canyon took on a desolate, isolated feel. From the rear window,

Stern looked out over the Southland spread below. The city was partially obscured by smog.

They wound up the canyon, seeing nothing but brush and a few trees around them. Then they topped a rise and suddenly they were at the chain-link fence that formed the boundary of the Martell Institute property, though they could not see any buildings.

The fare was enormous. Stern shelled out the money.

They got out and the taxi headed back down the winding road. The sun beat on them. *At least the air smells cleaner than it does in Manhattan*, Stern thought.

There was a guard booth at the gate entrance, but the gate was open and the booth was empty.

"Out to lunch?" speculated Reston facetiously.

Stern shrugged. Butterflies fluttered in his belly.

They plodded up a long asphalt drive, and as soon as they topped another small rise, the compound itself came into view.

The building was enormous: long and low with a flat roof, white stucco walls gleaming in the sunlight. Dark green shrubbery surrounded the base of it.

Reston seemed euphoric. "Here we are," he chirped, and reached for the buzzer.

Stern braced himself.

The door lock was released and they entered a cool, small foyer where a uniformed man presided over a desk with an electronic console. Reston presented themselves.

"Dr. Heineman is expecting no visitors." The guard gave them an icy stare.

So much for the California hospitality, Stern thought.

Reston said, "If you'll just tell him that Dr. Edward Reston—"

"Dr. Heineman is busy and cannot be disturbed."

Reston turned to Stern. "See, I was afraid of that."

Stern glanced up at the camera mounted in the corner of the ceiling. He wondered if someone else was screening them, and directing the reception guard through his control panel, which was tilted out of their line of sight. He said, "Can we wait?"

"That's not possible."

Reston was exasperated. "Then we'll make an appointment—"

"I don't do that," the guard said curtly. He reached into a drawer and took out a business card. "You'll have to call this person and explain your request." His attention was diverted by something on his control panel. He scowled and looked up at Reston and Stern. "Wait here a moment."

Within a minute, a tall, red-haired woman dressed in slacks and a shirt and wearing a long white lab coat appeared. "Dr. Heineman will see you," she said. "Come with me."

Stern and Reston trailed behind her down a wide hallway. "This looks a lot like the Klein facility in Purchase," Reston said to Stern. "A similiar research laboratory setup."

The smells reminded Stern of something else: a "hospital" at Auschwitz. His skin crawled and he wanted to get out of the building. Instead he forced his feet to continue ahead. They passed closed door upon closed door, and an occasional employee dressed in the research scientist's uniform of loose white jacket over casual clothing.

They were deposited in a comfortable, airy sitting room appointed in contemporary furniture and decorated in pastels. The bookcase and paneling were stained blond.

The woman disappeared. Stern and Reston had but a moment to look around them before a tall, lanky form appeared in the doorway.

"John!" cried Reston, rushing forward.

Stern's breath caught in his throat. He felt himself recede physically from the room, until he became a tiny point of consciousness floating in space, watching the tall man approach Reston, then extending a long, bony arm that ended in a skeletal hand. He watched them clasp hands, saw the light of reverence shining in Reston's eyes. A roaring sound like that of a train racing down a track filled his sphere of consciousness, while he moved through time, reliving memories he could never erase.

Reston pivoted and pointed to Stern, his words of introduction were lost in the roaring in Rainer's head. The older man shifted his gaze. Then Stern was looking full into the man's face, and it was everything he remembered. The eyes still glistened like blue ice, the cheekbones were high, and the cheeks hollow. The only changes were the wrinkles, the blond hair gone gray, and the short, trimmed beard covering the strong chin.

Heineman's lips parted in a thin smile, and it was the grin of a Deathshead skull, the emblem that had graced the uniforms of the Auschwitz guards. His arm snaked toward Stern, seeking a handshake. Stern was abruptly aware of his body again, and let his hand be seized. It felt like the grip of Death itself.

He wanted to say, *My name is Rainer Stern and my number is 55973, and I have come to make you pay for what you did to me, my brother, my family, and my people.*

But the words died in his throat.

Reston scrutinized Stern while Heineman shook his hand. The lawyer looked stupefied, his hand moving up and down limply in Heineman's strong grasp.

He tried to catch Stern's attention with his eyes. But Rainer seemed to be in a haze, responding mechanically to Heineman's questions about the pleasantness of their journey.

Reston took Stern's reaction to mean that Heineman was *not* Hans Messner. Stern evidently was shocked to discover how wrong he'd been. Reston breathed out a huge sigh of relief. He was vindicated, his faith in his longtime mentor restored. Now they would get help.

Heineman said, "Gentlemen, let's go outside to the patio, where we can enjoy the sunshine and fresh air. I am anxious to hear what brings you to Martell."

* * *

A hurricane of emotions raged inside of Stern. He fought for self-control. An animal side of him wanted to tear Heineman limb from limb, but the rational side of him urged him to stay cool. With great difficulty, the rational side prevailed. He must wait, do nothing rash. The right moment for truth would come, and with it justice. *His* justice.

Stern followed Heineman and Reston outside to a flagstone patio ringed by a garden of vibrantly colored flowers and emerald green shrubs and grass. Heineman draped his right arm around Reston's shoulder and they spoke like intimate friends. *Reston treats Heineman like a god,* he thought with disgust.

They took seats at a wrought-iron table on the patio. The cool of the black enamel-painted iron contrasted with the heat of the sun. In the distance, through bluish smog, Stern could see the valley below. He felt detached. Colors were heightened and sounds seemed amplified. It was as if being in the lion's den heightened his awareness of life—and the closeness of death.

A Mexican woman appeared with a silver tray and poured coffee into porcelain cups.

Reston launched straight into business. "It's about the embryo children, John. Stern and I are here in hopes that you, with your knowledge of them and your work here at Martell, can help us find a solution to the problem that confronts us..."

Reston droned on, summarizing the events that had happened. Stern was content to let the doctor do the talking. He wanted to conserve energy and strength. He sensed a test of his ability to survive was coming.

Heineman sat hunched over the table like a spider, his eyes closed while he listened to Reston.

"...and that's our situation," concluded the doctor.

An electric insect exterminator hanging from an eave cremated a fly with a hiss.

Heineman opened his eyes. His congeniality had vanished. He attacked Reston in a cold fury, his blue eyes glacial. "You gave me your word that you would never, *ever* discuss this matter with *anyone*."

Reston's mouth opened in astonishment. "But—"

"How can you do this to me, when I put myself on the line for you?" Heineman's whole body was taut with anger.

Reston looked miserable. "But John, I had no choice. Stern already had enough figured out, and I could see that a real problem had developed—"

Heineman turned to Stern. "A lawyer's gutter work. What are you after?"

Rainer kept his temper. "I don't call trying to stop a killing spree 'gutter work.'"

"Please, John," broke in Reston, "I only did what I thought was right." He added in a half whisper, "I kept the secret fourteen years. I would have taken it to my grave if these things hadn't happened."

Heineman was silent while his sharp eyes scrutinized Stern and Reston in turn. Rainer felt as though he were being X-rayed. The tension among them built. Reston, to Stern's dismay, looked like a puppy suffering the wrath of its master.

At last Heineman broke the tension. "Perhaps I overreact," he said in a calm voice. A measure of the congeniality was back. "The confidentiality of what I did fourteen years ago was important then, not so important now. I have left Klein and gone into another field."

Reston looked profoundly relieved. He started to apologize again, but Heineman dismissed it with a wave of his hand, saying, "What's done is done." He gave Reston a one-sided smile. "I have always regarded you as a son. That will never change."

What an opportunistic liar, Stern thought. He said nothing. His years of law practice had taught him how to keep a poker face in the most stressful situations. He was thankful for that ability now.

Heineman went on, "As for the children, it sounds like

they are in need of a psychiatrist. I'm sorry you have wasted your time by coming here."

"I thought—we thought—that you, having been involved in the original gene-engineering, might be aware of an Achilles heel, er..." Reston's voice trailed off.

Heineman shaded his eyes and looked out over his garden. "*Mein Sohn*, what are you talking about?"

"Didn't you—we thought the embryo children had been gene-engineered for amplified psychic ability."

"Edward, you are speaking fiction. Gene-engineered, yes, for a few things like eye color. But psychic ability?" Heineman chuckled.

Stern interjected, "But it is true that all these children from your source have advanced psychic powers."

Heineman raised his hands in a helpless gesture. "And so?"

"The odds for that to occur by coincidence are unimaginable."

"But not impossible."

"If the children had no special significance, why did you want to keep track of them?" Stern pursued.

Heineman shifted in his chair. "I was interested in them for a time because... well, for various reasons which are no longer important. Now I am involved in psychic research, which has always been a side interest of mine. When Martell invited me out—"

"What happened to Dr. Cernak?" Stern interrupted.

"Nothing. He is in Switzerland, at a symposium."

Reston said, "Perhaps, based on your current research, you might advise us how to deal with these paranormal powers beyond our control. We're here because I found out that Dr. Cernak's research might be applicable."

"Perhaps."

"It's crucial," Reston implored. "The children have a way of combining their power that puts them beyond the reach of ordinary people. Don't you see what can happen? They could hold anyone hostage to their whims and demands."

"Several murders already, as Reston has told you," Stern said.

"But there is no direct evidence the children were responsible. As a lawyer, Mr. Stern, you surprise me."

Stern clamped his jaws together. *Why is the bastard maintaining this charade?* He was losing patience.

Reston said, "John, for God's sake, what we say is true. You've got to help us."

Several minutes passed while Heineman was deep in thought. Then he said, "*Mein Sohn*, you have once again come to me for help and I cannot deny you. Let me show you something and you can judge for yourselves if it will be useful." He stood up and towered over them. Stern grudgingly admitted to himself that despite the man's age—he must be in his sixties—his figure was still strong and imposing.

Heineman led them back into the building and into white-walled corridors. Reston, with a bounce in his step, walked next to Heineman. Stern hung several paces behind.

Heineman said, "What I have been studying is a way to break down the barriers between the senses. You see, human beings differentiate between sight, sound, smell, and touch, for example. Perhaps this was an evolutionary necessity so that we are not overwhelmed by the constant bombardment of stimuli, but process only the information necessary for the appropriate physical or intellectual response. Animals, however, respond to stimuli much differently, integrating the senses."

"What does that have to do with psychic ability?" Reston asked.

"Psychic ability is but another sense. One most people do not use, but it exists in all humans. The psychic sense is more pronounced in individuals who can integrate their senses to some degree, and respond more instinctually—such as children and primitives. These individuals are able to let down the barriers between the senses and allow information to flood in. As children mature, and as primitive people become more civilized, they are taught not to rely on instinct and intuition, and barriers are erected.

Heineman continued, "That is most unfortunate because the psychic sense is more powerful than all the other senses combined. At its utmost, it is not limited by distance, nor is it bound by time. It has been my belief for years that mankind would benefit from the cultivation of our lost sixth sense. These theories of mine are not new; I have been working on them for years. Until recently, they have been a side pursuit."

"How does this work help us?" asked Stern.

"A little by-product you will see in a moment. It happens often in scientific research that one's search leads to the unexpected."

Reston said, "I understand Dr. Cernak may have been working on a device, a psychotronic generator, to manipulate psychic energy," said Reston.

"You are well informed, Edward." Heineman stopped in front of a door with a glass window internally reinforced by wire. "We'll go in here." He opened the door, flicked on a light switch, and ushered Stern and Reston into a small narrow storage room.

Stern distinctly did not like having his back to Heineman for one second. He quickly maneuvered in the narrow space to keep the German within his view. Heineman locked the door behind him and brushed by Stern. An involuntary shiver went through him.

The room was lined with gray metal shelves from floor to ceiling, upon which were stacked boxes and containers of various shapes and sizes. Some were labeled and some were not. The contents meant little to Stern; presumably they were related to work going on at the institute.

Heineman went to the back of the room and took down a square metal container about the size of a hatbox. He spun a combination lock and withdrew an object that looked to Stern like a cross between a video camera and an Uzi. It had a pistollike grip and trigger and a cameralike barrel and body with small buttons and a dial. Under the fluorescent light, its dark metal gleamed with bluish highlights.

"What is it?" Stern asked.

"A brilliant achievement," answered Heineman, the lines in his face crinkling around a triumphant smile. He held up the gun for his guests to see. "This is an Image Barrager."

"A what?"

"A psychotronic laser gun of sorts. It emits intense frequencies of psychic energy that impact the brain."

"What does it do?"

"It breaks down many barriers in the mind. I have found that in low it stimulates fear and disorientation. In high, it overwhelms to the point where brain function is impaired or destroyed."

It sounded like a terrible weapon. The consequences of its misuse . . . Stern shuddered.

Reston, the scientist in him taking over, was in awe. "How does it work?"

"To simplify a complex explanation, it impacts the pituitary and pineal glands and the hippocampus. The pituitary governs the release of adrenalin in response to stimuli. The pineal is a little understood gland which is a vestigial third eye, governing psychic awareness. The hippocampus, as you know, processes memories. It is the powerful fear memories which are unleashed."

"Why only fear? Why not happiness, even sorrow?" asked Reston.

"Fear dominates."

Heineman shoved the gun into Stern's hands. It was cold and surprisingly light.

"You are reminded of an Uzi, perhaps." Heineman said. "The design is borrowed from a little bit of this, a little bit of that. The economical streamlining of the Uzi nine-millimeter semiautomatic pistol for easy handling. The Austrian Glock plastic for lightweight and easy transport. And the design of a video camera for focus and lens. There are some other minor influences as well. It was years in the works, and much credit must go to Dr. Cernak."

Liar. He stole everything from Cernak.

Reston reached for the Image Barrager and took it from Stern. "How do you operate it?"

"The Image Barrager draws psychic energy from either the operator or another source, depending on how the controls are set, and magnifies it. When you pull the trigger, it shoots an invisible beam of energy. The laser light is added for accurate sighting, much like the laser sights on high-powered rifles. To operate, the gun must be electromagnetically charged. It can hold a charge for six hours. I have developed a portable battery pack that can give it a partial charge, if a full recharging is not possible."

Reston said, "Are the effects temporary or permanent?"

"That depends on how you use the instrument. It can go either way, from mild to extreme."

"Could this neutralize the children?" asked Stern.

"Destroy their psychic ability? Give them a 'psychic lobotomy'?" Heineman took the Image Barrager from Reston and cradled it in his thin hands as though it were a precious, fragile object. "I believe so, but I have never tested that particular application. My tests have focused on two applications: enhancing the psychic-factor of the operator of the instrument, and using it as a means of controlling and subduing others through disorientation caused by fear." He looked up at Stern. "Would you like a demonstration? On an animal."

Stern hesitated. He didn't like Heineman's keen attention to him. He said, "Yes."

Heineman led them out of the little room and down the hall to another room. This one was much larger and looked like a research area, with shiny stainless steel countertops and tables and jumbles of glass apparatuses.

On one counter was a small cage with a little brown field mouse crouched on a bed of straw. Heineman led his guests to it. "A field mouse such as this is the prey of hawks and snakes. If it is in the open, a typical response is to freeze, hoping the predator will not distinguish it from the surroundings." He thumped the cage to upset the mouse, which began darting about its prison.

Heineman raised the Image Barrager and adjusted several unlabeled dials. "I had this fully charged just before you arrived. I anticipated doing some experiments. For the mouse, because of the small size and primitive nature of its brain, I only need a low dosage." He pushed a button and a ruby beam of light shot out. He focused it on the mouse's tiny head. "It is best to aim for the head but not necessary," explained Heineman. "If the energy enters the body, it will travel to the brain. The effect is merely delayed a few seconds." Having sighted properly, Heineman pulled the trigger.

The gun hummed with the transmission of invisible waves of energy. The mouse froze, its black dots of eyes filled with terror, its nose twitching with the "scent" of danger.

"You see?" said Heineman. "It thinks it senses a predator, and has taken defensive action. Now watch what happens if we keep going."

The German kept the gun trained on the mouse, the ruby light striking the little skull. For a few seconds more, the mouse remained frozen, its sides heaving in and out in rapid breathing. Then suddenly it dashed, as though trying to avoid an imminent predatory strike. It struck the bars of the cage and toppled backward, stunned. Then it righted itself and tried to flee again, only to hit the cage a second time.

"Stop," said Stern. "It's terrified. It's trying to escape."

Heineman did not stop.

The mouse clawed frantically at the bars, pushing its little limbs out through the spaces, trying to get away from whatever vision haunted it. After a few seconds of clawing, it fell over on its side and writhed in the imaginary death grip of an enemy.

"Please *stop*."

With a shudder, the mouse died.

Heineman shut off the beam. The humming faded. "It probably had a heart attack out of fear."

"You didn't have to do that," Stern said angrily.

"It was a clinical demonstration," said Reston.

"But why kill it? We could see that the device was working, without having to destroy the poor creature."

Reston looked nonplussed. "This is science, Rainer."

"Gentlemen, please," broke in Heineman. "There is no need to argue over a mouse." He turned them away from the cage with its little corpse.

Reston said, "Does this work the same on people?"

"Apparently, though I have no way of knowing what an animal 'sees' under the influence of the energy."

"Can you show us?" said Stern.

Heineman frowned. "I'm afraid I have no volunteers until tomorrow. Unless one of you gentlemen would like to volunteer." He stared pointedly at Stern. "It will be a mild and temporary experience, though I cannot control what your mind conjures up from its own depths."

The gauntlet had been thrown down. Stern said. "I'll volunteer."

A slight smile curved Heineman's thin lips. "Excellent, Mr. Stern. We shall conduct our own little experiment. Immediately."

The setup reminded Stern of a small music recording studio. There was a control console filled with switches, levers, and lights in front of a narrow, thick window. On the other side of the glass was a single chair draped with wires whose attachments were not visible.

Heineman opened a small door on one side of the glass. "If you please, Mr. Stern. Take the seat in there."

Stern did not go in. Why had he agreed to this? It was as though Heineman was baiting him, as though he knew who Stern was, *Jude*, one of the "dregs of Europe" who escaped the Nazi death machine. He didn't like the look in Heineman's eyes. He felt his self-control slipping. Reston offered him no support, silent or spoken; he had become a scientist again, eager for the test.

"It's all right," Heineman assured him, his voice reminding Stern of the way he and Mengele used to cajole little twins before stabbing them with a needle. "This is the test chamber that allows us to monitor response to the Image Barrager." His hand swept the control panel. "We can read all your physiological and brainwave responses, and record any spontaneous utterances you make."

"The wires—?" Stern pointed to the chair on the other side of the window.

"Electrodes to be attached to your body for the monitoring I have just described."

"Where will you and Reston be while I am in there?"

"In here, the control booth. I will operate the I.B. from here. The energy transmissions go through glass, of course."

Stern still did not go in.

Heineman said, "Are you having second thoughts, Mr. Stern?"

Rainer took a breath, wondering what fears would confront him. "No, I'm ready." He entered the tiny chamber and let Heineman position him on the chair and attach electrodes to his temples and wrists.

Heineman asked Stern to unbutton his shirt so that he could attach another electrode over his heart. Stern complied. The touch of the man nauseated him. He wanted to shove Heineman away. He couldn't go on much longer.

His heart began to pound. Stern waited for Heineman to get set up on the opposite side of the glass. He felt claustrophobic in the cubicle. The electrodes were cold on his skin.

He stared at a red dot on the glass, as Heineman had instructed, which supposedly would help maintain good focus of the energy waves. Heineman bent over the control console and then straightened. He pointed the Image Barrager at Rainer's head and pressed the trigger.

Stern felt a jolt, like a small electric charge, course through his body. For a brief moment, he heard Heineman and Reston speaking, but the words were unintelligible. Then the voices faded as he felt a sensation which he could describe only as a singing through his bones.

Heineman said over the intercom, "What do you feel?"

Stern described the sensation. Heineman adjusted the controls on the gun.

Rainer felt his heartbeat jump and he broke out in a sweat of anxiety. He was beginning to feel dizzy. He saw a movement out of the corner of his eye, a darting gray shape. He looked but saw nothing. Then, with averted vision, he saw it again.

It was a rat.

He gasped. How did a rat get in the chamber?

There had been rats at Auschwitz, scavenging and stealing the crumbs the prisoners had to eat. At night, they would come and begin feasting upon those who were nearer death than life. He had been deathly afraid of them, terrified he would wake up one morning with his legs knawed through.

Stern saw the gray shape again, a blur moving toward him. Something clawed at the bottom of his trousers, going up his leg, and he kicked out.

"Describe!" shouted Heineman.

"A rat," said Stern, kicking out his feet again.

"Good," murmured Heineman as he touched the gun's controls.

Stern jumped as a new wave of energy seared through him. The chamber before him dissolved in shimmering waves.

He was at Auschwitz, a boy of five, standing before a small iron door in a wall. There were other iron doors in the wall, row upon row, like a beehive. The air was thick and hot, and stank with a sickly sweet smell. He was not supposed to be in this building, but he had wandered in and no one had stopped him.

A German soldier in uniform came up behind him and grabbed his arm so that he could not run away. With his other hand, the soldier swung open one of the iron doors.

The inside was a tube charred black, and Rainer could see flames in the far end of the tube. Using a hook, the soldier reached in and pulled out a steel flatbed trolley. Rainer stared at a human skeleton, the flesh nearly, but not completely, baked off the bones. One cooked eye stared sightlessly at him from its skull socket. The sickening smoke billowed out around him.

The Nazi yanked the skeleton off the trolley, brushing off bones as they distintegrated from the movement. "You're next," he told Rainer laughingly. It was a joke, wasn't it? But the soldier lifted the struggling boy and began to lower him onto the hot trolley.

The memory of his terror was crystal clear and so intense it overwhelmed him. Stern felt as though he were actually reliving the moment, feeling the heat, hearing the soldier laugh, certain he was going to be shoved into the tunnel of flames alive.

At Auschwitz, the soldier had stopped just inches above the trolley, dangling Rainer while he screamed for his life, then dropping him off to the side on the floor and yelling, "Get out of here! If I ever catch you in here again, I *will* put you in there."

But the memory abruptly changed.

The soldier did not drop Rainer on the floor but lowered him onto the trolley, still burning hot from the oven, and began to strap him down with chains.

Stern shut his eyes, but the memory was coming from within. "Turn it off!" he shouted at Heineman.

His arms and chest were chained and the metal of the trolley seared into him.

"Stop!" He couldn't take it anymore.

Chains went around his legs.

"For God's sake, stop it!" Stern tore off the electrodes.

The soldier began pushing the trolley into the oven.

Stern jumped up from the chair. The memory disintegrated.

Reston was pressed up against the window, an astonished

look upon his face. But Stern had eyes only for Heineman, who studied him with the same impassivity he had given the field mouse. Rainer shook with rage as he looked at Heineman. "You bastard! Nazi!"

CHAPTER Twenty-Six

Stern burst through the chamber door into the control room. "You bastard! You killed my brother! My family!"

Heineman backed away. "You're crazy."

Stern grabbed him by his loose-fitting jacket. Reston tried to thrust himself between the two, but Stern pushed him away. He shook Heineman. "You are not John Heineman, and your whole life has been a lie. You are Hans Messner, a Nazi!"

Heineman seized Stern's fists and tried to pry his fingers off. "I don't know what you're talking about."

"Butcher!" Stern felt the last of his self-control snap. For a terrifying moment, he teetered on the edge of a great dark violence, knowing if he let go, it would reach up and swallow him.

Heineman saw the look in his eyes and reacted. He quickly pinched the nerve at the base of Stern's neck. In seconds, Stern was unconscious.

Heineman lowered him to the floor. He straightened and said to Reston, "How dare you bring this lunatic onto my premises to make outrageous accusations. I should have him arrested for assault. Sued for slander!"

* * *

Stern waited in the darkness. He was prone on his back on a narrow bed in what appeared to be a dormitory-style room. He couldn't see much. He had no idea exactly where he was—still, presumably, within the Martell compound.

His head throbbed and his brain felt like a wad of soggy cotton. His throat was thick and dry. He was still in his clothes, and his shirt was unbuttoned partway down his chest, just as it had been during the experiment.

They must have given him something to keep him unconscious for a long time. *They're in this together, Reston and Messner,* he thought groggily. He could not muster the energy to get up.

This was not the way it was supposed to turn out.

Stern waited for what he knew was coming.

He sensed an invisible heaviness in the space around him. A foreboding.

He closed his eyes. There was nothing he could do about it. He let time wash over him.

He opened his eyes at the light pressure of a cold steel blade against his windpipe. A dark shape crouched over him. He lay still. He said hoarsely, "I've been expecting you, Dr. Hans."

"Dr. Hans? No one has called me that in many years."

Stern stared up at the figure. As his eyes adjusted to the darkness, he could make out the shadowy shapes of Messner's sharp features. The pressure of the knife blade increased. Stern said, "It has been many years, and I have not forgotten."

"You must have been a very small child back then."

"A twin. You don't remember? Rainer and Leon Stern, born March 20, 1939 in Munich, seized April 7, 1944 by the Gestapo, and shipped to Auschwitz."

The German was silent.

Stern swallowed, his Adam's apple moving painfully against the blade. "No, of course you don't remember. How could you? We were faceless, nothing but animals for your experiments."

The pressure of the knife lessened slightly. "A noble purpose for *die Juden*. A sacrifice in the name of improving the human race."

"Yes, we were sacrificed on your altar of tyranny, all right. Six million of us, including my brother and my entire family. But in the end, Messner, you still lost."

"Only the battle, not the war. The struggle goes on, Stern, among those of us remaining. I'm afraid it is you who have lost."

"You have the knife."

"Yes. I do not intend to let you turn me over to a monkey trial in Israel. I have work to do."

The knife blade left Stern's throat and the sharp tip raked down the center of his chest, splitting the skin in a shallow cut. A warmth blossomed there, but Stern felt no fear.

"That is your blood spilling, *Jude*." The blade returned to Stern's throat. "Where is the proof you have of who I am?"

"How do you know I have not already sent it to Israel?" Stern was thankful for the semidarkness, hoping his face would not betray the lie. Perhaps he had been foolish to take the matter into his own hands, instead of involving Tel Aviv, or Wiesenthal in Vienna.

"My instincts tell me you are alone in this."

"Perhaps. But the proof is in a safe place. If I do not return to New York within two days, it will be released to the authorities."

"You have nothing to gain by lying."

"You will have to decide." Stern shifted slowly on the bed. "Is Reston dead?"

"Reston is no concern of yours. Why don't you struggle? You lay here like a sheep, awaiting your death. You disappoint me."

Very slowly, Stern slid his hand along Messner's arm and grasped the wrist. The German's muscles were like bands of steel. The knife pressed harder against his flesh. Stern said,

"I remember the sign above the entrance to Auschwitz. *'Arbeit mach Frei.'* 'Work makes freedom.' For me, it is now *'Wahrheit mach Frei.'* 'Truth makes freedom.' I have learned the truth I sought, and it has set me free. There is no need to struggle."

"Sanctimonius Jew."

"You are sealing your own death warrant."

Messner laughed. "Do you really think the Mossad can catch me? Is that all you can come up with at the last moment to save yourself?"

"I'm prepared to die. Death has had one hand on my shoulder ever since I left Auschwitz. But it won't be the Mossad who gets you, Messner, it will be your own creations. The children." Stern felt the German tense.

Messner grunted disdainfully. "They are flawed."

"So you think you will get them with Cernak's invention? I should say the late Dr. Cernak. You killed him and stole his invention."

"How I resolve my work is my business."

"The children hate you, Messner, the instinctive way children sense and hate evil. They tried to kill you once, and they will do it again, because you threaten the very essence of their survival. They are not and never were slaves to be programmed. You created monsters and now they've gone out of control. You won't last two minutes if you go back to them, even if you try to get them one by one. They've got ways of knowing and ways of finding that you won't evade." Stern paused. "That's why you need me."

Messner roared. "*I* need *you*?"

"I have befriended two of the children who want out of the group. They will listen to me, and to me only. They know where I am, and if I don't return they will be on their guard against you."

"You're lying!"

"If I'm so full of lies, what are you waiting for? Use the knife." Stern let go of Messner's wrist and closed his eyes.

He was at his final Judgment, and a voice said, "Have

you dealt in life with integrity and faith?" And he answered, "I have tried." And the voice said, "It is written in the Psalms, 'turn away from evil and do good.' You pursued justice and mercy but surrendered to evil in the end." And he said, "I did all I could." He waited to see Leon, but Leon would not come.

Stern realized he was holding his breath. He let it go.

The knife blade was gone from his throat.

He opened his eyes and pushed himself up on his elbows. The dark figure of Messner towered over him.

The German said, "Perhaps there is room for a compromise. Your life in exchange for my permanent freedom."

"And the children?"

"They must be destroyed."

"Only their psychic power, not their lives."

"I will make that judgment."

"Except the two who have come to me."

Messner didn't answer.

Stern said, "What about Reston?"

"Reston will do whatever he feels he must to keep himself out of trouble."

Stern swung his legs off the bed and rose stiffly to his feet. The front of his shirt stuck to him with the blood from the shallow cut. Messner held the high cards. But at least he had bought his life and a little time.

"Agreed," he said.

The German started to go out the door.

"Messner," Stern called, halting him. "What makes you think I won't turn you in, anyway?"

Messner's teeth flashed in the semidarkness. "What makes you think I won't kill you—anyway? *Jude?*"

The next morning, a somber Stern joined Reston outside on the patio, where the doctor was enjoying coffee in the bright, warm sunshine.

"Are you feeling better?" Reston asked cheerfully. "I gave

you something to make you sleep. I was going to look in on you, but John said he would take care of you."

"He did." Stern poured himself a cup of coffee from the thermal pot sitting on the glass-topped table.

Reston was clearly oblivious to what had taken place in Stern's chamber. "I think this Image Barrager is just the thing we need. John has agreed to come back to New York with us. He says he thinks he can disrupt their psychic power permanently—"

"Shut up, Reston." Stern got up and walked to the edge of the patio. He could still feel Messner's knife point etching a line of blood halfway down his chest.

"Good morning, gentlemen." Hans Messner glided out onto the patio. His gray and white hair was combed straight back from his face, giving him a leonine appearance. His skin looked fresh-scrubbed and pink.

He looks like he just stepped out of a health spa, thought Stern. *Who would guess he nearly slit two throats last night?* He said, "Reston, your friend has something he wants to tell you."

Reston looked questioning at Messner. "Yes, John?"

Looking at Stern, Messner said, "It is not John, *mein Sohn*. It is Hans. My name is Hans Messner, and I was a scientist of the Third Reich."

Reston blanched. "I don't believe it."

"Believe it," said Stern. "This man has been a fraud for most of his adult life."

Reston was nearly speechless. "But—but why, John?"

Messner shrugged. "I had good reason. I did it in the name of a superior race to improve mankind."

Stern could barely restrain himself. He folded his arms across his chest. This was between Messner and Reston.

Reston said, "Then is it true about your... war crimes?"

"What crimes? I conducted experiments. It is no crime to be a scientist."

"Of course not," Reston mumbled, visibly shaken. "Hans

—" he had difficulty with the name. "You must have been forced to aid Mengele. Weren't you?"

Messner looked Reston straight in the eye. "No, I was not forced. Josef Mengele was a brilliant physician, and I was privileged to work with him."

That was not what Reston wanted to hear.

"I regret you do not understand, Edward. I acted out of free will—eagerly so, in fact. I am surprised that a man of science such as yourself cannot comprehend that. You see what has happened to the human race in the forty-odd years since. Interbreeding, a lowering of the quality of the genetic pool, inferiors breeding ever more inferior offspring, so dull-witted they do nothing but feed off society like leeches, adding nothing, contributing nothing.

"I had my reasons, Edward, and they were noble. They still are. I have always wished well for humanity, as do you and Stern. I believed the Reich had the best solutions for improving humanity. Mankind must be smarter and stronger in the nuclear age, or we will destroy ourselves."

Reston's lips were dry. "And the embryos you gave me?"

"Were the seeds for superior children who would grow up to begin the New Order. They were the surviving remnants of my work under Josef."

Reston struggled to accept this information. "You used me—"

"I saved you from ruin, *mein Sohn*. And gave you a place in history."

Reston stammered and looked at Stern for direction, but Rainer would not meet his gaze. Instead, Stern watched Messner, hating the arrogance on the man's face.

Reston mumbled, "I—I don't know what to say."

Stern unfolded his arms. "Dr. Messner and I have reached an agreement. I'll explain it to you. We'll catch the red eye to New York tonight. Now I must call Tommy."

Tommy's voice sounded thin and strained in Stern's ear. "Mr. Stern, I'm afraid. Brandon is acting real weird. He's getting stronger, and I don't know if he's been able to get through my shield and find out what I've been up to."

"Has he said anything to indicate that he has?"

"No. It's just a bad feeling I have."

"And Lori? How's she?"

"She's awfully upset."

"You won't have to hold out much longer," Rainer said soothingly. "Dr. Reston and I have found a way to prevent Brandon and the others from hurting any more people."

Tommy's voice raised. "How?"

"I'll explain later when I get back tomorrow."

"You'd better hurry, all right, Mr. Stern. We're having our regular club meeting tomorrow night, and Brandon has been hinting that something important is going to happen."

While Reston and the Jew were left under the supervision of an institute employee, Messner retired to his private quarters for his exercise. He worked out at his customized gym for an hour every day, doing weightlifting at a Universal gym machine and stretching exercises before a floor-to-ceiling mirror. One must stay fit, no matter what age. If he hadn't been in such good shape, he might not have survived the heart attack caused by the children. Little beasts. He would show them who was master.

He entered the gym and locked the door behind him.

He changed into gray cotton sweats and began a series of warm-up stretching exercises. He was satisfied with the outcome of events with his visitors. He would allow them to live a while longer.

He did side bends, counting. Then deep knee bends.

He didn't believe Stern about his "proof," and he also doubted his story that Stern and the two dropout children would be the key to overcoming the rest of them. He had decided to take no chances. Stern could prove useful in allowing him to get closer to the children and manipulate them before they could mobilize against him again. If the Jew was bluffing, his life would be taken immediately. He was going to lose it in the end, anyway. So was Reston, who had served his purpose.

The boy Brandon Evered would have to be killed. He was a nuisance, the one who instigated the mutiny in the park. The two dropouts would have to go as well. But Messner had no intention of ruining the psychic power of the rest of them. He would use the Image Barrager to control them until they learned discipline and the proper respect.

The beginning of the New Order was at hand at last. Through him, Hans Messner, would evolve a new race of human beings, stronger and smarter than anyone else, genetic wonders who would slowly overwhelm the inferiors on the planet. Without them, mankind was doomed. It was his duty to prevent that from happening.

He dropped to the floor and did twenty push-ups.

In his head, he recited a litany. *My will is resolute, my determination unshakable. I will overcome all obstacles. I will not fail!*

Messner went next to the Universal gym and proceeded with his workout. At precisely sixty minutes, he stopped. He swallowed a handful of vitamin pills stored in a cabinet on one wall.

He stretched. He felt glorious. A new power coursed through his blood.

CHAPTER
Twenty-Seven

The suite at the Alexander Hotel, just off Manhattan's posh Central Park West, was furnished in a rich blue and green color scheme with a slightly Oriental flavor. The main room looked like an elegant living room, with a comfortable sofa and armchairs and polished mahogany tables. Messner had insisted the three of them come here, where the staff knew him and would provide discreet service.

Stern wondered if the staff included some other Nazis-in-hiding. Especially the desk clerk whose name tag read "W. Becker." He made a mental note to remember.

He studied Messner as the German looked out their ninth-floor window. Reston was collapsed on the sofa, not yet recovered from the discomfort of sleeping on a red-eye flight from the Coast.

Messner turned away from the window. "Now, let's review. Edward, you will go to the museum and pick up maps and information about where the children will be holding their get-together tonight, and bring the information back to me."

"Yes."

"When did the boy say the meeting would begin?"

"Eight," said Stern.

"Then we will be there by seven-thirty." Messner studied Stern. "I understand you must meet with your two young friends. You will find out what children always know about the secrets of a place—the shortcuts, the doors that are supposed to be locked but never are, the things to be on guard for. Also, what sort of tricks we might expect from our rebellious little leader, Brandon Evered."

Stern nodded.

"I shall come with you."

"Absolutely not."

"I want to speak with them."

"You'll have all the time you want later. But these two kids are skittish to begin with, and if you show up with me, they might panic and run."

"Not if I use that." Messner pointed to the bag that contained the Image Barrager.

"Not on them, you won't."

Messner scowled. "Then I must trust you."

"It still works both ways, Messner."

The German went to his bag, which was on the floor next to the sofa. He rummaged around inside and drew out two candy bars. "Take them a little *Schokolade*. A token of my good will."

"They don't want your *Schokolade*," Stern said scornfully. Without another word, he strode to the door and left.

Tommy and Lori were a half hour late for their rendezvous with Stern at Riverside Park on the Upper West Side. He waited at the top of the stone steps with mounting anxiety, trying to watch a nearby group of five teenagers compete with each other on skateboards. They wore knee pads, but Stern still winced at every wipeout.

As the minutes went by, Stern worried that he had gotten the rendezvous point wrong. Riverside Park was long and narrow, paralleling the West Side Highway from Seventy-second Street to 152nd Street. Tommy had said to meet by the Soldiers and Sailors Monument near Seventy-ninth Street, hadn't he? Not the Joan of Arc statue at Eighty-eighth Street, or Grant's Tomb at 120th?

Just as Stern was beginning to fear that something had happened to the children, he spotted them coming toward him. Neither was dressed for Winston School, which meant they had cut classes. Tommy wore jeans and a dark green jacket; Lori was dressed in jeans and a fluorescent pink crewneck sweater. Her long dusty-brown hair was tied back from her thin face, making her appear more frail and tired than ever. *She won't be much help tonight*, Stern despaired.

"Sorry we're late," Tommy said. "We did the best we could."

"Don't worry," Stern answered, peering down at them. "Are you all right? Lori?"

"I'm just a little tired, Mr. Stern," Lori said with a tepid smile.

They walked down the steps into the park proper. The children sat down on top of a concrete wall that bordered a playground, dangling their legs over the drop. On the far side of the narrow park, heavy traffic roared north and south on the West Side Highway. Straight out ahead, on the other side of the freeway, was the Hudson River, a broad band of choppy, steel gray water flowing beneath light gray clouds, and across the Hudson lay New Jersey. Under other circumstances, Stern would have enjoyed the river view.

"Remember I told you Hans Messner wasn't dead? Dr. Reston and I found him, and he's going to help us tonight."

"I won't come if he's there," said Tommy. "He's a creep."

"Ditto for me," said Lori.

Stern wasn't surprised. *How do I sell them when I hate the setup myself?* He said, "Dr. Messner has found a way to, er, scramble thoughts so that Brandon and the others can't hurt anyone."

"How?" Tommy asked sharply.

Stern hesitated. Tommy was smart, and he would accomplish nothing with a condescending explanation. He summarized the principle of the Image Barrager.

"But that's dangerous," Lori said perceptively. "He might take away our power for good."

"I think you both realize that the only way to put Brandon and the others out of business is to change them permanently. We'll make sure both of you are out of the way."

Tommy said, "Messner isn't going to try to force us to go with him again, is he? I won't go."

Stern chose his words carefully. "He's agreed to help us in exchange for a personal favor from me. I won't let him take you away."

Lori looked frightened. "I don't know, Mr. Stern. That man scared me, and I don't want to be near him again."

"*I* don't want to end up like David," said Tommy. "And we will if we don't do something right away. We'll have to go along with it, Lori."

Lori gave Stern a pleading look. "You won't let Mr. Messner hurt us, will you, for sure?"

He smiled gently. "For sure. Now, I need you to tell me about the inside of the museum, where you meet. What the room is like, where the door is, what pathways and shortcuts you kids use in getting around, who else is in the building."

"I'll draw you a map," said Tommy. He took a folded sheet of notepaper out of his jacket pocket, and a stub of a pencil. He smoothed the paper out on the bench and drew a diagram for Stern, which he explained. Stern folded the map and put it in his pocket.

"You won't have to worry about the guards or the video monitors," finished Tommy. "We'll take care of the monitors like we always do. The guards and janitors avoid us, and they'll be happy the monitors are out. It's the same every week."

"What is Brandon likely to do?"

Tommy doodled on the paper. "Who knows? He's unpredictable. He can do a lot of things independently of the rest of us. You'll just have to watch out, Mr. Stern."

Stern patted the boy on the shoulder. "I guess we're all set then."

"Not quite. Remember when we were at the café, I said that sometime we should practice thinking alike?"

Stern nodded. "Thinking alike" was the children's term for communicating with each other mentally.

"We'd better practice."

"There isn't much time for me to learn anything."

"You're a better receiver than most people, except for us in the club, of course."

Stern nodded. "A long time ago, someone told me I had a certain ability. But I could never come to terms with it. I ignored it and denied it."

"It's like working a muscle," Tommy said. "It takes time to build it up. But we can do a few tests now to see how well you can tune in to me. I'm one of the best senders in the group." He leaned forward. "Let me see if I can send you pictures."

Lori slipped off the wall. "I have to go. You don't need me for this."

Stern reached down and caught her thin arm. "Are you sure you're all right?"

She gave him another wan smile. "I'll be better tomorrow." She slipped out of his grasp and began walking back up the steps toward Riverside Drive.

Tommy hopped down. "Okay, Mr. Stern, come on. I'm tired of sitting." Without waiting for Rainer, the boy set off through the park, heading uptown.

Stern rose and began following him. "Wait up."

"No, you stay here. I'm going ahead and get out of sight. Give your mind a blank spot."

As Tommy hurried ahead, Stern looked out across the river again, making himself conscious of the smell wafting off the water, the slow movement of the clouds, the fast roar of the traffic on the West Side Highway. He was tense, and his mind resisted shifting into neutral. This was hardly the best time to practice psychic games, but it might come in handy in a pinch.

He waited. Nothing popped into his head that struck him as a "message" from Tommy. Minutes went by. He cursed silently. It wasn't working. He was about to break into a trot and find Tommy when he caught an image of ripples on a glistening surface, like wavelets in a pond lit by the sun. It was gone before he could fully grasp it. Then another image appeared—a hand held upright with fingers spread. That, too, dissolved, and was rapidly replaced by a shiny red apple.

The apple disintegrated into a fiery circle of red and orange flames. It seemed to be a symbol, and it distressed him. *Was* it a sign? Of death? Purification?

The flames vanished and Stern "saw" himself walking toward Tommy. No sooner did he have the mental image than he began walking. Tommy stepped out from behind a tree and grinned up at him.

"I think it worked," Stern said. He described the images.

"You're a good receiver," Tommy said. "Brandon says this is the most common extrasensory ability in most people. It usually gets chalked up to intuition."

"When I was a small boy, I had a brother, a twin. We had a mental connection that must have been similar to what you have with the others, though not as pronounced or as powerful. I thought everyone was linked like that."

"Where's your brother now, Mr. Stern?"

"He—died some years ago."

There was an awkward silence. Then Tommy took Stern's hand and pulled him off down the path again. "Let's try words instead of pictures. I'll concentrate and you say whatever pops into your head."

They had very little success with this experiment. "Your thoughts are interfering too much," Tommy said. "Let go."

But Stern couldn't still his thoughts enough, especially now that they had been stirred by painful memories of Leon. The images Tommy had conjured up had been vivid. The words were fuzzy and vague, competing with the whirling stream of consciousness going on in his head.

"We'll stick with pictures," Tommy said. "Maybe I'll need to send you some tonight. You see, us kids will be together up here." He pointed to his head. "You won't know what Brandon might order everyone to do—until it's too late. A thought picture travels faster than spoken words."

Stern tried to feel reassured. Instead, he felt a growing sense of unease.

Brandon left his co-op building and headed toward Columbus Avenue. He was going back to the novelty shop where he had purchased the party goods. He had decided to get some balloons in his red and black color scheme. Balloons were always fun, and adults hated it when they were popped. Maybe he would pop a few at the guard on the way in.

He expected the store proprietor to "give" him another generous discount.

He had skipped school for the day, which meant he supposedly would have to make up an English test. Except, he didn't plan on taking anymore tests.

Brandon was looking forward to the party. He had informed Mr. Finley that the Junior Science Club would not be meeting this week, which meant they would be free of annoying adult supervision.

He turned the corner onto Columbus Avenue. Up ahead, he spotted a familiar thin figure in a pink sweater. It was Lori. What a surprise! She was all alone, without Tommy hovering over her.

"Hey, Lori," he called, breaking into a trot to catch up with her.

Lori looked over her shoulder. She was plainly not happy to see him. She kept walking.

"I can't believe it," Brandon said as he reached her side. "Miss Goody Two-Shoes skips class." He laughed.

Lori stuffed her hands in her pockets and hunched her shoulders. "Brandon, I'm not in the mood."

"Whatsa matter? You and Romeo have a fight and split up? Where is he? Aceing the English test?"

"Leave me *alone*, Brandon."

"I thought you'd be glad to see me." Brandon knew she was not. He probed a bit, but she was behind her barrier. He was not going to let her go. "How about pizza and Coke? On me." He gave her a big smile.

"I'm not hungry. I have to go *home*." Lori quickened her pace.

Brandon grabbed her arm and yanked her around. Her hand came out of her pocket. "Not so fast—" he began, and then a strange sensation swept over him, sparked by the touch. In a flash, he saw a picture of the doctor, the lawyer and . . . *Hans Messner* inside the American Museum of Natural History. They were there for *him*. Hans Messner was *alive*.

He recovered quickly, striving not to betray what he had experienced. If Lori had felt it, she gave no sign. He let go of her and said, "I'll see you later."

Lori hurried off down the street.

Brandon's thoughts churned as he reversed his direction and headed back home. To hell with balloons. He had something bigger to grapple with. *Treason*.

He walled himself off mentally. So the old man survived, and now he had teamed up with the other two grown-ups to try to spring a trap on him! He started to curse inwardly at their previous failures to get the enemies, but that did little good.

He thought of alternatives. The group would not meet tonight.

No, that was no good. That wouldn't solve the problem of the grown-ups.

They would meet and then play a war game.

Brandon liked that idea. One of the favorite park games he and the other boys had made up was "Double Trap."

When you found out the enemy was trying to trap you, you let them think they were going to be successful. Meanwhile, you planned a counter-trap. Yes, that was the solution.

This called for the establishment of an emergency war council. He would have to get hold of Jason and Jeff right away.

The party would go on as planned. It would start an hour earlier, at 7 P.M.

CHAPTER
Twenty-Eight

Brandon arrived at six-thirty at the American Museum of Natural History with Jeffrey, Jason, and Melissa in tow. Melissa, who was now officially his girlfriend, happily toted the plastic sacks full of party goodies. Jeff balanced a rectangular white pastry box that held a sheet cake he'd ordered from the neighborhood bakery. Jason carried two brown grocery bags full of plastic two-liter bottles of Coke and orange Slice.

"Hiya, Mr. Inferior," Brandon hailed to the guard at the door, making the big black man tense. Brandon knew how much the guards disliked them, especially this one.

Rupert Baines checked his clipboard. "I thought Mr. Finley notified us that the Junior Science Club was canceled tonight."

Brandon shrugged. "Must be a mistake."

Baines scowled. "I can't let your kids have a meeting without adult supervision."

"Finley's coming," Brandon lied. "It's your fault for the screwup. Look, we're having a party, and we already bought all this stuff."

Baines waved them through.

"That was easy," Melissa whispered to Brandon when they were out of earshot of the guard. "But won't he come and break us up when he realizes Finley isn't going to show?"

"He won't dare."

Their sneakers made crunching noises on the granite floor. They went through the Northwest Coast Indians hall, but instead of turning left to go to the meeting rooms wing, they headed straight out, then took a series of turns that led to the Hayden Planetarium, at the opposite end of the floor. Brandon said, "Does everyone know we've moved the party from the classroom to the planetarium?"

"Yes," answered Jeff. "Everyone was notified in advance except Tommy and Lori, like you said. Michael will get them at the last minute and tell them there's been a time change."

"Good."

Melissa said, "You still haven't told me what this is all about, Brandon. Is this a surprise for Tommy and Lori? Are they getting engaged or something?"

"It's a surprise, all right," said Brandon. He went on, "I bet I can figure out how to operate the planetarium projectors. They're all computer-automated. We'll have our own sky show and laser light show."

"Brandon, that's a great idea," Melissa enthused. She looked at him with adoration shining in her eyes.

Brandon returned her gaze. Maybe sometime soon they would go off by themselves and... He could see that she got the message, and liked it.

They headed for the planetarium, and had no trouble unlocking the door with their concentrated thought. They stepped into the round, domed room and turned on the low house lights. The massive black Zeiss VI projector stood in the middle of the room, looking like a stubby baton. It was ringed by rows of high-backed seats. Above was the white dome upon which the sky and light shows were projected.

They had barely set down their bags and box when a

guard appeared in the doorway. *He must be new*, thought Brandon.

"Hey! What are you kids doing in here? Don't you know this place is off-limits?" He tried glaring at them, but with his balding gray head and pot belly, he didn't look very menacing.

Brandon centered a thought at the man, scooping up the energy from the other three children in order to magnify it. "Sorry," he said. "The door was open. We're from the Junior Science Club."

A mellowness came over the man. "Okay, kids. You can have a look around, but don't touch anything. Close the door on your way out." He turned and ambled off.

Brandon said, "We've got to make sure nobody bothers us tonight."

"The monitors," said Jeff.

"And the other things we talked about."

"What other things?" said Melissa.

"Never mind right now. Okay, you guys, you know what to do."

"Right," said Jason. He and Jeff left.

Brandon said, "Melissa, you can help me set up the party decorations." He got out the red and black crepe paper streamers, and he and Melissa started stringing them around the door frame and the backs of the seats.

"Let's hang some from the projector," said Melissa.

Brandon vetoed the idea. "I'm going to run the projector, and it will twist and turn."

Soon the other members of the Secret Society of Loki began to arrive, delighted with Brandon's choice of site for the party.

Melissa gave him a quick, wet kiss on the cheek. "You're wonderful."

"Thank you," Brandon said matter-of-factly. *I know.*

When Michael arrived with the two in tow, Tommy said, "What's going on, Brandon?"

"I decided to throw a party tonight. Anything wrong with that?"

"What are we celebrating?"

"You'll see."

Jeff and Jason were the last ones in. Jeff nodded, signaling to Brandon that all measures had been successfully executed.

Brandon took a position in front of the Zeiss projector. "I call this meeting of the Secret Society of Loki to order."

His eleven followers grew quiet and dropped into first-row auditorium seats around him.

"Everyone is present and accounted for. We will dispense with the minutes of the previous meeting. As you all know, we're going to have a party tonight. First, there's some important business to discuss. We're old enough to take charge of our own lives." Brandon's tone dropped. "We don't need parents and other grown-ups telling us what to do anymore."

"Yeah!" said Jason.

"So I've developed a plan for us. With Jeff's help." Brandon nodded at his adopted brother. "Jeff's parents own some land in upstate New York, near Catawba on Keuka Lake. It used to be a farm, but the barn and farmhouse have been abandoned for a long time. Mr. Tate has been thinking of turning it into a horse farm. Well, after the Tates have their *accident*, Jeff will inherit that land along with everything else. And we're gonna move up there and take it over and live there."

"But what about school?" asked Sarah.

"Leave it to a girl to worry about school," Doug sneered.

Brandon said, "We don't need school. It's boring and slow. We can teach ourselves everything we need to know. Up at the lake, we'll be totally on our own. We can practice our exercises. We can set up our own businesses. There won't be anything we can't do."

"What if our parents don't let us?" said Jennifer. "You didn't think of that."

"Yes, I did. We can't get rid of them all, or it would look

suspicious. Some more of us will become orphaned, and some of us will run away. I'm giving you the big picture here. There are a lot of details that I will discuss with each of you individually."

"How can we stay there?" asked Elizabeth. "Some grown-up will come along and find out about us."

Jeff said, "The place is pretty isolated. We'll put up a fence and no trespassing signs, and a locked gate on the drive."

"That's the least thing to worry about," said Brandon.

"Do we *all* have to go upstate?" The question, not to Brandon's surprise, came from Tommy.

"Yeah, Tommy, we do. And there's a good reason why. We can't afford any more weak links like David. Or any *traitors* trying to leave the group. If we're all together, we'll stick together."

"Traitors?" said Michael incredulously. "Who?"

Brandon stared pointedly at Tommy while he answered. "Nobody yet, Mike. I was speaking of possibilities."

"What about the doctor and the lawyer?" asked Doug. "We haven't found them yet."

Brandon grinned. "After the party, we're going to play 'Double Trap' tonight. The doctor and the lawyer are coming here. And so is that Hans Messner, the man who met us in the park. He didn't die after all, and he's going to be with them." Brandon watched Tommy and Lori for reaction. Lori looked sad. Tommy's facial muscles barely twitched. Their mind shields were up.

"You mean we're going to get them at last?" said Michael.

"We'd better, or we'll never see the lake." Brandon continued describing his vision of their private utopia in glowing terms. He finished, "We have about half an hour until we have to get ready for 'Double Trap.' I'm going to start the show and the party."

Brandon walked into the control booth of the planetarium and examined the setup. Most of the sky shows were automated, so it shouldn't take long to figure out how to work the projector, he reasoned.

"Jeff," he shouted out the door. "Start passing out the plates. Melissa, cut the cake and dish it out. Sarah, you pour the Cokes."

The Masters of the Universe plates made a big hit with everyone, as did the Go-Bot centerpiece, which Jason unfolded and propped up next to the Zeiss.

Brandon found the computer programs and looked over the labels. He wanted to save the laser light show for last. "First, we'll take a little space trip," he said to himself. He lit a cigarette and let it dangle from his lips while he went to work. This was going to be fun. The Zeiss was a combination of more than one hundred projection devices that could create the images of thousands of stars, planets, and celestial objects. In addition, other projectors created hundreds of special effects, such as the surface of a planet or the inside of a galaxy.

Brandon doused the main lights. The white dome glowed then went black. A giant image of the red-orange planet Jupiter whirled across the "sky." Brandon could hear the oohs and aahs of the children as they craned their necks to watch.

"Damn," he said. He had meant to start the space trip show at the beginning. Jupiter was halfway out of the solar system.

The outer planets—magnificent ringed Saturn, gray Uranus, blue Neptune, mysterious dark Pluto—sprang into sight and whirled off the dome. The program was going too fast. It took Brandon a few jerky tries to get it rolling smoothly. He turned up the volume on the soundtrack, a voice-over narration with a New Age synthesized music background.

The children ate their cake and soda pop while comets, meteors, galaxies, and nebulae sailed spectacularly above them. Each new celestial object was met with cheers and scattered applause. Brandon's chest swelled.

After about fifteen minutes, he shut off the sky show. He

was bored with galaxies. A few shouts of protest rose from the audience. "Shut up," he hollered over the public address system. "I'm going to put on something else."

Everyone waited patiently while Brandon, with his cigarette jammed back in his mouth, set up another program. When he was done, he removed the cigarette and shouted into his microphone again. "Okay, everybody! Time to rock and roll!"

He pressed a button and laser beams of light in a rainbow of colors shot across the dome, gyrating and swirling in rapidly changing patterns. Heavy-metal rock, vintage Led Zeppelin in "Whole Lotta Love," boomed over the loudspeakers. Everyone cheered and whistled as they got to their feet and boogied around the room.

Brandon left the control booth and slammed the door shut. He went around the room and tapped Jason, Jeff, Doug, Michael, and Elizabeth on the shoulders. The kids nodded and slipped out. Brandon whispered in Melissa's ear. "We've got to go for a while—we want to make sure nobody bothers us tonight while we play 'Double Trap.' You make sure Tommy and Lori stay here."

Rupert Baines was not feeling well. He had been recently diagnosed as having a peptic ulcer, and it was acting up again, sending severe pain from his abdomen to his lower chest. Dang it, he knew he shouldn't have wolfed down that hot dog before coming to work. He rubbed his middle. He needed a good dose of antacid, and there was nothing to be had in the employees' lounge. He had used up the last of it himself the night before, and it hadn't been replaced.

Baines looked up as the three men came through the door to the museum. By his sights, they all looked a little wild.

"The museum is closed," he announced tersely.

The oldest and the apparent leader of the three addressed Baines in a German-sounding accent. "We are here for the young scientists' club."

Baines looked them up and down. These guys didn't look

like they had anything to do with science. But then, who was he to judge? "You mean the Junior Science Club?"

"That's right."

Rupert consulted several ragged pages on his clipboard, muttering under his breath. "First it's canceled, then it's not..." He looked up. "They didn't tell me about no guest adults showing up."

The man with the accent bowed deferentially. "Forgive me. It must have slipped someone's mind."

Baines shook his head. "Heh! Seems to be a lot o' mind-slipping around here tonight."

"My colleagues and I are from New Data Laboratories in New Jersey. We have been invited tonight to give a presentation on fiber optics." He patted the bulky bag slung from his shoulder. "My visuals."

Baines gave them another looking over. "All right. You know where the meeting room is? I can have someone escort you—" He turned to his tiny black-and-white video monitors. The screens were blank. "Shee-it," he mumbled. "'Scuse me, gents, but this monitor system is always going on the fritz."

"Never mind," said the gray-haired man. "We know where it is."

Baines waved them on through.

A few minutes later, the ulcer pain intensified to the point where Baines was desperate for relief. He picked up the phone to buzz Charlie, who was stationed down in the basement. Maybe there was someone around who could relieve him for a few minutes so he could run out to the drugstore.

But the phone was out of order. Not even the internal line was working.

Cursing, Baines crashed the receiver down. He was all alone on this end of the vast first floor, unless one of the janitors was around somewhere. The pain in his stomach burned.

He thought, *I'll just close up the station and leave for a few minutes. Nobody's meeting here tonight but those damn science kids, and they're all in.*

Baines got up and went out the door to the museum. He pulled it shut and locked it.

A few minutes later, Brandon and his team swooped through the halls, on a mission to say good-bye forever to Mr. Inferior and all the other night staff in the museum. Brandon had saved Mr. Inferior for last.

He stopped when he saw the deserted desk, swearing beneath his breath. "Check the can, Jason."

Jason trotted off. He came back shaking his head. "Empty."

Brandon dispatched Jeff to double-check the employees' lounge, but that yielded nothing. He leaned against one of the glass doors to think for a moment, and then realized the door was locked. He tried all the doors at the entrance, including the revolving doors, and found them locked.

"He left," Brandon announced, chagrined. Of all the night staff, Brandon had hated Mr. Inferior the most. He was angry at missing him, but there was nothing he could do about it. "Okay, let's jam the locks and get back to the planetarium," he commanded.

Stern, Messner, and Reston found the Junior Science Club classroom door ajar, the room empty and dark.

Messner said, "Good, no one is here yet. Let's get set up."

Stern kept thinking of a planetarium. It was an odd thought; he hadn't been inside a planetarium in decades. Maybe it was an association with being in the museum itself.

Messner was busy checking his Image Barrager. "Edward, see where the exits are, and which doors are locked. We don't want any of them slipping out."

Stern grew nervous. The clock in the classroom said twenty minutes to eight. Tommy and Lori had said they would meet them here at seven-thirty.

Messner made several dry runs of his plan. Tommy and

Lori would get Brandon out in the open *here*, and he would position himself *there* . . .

He acts like a field marshal in war, thought Stern with disgust.

At ten minutes to eight, no one had showed up yet. Stern was increasingly worried about Tommy and Lori. He paced up and down the corridor, acutely aware that his very worry might prevent him from recognizing a silent message from Tommy.

At five minutes to eight, Stern was certain something had gone wrong. At least one child should have showed up.

Messner started to fume.

"Where do you suppose they are?" Reston wondered.

Eight o'clock came and went, and not a soul approached the classroom.

At five minutes past the hour, Stern said, "I'm going to find a guard. Maybe they're meeting in another part of the museum."

"Sure," said Reston, strained by the anxiety of waiting. "It must have been a last-minute change."

Without waiting for Messner's approval, Stern left their post near the classroom. He was instantly lost. The museum was huge, and the halls all looked alike. He couldn't remember which direction they had come from. He wandered through the Northwest Coast Indian exhibits and then into the North American Mammals hall and finally came out into a cavernous open area with a round information desk set in the middle. No one was at the desk, of course, but on the far side was a guard desk at a revolving door. It wasn't the same man they had seen coming in. Somehow Stern had gotten himself turned around.

The guard appeared to be sleeping. He was folded over the desk with his red-haired head on his arms.

"Excuse me," Stern called out as he cut across the floor. His words echoed eerily. He had to admit that the museum, with some of its lights turned off for the night, was a spooky place. And chilly. "Excuse me," he called again, but the guard didn't stir.

The man must be a heavy sleeper. How on earth could he keep a night security job? Stern noticed that the video monitors on the desk were blank.

He called out a third time, and still got no response. By then Stern was at the desk, and he shook the man's shoulder.

The guard was dead.

CHAPTER Twenty-Nine

Stern backed away in shock.

"Tommy! Lori!" he shouted. The words were nearly lost in the echoing. He turned and began running back toward the classroom.

As the echoes of his words died, he heard faint, childish laughter. He halted and listened. The sound was soft, like children giggling in the back of a movie theater. It seemed to be coming from everywhere, reverberating around the high ceiling and walls.

"Tommy! Lori!" His shouts echoed and faded again into the giggling.

He started to run again but was disoriented. He stopped and listened, trying to determine the source of the laughter. It drew him toward a staircase. The sounds seemed to be coming from the next floor up.

"Tommy! Lori!" The laughter responded, louder.

Stern heard pounding footsteps, too heavy to be a child's. Like the laughter, they seemed to come from everywhere, echoing around and around. This was maddening.

"Stern! Where are you?"

"Messner? The main information desk."

The footsteps got louder. Messner, holding the Image Barrager, and Reston appeared out of a corridor.

"What's going on?" Reston was panicked. "Where are they? Where are the boy and the girl?"

"I don't know," Stern said. He pointed to the guard. "He's dead."

Reston blanched.

Messner was listening to the soft laughter. "They've got to be close."

"It's impossible to tell with the echoing," said Stern.

"Let's get out of here," suggested Reston.

"You fool!" shouted Messner. "We're going nowhere."

"It doesn't matter," Reston said. "They've jammed the doors locked so we can't get out. That's what they did to me when they set fire to my clinic."

"Listen!" Messner said.

"I think they're up there," said Stern, pointing.

Messner started up the stairs.

Reston looked questioningly at Stern. "Do you think the other guards are—?"

"Dead," Stern agreed soberly.

"But Tommy and Lori—?"

"Face it, Reston, we may have walked into a trap."

"Oh, Christ." The color drained from the doctor's face.

Stern prodded him. "Get going before Messner gets too far ahead of us." They ran past a bronze bust of Albert Smith Bickmore, founder of the museum, and took the stairs two at a time.

On the second floor, they emerged in the marble and limestone vault of the Theodore Roosevelt Memorial Hall, one-hundred twenty feet long by sixty-seven feet wide. Along the sides, eight Roman Corinthian columns rose forty-eight feet high, nearly half the distance to the ceiling. The walls were covered with murals depicting events in Roosevelt's life. In the center of the room was another empty information desk.

The sounds of the laughter and Messner's echoing footsteps drew Stern and Reston off into an adjoining exhibit hall, African Mammals. The hall was immense and relatively open, with animals in dioramas lining the walls, and eight stuffed elephants posed in the middle of the room in a line. No one was in the hall; the sounds of the children came from farther up ahead. They ran to the left of the elephants, past gorillas, okapi, zebras, and animals Stern didn't recognize.

They ran through a doorway at the opposite end bordered by elephant tusks, and suddenly were in a narrow corridor filled with photographs of Benares, India. They came out of that into another gallery, Man in Africa, cut up into small chambers with twisting pathways around exhibits. Each chamber was done in a different color, alternating among blue, olive green, and burnt orange. Everywhere around them glass display cases were smashed and exhibits ruined.

Stern and Reston rounded a turn and stopped in midstride. Coming at them, flying through the air, were primitive spears and arrows. Reston jumped, narrowly avoiding being impaled by a spear. They flattened themselves against one wall. The air became filled with flying objects as African masks, jewelry, and pieces of pottery joined the weapons. They whizzed crazily around, some of the objects crashing into each other and falling to the ground in showers of fragments. An arrow embedded in the wall just over Stern's head, sending him to the floor. The childish laughter was louder.

"I don't believe what I'm seeing," gasped Reston.

Stern looked cautiously around the corner. "Messner!" he shouted. There was no answer. "Come on," he said to Reston. "We've got to keep going." He crouched down and began to move ahead slowly.

"But—"

"Hurry!"

Reston obeyed. Fewer objects were flying through the air now, as though the psychokinetic power that propelled them was diminishing.

"There are no alarms going off," whispered Reston. "They've severed them—that's exactly what they did when they set fire to the clinic." He shuddered. "No one's going to help us."

"It's too late to worry about that," Stern said. "But we've got one thing on our side. They would have killed us by now if they had the power, but they don't—they're too scattered and there's three of us. They're trying to get us some other way."

The Man in Africa hall went quiet, except for the muffled sound of feet moving on rubber-soled shoes.

"Messner?" Stern called again.

"Here, Stern," said a voice in pain.

Stern sprinted ahead and found the Nazi slumped against a display pedestal, its glass case shattered. He had a spearhead embedded in his upper right arm, and he was still clutching the Image Barrager.

For a moment, Stern was tempted to grab the Image Barrager out of his hands and leave him, but he didn't know how to operate the weapon.

Messner was breathing hard. "I didn't get—any of them," he said haltingly. "I couldn't see them—I didn't want to fire blind and waste energy—"

"Don't talk," said Stern. He grasped the broken shaft of the spear and yanked. The head came out with a pop. Messner gasped and breathed harder as blood welled up out of the wound.

Reston had already pulled a cloth out of a broken display case. He tore it lengthwise and used one piece to staunch the blood and the second to wrap around Messner's arm. "Can you make it?"

Messner, his face pale, nodded. "I must," he said. "They have gone out another way." He got to his feet.

A boy darted out from behind a vitrine. Messner snapped up the Image Barrager to fire.

"Don't!" Stern said. "It's Tommy."

"Help, Mr. Stern," the boy pleaded.

Messner aimed his weapon and prepared to pull the trigger. "How do you not know he's still one of them?"

"I'm not, I swear," said Tommy. "Brandon's after us, too."

"Where's Lori?"

Tommy pointed to his hiding place.

"Get her."

The boy ran behind the vitrine and came out holding a teary Lori by the hand. *She looks like she's gone to pieces*, Stern thought. He said, "Stay with us and behind us."

"We might be able to help," said Tommy. "They've all gone up to the fourth floor."

There were two other ways out of the Man in Africa hall besides the way they had come in. Stern and Reston both were disoriented, but the Nazi had memorized the museum maps. "This way," he said, indicating straight ahead. "There is a staircase. We stay out of the elevators."

The exit Messner chose led to another exhibit hall, Birds of the World, and for a moment Stern was certain Messner had erred. But another left turn out of that hall brought them to a staircase, and they took the steps two at a time. As they neared the fourth floor, they heard laughter again.

The staircase brought them out between the entrances to two halls, Earth History to the right, Late Mammals to the left.

"Left," said Tommy. The laughter echoing around them increased.

"Be careful," warned Stern.

They stole into the hall and looked around. Unlike the Man in Africa hall, this gallery was long, wide, and open. The glass cases, containing skeletons of prehistoric beasts, were intact. Some cases were in the walls and some were free-standing. In the middle of the room and not under glass was a line of skeletons of mastodons and mastodonts, arranged like the stuffed elephants on the floor below.

They proceeded carefully, Messner and Stern leading the way, Reston behind and shepherding the two children. Their footsteps were muffled by the hard green carpet on the floor. There were plenty of hiding places behind some of the display cases, but the great hall hid no one.

On the way out, they passed the skeleton of a Great Irish Deer with eleven-foot horns, and then entered Early Mammals, a small, boxy room filled with vitrines of reconstructed skeletons. They had to choose between going right or going left, and Tommy pointed to the left.

That path led them to another large chamber, Late Dinosaurs. Stern found himself staring up at mammoth skeletons of some of the largest creatures ever to walk the face of the earth. Directly in front of him in the middle of the room and towering over everything else was a Tyrannosaurus Rex, more than eighteen feet high and forty-seven feet long, its gaping jaws showing rows of daggerlike teeth. Beside it was a Triceratops, its three sharp horns protruding from its broad skull armor, and behind were two Trachtodonts, duck-billed creatures that stood seventeen feet high by thirty-five feet long.

The remainder of the exhibit space was filled with freestanding glass cases with more skeletons.

There was still no sign of Brandon and the other children. Laughter came from ahead at the opposite end of the hall. They passed along the row of giant skeletons.

Stern caught a movement out of the corner of his eye. "Look out!" he cried, as the tail of a Trachtodont whipped out toward Reston and the children. The tail fell apart as a hail of bones were flung through the air. A large bone smashed Stern in the head, knocking him clean off his feet. The rest of the bones were diverted harmlessly around Reston and the two children as though they were inside a protective force field.

Stern rolled onto his side, seeing stars and fighting not to lose consciousness. Before he could get up, the Tyrannosaurus Rex shuddered and groaned to life, shearing loose of its moorings as its giant reptile feet moved forward. The huge jaws descended toward Stern, opening wider. He tried to push the heavy, four-foot skull away, but the force behind the skeleton had incredible strength.

He rolled over several times and scrambled to his knees, the dinosaur pursuing him, shaking with every step. He felt a strange buzzing in his head and pressure building in his ears. He thought he was going to black out. He caught a glimpse of Tommy and Lori and suddenly realized what was happening. They were using their power, and drawing on his.

Stern scrambled to his feet. The skull was swinging to the side, preparing to come back at him like a bat. He surrendered to the tugging feeling inside of his head.

The Tyrannosaurus Rex stopped and began to tremble. The tremble increased to a violent shaking, until the skeleton distintegrated in a tumble of bones.

Stern jumped out of the way of a huge hind leg bone and then sank to his knees. His head throbbed. He felt weakened, and didn't know if it was from the blow to his head or the strange experience. He looked at the bones rolling on the floor. Tommy and Lori had done that, but something inside of him had helped.

"Are you all right?" said Reston, pulling him up.

"Dizzy." He bent over and put his head down until the swimming sensation cleared. He noticed then that Messner had vanished.

"Come on, Mr. Stern." Tommy tugged at his sleeve. "They've all gone down to the third floor."

Brandon was high on excitement. "Double Trap" was working exceptionally well. They were running the adults ragged, all over the museum. He knew Tommy and Lori had dropped out of the group in the first hiding place they could find, but that was all right. Two of them could be of little help to the grown-ups, and Tommy and Lori would get theirs in the end.

The only thing he didn't understand was the weapon carried by Hans Messner. At first, Brandon had thought it was a high-powered gun, but it shot out red laser beams, not bullets, and it was nearly soundless. The light itself was harmless. But once Brandon had been close to the red beam, and a queasy feeling had overcome him. He didn't know if it was the early warning sign of another blinding headache, or if it had something to do with the weapon.

Whatever the device was, he decided, it would be useless against them and their combined power.

They unleashed the dinosaur skeletons and bolted downstairs to the third floor. Laughing, the ten children scattered through the dimly lit Gallery Three. The best part of "Double Trap" was about to begin.

Fueled by rage and adrenalin, Messner burst out of the stairwell onto the third floor. He was no longer aware of the pain throbbing in his right arm where the African spearhead had penetrated. He saw the map of the floor in his mind and instinctively guessed where the children were. He turned left, bypassing African Mammals and instead heading into the long hall of Reptiles and Amphibians.

They weren't far from him now.

He checked the settings on his weapon. He had wasted some of the charge by firing off in knee-jerk reactions. He would do no more of that.

Messner sped carelessly through the Reptiles and Amphibians, certain that no children were hiding behind the display cases.

He stopped at the entrance to Gallery Three. The hall housed a special exhibit of Medieval European culture. Beside the panel of introductory text stood a pedestal holding a small vitrine with an armored helmet inside. On the floor lay a man—a janitor, judging from his tan work clothes. There was a steel pail and a mop nearby. The man was either unconscious or dead. Messner didn't bother to check.

He raced inside the hall.

* * *

Stern, Reston, and the two children could hear Messner shouting all the way from the fourth floor. "I know you're in here! Come out!"

With Tommy guiding, they went down the staircase and through the Reptiles and Amphibians hall. At the entrance to Gallery Three, they stopped and Reston bent over the janitor, feeling his neck for a pulse. He shook his head. "He's dead."

They went into the gallery.

The exhibit space for Medieval European Culture was filled with a series of fan-folded panels colored charcoal gray. At various intervals in the panels were exhibit cases and text, featuring tools, jewelry, clothing, armor, and weapons. In the middle of the gallery was an open area set up to show a scene of daily village life inside a cutaway of a hut. The centerpiece in the one wall of the hut was a fake fire around which were gathered mannequins dressed in Medieval garb. A woman cooked in an iron pot hung over the fire. A man whittled a piece of wood. A young boy played with a dog. A hunter held out a string of slain rabbits to the cook. A girl set a crude table with wooden bowls and spoons.

Stern could hear Messner in the gallery, going from panel to panel, but couldn't see him. "I know you're in here!" Messner kept shouting.

Tommy said, "Mr. Stern, I have a bad feeling—"

It was too late.

The sound of laughter and running feet exploded into the hall. From the far end came a rumbling and crashing. "That's the exit," whispered Tommy. "They've blocked the far exit!"

The laughter enveloped them as the children ran behind the panels, cutting off the five from reaching the only other way out of the hall.

How can they stay so invisible? Stern wondered desperately. The children seemed to know every hidden nook in the museum.

Messner was turning in circles, pointing the Image Barrager. The red laser sighting beam shot out, sporadic and useless.

Vitrines shattered everywhere around them as Brandon and his followers unleashed a new wave of psychic energy. Tommy and Lori disappeared as exhibit artifacts broke loose from their mountings and hurtled around the gallery.

A spiked steel mace tore through the air toward Reston. He ducked behind a free-standing suit of armor, and the mace smashed into the breastplate, toppling the heavy armor backward into him. His wind was knocked out as he struck the wall and slid to the floor.

The mannequins in the center of the room were cut to pieces by flying swords, daggers, halberds, and boar spears.

"Come out!" screamed Messner as he dodged a rapier.

Slowly, the flying weapons were forcing them away from the walls toward the open center of the room. Then Stern saw flashes of movement as Brandon and his band scurried around the edges of the room, circling them like a pack of wolves.

Then Brandon and nine others came into the open, and Stern descended into pain. It was like being vised on the inside, and he could see that Reston felt it, too.

Messner fired his Image Barrager, sweeping it around the children. Nothing happened for a few seconds, and then a shocked look came over their faces as they responded to visions that only they could see.

"It's working," Messner cried in exultation. He swept the red beam in a wide arc around the room again and again.

The children began screaming and running in all directions, unmindful of the weapons that were still whizzing through the room. Stern had never heard such agony in his life, not even in Auschwitz. The physical pain inside of him subsided, to be replaced by another kind of pain, a response to the suffering of others.

They're monsters, he kept reminding himself. *They're monsters.*

He felt helpless. He spun around just in time to see a dagger—a real dagger—come at him, and it was too late to get out of the way. It struck him in his right thigh, ripped through a layer of flesh and exited.

He sank to the floor, his leg a mass of pain.

Reston, who had taken cover behind a panel, sprang out and dragged Stern back and propped him up against the panel. "Christ," the doctor muttered as dark blood flowed out copiously. "At least it's not the artery. Can you press down on it?"

Stern nodded and pressed both hands down on the wound.

Reston looked around him. Debris was scattered all over the floor. He spotted a wooden bowl and slid it under Stern's foot so that his leg was raised. "Don't move. I'll fix a bandage," he said. He worked fast.

Brandon was caught off guard by the effect of Messner's weapon. He was stunned as he saw a poleax, its curved blade glistening with blood, come sweeping down out of the air toward his head.

He threw up his hands and screamed, summoning up his mind shield. The ax blade struck an invisible bubble around him and dissolved. It wasn't real!

He looked around him, but his followers were in panic, flailing their arms as though they were fighting off attackers, only there was nothing in front of them.

Before Brandon could act, he was confronted by a sight that terrified him so much he almost fainted.

Standing in front of him were his dead mother and father, their burial clothes in rags and their flesh partially decayed away from the bones. They were swarming with cockroaches. They held out their arms to him beseechingly. His mother cried, "Why did you kill us, Brandon? We loved you."

"Get away!" Brandon shouted. "You're not real. Get away!"

He willed the visions to go away, but instead the decaying corpses came closer. He stepped backward, swinging at air. He called up more energy and more energy until he was nearly drained. Just as the hands of his dead parents were about to close around him, the figures melted away.

For a moment, Brandon felt like jelly, unable to do anything, reliving the awful sight of the corpses teeming with roaches. Then he sent out a silent command to his group, *mind shields*, as he dodged behind a panel to get out of sight. He felt a broken mental wall go up among them.

A few of the children were unable to protect themselves from the effects of the Image Barrager. Doug ran blindly and in total panic, crashing into pedestals and finally impaling himself on a sword held out in battle stance by another suit of armor. He moaned and jerked spasmodically as he died.

Melissa smashed into a vitrine, screaming as a glass shard stabbed her in the heart, killing her before the scream had left her throat. Blood from her severed aorta sprayed up in a red fountain.

Samantha backed into a crossbow, which released its arrow straight through her back and out her chest. She gave a strangulated cry and collapsed.

Brandon felt a white fury build inside of him. How dare these men do this! He began to summon up every ounce of power he could muster, connecting to the others and drawing on them. He had to get Messner and his weapon.

The energy was fragmented at first and then began to build, higher and higher, the pressure mounting like the inside of a volcano. He directed the force at the weapon.

The Image Barrager exploded in Messner's hands, sending the German flying backward off his feet and showering out a cloud of sparks and hot metal onto the centerpiece exhibit.

* * *

Out on the streets, Rupert Baines ambled back to the museum. He couldn't walk very fast due to his arthritis, so it had taken him a while to get down to the nearest drugstore where he could buy a remedy for his stomach pains. As soon as he had begun to feel better, he had started back to his post at the first-floor entrance.

He stuck his key into the lock, but it refused to go in. Try as he might, he could not get the key to work. The lock hole was jammed closed. "I'll de damned," he muttered.

He peered through the glass door. Everything seemed normal—the lights were on, nothing seemed out of place. How could the lock be jammed?

Baines didn't ring the night bell. He didn't want it to be known that he had left his post. He supposed he could trust Charlie, one of the other night guards, and headed around the enormous building to the entrance where Charlie usually sat.

Charlie wasn't there. *Must be in the john*, thought Baines. *Just as well. I'll slip in.* But his key wouldn't work in this lock, either.

Baines waited for several minutes. Charlie didn't come back to his post. Baines relented and pushed the night bell. It didn't work.

"Hell," he mumbled crossly. He would have to go around to yet another door.

At the third door, he saw a guard slumped over his desk, as though he were asleep. Oh, yeah, ole red-haired Pat. *Never caught him snoozin' off on the job before*.

Baines rapped on the glass, but the man didn't rouse. He tried his key in the lock. No luck. Some strange things sure were going on in this place tonight.

Baines banged on the glass, but the man still didn't respond. "Sleeps like the dead," said Baines, and then a horrible realization struck him.

He looked wildly around him. He had to get to a telephone, *fast*.

* * *

The sparks from the exploding Image Barrager quickly caught fire in the dry straw. The clothing on the mannequins began to smolder and turn to flame. "Fire!" Stern yelled, crawling toward the center of the room.

Reston scrambled up and looked for something he could use to try to smother the flames.

Messner came to his senses to focus on a boy in front of him—Brandon.

Stern caught the look in the boy's eyes, and it was the most unnatural he had ever seen. He could feel a tidal wave of force building up in the room. He held his breath.

But Brandon ignored him, intent only on Messner, who was getting to his feet. "You're dead!" Brandon shouted at him.

An animal growl came from deep in Messner's throat. "You can't kill me," he said, and advanced toward the boy.

Brandon retreated, stepping backward, as though luring the German toward him. Messner lunged at him.

Brandon jumped to the side. A nearby display case full of knives, daggers, and rapiers shattered, the contents exploding out into the air. Stern rolled back to the edge of the room as the sharp weapons tore through the air. He stopped and looked up in time to see a dagger slam through Messner's ribs into his right lung, burying itself up to the hilt.

Messner hunched over and fell to his knees, coughing on his own blood as it rose up his throat and spewed out of his mouth. He looked down at the dagger, stunned. He grasped the hilt and in two jerks pulled it out, giving a choked cry of pain as the bloody blade cleared his chest. He dropped the dagger and put his hands over the ragged hole in his flesh. Blood pumped out through his fingers and dripped down to the floor.

Brandon grinned. He picked a long, slim rapier from the floor and held it out on the flat of his palm. The rapier shot off and struck Messner in the chest near the dagger wound, piercing one hand and nailing it to his body. The German screamed and vomited more blood, and fell backward, dead. His gaunt features were twisted in a death mask of pain and astonishment.

Stern was horrified, but there was no time to dwell on it. "Reston," he shouted, struggling to his feet and wincing at the pain in his bandaged leg. "We've got to get out! Now!"

But Brandon, satisfied that Messner was dead, turned his attention to Stern. Some of the other children clustered around. An intense headache hit Stern and his vision went blurry. "Stop," he tried to say, but the word came out an unintelligible sound. He tried to imagine himself behind a mental shield but could not grasp the image and the power.

A thin, brown-haired body streaked out from behind a panel and tackled Brandon from behind.

"Tommy!" Stern cried. *Thank God he's still alive*.

Brandon crashed forward and down, throwing out his arms to break his fall.

The other children got out of the way, sensing that the struggle must be between the two boys alone. They rolled over and over on the floor, clawing at each other, their supernormal powers superseded by blind anger and fists.

Lori materialized next to Stern, and he hugged her. She pointed to the ceiling. He didn't know what she meant, until he felt the pressure and tugging inside his head. She was using his own meager power again to piggyback onto hers, and turn on the overhead sprinklers. As water cascaded down, the flames sizzled and smoked.

Brandon was on top of Tommy, pummeling him with his fists. Stern caught Brandon and tried to pry him off. The boy fought like a wildcat, and the three of them thrashed on the wet floor. The wound on Stern's leg bled with renewed vigor. The others ganged up on him, and Stern felt a bolt of pain go through him. He let go of Brandon and clasped his leg. With a flash, he knew the children were getting their full power back, and if he, Reston, Tommy, and Lori didn't get out, they were all dead.

He grabbed Tommy's arm and succeeded in pulling away

from Brandon. "Reston," he called out, still not seeing the doctor. "Let's go!" He held onto Tommy and began limping toward the unblocked exit of the gallery.

Reston quit beating at unextinguished flames. Like everyone, he was soaked by the sprinklers. He took Lori by the hand and followed Stern and Tommy.

But Brandon and his followers were combining their power, directing it at them. Reston doubled over in pain. Stern's skull felt like it would burst apart. Touching Tommy and then Lori, he became aware of a psychic union with them as they tried to counter the force being directed against them. *It's no use*, he thought, as he felt all of them ebb. They sloshed through the water that was building up on the floor.

Reston's foot struck a lance. "Bloody hell," he said through gritted teeth. He seized it and threw it at Brandon.

The lance rose in a curve and then abruptly changed course as it was deflected in mid-flight. Brandon laughed gleefully at what he had done. The lance flew up toward the ceiling and embedded where the wall and ceiling joined together, severing an electrical wire that was mounted along the niche. Sparking, the live wire dropped.

The tip of it stopped several feet above the floor. The wire was prevented from dropping all the way to the water by another bracket that still held the rest of it in place in the niche near the ceiling.

They were only a few feet from the exit, but Stern suddenly knew they would never make it. If they reached the exit, they still had to get out of the building. The odds were against them. His one consolation was that Messner was dead. If he and Reston died and Brandon and his group lived, at least they would not be pawns in a Nazi racial breeding plan.

Stern glanced over his shoulder and saw a wooden platform to the right of him. There was a pile of tumbled and broken mannequins on it, the remains of a display. He got an idea. They had one last chance.

"Reston, up here!" Stern pulled Tommy up on the platform, pushing off the mannequins. Lori and Reston joined them.

Stern formed a picture in his mind of the wire dropping all the way to the water-covered floor. There was no other choice. He concentrated with all his effort, and then felt the psychic union with Tommy and Lori return. They knew what he wanted.

"What are you doing?" said Reston anxiously.

Stern didn't answer. He was concentrating.

A screw came loose from the bracket in the ceiling and splashed into the water. The wire held.

Brandon picked up what was happening, and countered with a force to hold the wire in place. *Damn it*, Stern thought. *Now we'll never get it down.* He concentrated harder.

The rest of the children had mixed reactions to the danger confronting them. Doug and Elizabeth looked down at the water and then started to run, only to be collared by Jason and Jeff. Michael looked petrified. Brandon, too, looked around for an easy escape, but there was none, Stern knew. If they tried to run for it, the wire would come down. They had to keep it from making contact with the water.

"Let it go," Jeff said to Brandon. "I'll catch it."

"Are you crazy?" snapped Brandon. "You could miss." He pointed at Stern and the others on the pedestal. "Let's get them!"

The seven children flung themselves at the platform, pulling and pushing at Reston, Stern, Tommy, and Lori. Lori screamed and clung to Tommy. Stern, unable to concentrate on the bracket, reached down and grabbed a broken mannequin arm by the wrist and wielded it like a club, forcing Jason to keep at bay. He was acutely aware of the heaviness of the dangling wire, pulling on the bracket. *If the wire goes down and we're off the platform, or if any of those kids are touching us, we've had it*, he thought grimly.

Little hands grabbed at them from all sides as the children

attacked like animals. Brandon caught Lori by the ankle and yanked her away from Tommy. With a shriek, she tumbled off the platform.

Just as Lori fell, the bracket holding the wire gave way, and Stern saw the wire drop toward the floor. *Oh, my God, no!* In the same instant, he felt a renewed charge of energy between himself and Tommy. It happened so fast he barely knew what was going on, but he felt the energy reach out to the wire. It stopped inches from the floor and hung suspended like a thin black snake in a magician's act.

Brandon shouted and ran toward it, the rest of his troop following him. Stern quickly snatched Lori up off the floor and lifted her back on the platform. *Not yet . . . not yet . . .*

"Grab it, Jeff," Brandon said. "Just don't touch the end."

But Jeff was frightened of the wire now. "I don't know," he said helplessly.

"Get it out of here!" shouted Brandon. He shot out his hand to grab the wire. The instant before he touched it, the live end fell into the water.

The water hissed and vibrated as the current shot through it. Brandon and his followers—Jason, Jeff, Michael, Doug, Jennifer, and Elizabeth—were immobilized, screaming, terror in their faces.

Death came swiftly, but the slender bodies remained standing, frozen in place by the electricity that coursed through their flesh and seared their sightless eyes. Then, in what seemed like slow motion, the seven bodies toppled rigid onto the watery floor. Brandon struck his side and rolled onto his back. His eye sockets were black holes, and his hands were clenched like claws out in front of him. His mouth was stretched open in a soundless howl.

Jason and Jeff fell forward onto their faces, their limbs contorted. Doug, Jennifer, Michael, and Elizabeth lay like broken dolls whose hearts had stopped in a moment of unspeakable fear.

Around them all, smoke rose from the hissing water.

Stern covered Lori's face and turned away.

"My God," Reston managed to whisper.

Tommy said nothing, but stared at the bodies.

For what seemed like a long time, the four stood motionless on the wooden platform, as if the slightest movement would somehow send the current racing up through their own bodies. Then Stern pulled himself together. "Let's get the wire out," he said in a raspy, choked voice. Tommy and Lori obeyed. The wire came out of the water and snaked up to rest on an unbroken display case, safely out of the way.

CHAPTER Thirty

Stern was numb, beyond thought and words. Mercifully, so was Reston. Neither spoke as they followed Tommy and Lori out of Gallery Three, leaving the bodies and wreckage behind them. They went down the stairs to the basement level of the museum, Stern limping, keeping one hand pressed to his wound. Not a human being stirred anywhere. *They're all dead*, Stern thought with horror. *Everyone who was in this museum tonight. Except us.*

He couldn't even begin to grapple with what had happened.

Tommy and Lori seemed buoyant. Holding hands, they walked with a spring in their step. Tommy called out to Stern and Reston behind them, "There's an exit to the outside down here that's used only by the staff. It's the best way out."

Good. Let's get out of here before someone comes, Stern thought. Sirens wailed in the distance. They could be going anywhere else in the city—or coming to the museum.

In the basement, Tommy and Lori left the public rooms and led Stern and Reston into the off-limits storage and office areas. All the lights were out. Tommy and Lori seemed sure of themselves in the dark, but Stern and Reston fumbled along, hugging the wall for bearings.

They came out into a hallway where visibility improved a little. The children awaited Stern and Reston.

Stern said to them, "You saved our lives. But, God, I'm sorry about—"

"Mr. Stern," Tommy interrupted, "they all got what they deserved."

The sharpness in the boy's voice caught Stern off guard. He looked down at Tommy and Lori. Their eyes shone in the dark like animal eyes.

"There's the exit door, to your left," said Tommy. He started to turn away, but Stern took him by the hand.

"Aren't you coming with us?"

The hand slipped from his grasp. "No. You'll hear from us."

Lori giggled.

Stern tried to fathom the meaning behind the words, but the psychic rapport he had felt before with the children was blocked. *They've cut me off*, he thought in bewilderment.

"We'll see you," Tommy said.

"'Bye," said Lori.

Suddenly the eyes were gone. Footsteps ran off into the darkness.

"Wait," Stern shouted hoarsely. "Don't leave!" He foolishly started to run after them but couldn't manage more than a hobble. He was blind in the darkness. The footsteps receded rapidly.

He groped his way back to Reston. "Gone," he said with disbelief.

The doctor pushed the bar on the door. "Let's get out of here before you lose any more blood. Into the park." He pointed across the street to Central Park.

They stepped out. The night air was cool and refreshing. Stern felt like he had exited a nightmare and come back to reality. He realized what a sticky mess he was. He and Reston were wet, their clothing was torn, and they were streaked with blood and dirt. His swollen throat ached. He limped, and Reston took hold of his arm to support him.

It's over, Stern thought. *My unfinished business. It's finally over.* For the first time since Leon had died, he relaxed his guard and welcomed the inner voices to him. *Tell me it's over.*

Silence greeted him.

Well, what did he expect, after years of denial?

He and Reston crossed the street and entered the park. The sirens were coming closer, shrieking through the night.

Leon, Stern thought. *You've known all along. Hans Messner is dead now. Tell me it's over. Please.*

The silence in his mind was ominous.

"Let's get off the path," said Reston, prodding Stern off into grass, deeper into the darkness.

Slowly, a thought formed at the back of Stern's head and pushed its way forward. He wanted to deny it, but it was insistent. "Reston," he began.

"Yes?"

"What if—Tommy and Lori planned it to end this way?"

Reston's grip on his arm tightened as the doctor tensed, then relaxed. "I think your imagination is working overtime. How could they have planned this?"

"I mean, what if they decided they wanted out of the group because they had their own schemes? According to their little death pact, that meant either them or the rest of the group, and they couldn't manage to get rid of everyone else by themselves. We conveniently provided the means. Now Tommy and Lori are the only ones left. They've still got their power."

"Yes, but—" Reston's voice broke off. A moment passed before he spoke again. "No," he said with finality. "You're wrong."

They went on into the depths of the park. The sirens were very close, heading, it seemed, straight for the museum. Stern's leg was in burning pain.

The voice in his ear started very low, a whisper that grew

louder, Leon's voice. It sounded sad, but Stern didn't care, he was relieved to hear it and didn't try to shut out the words.

Until the words became clear.

"Rainer, it isn't over."

Mystery . . . Intrigue . . . Suspense

__BAD COMPANY
by Liza Cody   *(B30-738, $2.95)*
Abducted by a motorcycle gang, Anna discovers she has shaken an unsteady balance in the London underworld—and now must fight for her life.

__DUPE
by Liza Cody   *(B32-241, $2.95)*
Anna Lee is the private investigator called in to placate the parents of Dierdre Jackson. Anna finds motives and murder as she probes the unsavory world of the London film industry where Dierdre sought glamour and found duplicity . . . and death.

__STALKER
by Liza Cody   *(B32-807, $3.95)*
In a peaceful village, Anna finds a corpse with a bolt from a crossbow piercing its side. In an unfamiliar world of city princes and country poachers, she pursues the Stalker.

WARNER BOOKS
P.O. Box 690
New York, N.Y. 10019

Please send me the books I have checked. I enclose a check or money order (not cash), plus 50¢ per order and 50¢ per copy to cover postage and handling.*
(Allow 4 weeks for delivery.)

_____ Please send me your free mail order catalog. (If ordering only the catalog, include a large self-addressed, stamped envelope.)

Name _____

Address _____

City _____

State _____ Zip _____

*N.Y. State and California residents add applicable sales tax.

Mystery & Suspense by GREGORY MCDONALD

__**FLETCH AND THE MAN WHO** (B34-371, $3.50, U.S.A.)
(B34-372, $4.50, Canada)

America's favorite newshound has a bone to pick with a most elusive mass murderer! From the bestselling author of FLETCH'S MOXIE and FLETCH AND THE WIDOW BRADLEY.

__**FLETCH AND THE**   (B34-256, $3.50, U.S.A.)
WIDOW BRADLEY   (B34-257, $4.50, Canada)

__**FLETCH'S MOXIE**   (B34-699, $3.95, U.S.A.)
(B34-700, $4.95, Canada)

__**CARIOCA FLETCH**   (B30-304, $3.50, U.S.A.)
(B32-223, $4.50, Canada)

__**FLETCH WON**   (B34-095, $3.95, U.S.A.)
(B34-096, $4.95, Canada)

__**FLETCH, TOO**   (B51-326, hardcover, $15.95)

WARNER BOOKS
P.O. Box 690
New York, N.Y. 10019

Please send me the books I have checked. I enclose a check or money order (not cash), plus 50¢ per order and 50¢ per copy to cover postage and handling.* (Allow 4 weeks for delivery.)

_____ Please send me your free mail order catalog. (If ordering only the catalog, include a large self-addressed, stamped envelope.)

Name _____

Address _____

City _____

State _____ Zip _____

*N.Y. State and California residents add applicable sales tax.

FIRST-RATE 'WHODUNITS' FROM MARGARET TRUMAN

__MURDER IN THE WHITE HOUSE
(B31-402, $3.95, U.S.A.)
(B31-403, $4.95, Canada)

A thriller about the murder of a Secretary of State... Could the President himself have been the killer? All the evidence pointed to the fact that the murder was committed by someone very highly placed in the White House...

"Terrifically readable... marvelous... She has devised a secret for her President and First Lady that is wildly imaginative... The surprise ending is a dandy..."
—*New York Daily News*

__MURDER ON CAPITOL HILL
(B31-438, $3.95, U.S.A.)
(B31-439, $4.95, Canada)

The Majority Leader of the U.S. Senate has been killed with an ice pick...

"True to whodunit form she uses mind rather than muscle to unravel the puzzle. Ms. Truman's writing is bright, witty, full of Washington insider insight and, best of all, loyal to the style of the mysteries of long ago. She may bring them back singlehandedly. Here's hoping so!"
—*Houston Chronicle*

WARNER BOOKS
P.O. Box 690
New York, N.Y. 10019

Please send me the books I have checked. I enclose a check or money order (not cash), plus 50¢ per order and 50¢ per copy to cover postage and handling.* (Allow 4 weeks for delivery.)

_____ Please send me your free mail order catalog. (If ordering only the catalog, include a large self-addressed, stamped envelope.)

Name _____
Address _____
City _____
State _____ Zip _____

*N.Y. State and California residents add applicable sales tax.   116